Tenderness and Tears

Eventually Jessica's sobs subsided and, looking at him with glistening violet eyes, she moaned, "What will happen to me? How can I possibly stay here with that monster?" Her sobbing renewed; he felt her tears through his wet shirt.

"My father will not treat you so again. That much I can promise you." But Jonathan knew those words did not ease her agony. Holding her as though comforting a wounded child, he patiently rocked her until her sobs abated. He kissed her hair and caressed her arms and shoulders. Jessica looked at him through teary lashes. He sucked in his breath at her dazzling beauty. Impulsively his mouth closed over her quivering lips in an urgent kiss that took her breath away. Without realizing what she did, she lifted her arms and put them around his neck. His lips caressed her eyelids, moved to her nose and nibbled at her ear, murmuring soft, unintelligible words. Jessica's body melted against his strong chest, and with a low groan his lips found hers again. Emotions she never knew she possessed whirled within her and Jonathan felt her body tremble as he carried her to the bed. . . .

FLOWER OF LOVE

Rachel North

Book Margins, Inc.

A BMI Edition

Published by special arrangement with Dorchester
Publishing Co., Inc.

Printed in the United States of America.

Chapter One

"I won't!"

"Yes, you will!"

"I won't marry a stranger!"

"You will do as I say!"

"You can't make me!"

"But I can," he answered deliberately. Suddenly Jessica recoiled with the realization that he could; Geoffrey could force her to do anything he chose to have her do. She slumped into a chair and buried her face in her hands.

Over her sobs she wailed, "Why? Why must you do this to me? Do you hate me so much?"

Inching onto the edge of the chair opposite her, he reached across and gently took her hands into his own. His heart wrenched at her misery. He had not meant to deflate her so completely. Cruelty was not his style, especially with his petted and pampered little sister.

It seemed as if the battle had raged for hours instead of a few minutes. Actually the battle within himself had been the long fight; and when he had finally made up his mind, he acted hastily. Now he could see that, try as he had to be kind, to break the news gently, he had done it all wrong. How could he tell his sister she was a valuable commodity he was selling? Stiffening with resolution, he spoke softly because he had to gain her cooperation. Trying to fill the chasm between them, he said, "I know we have not been close these several months. If I explain, will you listen without interrupting?"

"I'll die, Geoffrey. I can't stand the thought of marrying someone I don't know. I've never even heard of him."

Looking at her forlorn face, he pulled her over beside him and encircled her shoulder with his own. Ever since their parents' death almost six months earlier, Geoffrey and Jessica, once close siblings, had become more and more estranged. As older brother and indulged little sister, they had had many good times together. As guardian and ward, they fought incessantly. Because of the ten years' difference in their ages, he had often good-humoredly let her tag along with him and his friends. They had taught her to ride and endured her presence with amusement while ranging over the Germayne estate on quiet afternoons. They had entertained her with stories, teased her about her scrawniness, and spoiled her completely. They had unwittingly fed her with self-importance until she became a very willful young lady. Realizing how spoiled she had become, Lord and Lady Germayne sent her to Miss Trent's Academy, the ideal school for transforming wild girls into correct young ladies. It was far too late. No girl—or boy either, for that matter—can have everyone yield to her slightest whim for fifteen years without thinking it can go on forever. Her parents had hoped she would return to them amenable and unassuming. Reports from Miss Trent herself labeled Jessica headstrong and unruly, strong words to describe the daughter of a Lord when written by a spinster whose livelihood depended on her keeping the school open by catering to the best families in England. Truly Jessica had been a trial. Geoffrey smiled at the brief memory of her face when he had told her she need not return. Indeed, he should have told her then she could not, even if she had wanted to.

How could he make her understand? Only with the

death of their parents in a carriage accident had Geoffrey become aware of the precariousness of their lives. Lord Eden, his father's attorney, had asked for a reading of the will immediately following the funeral services. "His long face should have foreboded his news," Geoffrey mused. "And I thought only that his demeanor matched the seriousness of the task. How can anyone be so naive as Jessica and I have been!"

He still recalled the afternoon vividly. Lord Eden droned through the expected bequests—varying amounts of money to the longtime servants, mother's jewelry and a generous settlement to Jessica, the estate and everything else to Geoffrey. As the servants filed out of the library, Lord Eden cleared his throat, "Geoffrey, could I speak to you alone?"

"Of course. I'll be right with you. Jessica, can you see to our guests?"

"Yes, Geoff. Join us as soon as you can," she answered demurely, for what may have been the first time.

While the new Lord Germayne closed the door behind her and turned to face Lord Eden, that man cleared his throat again.

"Geoffrey," he began hesitantly. "As the new master of this estate, you will have serious difficulties thrust upon you at once. The will is iron-clad, yet we cannot adhere to it."

Seeing the young man's frown, he rushed on, "Your father did not want anyone to know about his troubles because he was positive they were temporary. However, with his untimely death, uhm. . .his uhm. . .expectations. . .disappeared. Your father sought to protect all of you. He never allowed anyone to share his troubles, only his good times." The older man shuffled the papers on the desk. Finally he looked up at the young man and said in a flat voice, "Quite simply, there is no money."

"What?"

"There is no money even to pay the legacies to the staff, let alone such a generous settlement to Jessica."

"You must be mistaken!"

"Come now, Geoffrey. Do you really think this is the time for levity or that I would indulge myself with such a cruel joke?"

"No, no, of course not. I apologize. You might as well tell me all of it," he said as he poured two rather stiff drinks. "I think we'll both need these before you're finished." He sank into a chair across from the man and sipped his drink thoughtfully.

Nodding sympathetically, the older man continued, "Your father, like all healthy men, expected to live forever. He wanted you and your sister to enjoy yourselves. Even you must realize that both of you have certainly been overindulged. It's a wonder you've turned out as well as you have. I realize you have never before had to think—about anything—and certainly not about money. Your most serious problems has been what to do with an evening, whom to see, or where to go. I also realize you did not always want it this way, that you tried to learn about responsibility. Your father's one fault was that he did not let you."

At the mention of his father the young man jumped to his feet, finished off the drink and poured himself another.

Lord Eden continued, "Your father always used to say, 'There's plenty of time to learn responsibility. Let him enjoy himself a little longer.' How can you manage an estate of this size and settle financial problems?"

"I don't know," Geoffrey replied, drinking deeply of the whiskey and flopping into a chair. Dangling one leg over the arm, he continued, "Go on. What must I contend with and how did all this come about?"

"Your father invested heavily in certain ventures that failed. The papers are all here for you to read later." Lord Eden stared at the desk as if he could not look the young man in the eye. "You have inherited this estate

8

and a multitude of debts. I have been able to persuade your creditors to defer payment of these debts for six months, for all the good it will do. I suppose they have agreed to this plan because receiving the money is better than taking over an estate they don't want or need. In the meantime they will be applauded for their generosity. And you will have the time to sell your property as advantageously as possible."

"Sell Briarly Hill? Never!" he exploded and strode to the door. "You can tell my father's creditors I will assume his debts and pay them somehow. But I will never sell Briarly Hill. Now, if you will excuse me, I must join my sister."

Geoffrey slammed out of the library and strode to the parlor with a bravado he did not feel. Hearing the faint whispers as he neared the door, he paused in the doorway. He surveyed the room and saw Jessica, his adored sister, answering questions politely with tears in her eyes. She must be protected. Gulping to pull himself together, he rushed into the room with a smile on his face.

Now his time was almost gone and, miraculously, a solution had been offered to him. He had worked these past six months—oh, how he had worked. The night of the funeral, after sending his sister to bed, the new Lord Germayne had studied all the papers the executor had left. "I am Lord of nothing," he thought derisively. No wonder the creditors did not want to foreclose. They were his father's best friends. Were they friends or had they delibertely set out to ruin his father? Even though he knew little of financial matters, he was not stupid. Either these men had systematically plotted his father's downfall, or his father was a fool. The latter he would never believe. Well, he was not a fool either, and they would be paid!

One week later, a week spent establishing his authority in the running of the estate, Geoffrey journeyed to London. There he had an appointment with Mr. Jeremiah Selby. Geoffrey understood immediately upon seeing Mr. Selby that only with the truth could he gain the aid of this man who was rumored to be a financial wizard. Having laid all his problems and suspicions before this shriveled old man, Geoffrey had asked for his help. For reasons of his own, Mr. Selby had readily, in fact eagerly, agreed.

Returning to Briarly as instructed, Geoffrey had worked hard and the estate had become more profitable than ever before. He had made money these six months, but not nearly enough. Now he also finally knew Mr. Selby's reasons. He must make her understnd, as gently as possible, that she simply had no choice. If she did not marry this Yankee, all would be lost and their father disgraced. Though nothing had been said to him, he could even picture their so-called friends' anticipation of the downfall.

Tenderly he looked at his sister and tightened his arm. "Jessica," he started. "You know I have always taken care of you. Why will you not rely on me in this?"

"But this is unspeakable," she cried as she wrenched herself free and sobbed into the arm of the settee.

"You think I'm putting you into a detestable position. You're right. I am. Would I do this just to be hateful? Am I really that despicable?"

"You never were before Mama and Papa died," she mumbled, her sobs ebbing to occasional hiccoughs.

His sister was more precious to him than any of his possessions, including Briarly, so he wanted to gain her cooperation to save their father's reputation. Desolate that no other solution offered itself, he knew he could put off telling her the entire story no longer.

"Try to comprehend what I tell you. I was advised to tell you immediately, but I have been as mistaken as father by trying to protect you. Now you must know."

"Father? Mistaken?"

Finally he seemed to penetrate the soft shell of tears. He looked into her wondering eyes with sadness before continuing. "Prior to the accident Father made some unfortunate investments, borrowing heavily to do so. The investments failed and the accident occurred before he could recoup his losses."

"Oh, Geoff, what has that to do with my marrying a man I've never met?" she asked, sniffling anew into her handkerchief.

"I had never before that time even tried to accomplish anything serious. When I was faced with all Father's debts, there wasn't even enough money to pay the staff their inheritances. His creditors kindly extended the terms of the loans for six months in an effort to get a maximum return on their money," he said sarcastically.

"Oh, Geoff, is that why you've been so mean?"

"I'm sorry but I couldn't allow you to continue your frivolous ways—spending money as if there were no bottom to the well when, in fact, there was no well."

"You should have told me right away. How bad is the situation?"

"I was given the six months so I could sell Briarly at my leisure. Selling rapidly would surely lower the return."

"Sell Briarly? Never!"

"My reaction exactly," he commented dryly. He admired the stiff set of her shoulders. She rose and straightened. Seeing her holding her hand out to him, he rose and followed her into the library where she closed the door deliberately.

After they had sat down across from each other, she continued, "I think I had better hear the whole story without worrying about our being overheard."

"The servants already knew most of it. I had to tell them there would be no inheritance after all, at least for the present."

"How humiliating that must have been for you."

Her brother had always been a man proud of keeping his word. This he had learned from their father. What could have gone wrong?

"It wasn't nearly so bad as it might have been. I expected bitterness and recriminations, but got kindness and understanding. While I feared all of them would pack up and go, Raines spoke up immediately and said they would stay. They had always received good treatment here and knew I would see that they got their retirement—that's what he called it—when they needed it. In the meantime, since the accident had been so sudden and none of them had planned to retire so soon, they would continue to work as before."

"Papa was right. Respect and love *are* more important than money and obedience."

"Yes, he was. That's one of the reasons I believe his ruin was deliberate. Could he be so right about people and a complete fool about money?"

"Papa was no fool," she answered quickly.

As she echoed his own feelings, he wondered why he had not confided in her earlier. So much misunderstanding could have been avoided. She was not a seventeen year old scatterbrain; she was a young woman. With the same parents why had it not occurred to him that she was as strong as he?

Suddenly a look of pain flashed across her face. "The accident—it was an accident, wasn't it? You don't think. . .?"

"Yes, it was. Don't ever think anything else, Jessica." He crossed the room to kneel in front of her. "Father would never have left all these problems to us—not when he would never even let us worry when he was alive."

Her frown disappeared immediately as she realized the truth of that statement. "This accounts for all the changes around here, I suppose—the preoccupation with breeding horses rather than riding and hunting with those we already had. The farming, too. I'm sorry I sniped at you that day about not wanting to live on a farm. You were trying to help the tenants farm better so we would be better off. The six months extension is almost passed. How much progress have you made?"

"Not nearly enough." Folding his hands behind his back, he paced across the room and back. "That is what caused me to suggest you marry Jonathan Selby."

"Go on. I'm listening this time," she said quietly.

"Once in London I saw Jeremiah Selby at a gaming hall. He left early with huge winnings, and I heard someone, I don't remember who, remark that everything he touched turned to money. After the initial shock of our extremely reduced circumstances wore off, I went to London to see him. I told him everything."

"Oh, Geoff, how could you?"

"It was not time to be proud. I also told him I suspected someone had tried to ruin us deliberately and I wouldn't allow it. He studied the papers overnight and agreed the next day to help for reasons he would divulge later. All the changes here have been with his approval, though many of the ideas originated with me. Since I had some ideas, he seemed to decide I was more than the fop I appeared. Certainly Briarly is a successful estate that brings in a profit now. I have enough money secreted away to pay the staff's 'retirements'—the faithful must be taken care of first. I don't have nearly enough money for the other debts."

"Maybe the loans can be extended further?"

"No! I wouldn't lower myself to ask just to be refused."

"Refused? Surely anyone can see you have made progress. If they could afford to wait six months, won't they wait longer?" she inquired.

Charging to the desk, he grabbed a handful of papers and shook them at her. "Here are the notes—all of them. Do you know who holds them? Roger Trevaly, Henry Courtney, Arthur Williams," he read as he slammed the papers on the desk in turn.

"But they're Papa's best friends," she gasped.

"Friends! They don't even speak to me. They speak only through Lord Eden."

"You said 'deliberate ruin' earlier. Do you mean these men contrived against us?"

"Yes! That's what I mean."

"And I have truly been deserted by my friends. How foolishly I thought they respected my grief overlong." She set her shoulders and said with determination, "We cannot allow these back stabbers to disgrace us or our parents."

"No, my pet, we can't."

Somewhat calmed by now he walked around the desk and back to her. He looked at her sadly and turned away. He could not do it; he could not sell her for money. If only he knew to what kind of fate he might be condemning her.

"How will my marriage help?" she asked hesitantly. She had seen the change of heart written on his face. She surely knew her brother well enough to be aware that he would never have suggested such an act before he had considered and rejected all other possibilities. Since she was no longer marriageable to one of their friends, she might possibly be of some use. "Geoff, do not shirk now. Finish your explanation."

"Mr. Selby has revealed his reasons. He wants you to marry his son Jonathan."

"What kind of man would allow his father to buy him a wife?" she scoffed.

"I've not met him. He lives in America. He is here for his annual visit. His father may be telling the same story to him as we sit here now. However, if the marriage takes place, his father has offered enough money to pay off all the debts. He will also continue to advise me so that I too shall be wealthy shortly. He has assured me you would always have a home with him if the marriage did not work out."

They sat quietly, each with his own thoughts. Straightening his shoulders, he said firmly, "Forget it. It is unthinkable that I should even have considered it. Until I said it aloud, I did not really think of it as selling

14

you. Selling a person is slavery. I want no part of it." He added in a safer tone, "Forgive me?"

"Why forget it? It is the obvious solution. The only thing I have to forgive you for is not confiding in me earlier."

"No, I'll not allow it." He had forgotten Jessica bristled when given orders and watched her do so now. "I will arrange something else for Mr. Selby. The bride does not have to be you—only someone of our class. Probably our creditors will be put off a while longer with part of their payment."

"You know they won't. Oh, Geoff, there is no other way." She had already resigned herself. "Maybe he will not be so bad as we think."

"Jessica, you will not do this."

"I most certainly will!" Giggling aloud, she continued, "How did we ever change sides in this argument?"

"Maybe he won't agree," he said with some hope in his voice.

"What will happen then?"

"The agreement is off; I will sell Briarly and pay all the debts."

"Are you saying that, in addition to all else, I have to make myself agreeable and enticing?"

"No, he is probably at that chore now. Do not humble yourself more."

"I'm not at all sure I shall like America." She had heard to many stories of the wild land, all of them somewhat frightening.

"If you don't, come back to me," he said disconsolately.

"When is the wedding? Did Mr. Selby plan that, too?"

"Jonathan Selby plans to return soon. You may have as much as a week."

"A week! How can I ever get used to the idea in a week?" Standing and moving to the door with great

15

dignity, she said over her shoulder, "Don't worry, Geoff. One step at a time. First, we must secure Briarly Hill. Then we must deal a crushing blow to those who would blacken the Germayne name. After that is done, we will concern ourselves with seeing that Mr. Selby gets an equitable reward."

He watched her leave the room, knowing she had made up her mind and he could not change it. But he loathed himself for ever making such a suggestion to her. How could he sacrifice his lamb of a sister for a house—he suposed he must remind himself often that his father's reputation was the real stake and that he did not want besmirched. He slumped into a chair with a bottle in one hand and a glass in the other and purposefully proceeded to drink himself into oblivion.

Chapter Two

Geoffrey Germayne might have been surprised if he realized how well he had guessed at the scene in London. Jeremiah and Jonathan Selby were dining at home tonight. Jeremiah had asked Jonathan to dinner three days earlier so his son would be sure to be available. Since his father did not usually stand on such ceremony, Jonathan knew his father had something on his mind. Why didn't he get to whatever it was? Throughout all the courses of the extremely formal dinner, his father had talked about business and world affairs. Undoubtedly the state of the world was on the brink of disaster, but Jonathan knew this dinner and table conversation were only a prelude to the actual point of this get together.

After Edward had cleared the table and served their brandy, he lighted their cigars and quietly left the room. The servants here are certainly unobtrusive, thought Jonathan. They knew their place and there was none of the easy commaraderie that existed between him and his housekeeper Callie. Maybe it was time to take a wife; then Callie wouldn't badger him so. Oh, God, no! Suddenly he knew what his father wanted. How could he not have known! Every year when he brought the ship home, his father questioned him about a wife. He had long known his father wanted him married. "I want grandchildren," he was fond of repeating, "someone to make this accumulation of wealth worthwhile."

A nagging thought that something had changed plagued Jonathan during this trip. Even though he resided at his father's home when in London, they had seen little of each other, except to speak while one or the other was on his way in or out. To be sure, Jonathan's business affairs and night life did not allow him much spare time. He should have been wary when Edward delivered the invitation. Actually he had laughed aloud when he read it, recognizing his crusty father's sense of humor. The old man probably thought the situation so ridiculous he might as well go all the way and make an appointment. He had been cleverly lulled into this, so he might as well sit back and take it.

"Well, Sir, I assume you will soon tell me the purpose of this formal occasion."

"Surely. I am announcing your engagement."

"You are what?" He leaned forward, laying his arms on the table.

"I am announcing your engagement. To you." The old man was full of surprises. "I have bought you a wife."

"Well, you can return her. We've been through this before, and I will choose my own time to marry. Positively, I will choose the woman. You've really done it this time." Jonathan stormed to his feet and threw his napkin to the table.

"Sit down," his father said calmly.

So startled at being told what to do at his age, Jonathan did just that—sat down. "Sit down and hear me out. Then I will listen to you." The old man frowned and paused as if unsure of how to proceed. Finally he looked up from the table. Obviously he had decided to plunge forward, thought Jonathan. "I have become a wily, selfish old man," he began. "I have more than enough money to get whatever I want, but I can only partially buy the only thing left to desire. Always before I thought I was honorable. Now I find that I am lonely." As the younger man started to interrupt, his father raised a hand to silence him and continued, "Ten years ago you asked my backing for a venture in America. Although I did not want to lose my only son at eighteen, I purchased your ship which you have surely mastered and turned into a fortune of your own. You have a ship, warehouses, a fine plantation, and other business interests as well. You are the model of a successful man. I know you have tried many times to repay the money I gave you. If you remember, I refused, saying I would think of something you could do as I had no use for the money. You will please do this for me."

"Why? Why have you put me into such an uncompromising position? God, that's always been a woman's line," he mumbled. "You do not even leave me an honorable way of refusing."

With twinkling eyes, his father answered, "I have tried to cover all contingencies." Jonathan scowled but his father, sad-eyed once again, rushed on, "I am an old man. I want grandchildren and you are my only child. We have talked of this before, but you have taken no initiative yourself. I'm tired of living alone in this big house. My work no longer interests me, though I have one rather interesting project to complete."

"How will grandchildren in America overcome your boredom? Do you plan to come live with us?"

Ignoring his son's sarcasm, Jeremiah Selby replied, "No, I know you would not allow anyone to choose your way of life for you. If you consent to marry Jessica, you can go back to your business as usual and let her stay here with me. She would probably prefer it that way too."

"Who would marry a girl willing to sell herself? What kind of woman would cold-bloodedly make such a bargain?" My father certainly is an old man if he thinks I would submit to this, his thoughts continued. Jonathan had always regarded his father a gentleman in

19

all ways but one—his birth. In spite of or maybe because of his low birth, he had amassed a fortune. Making money had driven him all his life, and now it bored him. Ever since Jonathan could remember, his father had avoided people socially. He must have been different once or his gentle mother would never have married him.

"Jonathan, my son, I know the type of woman with whom you spend your time. I am also aware that you will never marry one of them. I have been informed that you are feeling the pressure to marry one only slightly better. This can be your excuse to the full-blown Carolyn you left behind you."

"You spy on me, Sir?"

This was too much. He must discover who his father's informant was. Then he decided his father could check up on him from any number of sources. Certainly his liaison with Carolyn had been no secret. She had seen to that.

"No," the old man continued. "But I did inquire before I made any arrangements. I was assured you were about to be a most reluctant bridegroom on your return. I have at least chosen wisely. Jessica Germayne is a beautiful, refreshing orphan of seventeen. Her parents died suddenly and left a mountain of debts, and her brother came to me for help. Did you ever meet Geoffrey Germayne in your younger years? You are about the same age."

"We did not attend the same school; and since, as you are so quick to point out, I've been busy with women of the lower classes, where would I come across him?"

" 'Tis no matter. Think Geoffrey and me scoundrels if you want. We made the bargain—he is probably holding the same conversation with his sister at this moment. You can't think she would like this kind of settlement any better than you."

"I suppose in return for his sister as a daughter-in-law, you will pay his debts."

"Among other things."

"He will probably meet with as much resistance as you have, or is she as malleable as most of her kind? All the so-called ladies I have met are either pliable as putty or as spoiled as children."

"Won't you at least meet her?"

Relenting somewhat, he replied, "I supposed meeting her can do no harm. But don't assume this is submission," he added quickly at his father's knowing smile.

"Oh, no, I would never do that. You are expected for tea tomorrow."

What an agonizing interview this had been! Little did Jessica and Jonathan know they echoed each other's thoughts. Thank heaven someone had decided they should meet before the ceremony. Jessica glanced at the tall, muscular build of the man standing across the room from her. He was much better-looking than she had expected. He wore a green velvet coat that deepened his green eyes and an ivory waistcoat over his white ruffled shirt. His matching green breeches fitted snugly about his narrow hips. Handsome though he was, she loathed him for what he had done to her. Expected to arrive at four for tea, he had in fact arrived two hours early. How dare he demean her like this! Well, she would sit here, but he could carry on the conversation; she would not struggle with small talk.

His father had been correct, as usual. She *was* beautiful. She can only lose by marrying me; why did she become a party to this? There she sat on the edge of the settee—ramrod stiff. Does she ever bend or wilt? Probably no, he surmised. Nervousness threatened to overtake her slight frame. Despite her rigid back, her teacup rattled in its saucer, betraying her calm as the sham it was. Tea! That, a drink? Thank God I'm no longer English. His thought flew on—how did I ever let my father talk me into coming here?

Here they sat in the confoundest, awkwardest long silences. How long could this go on? I should do something, say something to ease the strain for her. I might be cruel enough to arrive two hours early to embarrass her, but I cannot just sit here and watch her stare at me defiantly. Taming her might be amusing and I do have a few days left before I sail. How much of the truth did she know? The tilt of her chin revealed her to be no more submissive than he. His ploy did not leave her discomfited for long. Yes, Father, she is a beautiful girl, for girl she is—not a woman. She would make a beautiful decoration on any man's arm. No, he would not relent; force, no matter how subtly applied, strengthened his resistance. She's probably a stubborn, spoiled brat. Still, he hated a milksop.

As she sat her saucer on the table in front of her, the cup rattled again, and her back straightened even more. Very stiffly she asked, "Why did you agree to this? You don't look as if you had to bribe someone to marry you."

"Bribe you? My dear young lady, I am not really interested in marrying anyone, especially some chit of a girl."

"I suppose you'd prefer someone more experienced," she retorted scornfully.

"I prefer no wife at all!" he roared.

"Then why are you here? To laugh at me? To gloat over my misfortune?"

"No, one does not gloat over pathetic creatures," he snarled.

Smack. She jumped to her feet and slapped him so hard his head jerked sideways. Grabbing her wrist as she swung a second time, he threatened menacingly, "I've never thought to hit a woman, but you do tempt me. Don't ever swing at me again."

"Maybe you don't want to marry me, but. . ."

"Maybe! Ha!"

"All right, why are you here?"

"I agreed to meet you to satisfy my father. I could hardly wait to meet a woman who would sell herself," he sneered.

"Sell myself?" She wilted before his eyes. Hopelessness covered her face. Her bright blue eyes darted around the room, refusing to meet his.

"What would you call it?"

Did she have to take this? Now she did, but he would pay, she vowed. As if the vow gave her strength, she said, "Maybe we had better both calm down and try to discuss this as rationally as possible. It is perfectly clear that we have not been told the same story. Since this entire farce concerns only us, maybe we could at least compare stories and determine our actions later."

Chagrinned because she, not as he intended, had called for reason, he led her to a chair and sat down opposite her. Holding their tempers in check, they told each other the stories they had been told to convince each of them to bend to another's will—he explaining the grandchildren and she the debts and treachery of their friends. They were not two who could easily be used. Hopelessly she moaned, "What can we do? Because of your father's stubbornness and my brother's desperation, we have really been backed into a corner."

"I may be willing to help you, but I will not be forced to do so," he murmured. He watched her with a sickening feeling. The weight placed on her was much too heavy for such narrow shoulders. "Could we strike our own bargain?"

"Do you mean you would go against your father?" she asked.

"Not openly. That would ruin your family. All my father is interested in is grandchildren. We can easily sabotage that plan. First, we could agree to the marriage. That would solve the Germayne problems."

"Will we really be married? I mean will it be a marriage?"

"Don't worry, Jessica. It will be binding. You will

23

have the respectability of being married—but in name only. A bride in *absentia* will serve me well."

"In *absentia*?"

"I told you I didn't want to marry anyone. We will get back at my father by not living together. If you stay here in London with him and I go back to America, his grandchildren will remain a dream."

"What will happen to me?" she asked as she stared at her hands in her lap.

"Nothing will happen to you. You can have any kind of life you want. London is an exciting city for a young woman, and my father isn't a complete ogre, at least not often. You may even learn to like him."

"Well," she almost whispered, "that couldn't be so bad. I must help Geoff and this may be the perfect way."

"Could we walk over this estate so that I could see the precious Briarly Hill you love so much? Besides, since the wedding will have to take place in three days, we need to appear terribly enamored of each other."

"I've been too stubborn and shrewish since my parents' death for anyone here to think I've fallen desperately in love in less than an hour."

Extending his hand, he helped her up from the chair and said smiling, "Can you not pretend? Come, we will put on the first of our magnificent performances for the week."

She gazed longingly into his eyes while they walked into the hall, past a gaping Raines who quickly recovered in time to swing the door open. Jessica and Jonathan stared adoringly at each other until the door closed softly behind them. She giggled with pure delight as she cried, "Was that convincing enough, do you think?"

"What a little minx!" He felt much more lenient with her as they strolled through the gardens and stables. When she called Jimmy to saddle horses for them, Jonathan could not help noticing how quickly and willingly they idolized her. He observed, too, that she asked, not ordered, those around her. As they rode through the tenant village, not only the men but the women too smiled at her passing. She, in turn, waved or spoke to each, calling many by name. Clearly, the villagers respected the young lady of the manor.

When they returned to the house, Jimmy rushed forward to take their mounts. However, Jonathan motioned the boy away from him. "There is no need to bother. I'm leaving now."

Having started up the front steps, Jessica spun around to face him. "You're leaving? What will I tell Geoff? He wants to meet you and planned to have tea with us."

"We already had tea, remember? And I'm not standing for inspection by the likes of your brother."

She most certainly did not care for his tone and rose to her brother's defense, "He wasn't going to inspect you."

"No? Well, then, tell him I'll meet him at the wedding Thursday at four o'clock."

"Thursday! He said I would have a week."

"I'm sailing with the morning tide Saturday. So if we are to carry out this little charade, we must get started. We can't disappoint our families, now, can we?" he jeered.

Jessica had thought they were becoming friends because he had behaved so gallantly toward her on their tour of Briarly and the village. Now at his jeering tone her head snapped up and her eyes blazed. Seeing her harden herself against his mocking, he added, "Besides, I have the feeling you don't need the approval of your brother. You will do as you please. I'll see you Thursday at four in the chapel."

"I won't be there!"

"Yes, you will," he barked as he mounted and rode off while she trembled with rage.

The afternoon thoroughly confused Jonathan. He had purposely arrived hours early to show his contempt for her. That move had only partially succeeded. She had suffered the intended embarrassment, but briefly. She responded to his arrival with dignity and put him on the defensive by accusing him of bribing her. As if that were not enough, she sneered at his not being capable of finding a wife. Jonathan was not in the habit of being on the defensive and did not like it. So he had attacked her with cruelty. "I didn't win that battle either," he admitted to himself.

Jonathan sat late into the night contemplating the events of the previous twenty-four hours. After leaving Jessica glaring at his back, he had ridden only halfway to London. He had stopped at the inn, knowing that he must settle the turmoil within himself before he could endure the persistent questions of his father about what had happened.

Sitting at the small table in his room, he poured from the bottle of whiskey and gulped it down. Still, the turmoil was worse than ever. He did not know why he acted as he had at this inn. He had charmed the serving girl into giving him a private room by practically promising her pleasures to come. He had refused to notice her, however, when she bent low to serve him, almost baring her breasts. He remained unmoved when she brushed her breast against his shoulder while setting his plate before him. He stared into his glass and brooded, ignoring the bustle and confusion in the room. Finally, he climbed the stairs alone. When he closed the door to his room, he lighted a candle and dropped the bar across the door. Later when he heard the wench softly turn the knob, he ignored her again. "Why?" he said to himself. "I have always taken anyone I fancied. I fully intended to have her tonight when I enticed her into giving me this room."

He stripped and pinched out the candle. Lying alone in bed, Jonathan could not sleep. What would she do if I broke our agreement and forced her to go home with me? No, that would not do. If he had any notions of truly making her his wife, he would put his life in America in order first. Carolyn would rave because he had allowed her to believe he'd marry her when he returned. It was true that he had never asked her to marry him and that he had instructed Callie to guard the house against her, but he had said nothing, absolutely nothing to Carolyn. It had seemed easier at the time to take what he wanted from her and sail away, letting her believe what she wanted. He had told himself he would deal with her when the time came. Deal with her he must before he could do anything about Jessica.

Why was he considering such a move anyway? He didn't want a wife, except to relieve himself of Carolyn's overbearing presence in his life. Last night he had railed against his father for interfering in his life. He had thought Jessica the most sluttish of temptresses for selling herself in exchange for a house. Today he had callously plotted with her to thwart his father's careful planning—a plot to which she readily agreed. If possible, she schemed as much as he and his father. If his father was lonely, her presence in his house would relieve that loneliness. This afternoon he had salved his conscience with this idea. Why should he honor his word to a schemer? Yet he admired her fortitude, though he did prefer his women a little more easily influenced than she. She would never cling and simper as other women, and he would be proud to have her at his side. He supposed she would not agree to come to America and let him continue with his rutting ways. Marriage could be the perfect haven for him, women could no longer press for more. Still, he knew she would not be shamed by living with him and turning her head at his behavior. She would not care if she were in London and knew neither his friends nor the details of his actions. Besides, Jessica was assuredly vexed with him now. Perhaps, if he left her here to cool her heels, she would be more agreeable when he came back next year. Those were more plans that he had to change.

27

Tiring of these annual trips across the Atlantic, he had hoped to convince his father to go back with him this time. His father's wild plan had driven that idea from his mind, but the man was getting too old to be left alone with only servants for company. "Let them both sit in London and fume together. When they are calm after a year, I'll come back and then we'll see."

With a decision reached, Jonathan rolled over and slept.

Chapter Three

Jessica spent the next two days saying good-by to her home. Though many of her and Geoffrey's friends and their parents thought her a flibbertigibbet, everyone on the estate knew her to be kind and friendly. In the servants' quarters there was constant chatter about the preparations for the wedding. As Jessica rode for many hours over the fields and through the trees of her beloved Briarly, many wondered momentarily at her long face and sad eyes—definitely not the glow of expectancy on a bride's countenance. Most assumed it to be caused by sadness at leaving the only home she had ever known and quickly returned to their dusting and scrubbing. If anyone had realized the great torment in her slight body, he would have really been horrified, for Jessica was and always had been petted and pampered as everyone's darling. What else could be expected for the little Miss?

The day after Jessica and Jonathan had made their own bargain, the house became a flurry of activity. It had to be turned out from top to bottom, decreed Mrs. Hopewell. Jessica could not imagine why, as the only guests would be Lord and Lady Eden—the closest anyone came to being family—and Jonathan's father. The tenants were invited to the ceremony, but even Jessica would not invite them to the house for dinner, nor would they have come if she had. Mrs. Hopewell was not to be denied as this was the only wedding she would ever see at Briarly Hill. Tuesday morning, after a sleepless night spent considering the wisdom of calling off the affair and rejecting it for Geoff's sake, Jessica lay in bed later than usual. Almost before she had awakened, Polly burst into her room.

"Are you up yet, Miss?" she questioned and strode across the room to arrange Jessica's breakfast on the table by the window. "Everything's in such an uproar downstairs I thought you might like breakfast here. Raines took a message about someone's arriving at nine o'clock to get you ready for the wedding. It's eight thirty now."

"Get me ready?" Jessica squealed as she bounded out of bed and struggled into the robe Polly held for her. "Whatever does that mean?"

"I don't know, Miss. Even Raines couldn't get much more information, and you know how fussy he is about messages. Someone rode all the way from London."

Yes, Jessica knew that well. She giggled as she pictured the stiff-necked butler and his frustration at not making sense of a garbled message. "Well, if someone's coming from London, I suppose we'd better be ready when they get here." Sitting down, she hastily gulped her breakfast and then dressed as quickly as possible. Polly scurried around the room, straightening things here and there, chattering all the while. After fastening her mistress's gown, she left the room only to return before she had had time to reach the staircase.

"They're here, Miss. I couldn't stop them," she said as a troop of strangers pushed into the bedroom immediately behind her.

"Miss Germayne, I'm Mrs. Mattingly and these are my assistants. Mr. Selby said you are to be the most beautiful bride ever and sent us to see to it."

Overcome with amazement Jessica stood still and stared as the assistants carried in bolts of cloth, scissors, needles and thread, trimmings, and drawings of gowns.

One set a stool in the middle of the room. Jessica stood as if in a trance while Mrs. Mattingly unfastened her dress, helped her out of it, and cast it aside. Leading the girl to the stool, the woman ordered, "Step up here while I take your measurements."

While Jessica lifted her arms and straightened her back at the woman's commands, Mrs. Mattingly exactly and skillfully measured her. Folding her tape, she crooned, "It will be a pleasure to work on someone so lovely. Considering the haste with which Mr. Selby said we must work, I expected you to have more of a belly." Not waiting for Jessica's reaction, the outspoken woman commanded, "Show us where we can work."

As she dressed anew, Jessica said, "Don't you want me to choose a gown from the drawings?"

"There is no need. Mr. Selby made it clear I was to choose."

Seething with rage, Jessica said haughtily, "Follow me," and strode down the hall to the sewing room in the back of the house. "You may work in here."

"Don't go too far away, dear," said Mrs. Mattingly sweetly. "We'll need a fitting later."

Jessica swept back down the hall and down the front stairs. How could Jonathan send that woman here? She's unbearable and condescending. How dare she comment on the hastiness of the marriage! Thought I'd have a full belly, did she? We'll see who listens to her, Jessica thought as she walked into the stable and told Jimmy to saddle Jezebel. Slashing the crop to the mare's neck, she and the horse tore across the field. Traveling at breakneck speed, they raced into the woods. The horse jumped a tree fallen onto the path and barely missed stepping into a hole. Finally, both horse and rider calmed down and soon approached the stream at the far edge of the woods. Slipping from the saddle, Jessica patted Jezebel and mumbled, "I'm sorry, girl. It's not your fault, but we'll not rush back."

Jessica sat in the sun at the back of the stream to reconsider the state of her affairs. Last night she had convinced herself that this plan would work. She and Jonathan would marry and he would return to America while she stayed in London with his father. In that way she could do as she pleased and have the respectability of marriage. In the meantime Geoffrey could settle his debts, for she knew he would make a respectable living if he didn't have to worry about the thousands of pounds their father owed. Jonathan could also have what he wanted—revenge against his father. Since she had no other marriage hopes, she had decided to help solve everyone's problems by going through with Geoff's plan. Now, how could she? Why had she ever thought this a solution rather than a new problem?

She had realized as soon as she saw him that Jonathan Selby was a handsome man. She had also soon learned that he could be ruthless and cruel. Only a cruel, ungrateful son could so deceive his father. Still he had been clever enough to lull her into becoming a partner in his scheme. She had never thought he would be this overbearing—not even to allow her to choose her own wedding gown. "He probably even told that witch to treat me so disgustingly," she thought.

Well, he's not going to get away with humiliating me so again. I'll cut a swath through London so wide he'll be able to see it from America, she promised. Resolutely she rose and paced up and down beside the stream and the warmth of the sun relaxed her enough that she could serenly return to the house.

As she walked into the house, Polly rushed up to her and exclaimed, "Oh, Miss, where have you been? That woman has had us looking everywhere for you. Over an hour it's been."

"I went for a ride. What does the good Mrs. Mattingly want?"

"A fitting. You've been gone all morning and we were worried about you." Polly fluttered beside her as Jessica ascended the stairs. She most definitely was not about to rush for that uncouth woman.

"There's nothing to worry about. I'm fine. Tell Mrs. Mattingly I'm in my room."

"She's already there."

"Oh!" Jessica gasped as she walked into the room, "It's beautiful!" The heavy ivory satin was cut in simple slender lines. A hood fell back and draped itself into a wide layback collar. The slim sleeves came to a point on her hand, she noticed as she slithered her arms through to the end. The skirt flares slightly at the floor. As she turned for Mrs. Mattingly to hook the back, she glimpsed her reflection in the mirror. The gown flattered her slim figure and made her feel and look more like a woman than a girl. It fit perfectly.

"Mrs. Mattingly, I am certainly glad you bullied me into letting you choose. I would never have chosen so well."

"I am sorry, my dear," apologized the woman. "But Mr. Selby said you were only a girl and must become a woman quickly."

Jessica softened completely toward the seamstress. "I didn't realize that he knew me so well."

"We will finish this now and make the appropriate undergarment. And when you come to London, the others will be ready."

"The others? What others?"

"Mr. Selby has ordered an entire wardrobe, Miss."

"I'll forgive you, madam, but I'll not forgive Mr. Selby for behaving in such a heavy-handed manner." Well, she thought, at least I'm not too angry with him to be afraid of him.

How this week had flown! Tuesday had been spent with the seamstress, at least the afternoon. Wednesday she had ridden over almost every foot of Briarly, saying good-by as if she would never return. Thursday, her wedding day, dawned with the earth bathed in sunlight. Jessica stirred as Polly flung open the door, bustled across the room, and brushed aside the draperies.

"Time to get up, Miss Jessica," she called softly as she laid a robe on the end of the bed. "This is a really exciting day," she rambled. "Your bath is on its way."

"Tell them not to bother yet, Polly. I'll bathe later."

Exciting? Jessica rolled onto her back and stretched her arms above her head. Plumping her pillow behind her, she muttered to herself, "I hope it's exciting. If I could only make him love me. How could I do that in less than two days? No, I don't even know how to start." It would, however, be eminently satisfying to have him pine for her.

Jessica, having dressed, eaten breakfast, and packed, walked to the door of the library and knocked. When her brother had called for her to enter, she turned the knob and opened the door. "Raines said you wanted to speak to me, Geoff."

"Come on in and sit down."

"What did you want?" she asked as she closed the door behind her. She slid into a chair and waited expectantly.

"Jess, are you sure you want to go through with this?" he asked with a frown on his face. "It's not too late to back out, you know. I can find some way to raise the money."

"Are you having second thoughts, Geoff? Don't worry. I'll be all right. Jonathan Selby doesn't know what he is in for yet," she said determinedly.

"I almost feel sorry for him," her brother smiled.

"He needs your pity more than I do," she retorted with a stiffening of her spine. "But beware, he may return the merchandise," she flung over her shoulder as she left the room.

Jessica then walked down the hall, through the dining room, and down to the kitchen. All the workers smiled but kept busy. Jessica asked about preparations for the wedding supper and was assured all would be ready. Saying she would return later, she went on outside through the kitchen door for one last stroll in the gardens. Stepping carefully through Mrs. Jamison's herb garden, she wondered when she would see it next. She proceeded on through the flower gardens, drinking in their beauty and fragrance. In the maze she met the gardner who wished her a happy marriage from him and his wife. Accepting his good wishes, she continued through the maze, remembering fondly the many times she had played here as a child.

Everywhere she went brought strong but intolerable memories. She hated to leave her beautiful home. "What lies in store for me now? Can I build a life on getting even—not one that is lasting, but one that will do for a time? Enough of this moping," she thought. "I must get back to the house and get ready."

Retracing her steps, she walked into the kitchen and slumped at the table. "Do you have one last treat for me, Mrs. Jamison?"

The cook, sensing instinctively that all was not well with her darling little Miss, set a cup of tea in front of her.

"Cheer up, Miss Jessica. You have going to have the grandest wedding supper you've ever seen."

"Oh, thank you, Mrs. Jamison. I was just thinking how much I'll miss all this. You've always had a kind word and a crumpet or two to patch up my ills."

"But you're grown up now, Miss. You're no longer the little girl who came to my kitchen hunting treats. One day soon your own little darlings will be here asking me for crumpets."

"If that were only true," Jessica thought as she hugged the chubby woman and left the room.

"Your bath now, Miss?" Polly asked as Jessica walked into her room.

"Yes, Polly, now. I can't put it off any longer. Where did this day go?"

Polly helped Jessica undress and arranged her raven hair high atop her head with ribbons. A large brass tub was dragged into the center of the room and filled with steaming water. She stepped into the tub and sat so only her head showed above the side. She poured lavender scent into the tub with her and leaned back to relax. "Well, this is at least one pleasure I can still have in London," she thought. She bathed as leisurely as she ever had and soon stepped out of the tub into the towel Polly had ready.

After drying her mistress, Polly dropped the towel and helped her into her shift and gown. "Never had I thought I'd be married in such a dress as this," Jessica murmured. She went downstairs to meet Geoff so they could proceed to the chapel in the village.

He awaited her at the bottom of the stairs with a box in his hand. Opening it, he said, "I thought you'd like to wear these."

"Mother's pearls! I thought you had sold them."

"No, Jess, her jewels are here waiting for you and will accompany you when you leave here. I couldn't send you away with nothing."

After clasping the pearls around her neck, he took her arm and led her outside to the waiting carriage. She huddled in the corner all the way to the chapel, wringing her hands and twisting her handkerchief. Goeffrey jumped out first and held his arm out to help his sister from the carriage. Mechanically she put one foot in front of the other as her brother led her inside.

Polly, having come ahead, fussed about her and straightened her gown. Last of all she fastened the heavy bridal cape around her. "Oh, Miss Jessica, you're so beautiful!" Bobbing quickly, she scurried away to her seat in the rear of the chapel.

"Is he there, Geoff?"

"Yes, darling."

"Why am I so nervous?"

The music changed tempo and Geoff said, "It's time if you're still sure."

Jessica stepped forward, saying, "It's too late to stop now."

As she walked toward the front of the building, she felt the heavy train pull her back. Jonathan's face loomed before her. He reached out to her and she took his hand in hers. Kneeling together, they repeated their vows quietly. Neither sounded eager or sure. Then somehow it was over and they rose shakily. Jessica turned to leave but Jonathan held her firm. When she turned back to him, he crushed her to him, looking at her with mocking eyes, and lowered his lips on hers. Startled by his deepening kiss, Jessica struggled half-heartedly. At that moment she hated him and vowed once more to get even with him for humiliating her before these people.

"Be careful, dear," he taunted. "You wouldn't want your friends to think you aren't a willing bride."

Just as quickly he released her, put her hand through his arm, and almost dragged her toward the door at the rear of the chapel. Outside stood three carriages. Jessica started toward the one in which she had arrived; however Jonathan quickly guided her instead to the last in line. "We'll take this one. Your brother and my father are such good friends they can ride together." He quickly lifted her into the carriage and climbed in behind her. When the others stepped out of the chapel, the bridal couple was already pulling out of line to make the short journey to Briarly. Jessica sat primly in the corner and watched the countryside move by, completely ignoring the man beside her. When the carriage stopped in front of the manor, she flung open the door and almost fell out. Jonathan thrust his arm around her and set her on his lap.

"Is being married to me so bad you must throw yourself to the ground?" he shouted.

"Let me go!" she cried, beating him on the chest. "I hate you!"

"I told you once before never to hit me again." Grabbing her arm tightly, he shouted, "You wanted this marriage and you will behave yourself. We'll see how you like it now."

"You're hurting me," she sobbed and threw herself back into the corner. He stared at her back and heaving shoulders. Gently he reached for her and pulled her small body into the shelter of his strong arm and shoulder. Jessica, surprised at his tenderness, sniffled into her sleeve until he put a finger under her chin and tilted her head so far she had to look into his snapping green eyes. He felt his heart soften as he stared at those water pools. When she blinked away the last of her tears, he kissed her gently.

"I'm sorry, pet. I really have treated you badly. In less than two days I'll sail away, and you'll be free again. Do you think you can tolerate me that long without a battle? Monday I was such a villain, but you weren't much better. I really wasn't sure you would be here today."

She relaxed in his arms and leaned against him. He hugged her briefly and jumped through the open doorway to the ground. As he turned to help her down, he said, "Come, Madam, we have one more ordeal to go through before we can be on our way." As they walked into the house, he continued, "Don't worry, little one. Your friends will think only that I'm an overanxious bridegroom."

She jerked her arm away, her anger again rising quickly. As she walked through the doorway, the entire staff stood inside as a welcoming committee. Each of them curtseyed or bowed, congratulated her, and whisked away to attend to his assigned duties. Soon the other carriages appeared, and the feast was already on the table as they filed into the dining room. Geoff took his place at the end of the table with Jessica and Jonathan on one side and Lord and Lady Eden and Mr. Selby on the other. They lifted their wine glasses in a toast to the young couple.

"To a happy and satisfying marriage," Geoff offered. He seemed about to go on, but changed his mind abruptly. Jessica realized he kept his silence to avoid embarrassing her further in front of the Edens. She could not help noticing Jonathan smiled as if amused and drank the champagne down easily. She glared at him with repugnance.

The meal was over much too soon for Jessica. As the men sat at the table with their brandy and cigars, she and Lady Eden started upstairs. Jonathan spoke, loudly enough for everyone to hear but sweetly for all that matter, "Jessica, as soon as you've changed your gown, we will be on our way."

Jessica blanched at the words. She had thought they would remain here overnight. She was to spend the night with him alone? She definitely had not counted on this. She gasped, about to retort, but clamped her jaws shut as she saw the amused glances of the other gentlemen. They did think he was an eager bridegroom! She turned and flounced up the staircase with Lady Eden bustling to catch her. "These impetuous men," the woman muttered as they entered Jessica's room.

Polly awaited her mistress and, upon hearing of their imminent departure, cried, "Oh, Miss, what will you wear?"

"I will have to wear the outfit I had planned to wear tomorrow. Pack everything else and have it taken to the carriage. Surely I'm not to travel without my belongings."

Geoff and Lord Eden were coming from the library as she descended the staircase. When Lord Eden smiled at her contentedly, Jessica knew Geoff had paid his debts, probably with money obtained from Mr. Selby while they rode back together. Her brother walked over to face her with a casket under his arm. "These are yours. No one else will ever deserve them so completely."

She knew he was placing her mother's jewels in her arms. She also thought that someday his wife should have them, but at this moment she couldn't agree with him more as to who deserved them now. With a shake

39

of her head and a brave smile, she whispered, "Geoff, will you send Polly to me if she is willing to come? I just can't face living alone with strangers after all."

"You know I would send anyone who would be a comfort to you," he said with tenderness. "And I am positive Polly will be willing."

"Thank you, Geoff," she uttered as Jonathan moved to her side.

"Are you ready? Good," he replied at her nod. "Let us be on our way."

Leading her outside, he clasped her around the waist and swung her into the carriage. He sprung in after her and yelled to the driver. Jessica turned for one last glance at her childhood home as the carriage rolled down the drive. Not one of those remaining on the porch seemed surprised at her husband's eagerness.

Chapter Four

Jessica nodded in the corner of the carriage, wishing she could sleep through all this jolting as easily as Jonathan. He had fallen asleep almost immediately after they had started their trip, and he still slept even though the entire carriage shook from some of the ruts the wheels hit. Eventually they stopped at a posting inn. Promptly Jonathan was wide awake and leaped to the ground.

"Come, my dear, we will rest inside tonight." Jonathan assisted her from the carriage and led her inside. Thinking that he meant they would rest inside while fresh horses were exchanged for their tired ones, Jessica complied with his wishes docilely. However, Jonathan's man rushed up the stairs while they followed more leisurely. As they trod down the hall with Jonathan firmly propelling her forward, Donald threw open the door of a room gleaming with candlelight. Jessica drew in her breath sharply when she saw the bed. Closing her mouth immediately, she stared at the floor.

"Will you see about the baggage, Donald?" Jonathan asked; and Donald, with one brief glance at the misery in the girl's face, hastily left and closed the door. "Surely, my dear, you did not think I planned to travel all those miles to London tonight?"

"I didn't really think about it," she mumbled. She raised her eyes and looked at the room more carefully. The bed was certainly the most prominent piece of

41

furniture. However, the room was quite large and at one end Jessica noticed a table with two chairs. The table was set as for a meal. "Does he do nothing but eat?" she thought. She sat down in a large chair that faced the blazing fire. She had not realized until this moment how chilly she had been in the carriage.

Jonathan answered a soft rap on the door and Donald entered, saying, "I've brought some refreshment, Sir," as his master frowned. When he had finished laying the table, he spoke to Jessica who had turned to watch. "I hope everything is to your liking, mum," he said with a quick bow.

"I'm sure it will be. Thank you, Donald." The servant smiled encouragingly and Jonathan frowned again. Noticing Jonathan's discomfort, he continued, "I'll return with your belongings shortly, mum." When he saw the color rise in her cheeks, he left discreetly.

What is he doing? thought Jonathan. Can this little girl have captivated him already? Never before had Donald bowed—to anyone that Jonathan knew of—and they had been together a long time. With one glance he has decided I'm a villain about to do the worst to a sweet young innocent, he thought, and so does she. Shrugging his shoulders against his annoyance, he deftly opened the wine and filled the glasses which he set on the table.

"Come, Jessica, you must be hungry by now. You ate nothing before we left."

Suddenly she was hungry, almost starved in fact. He was right, of course. At Briarly she had eaten little and pushed her food around the plate to hide the fact. Surprised that he had noticed, she rose and walked over to the chair he held for her. Noticing her brooding silence, Jonathan said nothing but merely sat down across from her and started to eat. Finally he saw Jessica relax and eat, too. Little did he know grim reality had reared its ugly head before her and she had resolved to keep up her strength.

Jessica returned to the chair by the fireplace when she had finished. She stared at the flames while Donald tiptoed in with her valise. Shaking his head all the while, he cleared the small table and tiptoed back out with a full tray. Jonathan closed the door, excused him for the night, and sat in a chair next to her.

"Jessica, we must talk. We will be in each other's company almost constantly for thirty-six hours more. We cannot avoid each other and these continual silences make us both uncomfortable," he said quietly.

"I know, but I did not expect this," she moaned.

"What did you expect?"

"I, I don't know. You didn't even mention leaving Briarly tonight. I expected to stay there, for one more night at least. You tricked me."

"Tricked you!" His anger rose rapidly and Jessica shrank into her chair even more. "Think, girl, think! Both of us saw Lord Eden and your brother leave the library. Both of us know what occurred in there. Did you want him to guess how your brother suddenly possessed all that money? He would have, you know."

"What has whisking me off before his very nose have to do with that? You humiliated me!" she wailed.

"Ah, the fight has gone out of you. I'm sorry for that. I was beginning to think you might be interesting," he retorted sardonically.

She jumped to her feet and strode to face him with fists clenched. "Oh, did you!" she railed. As she raised her fist, he caught it in mid-air.

"Be careful," he threatened. "I've warned you twice. I'm not in the habit of giving more than one warning. But with you I've been extremely generous."

Her anger wilted as rapidly as it had bloomed. With her retreat into dejection once more, he turned her around. As he unfastened her gown, he continued in a gentler tone, "Since you have no maid, my lady, I do not mind acting the role."

Jessica clutched the bodice and spun around again,

fire dancing in her eyes. "You are insufferable!"

"That is true. I will leave you now to dress for the night," and he stalked from the room.

Surprised, but pleasantly, to find herself alone, Jessica shot the bolt on the door. She stood shaking in anger for some minutes until the fire raging in her burned out. With renewed determination she opened her valise to see what Polly had packed. How had Polly known she would need a valise for tonight? She's much more realistic than I, thought Jessica. Jonathan played his part so well Polly knew he would not travel all night. The valise contained all the toilet articles she could possibly need, her prettiest gown, though it bordered on being unsuitable for travel, and a filmy, transparent night garment and robe of a violet that Jessica knew would match her eyes. Where did the girl find this? Mrs. Mattingly again, I presume. That woman's presumption is extremely irritating.

A knock on the door interrupted her thoughts. When she opened it, Donald pardoned himself and walked in carrying a tub followed by several servants bearing pails of water. "Mr. Jonathan thought you might like a bath, mum," he said while he oversaw the procedure. "I'll be right outside when you are finished." He backed out of the room with a bow and Jessica was alone again.

"Polly really knew what she was doing," thought Jessica as she poured lavender scent into the water and put the same perfumed soap on the edge of the tub. She squeezed the sponge over her shoulders and arms until the warmth eased all the tension within her body. With a start she thought, "I must wash quickly before he returns."

Shortly after the room had been restored to order, she heard another tap.

"Who is it?"

"Jon."

She walked slowly to the door and lifted the bar that locked it. "I almost didn't know who you were. Do many people call you Jon?"

He gasped at the sight of her. As she quickly scuttled back to her chair by the fire, he masked his feelings with a "Come now, man, cool yourself" under his breath.

With a feeling of *deja vu* he crossed the room to her. Through the years there had been so many, but none like her. "God, she's beautiful. I like this bargain less every second I'm with her," he told himself. Pulling the other chair close to hers, he saw her shrivel further into hers as he sat down. Taking her hand in his, he said, "Jessica, can we not declare a truce for the remainder of my time here?"

The gentleness of his voice drew her eyes to his. "Jonathan, what have we done to ourselves?" she sighed. "This will never work."

"I am at fault much more than you," he apologized. "You were desperate while I took advantage of the desperation for the sake of convenience. Now we must try to find a way to live in peace, if not happiness, with the situation in which we find ourselves."

"But how can we? We don't know each other. We don't even like each other. We fight constantly when we are together."

"We will find a way. We must both hold our tempers, and I must stop baiting you at every opportunity. I will freely admit that I take out my resentment on you because I have tried to blame you for this mess when all the while I have only myself to blame."

"Why do you blame me? I never offered to make a bargain."

Sensing she might soon be angry again, Jonathan mollified her quickly. "I know. None of this is your fault. At first I thought I would hate you for meekly offering your body for your brother's use. Then I tried to hate your brother for using you so badly." Feeling her body stiffen, he patiently continued, "But after I met Geoff, I realized his greatest concern was for you, not for your home. Then I hated my father for forcing all three of us to bow to his will and selfishness. Downstairs, after much consideration of all these shifts of hatred, I finally acknowledged that I could have refused him.''

"Why didn't you?'' she asked meekly.

"I don't know—probably because of my own selfishness. My father is wiser than I care to admit. He knew I might jump at the opportunity to escape another marriage when I returned to America. I have always thought I controlled my life since I moved out of his house ten years ago. In truth my personal affairs only drifted, and I left for this trip without telling my so-called intended that only *she* intended. I never seriously entertained the thought of marrying her. This marriage to you offered me an excellent excuse to extricate myself from her clutches.''

"Oh, Jonathan, how could you be so cruel to her?''

"Do not concern yourself with Carolyn, my dear. I did nothing but let her assume what she wanted. I promised her nothing.''

"But still. . .''

"She is my problem. I married you and will keep my word. But I dislike seeing you either frightened of me or angry with me. I would not distress you further, Jessica,'' he continued tenderly, "even if we do not live together, we are married. Since I will have a wife in London, I certainly intend to return to England each year as I have always done. We cannot be at each other's throats on those occasions.''

Feeling much more comfortable with his tenderness, Jessica stood, not realizing how the fire silhouetted her body within its gauzy coverings. The effect on Jonathan was instantaneous and he jolted to his feet to look down on her. Jessica molded her body to his when he encircled her with his arms. His will power disappearing rapidly, Jonathan led her to the bed and tucked her under the covers as if she were a child. "Try to sleep, Jessica. Tomorrow will be soon enough to decide what to do.''

Somewhat surprised but too tired to care, Jessica soon slept while Jonathan dropped into a chair to brood into the fire.

In the morning Jessica jumped from the bed quickly when she awakened in an empty room. She washed and dressed, wondering where Jonathan could be. Just as she thought he might have left her alone, he came into the room. She turned to face him. Seeing her questioning eyes, he smiled and was rewarded with a delighted grin from her. "I thought I would be back before you awakened. Are you ready to go down to breakfast? We will be leaving shortly."

"I'm almost ready," Jessica answered nervously as she turned away to lay her few things in the valise. She heard him move behind her and quieted as he hooked her dress.

When they went down to eat, Donald pulled out a chair for her. "Morning mum," he mumbled and left the room quickly. Following his departure with her eyes, Jessica wondered what he thought of his master's marriage. "Has Donald been with you long?" she asked.

"Ever since I've had my ship," her husband replied. "You need not worry about him; he seems quite taken with you. If he becomes as devoted to you as he has been to me, I may become jealous," he teased.

Not knowing what reply was expected, Jessica attacked her food which the serving girl placed in front of her. After the silent meal Jonathan stood and helped her from her chair. "If you are ready," he said as he tucked her hand through his arm. Jessica followed and soon the carriage once more rattled toward London.

Nervous because he insisted on watching her with half-closed eyelids, Jessica groped for conversation. "How long will we be on the road?"

"It's not all that far, my pet, about two hours."

"Will we be going to your father's?" she questioned quickly. The quiet made her fidgety. They were not comfortable enough with each other to lapse into silence.

"I will deposit you at his house while I finish my business in town. That will give you some time to settle in. However, I will have completed my affairs by the noon meal and thought you might enjoy seeing some of the sights of the city afterwards, if you're not too tired."

His heart tugged as she looked at him, wide-eyed with pleasure. He watched the delight spread over her face in a beautiful smile. How little it takes to please her. Would she ever look at him that way without bribery?

Jessica now found a wealth of questions and chatted gaily the rest of the journey. As the horses pulled to a halt in front of his father's imposing house, she quieted once more. When they alighted from the carriage, he put his arm around her waist and reassured her with a gentle squeeze. Once inside, he introduced her to Edward, who said, "Good morning, madam." Then to Jonathan he added, "Your father thought you would be more comfortable in the blue room, sir. Your things have already been moved."

She felt Jonathan stiffen but he merely replied ever so formally. "That will be fine. See that my wife's things are brought up at once."

"They are already there, sir."

Jonathan led her upstairs, muttering, "It seems my father thinks of everything."

Realizing he was in a foul mood, Jessica trotted to keep up with him. Just as suddenly as his temper flared did it die out as if it had been doused with water. He turned to wait for her in the middle of the staircase, and they ascended to the top together. He took her down the hall saying, "My father certainly does irritate me greatly. Once more, I apologize."

"Jonathan, if you don't want to move, you can move back to your old room, can't you?"

"Are you trying to escape me, my pet?"

"Do I need to?" she asked impishly.

"No, my dear, you are quite safe," he answered as he opened the door.

"Oh, it's a beautiful room!" Jessica exclaimed as she darted in and spun around looking at everything. Sunlight poured in the windows and danced off the mirrors onto the delighted girl. She had thought the room would be as masculine as the rest of the house—what little she had seen as he spirited her past—but this room was utterly feminine. Blue for the blue room—blue wallpaper, blue draperies, blue carpet. "I'm surprised the furniture isn't blue," she giggled as she ran her hand over the smooth top of the white oak dressing table. She looked out the window briefly and sat down even more briefly at the small desk by the other window. She opened the wardrobe and was surprised to see Jonathan's clothes hanging next to hers. She opened and closed drawers and finally noticed one box set out of the way in the corner. "I'm glad they left me something to do," she stated.

Jonathan, grinning at her happiness, thought wryly, "Well, old man, you were right as usual." To Jessica he finally said, "No, sweet, I cannot move back to my old room. Though it is customary for a man and wife to have separate rooms, separate but connecting, the servants would surely gossip if we separated the second night of our marriage, especially since I am leaving tomorrow. You will just have to put up with me one more night."

"Beg pardon, mum," Donald said as he set down both of their valises. Jonathan turned and said, "I'll be down shortly."

Turning back to Jessica, he went on, "Shall I send someone to help you? We don't have a lady's maid, I'm afraid."

"Do you think your father will mind if Polly comes down from Briarly?" she asked. "Geoff said he'd send her."

"I'm sure anything you do will suit my father." At her crestfallen gaze, he continued rapidly, "I'll send Mrs. Winters up to show you the house. Be ready for our grand tour when I return." He strode from the room, knowing he had been more abrupt than necessary. I will not forever be apologizing to her, he thought. After all she can hardly wait to see me gone.

"That sly old fox," Jonathan said to himself as he opened the door and looked into the room that had been his since childhood. "What did he hope to accomplish with that maneuver?" The room looked as if no one had used it in years. "He has me gone already."

Downstairs he walked to the back of the house and asked Mrs. Winters to make Jessica feel welcome. After the housekeeper assured him she would take care of everything, he and Donald left to tie up the loose ends of his affairs.

Meanwhile, Jessica unpacked the articles from the box, fondling each in its turn. Someone here was thoughtful. It might not be so bad after all. They had unpacked her clothes, but would not presume to put away her few personal treasures—her books, her pictures of her parents, her mementos from her happy childhood days—nothing really valuable but the placement of which required a decision on her part. She spent the next half hour hanging away the clothes she and Jonathan had brought with them and deciding how she wanted her toilet articles on the dressing table. When she thought everything was where she wanted it—at least for now—she sat down in the lounge chair to await Mrs. Winters.

"Come in," she called in answer to a hesitant knock.

"Congratulations on your marriage, ma'am. I'm the housekeeper, Mrs. Winters." A middle-aged woman, so efficient looking that Jessica wondered she had bothered to knock, moved to the center of the room. "I see you have finished unpacking. Would you like to see the house now?" she asked crisply.

"Yes," said Jessica. "I want to learn my way about at once. It would never do for the mistress of the house to get lost." Two can play at this game she thought as she continued imperiously. "My husband said you would show me everything."

Realizing immediately that her mistress was not a little girl one could easily push around, though she did look it, Mrs. Winters softened her tone somewhat. "Is there anything you need? I can have one of the maids help you."

"No, thank you. I'm sure you need all your staff to run the house. My maid from home is coming here to help me. I would appreciate your finding a nice room for her in the servants' wing, but don't inconvenience anyone else to do so. Polly is very congenial and will make do with whatever you can provide."

Their battle had been joined and the armistice declared. "If you are ready, Miss Jessica, would you like to start with the upstairs?"

"I would like to meet the staff first and find suitable quarters for Polly next. Is everyone so imposing as Edward?"

Jessica's answer had been perfect. Completely pacified because the mistress was so concerned about the staff, Mrs. Winters surrendered. The two women—one very young and one considerably older—passed away the rest of the morning as Jessica became acquainted with the house and the operation of the household. The morning had vanished when Jonathan returned.

They ate the noon meal quickly and left the house. Jessica commented on a new driver for the coach, but Jonathan said only, "Donald is seeing that all is ready for our departure tomorrow. This is my father's coachman." As the coach pulled out to start its journey, Jonathan said dryly, "It seems we must stop at a Mrs. Mattingly's to have some gowns fit. We will go there first."

Jessica wondered why he acted so odd since he had

51

ordered the gowns, but said nothing. At the shop Mrs. Mattingly rushed to greet them. "Come in, my dear. Was the bridal dress a success?"

Jonathan answered emphatically, "It most certainly was. She was a beautiful bride and I thank you, madam," he added gallantly.

"And you, sir?"

"I am Jonathan Selby, this young girl's fortunate husband. My father said we have business here."

"Oh, I should have known," the clothier replied. Ah, she thought, he does not want to waste time here. No wonder he was in such a hurry for the wedding. "Come this way. The work has only to meet with your approval. Do you want to try them, madam?"

"I should probably try at least one," the girl answered as she followed Mrs. Mattingly to a dressing room. There the woman motioned Jonathan to a chair as she unhooked Jessica's gown. Jessica's cheeks turned scarlet when Jonathan murmured, "I want to see all of them on her."

"Yes, sir." He certainly takes care of her, she thought. "Here is the first," and she helped Jessica into the dress then turned her around to fasten it.

How does she do it? Jonathan thought. The woman does know her business. If Jessica was a pretty girl, she is a beautiful woman. Jonathan felt as if he were seeing a preview of her in the full bloom of womanhood. Jessica seethed as Jonathan continued to watch her dress and undress. Why couldn't he leave?

Little was she aware he was having as much difficulty as she. He soon wished this would be over. He shifted in his chair thinking, I may attack her like an animal if she doesn't stay dressed soon. He crossed his arms in front of him and shifted again. He smiled as Jessica turned to look at him and then jumped to his feet. Why the Hell did I insist on seeing all of them? "How many more?"

"Do you not like the gowns, sir?"

"The work is satisfactory and you have chosen the

styles well. My wife has never been in the city, and we have many places to visit today."

"This is the last, sir." She glanced at the pair knowingly, but sensing the girl's lack of ease, she said nothing. Jessica, knowing what the woman thought, reddened more.

When they left the shop, Jonathan said, "Let's walk." They went into many shops on that street, Jessica exclaiming with wonder at the vast array of offerings. Soon she was pulling him and he was following her. Jonathan gave her some money to make small purchases, but she bought nothing. Towards the end of the afternoon she headed into a men's shop. "You can't go in there, my dear."

"Why ever not?"

"Ladies don't go into men's shops," he answered with a grin, "not if they are ladies."

"Oh, pooh! However do wives buy their husbands gifts?"

"They send a servant."

"Oh, take me in, Jon."

As he propelled her down the street, she sulked until they entered another store when he said, "Let's try this."

Jonathan sat silently in the coach on their return. Jessica wondered at this briefly, but was too joyful over these new experiences to contemplate his silence long. Innocently she leaned against him and felt him shudder. "Is something wrong? What did I do?" she asked as she jerked back to the corner of the carriage. ·

Hardly able to control himself, he snarled, "I'm all right."

Jessica cringed at his tone. "Jonathan," she begged, "don't spoil it. This has been the most wonderful afternoon of my life."

"Most brides would say that about their wedding day," he growled.

She sat in the corner of the carriage and stared at the

floor, tears filling her eyes. As the tears trickled down her cheeks, Jonathan drew her back to him. He quietly dried her eyes with his handkerchief and delicately caressed her cheek. Softly he kissed the tip of her nose and held her in his arms until the carriage stopped.

When they alighted from the carriage, Jessica, now completely recovered, ran unceremoniously past the gaping Edward, squealing, "I must speak to Mrs. Winters."

Feeling very pleased with herself, Jessica burst into their room a few minutes later, but stopped short when she saw Jonathan in the tub in the middle of the room.

"Come on in, my dear," he drawled. When she hesitated, he added, "We don't want gossip among the staff." She closed the door behind her and busied herself around the room, keeping her eyes averted from the tub. She hung up the clothes he had discarded here and there. Then she opened and shut drawers hunting clean clothes for him. When she finally had gathered what she thought appropriate, she said over her shoulder, "Mrs. Winters says we are to dine with your father."

"It was to be expected," was his only comment.

Still not able to face him, she pushed aside each of her gowns in the wardrobe, discarding all of them. "What will I wear? Oh, Jonathan, I'm so on edge."

"My father is only a wise old man, not a wolf. He never eats fair young maidens," Jonathan continued as he stood in the tub.

Jessica, who had finally turned to answer him, gasped at her first sight of a naked man and fled from the room. In the hall she heard him roaring with laughter. Her temper flared and she fed it as she furiously paced up and down the hall. When Jonathan opened the door and called to her, she stormed into the room. But her anger subsided quickly when he said, "Forgive me, dear, but that was the quickest way to give you courage. When you are angry, you are very brave."

Still not relenting completely, she flounced into the

chair at the dressing table and peered at herself in the mirror. Coming up behind her and unfastening her dress, Jonathan went on, "You must not cower before him. He most admires strength. Since you want to change for dinner, it would please me if you would wear the gown in the box on the bed."

As she rushed toward the bed, she tripped on the hem of her loosened dress and fell headlong into her husband's arms. Only his quick action saved her from crashing to the floor. He held her tightly for a few seconds then released her. Her dress fell to the floor, and he lifted her from among the folds and set her down again beside them. "You should be safe now, little one," he teased. "Call me when you are ready to have your gown fastened," he growled as he strode from the room.

"What did I do now? I will never understand him," Jessica muttered as she neared the bed. Having pulled the box to the edge, she raised the lid. She lifted the ice-blue fabric from the box very carefully and held it in front of her. "Oh! It's more gorgeous than any of Mrs. Mattingly's gowns." The soft fabric shimmered in the light almost as if it were iridescent. She could hardly wait to see it on herself, so taking special care with her toilette, she dressed for dinner.

Jonathan meanwhile paced the hall as she had previously. I don't know whether I can hold out even this one last night, he brooded. This girl reduces me to jelly with the slightest touch. And she is completely without guile, she doesn't even know what she does. I watched all kinds of men turn to stare at her this afternoon, and she never noticed. How can she be so unaware of the effect she has on those about her?

Instead of calling him, Jessica slipped into the hall and presented him with her back. "Jonathan, this is the loveliest dress I've ever seen," she whispered. "How can I ever repay you?"

When he had finished the buttoning, he patted her

shoulder. "We'll think of a way." Offering her his arm, they descended the stairs together. He drew her to the settee in the drawing room and they sat there quietly for several minutes. "Where in America is your home?" she queried timorously.

"My ship sails to and from New Orleans in Louisiana, but I own a plantation several miles from the city," Jonathan answered, watching her calculatingly.

"A plantation?" she questioned.

"A plantation is the American term for an estate," he explained.

"Is your plantation as large as Briarly?"

"Many times larger, my dear. One definite advantage to America is the wealth of space. It would take me many days to ride the boundaries of my land."

"Is Louisiana pretty?"

"I think so." Jonathan quietly told her about his home and about Callie. In her turn she described her short life at Briarly Hill. Thus they sat companionably on the settee when Jeremiah Selby entered. Jonathan patted Jessica and covered her hand with his own to reassure her. Jessica glanced at him tenderly and returned her gaze to his father.

"Well, well, my dear," said the old gentleman. "How do you like London?"

"What I've seen of it is very exciting, sir."

"Hrumph! Exciting? My son did not take you to see all of the town then."

Not understanding, Jessica replied, "We had a good time today, didn't we Jonathan?" Her eyes pleaded for his support.

"Yes, we did, love," he answered with a quick squeeze of her hand and a smile.

Catching the intimacy between them, Mr. Selby smiled gloatingly. Jonathan, when he saw his father's grin, glared at the old man. Before he had the opportunity to say another word, Edward appeared in the doorway, and the three of them went in to dinner.

Throughout the meal Jeremiah Selby was as disagreeable as possible. When Jessica asked him a question, he either grunted or ignored her. Soon she retreated within herself and concentrated on her food. When he realized she had given up, he badgered her with a barrage of questions, hardly allowing her time to answer one question before he shot another her direction. Each question was calculated to irritate her more than the preceding one. Jonathan came to her rescue several times, but even he could not control the man's rudeness. "Father, that's enough!"

"Enough what?" the man asked innocently. "Well, girl, why don't you answer? Can't you speak about any topic sensibly? It's going to be dull around here with you spouting gibberish through every dinner!"

Tears springing to her eyes, Jessica ran from the room. Jonathan followed at once, but she was already running up the stairs.

Mrs. Winters rushed to the bottom of the stairway and stood with him, watching the fleeing girl. "Is anything wrong, sir?"

"My father has just been his usual nasty self," he answered disgustedly. "Take care of her, Mrs. Winters. He has wounded her deeply."

Returning to the dining room, he shouted, "That was the most disgusting display of uncivil behavior I have ever witnessed. You have outdone even yourself tonight. What did you hope to accomplish?"

Without a word Jeremiah Selby rose and walked from the room. Jonathan stamped after him to his father's study where he slammed the door violently. "I will have an answer, sir." He pounded his fist on the desk as the old man sat behind it. "Why?"

"Why are you so concerned about the feelings of this girl I forced you to marry? Could it be I didn't force you, as you so often like to remind me?"

Jonathan clamped his jaw tightly. Struggling to control his rage, he shook visibly and clenched his fists.

He threw himself into a chair across from his father to keep from hitting the old man. Gradually he regained control of his emotions. Finally, he rose and stared at his father who had said nothing else during the interview.

"You will not repeat this magnificent performance, sir!" He punctuated his words with further hammering on the desk.

"You are right, son. I shall not repeat this episode." Somewhat reassured Jonathan stalked from the room and up the stairs. Lavender scent greeted his nostrils as he entered the room to which Jessica had escaped. He quietly closed the door and regarded her while he leaned on it. Mrs. Winters had obviously ordered a bath to relax the girl, but the desired effect was not accomplished. Jessica, in a blue negligee, lay on the lounge chair, sobbing her very soul into the arm. Jonathan crossed to the chair and lifted her into his arms. Then he sat down, holding her on his lap. She turned to him and cried into his chest. Knowing nothing he could say would help, he embraced her quietly and hoped she would draw some strength from him. He gently brushed her tousled hair from her wet face. Eventually her sobs subsided and, looking at him with her glistening violet eyes, she moaned, "What will happen to me? How can I possibly stay here with that monster?" Her sobbing renewed, he felt her tears through his wet shirt.

"He will not treat you so again. That much I can promise you." But he knew those words did not ease her agony. Holding her as a father comforting a wounded child, he patiently rocked her until her sobs abated to occasional sniffs. He kissed her hair and caressed her arms and shoulders. She looked at him through teary lashes. He sucked in his breath at her dazzling beauty. Impulsively his mouth closed over her quivering lips in an urgent kiss that took her breath away. Without realizing what she did, she lifted her arms and put them around his neck. She felt his hands caress her back and finally pull the ribbon on her head. Her hair tumbled down over her shoulders. His lips caressed her eyelids, moved to her nose and nibbled at her ear, murmuring soft, unintelligible words. Jessica's body melted against his strong chest, and with a low groan his lips found hers again. Emotions she never knew she possessed whirled within her and Jonathan felt her body tremble as he carried her to the bed.

"I don't know what to do."

"Sh. Don't do anything," he whispered as he lay beside her. He took her in his arms and held her close to him. When he felt her relax against him, he tilted her head so she gazed at him. Her heart caught in her throat as she saw his expression. She reached out and stroked his cheek softly. The gentle touch unnerved him so much his whole body shook. She could feel his heart beating in rhythm with hers. He kissed her again until his warmth penetrated her body and she began to kiss him back. Once more his lips trailed over her face to her earlobes and she felt him briefly bury his face in her hair, raising and dropping the long tresses on the pillow. Hardly aware of what was happening, she lay still while he tenderly undressed her and threw her garments on the floor. His hands fondled her breasts and moved down the length of ther body. His lips followed his hands to her breasts, up to her lips, to her throat and back again to her breasts. She hesitantly moved her hand to his chest but caught it in a button on his shirt. He withdrew his arm from around her and helped her unbutton the shirt. Then he rolled from the bed and stripped his clothes from his body and dropped them on the floor beside hers. When he joined her again on the bed, he pressed the full length of her body to his. His lips softly pressed her temple and moved down her face closer and closer to her mouth, each kiss making her shiver. Her pulse quickened as his mouth closed over hers and opened her lips. He was gentle with her, taking time to arouse her and allay her fears. His hands fondled her breasts, then slipped to her thighs and moved upward along the inside while his lips traveled to her throat and breasts, slowly caressing the pointed peaks. Jessica moaned and clung to him, pulling him to her mouth once more. Waves of pleasure swept over her entire body and she offered herself, never realizing the meaning of the movements, all her senses swimming and swirling through her. When he took her, the violet eyes opened wide, but she did not cry out as his mouth again crushed to hers. Gradually he moved within her, gently at first; his movements quickened and suddenly her body moved with his. She did not want to think of anything but that he wanted her and called her "my love." Her hands roamed over his back and up to his hair. His flesh seemed to burn her soft breast. The sun burst within her and spread its surging heat in eddying swirls to the limits of her senses. She arched against him in an ecstasy she had never imagined possible.

As she floated back to earth, she felt a delicious sense of well-being. Sated and cradled in his arms, Jessica thought, life is perfect and he loves me. She was so weak she hardly had the strength to return his kisses. She closed her eyes and fell asleep in his arms and he held her throughout the night.

Jessica awoke, blinking away the bright sunlight that flooded the room when Mrs. Winters opened the draperies. She stretched languously and blushed, remembering the night before. She fingered the empty space beside her and jumped out of bed.

"How long ago did Jonathan arise?"

"He came down just a little while ago. He and Mr. Selby are in the dining room."

Jessica threw on her clothes and rushed from the room. Once in the hall, she stopped short and then primly walked down the stairs. Loud voices from the dining room bombarded her ears. Thinking she could do something to forestall further argument, she made her way to that room. Just as she reached the doorway, Jonathan shouted, "I have done everything in my power to insure she bears you a grandchild! I will do nothing more this trip!"

Aghast Jessica stood in her tracks. Her hand flew to her mouth and tears filled her eyes. The love that had just begun to bud was instantly crushed to death before it ever had a chance to bloom. She twisted around and sprinted back up the stairs, suffering an agony worse than any she had ever known.

Jonathan with a final, "See what you have done to her now?" stamped from the room and house to sail for America.

Chapter Five

Jonathan, after the scene at his father's house, returned to his ship. "Let's get underway as soon as possible," he growled to Donald as that man took his master's belongings to the captain's cabin. Jonathan remained on deck to oversee the sailing. As he watched the shoreline recede, his thoughts returned for the first time to his wife. Why do I let my father anger me to the point that I say such horrible things? She completely misunderstands—she thinks I only used her last night. Well, that can't be helped. My life has too many complications that must be put straight before I can consider introducing her into it. Still—no, maybe, next trip.

Leaving the ship in the capable hands of his crew, Jonathan went below. He crossed the room to his sea chest, thinking to change to clothing more practical for the ship. As he threw back the lid, right in the middle on top of all his belongings, he saw a gift-wrapped box. "Where did this come from?" He moved the box to his bed and proceeded to change his clothing. When he had finished, he sat at the desk to record the sailing and complete some other paper work. But every time he raised his eyes from his books, they travelled naturally to the box. "This is silly. I'm not some child who can't wait for Christmas morning." Finally his curiosity got the better of him. He rose from the chair and strode to the bunk. He opened the box and saw a pipe, exquisitely hand tooled. Now he was really confused. Lifting it from the box, he noticed an envelope on the bottom. Not recognizing the handwriting, he opened the letter. His heart flip-flopped as he read:

Dear Jonathan,

Thank you for being so kind and considerate. These last two days have meant much for me, and I will never forget them because of your kindness to me.

Jessica

He sank into a chair and remembered his kindness ironically. He had thought her as scheming as the other women he had known. And when he had discovered his error, he had humiliated her for allowing herself to be a pawn. Then he had discovered she had spirit, but was only slightly remorseful over his treatment of her. It had taken no sacrifice for him to treat her decently, though it did take a great deal of will power at the inn. His blood rose whenever he looked at her. Did he just want her? He surely wasn't falling in love with her. He who had escaped the clutches of countless females and more or less done what he wanted so far as women were concerned. How could he fall in love in less than a week with a mere child? Mere?—a lovely and beautiful girl. She would not be cowed for long. She enjoyed life and was so naturally exuberant when she was happy. Thank God she wasn't stiff and prim and proper. He had intended to sail without touching her. How could he have let matters get so far out of hand last night? First his father and then he had taken advantage of her. He certainly should have removed her from his father's company. The exhibition at dinner had wounded her terribly. Why had he ever let it continue? I never thought he would go so far, he brooded. And later—ah, later—was magnificent. But this morning! It's no excuse that I didn't know she was there. I will forever make statements I regret. Now she thinks last night meant nothing to me and is humiliated again. God, she must hate me now. It was bad enough that I left her behind, but now she has humbled me even further by spending all her money on a gift for me because of my "kindness." I don't even know how she managed it. We got back fairly late in the afternoon, yet she found a way to surprise me.

Well, the least I can do is let her know I got the gift and am using it. I'll write her and send the message with a passing ship. If I had any sense at all, I'd just go get her and take her back with me. No! I must get my affairs straightened out first. I sat like a stupid ox and let her suffer my father's badgering. I must settle with Carolyn before introducing Jessica to my home.

Yes, Carolyn. What a bitch she could be and would be to someone as gentle as Jessica. One has to fight Carolyn with power, not a flaring temper or tears. Carolyn would surely prevail in any confrontation with Jessica whom she could easily reduce to tears. Though Jessica doesn't realize what a weapon tears are against me and can rant and rail at me, she would be helpless against the feminine wiles Carolyn was used to employing. Yes, that must be settled.

Callie will be beside herself with Jessica to fuss over. That's one person who will wholeheartedly approve. She will certainly be glad I'm not marrying Carolyn. Thank heaven that discussion will be ended. With a loud sigh he returned to the desk and continued his work; but even with his decision made, concentration was difficult. Pictures of Jessica smiling, trembling, and crying flashed through his mind.

When Donald came in with his master's lunch, he wondered at the turn of events. Who would marry a sweet girl like Miss Jessica and leave her behind in a foreign country two days later? Surely his master wouldn't do her wrong and go back to the likes of Miss

Carolyn. Shaking his head in confusion, he left the room. When he returned for the empty dishes, Jonathan said, "Let's make this a fast trip, Donald. I've got things to do at home and I want to hurry back for your mistress."

Donald burst into a wide grin, saying, "Yes sir!" and hurried out.

"Donald has really been taken in," Jonathan thought. "He could barely speak until he knew I was coming back. Between Donald and Callie, I never stood a chance, nor did Carolyn."

Almost two months later the *Raven* slipped into the channel and ground to a halt against the dock. Jonathan left the bridge and made his way to his cabin. He made a final entry in the log and tied all the ledgers together. As if an afterthought, he set them down and grabbed the bottle from his desk. He poured himself a drink and gulped it down. Then he poured himself another. This too he gulped as if gathering courage. Returning the bottle to the drawer, he picked up the ledgers and again stalked determinedly from the cabin and the ship. As he descended to the dock, a woman rushed through the crowd to him and threw her arms around him. "Welcome home, darling!" Jonathan stood hugging his books to his chest while she kissed him over and over. She never noticed his lack of enthusiasm.

"Shall we go to your house or mine? We have so many plans to make. I told everyone we'd be married a week after your arrival." Jonathan could not get a word in edgewise. She slid her arm through his and started to lead him away as if in total command. Jonathan stopped short and put her aside.

"Why don't you go on to your house? I'll be there as soon as I can. Before I go anywhere, I must talk to Steve at the office."

"You can talk to him later," she insisted and started to pull him to the waiting carriage.

He went along with her, but surprised her by helping her in and closing the door after her. "I'll see you later, Carolyn—not more than an hour if I can get Steve to ignore the unloading long enough to talk." He had to get her out of here before she made a scene on the street. The last thing he wanted was a private interview, but he certainly could not tell her the news here.

Flouncing her skirts beside her, she resettled in the seat, pouting all the while. Then a wide seductive smile covered her face. "Come as soon as you can, darling. I'll be waiting." Jonathan motioned to the driver and the carriage rolled down the street.

Jonathan turned back to his ship, and his eyes traveled over the crowd until they spied his friend and partner. They had worked together many years now and were more like brothers than business partners. Steve hailed Jonathan at about the same time as Steve turned, as if some kind of telepathy told him Jonathan was watching him. Leaving the work behind him, Steve rushed over and clasped Jonathan's hand. "Well, I guess you got disentangled from the fair Carolyn. You didn't seem nearly so enthralled as she," he muttered with a sardonic grin.

"That's nothing compared to what is to come. Let's go inside."

The two men, both tall and lean, strolled into the office of the warehouse. Steve poured each of them a drink and toasted, "To the fair Carolyn," and drank the whiskey with a shudder. Only as he poured his second drink did he notice that Jonathan had set his own down without touching it. "Oh, not drinking to Carolyn? I thought the wedding was next week."

"Don't joke, Steve. Carolyn will screech when I tell her."

"Tell her what?"

"Come on now, Steve. You know I never asked her to marry me. I never said I would marry her. Well. . .well . . .the truth is. . ."

"You don't intend to marry her?"

"I'm already married," he blurted out.

"What!" Steve drank his second whiskey and slapped his knee with delight. "I'd love to be there when you tell her! She's told everyone in town about your coming marriage."

Jonathan finally put his ledgers down and slumped into a chair. "I might have known she would. I had hoped she wouldn't."

"She really thought she had trapped you. But tell me how you escaped her clutches."

"I got married two days before I sailed. I want to settle with Carolyn and sail back to England for my wife quickly. Can you get me cargo?"

"Oh, yes, that is no problem. I can get you all the cargo you want. But there is another difficulty, maybe worse."

"What could be worse than facing Carolyn with the news I have?" They agreed on the difficulty of that chore. Steve breathed a sigh of relief that Jonathan and not he had to handle that problem.

"You must take a trip into the interior before you go. I understand there is trouble in that territory, and no one has heard a sound from your men. Do you want me to go?"

"No, I'll go, but have the *Raven* ready to sail the day after I return. I should take me no more than two weeks. Can the ship be unloaded and reloaded in so short a time?" Steve nodded and Jonathan rose from his chair and looked as if he were fifty years old. Shrugging his shoulders, he straightened and took twenty years from his appearance. "Will you tell Donald to take my things out to my house? I'll be there soon," and he strode to his carriage with renewed purpose.

After the short ride he arrived at Carolyn's and, after telling the driver to wait, went into the house. The butler pointed toward the drawing room and disappeared.

When he entered, Carolyn rose and walked to him deliberately and entwined her arms around his neck, "I thought you would never get here," she whispered huskily and kissed him. This time she noticed the perfunctory kiss and the slight stiffening of his body. His arms did not embrace her but went to the back of his neck where he unlocked her grasp.

"Surely you're not worried about the servants. Cook has prepared a cold supper for whenever we get to it. Everyone is gone for the night but us."

Once more she tried to wrap her arms around him, but he caught her wrists and turned her around. He led her to the settee and returned to the bar for a drink. "Do you want some madiera, Carolyn? Or something stronger?"

"That will be fine. Sit here," she said as she patted the seat beside her. However, he handed her the glass and sat in a chair facing her.

"What the hell is going on, Jonathan?" She was no longer teasing or pouting, she was angry.

"What's this about a wedding next week?" he asked equally angry.

"Jonathan Selby, you aren't going to back out now!" she said with eyes flashing.

"Back out of what? I never said I would marry you and I have no intention of doing so."

While she gasped in fury, Jonathan unwittingly took his pipe from his pocket and filled it. Seeming to capitulate but only to attack from another direction, Carolyn asked sweetly, "Where did you get the new pipe? That's not the one I gave you."

"No, it's not. My wife gave me this pipe."

"Your wife!" she rasped. "What wife?"

"The wife I left behind in London and am returning for soon."

Carolyn jumped to her feet and strode, more like a man than a woman, the few steps to his chair. "You damned bastard. You are trying to make a laughing stock of me. You won't get away with this." She swung so hard she would have lost her balance had he not caught her arm before she hit him. As it was she fell into the chair on top of him and was very much chagrinned when he immediately arose but turned and set her into the chair alone.

"What about my reputation?" she wailed. "Everyone thinks we are to be married."

"I was never aware, Carolyn, that your reputation was important to you. In fact, I thought you enjoyed shocking everyone in the city."

"I still don't believe you. If you don't want to get married, we can go on as before."

"No, we can't, Carolyn. You don't seem to realize I *am* married." He looked at the bitterly angry eyes and continued, "I didn't say I didn't want to marry, but that I definitely did not intend to marry you."

Rage overcame her again and she sprang from the chair like a tiger with claws bared. This time he did not move quickly enough, and her nails raked the side of his face. Without even hesitating, she pounded his chest. Jonathan took it stoically for a while until the worse of her malice had been vented. Then he grabbed her arms and stood back from her. "Listen to me, Carolyn. And hear me well. You have no one but yourself to blame. You thought to trap me into marriage by broadcasting it while I could not deny it. You are the victim of your own trap, not I. I was married, by my own choice, only two days before I returned to Louisiana. When my wife arrives, you will be civil to her or you will not be welcome in our home."

"Never!" she spat. "You were mine. That slut you married had no right to you."

"She had every right. I asked her to marry me. I am going upstate tomorrow, so you may spread whatever story you want to save face. When I return, I will sail for my wife. So do your worst. You cannot hurt us because I do not care what people say behind my back."

As he started for the door, Carolyn looked at him with pure venom in her eyes. "You'll not get away with treating me so shabbily, Jonathan." He did not even break stride and slammed the door on his way out.

As the carriage rolled up the drive, several children standing out front gave up the cry, "Mr. Jonathan's home! Mr. Jonathan's coming!"

A flurry of excitement hung in the air as Callie, the good-natured housekeeper, waddled through the door and down to the drive. When Jonathan descended, he flung his arms around her wide girth and said, "Callie, I've missed you. How are things here?" and lifted her off her feet.

Callie squealed, "Put me down afore you drop me. Always showin' off, aren't you, Mister Jonathan?" Everyone in the yard giggled because lifting Callie was no easy feat and they could see her words belied her happiness.

Jonathan complied and walked into the house with her as Callie turned back a couple of times to make sure no one else was in the carriage.

Callie issued orders for a bath for Mister Jonathan, but never stopped her chatter as she followed him all the way to his room. "Everything here is jus' fine. Don't you know I can take care of the place for you yet? Miss Carolyn came to look at supplies—count the silver, most likely—but I wouldn't let her in like you said. Mr. Jonathan, are you really marrying that woman next week? We don't need a mistress here that bad."

Jonathan watched Callie move about the room, throwing clean clothes for him over her arm and putting a few of the last items she had been unpacking away. "Callie, rest easy now. You already have a mistress."

For the first time Callie stopped in her tracks. Hands on her hips, she said, "What do you mean? You already married her? Today? Humph!"

Jonathan threw back his head and roared while she

scowled. "I can see you will never let me alone to bathe if I don't explain. No, Callie, you were right. That woman, as you insist on calling her, is not for me. I married a charming young lady, of whom you will most certainly approve, before I left London."

"If that's so, where is she?"

Unbuttoning his shirt, after already dropping his coat on the bed, he added, "She's still in London. I thought it best to break the news to Carolyn and then return for her, but now I must go to the northern plantation to see about the trouble there, so I'm not sure when she will get here." His eyes clouded over and the housekeeper, having been with him so long, knew he regretted leaving his wife behind. Snatching his coat from the bed, she put it away and left him alone to bathe.

Jonathan thought, "What a mess I have made out of this whole affair," as he lowered himself into the tub.

Later Jonathan made his way to the stables to make sure all would be ready early in the morning. Then he went to find Callie, coming upon her in the dining room. She clattered dishes to the table, and Jonathan recognized her anger.

"What now?"

"Why did you leave that poor little girl in London? Didn't you know we could protect her from that woman? She couldn't get past me to hurt your baby."

"Callie, leave it. Carolyn already gave me a terrible time. I'll not go through another one with you. Jessica never thought of coming with me, and I could not bring her here to face Carolyn in any case. I'm not even sure when I go for her that she will come back with me. But I'm going to try."

"Don't you worry, Mister Jonathan, she will come. You just hurry up and get back so you can go for her."

With her usual calm assurance she left the room. Jonathan only wished he was as sure as she seemed to be that Jessica would be willing to come here. He wouldn't blame her if she never agreed, but he must try. Even if

71

she refused this trip, there would be more and he was not in the habit of giving up easily. Eventually Jessica would be sitting across from him at this very table. He could hardly wait.

Chapter Six

Life at the Selby house was extremely quiet for the next few days. Jessica sat in her room continuously Saturday, not answering any of the taps at the door with more than an agonized, "Go away." Trays were set outside the door at mealtimes and removed untouched hours later. The servants whispered among themselves and shook their heads when an untouched tray returned to the kitchen, but obeyed when Mrs. Winters said, "Let her alone."

Throughout the weekend Jessica alternately cried, threw tantrums, resolved vengeance, and bemoaned her fate. She was too humiliated to face anyone. Though she needn't have worried because no one intruded on her privacy.

Monday morning she was awakened by a sharp rap on the door. As she rolled over in bed, intending to ignore whoever was there, the door burst open and Polly swished in with a "Good morning, Miss Jessica. Here's your breakfast."

Happy to see a familiar face, Jessica crawled out of bed and reached for her robe. Polly arranged the breakfast on the table by the window, chattering all the while. "I arrived last night. Mr. Geoffrey asked me to come. At first I wasn't sure I wanted to leave Jimmy, but I finally decided I could go back if I wanted. Did you know about Jimmy and me? We have a sort of understanding. O, Miss Jessica, what happened to you? We thought you'd gone to America, and I find you here with the room a mess."

While Jessica ate her breakfast, Polly fussed with the room. Then she pushed aside the draperies and said, "It's going to be a beautiful day," as sunshine poured into the room.

Jessica thought, "Thank heaven she doesn't wait for answers. Beautiful! How can a day be beautiful when I feel like this!" Jessica started the plunge into despair all over again, but Polly would not stand for it.

"I shouldn't have asked because I know. I didn't want you to think the staff here were gossiping about you. They really aren't, you know. They already like you and are very worried. You can't go on this way, so we are going to town today for a ride in the park. What do you want to wear?"

Appalled that Polly should speak to her so, Jessica answered, "I'm not going anywhere." Polly looked at her mistress and walked over to the wardrobe to look over the gowns inside.

"This will do. Now let me help you dress. Then I will do your hair. The carriage will soon be waiting out front."

By mid-morning Jessica and Polly climbed into the carriage. Jessica was somewhat surprised that she had allowed Polly to bully her this way, but she didn't seem to have the energy to resist Polly's boundless enthusiasm. The ride was pleasant enough and they returned to the house with Jessica in much better spirits.

Edward opened the door for them and Mrs. Winters met them before they had a chance to start up the stairs. "Mrs. Selby, we need your advice in the kitchen. Would you follow me?" She started off and Jessica could do little but follow. Mrs. Winters detoured on the way and led her to the servants' quarters. "I thought you might want to see what I was able to arrange for your maid."

74

Mrs. Winters proudly opened the door to a small room which had been made very comfortable-looking with the standard bedroom furniture plus a large chair with a table beside it. The covering on the table matched that on the bed. The room was light and airy.

"Oh, Mrs. Winters, this is so nice. How did you manage something so lovely?"

"We are your people now, and Gwen, the first maid, volunteered to let Polly have her room."

"All of you have been so kind to me," Jessica exclaimed.

"Madam, will you look over the menu for dinner now? There will be only you and Mr. Selby."

"Anything you serve will be fine with me. I'll have my dinner in my room," Jessica continued with a shudder.

"May I offer some advice, Madam?" asked the housekeeper.

"I suppose so," Jessica said as she shrugged her shoulders.

"Mr. Selby may not say so, but I know he is sorry for what has happened. Why not eat dinner with him? You can always go to your room if it doesn't work out."

"But, Mrs. Winters, I can't possibly face him. He's responsible for this entire mess and it would be too embarrassing," Jessica moaned.

"He has humiliated you, but he is not a monster. He is concerned about you. He is also the one who made sure you were left alone all week-end, but he admires a fighter and thinks you are one. Show him you haven't been cowed by the recent events."

"All right, Mrs. Winters. I will be there, but not too much too fast. Just tell me what you have planned for dinner. I'm sure whatever it is will be satisfactory." She started back to the front of the house, then stopped to say, "Please thank Gwen for me, too. I know Polly must have been surprised and I need her company these days."

Jessica whiled away the afternoon writing to Geoff. It was difficult to maintain a cheery manner, but she didn't want him to know how bad the situation was already. She told him about her trip to town and her tour of the city. It was easy for her to sound excited about Friday. She mentioned only that Jonathan had left Saturday and she had spent a quiet weekend. Ending with thanks for his sending Polly, she closed the letter, hoping she had disguised her feelings successfully. Then she read a little until it was time to dress for dinner. After taking particular care with her toilette, she made her way down the stairs.

Her father-in-law stood at the bottom and held his hand out to her. Ignoring his hand, she stood on the bottom step and looked straight into his eyes until he said, "Let's go into the drawing room until dinner is announced."

Jessica nodded and stepped down the final step and swept off in the direction of the drawing room. Jeremiah Selby followed; but when he took her arm, he felt her stiffen perceptibly. This was not going to be easy for him either. Jessica squirmed in her chair, hoping he would just sit quietly. Clearing his throat, he ignored her wishes and started, "I know you blame me for all that has happened, and I don't think we should pussyfoot around the house, pretending all is well."

"Oh no. . ."

"Why do young people always want to interrupt?"

Jessica clamped her jaw shut and let him continue. He could talk all night as far as she was concerned before she would say another word.

Her father-in-law noticed her resolve and added, "I'm happy to see you still have a little spunk left. You will need it. What occurred between you and my son I can only guess, considering the shouted remark you overheard." Jessica started to her feet, but he gently but firmly set her back down. "Don't run away yet. We may have common goals. I suppose you think you hate him, but you don't. I could also tell he admired you."

"But. . ."

"Forget what you overheard. I provoked that vile remark by pushing too hard. He didn't mean such a despicable thing as he said. He resents my telling him what to do, and well he should. I never listened to advice from anyone either. Whether you believe it or not, he was really protecting you."

"Protecting?"

"Yes, protecting you. You see he does care enough about you to want to clean up the dirty mess he has allowed his personal life to become. I thought he should take you with him."

"But it was agreed from the beginning that I stay here —but you were so mean and rude I didn't think I could stand it here." She looked around her, but couldn't force herself to look at him. She knew he wanted to meet her eyes but she was too embarrassed.

"I hope you won't hold that against me, my dear. I was at my nastiest, but Jonathan recognized what I was doing—trying to force his hand. He knows I am not naturally so mean. After I met your brother, I inquired about you and had you observed. Both of you had pride, but not so much that you would be silly rather than bend. You are survivors. I really think you and Jonathan would be good for each other. I must admit I am guilty of more concern for my son than for you. So many women have fallen in love with him through the years that I assumed you would also—especially if he loved you, and I think he does, but he may not yet be aware of it."

"But he was to be married when he returned to America."

"Forget that woman. I am now convinced she is the reason he left you behind. No—not so he could return to his relationship with her. She is a mean, vindictive woman when crossed and he fully intended to cross her, whether or not he met you. I am sure he wanted you out

77

of the way of harm from Carolyn until she realized the
futility of her quest for him as a husband.''

Edward appeared as if from air and the older gentleman offered Jessica his arm, "Shall we go in to dinner?
Jessica, all I ask is that you think carefully before you
commit any rash act.''

"I promise nothing," Jessica answered as she took
his arm, but she had to admit to herself that he was not
nearly so awful as she had thought.

The remainder of the evening passed quickly. When
Jessica finally retired, Polly waited for her in the room.
"Oh, Polly, things may not be so bad after all. That
man does care about people.''

From that day on, Jessica settled into a routine. The
relationship between her and Polly flowered as one between friends almost like sisters, rather than as mistress
and servant. Though she did not keep her vow to cut a
wide swath of scandal across London, she did seem
content both to run Mr. Selby's household and to await
Jonathan's arrival almost a year away.

Jessica knew Mrs. Winters was responsible for much
of her contentment. The older woman saw to it that
Jessica did run the household, even though she herself
knew more about it than Jessica. Every morning she
came to the new mistress to go over the day's menus and
plan the day's work for each member of the staff. Many
times Jessica wanted to say, "Whatever you've done the
last ten years will be fine. Why bother me?" But Mrs.
Winters steadily maintained the attitude that she could
not proceed without her mistress's approval, and Jessica
could do little but involve herself in the daily plans.

Almost every afternoon Jessica, with Polly accom-
panying her, rode out in the carriage, sometimes merely
for a drive in the park, and sometimes to the dressmaker
or to some other small shops to perform small errands
for herself or the household. Jessica spent many hours
in the library, for Jeremiah Selby had a vast collection
of books and added the latest novels to it regularly—for

her benefit, she was sure.

After several weeks during which she and her father-in-law had maintained a sort of armed truce, her defenses gradually disappeared and a true companionship developed. Jessica's heart went out to the lonely old man who had always been so busy making money that he had not time for people, even his family. Now, when it might be far too late, he realized his folly and had once again used his business acumen to correct the situation—thus making two more people resent him. At least he recognized the fact that, no matter how successful he was, he couldn't handle people. Finally, throughout the weeks Jessica lived in his house, he quit trying to manipulate the course of her life and simply enjoyed her.

At first his household changed only because he had a companion at dinner, because Jessica always ate in silence, then excused herself, and retired immediately to her room. One evening he inquired about her day, mentioning her afternoon rides, and she told him about having seen a former school friend. When he told her she could invite her friends to the house, she replied, "They really no longer interest me. I don't care to have friends that recognize me only when I am wealthy and respectable." The silent dinners were ended.

Soon Jessica took to retiring to the drawing room rather than to her bedroom. And Jeremiah joined her rather than remain in the dining room with only brandy and a cigar for company. Both of them changed considerably in those weeks; Jeremiah Selby learned to have patience with the young, and Jessica learned tolerance and understanding. By tacit agreement one subject remained taboo—Jonathan. But they discussed almost everything else—business, people, styles—and agreed completely that most people were "darned fools" as he put it.

One evening the conversation took another course. Jessica could tell her father-in-law was hemming and hawing, trying to find a way to state a problem. Finally she said, "Mr. Selby, why don't you just speak what is on your mind? This talking around the topic is silly."

He stared at her a moment and shook his head. "And I thought I was being subtle," he admonished. "You do know how to set a man down. I would like to invite a business associate to dinner tomorrow. Since he must travel in from the country, I would like to invite him to stay here overnight."

Jessica sat quietly, wondering what she could do to avoid a confrontation with a stranger. "Well, what would you like me to say? This is your house."

"No, Jessica, this is your home, too. You are the mistress here. If you feel you are not yet ready to meet people, we will forget it, and I will go out to dinner with him. But whatever is decided about tomorrow, I do not wish you to hide yourself away in your room."

Jessica's hands twisted in her lap and she stared at them, not realizing how the silence between them had extended. Finally, she looked at the older man and saw his sincerity. The way she felt was the most important aspect of the request, at least as far as he was concerned. "Do I know this man?" she asked.

"Yes."

Stiffening her shoulders, she replied, "Well, I can't hide forever, can I? Invite the man, and I will endeavor to be the proper, gentle hostess."

The next day Jessica made all the arrangements for a guest. A room was readied and an elegant dinner planned. When Polly suggested they ride out as usual, Jessica would have none of it. She realized Mr. Selby was right last night—she had been hiding for almost two months now. She was so nervous she decided she must rest in the afternoon. But she rested little, if any. She had been walking around as if in a stupor all day; but once she lay down, her mind became a beehive of activity. Unwelcome thoughts raced through her brain —who could it be? What would he think or say? Everyone in London knew about her hasty marriage, and no one believed it had occurred because of Jonathan's intense ardor for her or he would hardly have left her behind two days after the ceremony. Could she confront a smirking face? Maybe he would not be that unkind, but at best he would give her knowing or pitying glances. Well, let him. I will appear my haughtiest and remain aloof throughout dinner and can escape immediately after.

However, when Polly arrived to help her dress for dinner, much of Jessica's resolve and courage had disintegrated. She had planned to meet the guest head on inside the door, but was still fussing with her gown when there was a soft tap on the door. Jessica jumped as Polly rushed to open the door for Jeremiah Selby. As if he knew her state of mind, he crossed the room to take her hands in his. "You look beautiful, my dear," he said as his eyes grazed over her. "Remember, you are mistress here. Come, it will be all right," and he led her from the room and down the stairs.

When they reached the bottom, she saw the man in the drawing room rise. As he turned, she flew into his arms. "Geoff, he didn't tell me it would be you!"

The brother and sister hugged each other, then separated to look at each other, and then hugged each other again. With twinkling eyes, Mr. Selby beamed at the pair. He was happy he had pleased her so much. She certainly held no resentment toward her brother, and she had recovered from her embarrassment enough to face her problems. Yes, the cure was working nicely. While he sat contemplating, Jessica and Geoffrey sat on the settee and chattered, or rather Jessica did, incessantly. Geoff had just enough time to reassure her that everyone and everything at Briarly Hill was doing well before Edward announced dinner.

When they entered the dining room, Mr. Selby raised his eyebrows. The girl really does have spunk, he told himself. She had set only the one end of the table with three places grouped together. He had fully expected her to sit at the opposite end of the long table. Noticing his surprise, Jessica rushed in with, "I thought sitting like this would be friendlier. I hope you don't mind." She shrugged her shoulders and stood by her chair while the men all but fell over each other trying to help her.

Dinner was a complete success until Geoffrey asked, "When do you expect Jonathan to return?" He could have cut out his tongue as the pleasant atmosphere died immediately.

Jessica's bubbling excitement disappeared as she and her father-in-law exchanged quick glances. Determined to put up a good front, she quickly replied, "We're not sure. He has barely had time to reach America. I'm sure he will let us know how long it will take to settle his business and return." She appeared completely unconcerned, but her brother noticed the look she had given the older man to keep him silent.

"Must you go home tomorrow, Geoff? There are so many things to do in London, and I've been dying for an escort to the theatre." With the possibility of his staying governing the conversation, the tension lessened, and Jessica bubbled again with her delight at seeing her brother.

Jessica started to excuse herself, but Mr. Selby interrupted, "Both of you go to the drawing room while I look over the papers Geoffrey brought me."

"Don't you and Geoff need to talk business?" she asked.

"If he stays over to take you to the theatre tomorrow night, we can talk tomorrow," he said as he left for the library.

"Jessica, what is wrong?" Geoff asked as soon as she was seated in the drawing room.

"Wrong? What could possibly be wrong?" she replied too quickly.

"Why are you here? That's what comes of being buried in the country as I have been. I thought you had

82

left with your husband."

"Oh, no. We agreed on that from the start. There was never any question of my returning to America this trip. It seems my husband had to extricate himself from the clutches of his mistress before he could introduce a wife into his life."

"Good God! What have I got you into?" he looked agonizedly at his sister.

"You have got me into nothing. I wrote you about the decision right after he left, but I never got around to sending the letter. Jonathan and I discussed the entire situation the first time we met. His father thinks leaving me behind is his way of protecting me from unpleasantness. Everyone protects me," she added with sarcasm. "Anyway, it doesn't matter. What does matter is that I am content, for the time being, here in town and I am truly delighted to have you here for however long you can stay."

Try as he could, Geoffrey could obtain no more information from his sister. However, not content to leave well enough alone as far as she was concerned, he obliquely steered the conversation in another direction. As Jeremiah Selby walked into the room unnoticed, Geoff was asking, "Why don't you come to Briarly for a few days?"

Without hesitating, Jessica replied, "No, thank you, Geoff, this is my home now. Maybe next month if the heat gets unbearable in town." When her father-in-law, pleased though he was with her reply, urged her to reconsider, she remained adamant. "I belong here."

Geoffrey did stay over and escort her several places, the theatre being the most exciting for her. During the first intermission she preferred staying in their box, looking down on her former friends. She nodded coldly to some and ignored others. She was well aware Jeremiah Selby had managed the box for them and was grateful he had given her an opportunity to be condescending to those who had hurt her before her mar-

83

riage. Finally, she asked Geoff, "Why are all those people who ignored us trying now to be so friendly?"

"I imagine many of them are beginning to feel as we did," he answered noncommittally.

"Don't talk riddles please. Explain yourself."

But Geoff would say nothing more than, "The last part of our plan is beginning to bear fruit."

With that remark the play began anew, and Jessica became engrossed in the drama once more. Her absorption gave her brother ample opportunity to study her, but even in such unguarded moments she revealed nothing. She laughed at the proper lines and seemed to be truly enjoying herself. Could she enjoy herself so if she were unhappy he wondered. "Probably not; so at least she isn't miserable."

When they arrived home, Jessica raced to tell Mr. Selby all about the play, and Geoff was pleased to see how much the two obviously liked each other. When he returned to Briarly two days later, she still would not accompany him; but he felt much more relieved than he had when he came. Grasping her hands, he squeezed them gently, "All will be well, Jessica—just keep in the fight."

"Go home, Geoff, and don't worry about me," she replied with more confidence than she felt. He looked back once after climbing into his saddle, but she flashed a wide smile and waved him on.

As she turned to go back into the house, she reeled slightly and grabbed for the railing at the side of the steps. She did not see Edward lose his aplomb and rush down to pick up his fallen mistress from where she lay unconscious.

Chapter Seven

At about the same time Jonathan rode north from his home to his new plantation, everyone in her London world was fussing over Jessica. She sat in bed giggling at Polly's description of the staid Edward in a state of panic. "Can you imagine, Miss Jessica, he actually shouted for Mrs. Winters? Then she flew into a tizzy and ran, I mean ran, to get me. I finally asked Edward to carry you up here. You had them all scared proper, miss."

"Well, I'm just fine now and you go right now and tell them that."

"Oh, miss, they will never believe me unless they see for themselves. Besides, I think Mrs. Winters sent for the doctor."

"I certainly don't need a doctor. I just turned too fast and got dizzy. Go tell her not to bother. Better yet, I'll do it myself," Jessica said as she pushed the cover away.

"No, you stay right there. I'll go," Polly said as she pulled the cover back over her mistress. She had taken only one step when the door opened after one faint knock and Mrs. Winters strode purposefully across the room following by a stranger.

"This is Doctor Forsythe, Miss Jessica."

"But I don't need a doctor," said Jessica as she pushed the covers aside once more and moved to the edge of the bed.

"Just let me make sure nothing serious is wrong," he said sitting in the chair next to the bed that Polly had just vacated. "You certainly look healthy. I wouldn't be surprised if my trip to this house is a complete waste of time."

Somewhat mollified, Jessica sat still on the edge of the bed and looked at him. Seeing in his eyes friendliness and humor, rather than the panic and fright of Miss Winters, she surrendered to them, saying, "All right, doctor. I don't know why everyone is so upset about a little fainting spell. I told Polly I spun around too fast and got dizzy."

The doctor checked her over while she sat quietly. He took her pulse and felt her forehead and asked whether she had ever fainted before. When he was about to speak again, Jessica shook her head. Finally, he looked around and said, "May I confer with my patient privately?"

Mrs. Winters and Polly exchanged glances and the older woman said, "We will wait in the hall. Just call if you need us." Both of them left the room as if they had been insulted.

When the door closed behind them, Jessica asked, "I'm pregnant, aren't I?"

"Well, you are certainly matter-of-fact, young lady. It is a distinct possibility."

"Doctor, I am a young woman with no female relatives. There are not women around me but servants. I know nothing about these things, so I would like as much information as possible from you."

"Surely Mrs. Winters can take care of you. I'm sure your husband. . ."

"My husband left two months ago for America after a marriage of two days. He will not return for months. I presume it is possible to breed in such a short time?"

"Oh, yes, but it's highly unusual unless you spent the. . .uh. . ."

"Come on doctor, be frank with me. I have much to

learn quickly so that I may make plans."

"Plans? Most women do nothing but sit and wait their time out. What kind of plans?"

"What I do need not concern you. Just go on with what you were saying. I definitely am not like most women and there is no time to be delicate."

"I started to say one does not usually have a baby after two days unless the couple spent the entire time in bed."

"You are saying that if my husband is well acquainted with the ways of women and had me only once, he would not reasonably expect me to be with child?"

"No, he certainly would have no reason to expect it."

"If I am to have a baby, and I expect I am, do I have to expect to faint as I did today very often?"

"You may never faint again. Did you eat this morning?"

"I skipped breakfast because I slept late and my brother was leaving."

"That plus the spinning around probably made you faint. In any case, after three months fainting is rare."

"When will the baby be born?"

"Well, if your husband has been gone two months, I'd say toward the end of March."

"How long will it be before I start to show?"

"Now, young lady. . ."

"Don't bother to admonish me, doctor. Just answer the question. How much time do I have before my condition will be obvious?"

"It depends, but about two months, give or take a little. If you really want to hide your condition, you can do it pretty well for quite a while with loose fitting garments."

"Thank you for being so frank. Now I want your promise that you will not reveal what we have discussed to anyone."

"But Mrs. Selby, surely the other women in the

87

household will guess after your fainting spell today."

"I prefer to keep it just that, a guess, at least for now. Is there anything else I should know?"

"You may be nauseous in the morning for the next month or so; but if you haven't been yet, you will probably be spared that discomfort. May I suggest you keep to your bed the rest of the day. That will satisfy Mrs. Winters that I have done something. I will tell her you need rest after receiving a bump on your head from the fall. If you are really interested in collusion, tear the hem of your gown and we can say you tripped," he added conspiratorily.

"What a great idea, doctor!" Jessica cried with glee. "Now go allay Mrs. Winters' concern and send Polly in to me, please."

The doctor left the room, and she could hear whispering outside the door. Polly opened the door and quickly slipped across the room to her. "Doctor Forsythe said I'm to help you undress and you are to stay in bed today." She helped Jessica out of her dress and into her dressing gown. "Now you just lie down, miss. Can I get you anything else?" Polly as usual chattered without expecting any answers. She pulled the draperies closed and continued, "You should be able to rest without all that sun in your eyes. I'll stay close in case you want me."

Jessica sighed and finally found a pause long enough for her to say, "Polly, will you bring me the novel I was reading? I think I left it in the library yesterday."

"But, Miss Jessica, you are to rest, not read," Polly reproached her.

"Yes, yes, Polly. I may not even be able to read, but an entire day in bed stretches out forever. Please go."

Once Polly had returned with the book and been firmly dismissed, Jessica settled down to some serious thinking. What should she do now? What could she do? She really didn't believe that either Jonathan or his father was merely interested in her having a baby. Did Jonathan really care for her as his father insisted? He had been kind to her, but was that because he cared or because he was basically a polite man? No, if he wanted, he could be as cruel as anyone could imagine. Still, he had treated her roughly only when provoked. He certainly was not a man who would allow a woman to dominate him. Still, what about Mr. Selby? Would he be able to tolerate the changes in his life that a baby would bring? How would Jonathan react when he returned and found he really had done all he could to father a child? She tried to picture Jonathan as a father, but she just didn't know him well enough to guess what kind of father he would be. Then again why should I bear the responsibility for a child alone? What will I do if Jonathan doesn't return? What would he do if I just appeared on his doorstep? No, that's a ridiculous idea. There is no way I could manage such a feat. Should I write to tell him about the baby? Definitely not—we agreed he'd return to America while I remained with his father. I really have no choice—after all, this entire situation came about because Mr. Selby wanted grandchildren. I hope he really did because this is what he is going to get. I can do nothing but wait and hope that my husband eventually wants me for a wife. Whether I like it or not, wait I must. Maybe when Jonathan is a father, he will be interested enough in his child to take both of us home with him.

Jessica rested briefly and soon Polly came with lunch. Jessica ate hungrily, causing Polly to comment that she seemed much better but to be safe she should stay in bed. When Polly left with the tray, Jessica picked up her novel. After opening the draperies, she sat on the lounge chair until she finished her book. Now, she was finally tired. Lying down on the bed, she napped until she was awakened by a knock on the door. "Come in," she called as she stretched her arms over her head. "Oh, I thought you were Polly," she gasped, grabbing the covers and pulling them up to her chin as she sat up against the headboard.

"Did I awaken you? I am so sorry. I will come back later." Mr. Selby turned to leave.

"No, come on in. Are you home early or did I sleep such a long time?" Jessica nodded toward the chair, so he slid into it, without answering her question, and took her hand.

"I was so worried when Mrs. Winters sent me word about your accident. I wanted to see for myself that you really are all right." She had to believe he had been worried about her. The frown creasing his brow, his darting eyes and nervous hands lent credence to his statement.

"Don't even think about it any more. I am just fine. I stayed up here only because that silly doctor insisted and told Polly. Otherwise, I would have gone downstairs for lunch. No, don't look at me as if I were a naughty child. I'm not, you know—only a clumsy one."

He patted her hand and stood up, saying, "I shall miss your delighted company at dinner tonight, my dear. I am definitely out of the habit of eating alone."

"Then don't eat alone. Have your dinner brought here too, and we can still have dinner together. Polly will never allow me to come down."

A wide smile crossed his face as she initiated her first invitation. "Do you really think I would not tire you too much?"

"Of course not. Besides, you can watch me for all the spies in the household. No one believes Polly that I feel just fine."

The older man crossed to the door and turned once more. "You're really sure?" he asked.

"Yes, I'm really sure. And would you please tell Polly I need her? She is probably hovering close by the door."

"Certainly, my dear. Is there anything else I can do for you?" Mr. Selby sounded anxious. Jessica shook her head as she watched the old man move again toward the door. He looked so tired. He had seemed so much younger lately than he had appeared when she first came here. What caused his stooped shoulders today?

"Mr. Selby, is there anything I can do for you? You look so tired today."

"No, my dear. You just take care of yourself. I was worried about you; but since I see that you are not seriously hurt, I am feeling much better myself." He straightened his shoulders as if the action would support the words.

"Well, you rest before dinner. I want to dine with someone in good spirits tonight."

After Mr. Selby left the room, Jessica rang for Polly. However, she heard a soft tap at the door and knew Polly would have burst in. "Come in," she called as she lay back on the lounge chair.

Edward opened the door and called in, "I have some mail for you, madam. In all the confusion this morning I quite forgot about it."

"Bring it on in, Edward." She sat up to reach for the letter, wondering who could possibly be writing her since Geoffrey had left just this morning. When Edward handed her the letter, she did not recognize the handwriting. "Now I'm really confused. I wonder who could be writing to me," she murmured.

"It's from Mister Jonathan," replied the man as if she had been speaking to him.

"Oh. Tell me, Edward, do you think your master, Mr. Selby, looks well today?"

The butler stood still and said nothing. She thought he was trying to decide whether or not he should answer such a personal question about his employer.

"Isn't he home early today?" she continued.

"Yes, he is, madam. But I expected him when we sent word to him about your being ill."

"Why did you do that? I am perfectly all right." Jessica sounded as irritated as she felt. There was too much fussing over one little fainting spell.

"Mr. Selby looked tired when he left today. I knew he would rush home early when he heard about you."

Jessica smiled at the servant. "Thank you, Edward. You do take very good care of your master." Edward bowed without smiling and backed out of the room. Jessica again looked at the letter. How could Jonathan be writing to her so soon? He barely had time to be home. Why would he be writing to her? "Well, if I don't open the letter, I'll never know," she thought as she ripped open the envelope.

Dear Jessica,

I found your gift the morning I sailed and have enjoyed it very much. Thank you, my darling.

A ship going to Europe has been sighted so I am sending this with them as they are about to pull alongside the *Raven* now.

It will take about another month to arrive in Louisiana.

As soon as I can get another cargo loaded on board, I will sail again for England. Please forgive me for the words you overheard me shout at my father. Why do I let him goad me into saying things I do not mean? You must know that any night as perfect as our last night together is very important to me. I am looking forward to many more such nights.

When I return, I want to renegotiate our bargain. Will you seriously consider the possibility of returning to my home with me? Please don't refuse without giving it much thought.

I will return in approximately three months from the date of this letter. We will be together soon.

Love,
Jonathan

Jessica almost reeled with pleasure. Whatever should

she do now? She looked at the letter again and realized she had only two months more to wait. When he returned, she would be four months along. Could she then travel to America, or would she be too far along for an ocean voyage? I must remember to ask the doctor when I next see him.

Just then Polly knocked on the door, but entered without waiting. "I hear you are to dine with Mr. Selby here in your room. Do you want help to get ready for dinner, or are you not going to change?" Jessica was thinking too deeply to answer the girl. "Miss Jessica, are you going to dress for dinner?"

Shaking her head, Jessica came out of her reverie, "What?"

"Do you want to dress for dinner? What is wrong with you, Miss Jessica? What are you thinking about so seriously?"

"How would you like to go to America, Polly?" Jessica asked in a far away tone.

"Are you thinking about Mister Jonathan? Maybe you will go to America some day, but I never will, so I don't have to think about how I would like it. Why don't you rest, if you are to have dinner with Mr. Selby?"

Throwing the cover to the side, Jessica jumped to her feet. "I'll be really sick soon—from resting—if this keeps up. Look, Polly, I have an idea that I haven't worked out yet. If I talk to you about it, will you promise to keep it a secret and tell no one?"

"Sure, Miss Jessica. Is this to be a mystery? I do love secrets." Polly plopped into a chair while Jessica paced back and forth across the room.

"Did you know that I had a letter from Jonathan today?"

"No, ma'am. How could you have had a letter so soon?"

"He sent it to London on a passing ship. I never knew they could do such things."

"Me either. What on earth could that nasty man want?" scowled Polly.

"It seems," retorted Jessica, "he's sorry I heard what he said to his father and is returning almost immediately to see me, possibly to beg for my forgiveness."

"Oh, Miss Jessica, things may work out for you after all. Will you really make him beg?" She clapped her hands in glee.

Jessica stopped her pacing and spun to face her cohort. "He certainly deserves it, but maybe his father was right after all. Both he and his father insist Mr. Selby did goad him into blurting out such a despicable remark. In his letter he says he is coming to renegotiate our agreement and wants me to consider returning to America with him."

"Oh, Miss Jessica, that's wonderful news." She hugged her mistress tightly.

"Maybe. Tomorrow I want you to go to the doctor's office and question him for me. Find out how much longer I may safely make an ocean voyage. If I cannot return with Jonathan in another two months, then I will have to plan something else."

"You and he will just have to wait here until the babe is born, ma'am."

"That seems to be the obvious solution, but maybe there is another possibility." Jessica did not notice that Polly was aware of her pregnancy.

"What else can you do, Miss Jessica?" asked Polly as she watched her mistress carefully. She could see Jessica frown and knew the girl to be thinking again. Too often Jessica thought of answers that caused problems. I might need help with her this time, she thought.

"Polly, I will not change for dinner. Please be sure to check with the doctor the first thing in the morning."

"Yes, ma'am," she bowed as she left the room.

Jessica and Mr. Selby dined amicably an hour or so later. He appeared rested and much more relaxed while she seemed not quite well.

"You seem to have recovered, my dear," he muttered

with a slight smirk. "Are you sure you have told me everything?"

"Quite sure, sir. Did you know I received a letter from Jonathan today?" she asked noncommittally.

"Edward mentioned it." He waited for her to go on, but eyed her carefully.

As if nervous or unsure what to say, she hesitated. "It seems as if you were correct about his feelings, or so he says." She stared at the table as his face broke into a wide grin. "He says he is returning immediately—as soon as a new cargo can be loaded."

"See. I told you he would come to his senses and it didn't take long for him to get home." He reached across the table and covered her hand with his. Finally she raised her head and their eyes met.

"How can you keep such close track of him when he is so far away? What do you know about his business?"

His face sobered at her questions. With a sigh he said, "I know all about him and his business because I have paid informants. I don't spy to meddle, but I do care what happens to him. I have always been waiting in abeyance in the event he needed me. He never did—not since the first time he left home. He would have been successful even without my initial help. He's made mistakes, but has never repeated a mistake. We've been through this before. Why rake over cold ground again?"

Jessica sat with her heart wrenching her whole body. "Are Jonathan's affairs so complicated that he could not stay here for a year or so?"

Mr. Selby frowned questioningly as he said, "No one's business can get along without its master for that long a time—even with a good partner like Steve O'Neill. He has a great deal of expertise, but he and Jonathan complement each other. They cannot replace each other. Why is it so important?"

Jessica stared at the table again and fingered her cup. She was too embarrassed to continue. He pulled his hand back and placed his napkin on the table. Pushing back his chair, he rose and walked around the table to her chair.

"Jessica, I think of you as the daughter I never had. I would be honored to talk or to listen any time you want to confide in me. You have brought my existence back to life with your presence in my household. I will not press you now if you cannot continue, but I want you to know I am as available to you as I am to my son, not because you are his wife but because you are my daughter." When he finished, he stood behind her chair and dropped both hands on her shoulder, squeezing gently. "I only hope you have come to care for me enough not to shut me out of your and Jonathan's lives."

She quickly reached a hand to his and turned to look at him. With tears in her eyes, she whimpered, "Father Selby, you are so kind to me. I don't want to hurt you. You have been a father to me when I needed one so desperately, and you are entitled to the grandchildren you desire. But Jonathan wants me to go to America with him."

"I should think so. And you should most certainly go with him. When my grandchildren are born, I will come to America to visit them. My affairs are about finished because I am planning to retire." He smiled at her lovingly. "I only hope you can love my son and provide those grandchildren, if there are any, with a loving home."

She smiled at him in return, saying, "You heard Jonathan. If I go, there will most assuredly be children. But I can't go unless I know all will be well between us." She stood as the old man started for the door. "I'm so glad we had dinner together. I was getting lonely cooped up in here by myself."

"I'm glad as well, my dear. Think through your decision as you usually do. But don't be afraid to be selfish. Your happiness is important too."

Chapter Eight

After pacing the floor most of the night, Jessica slept late the next morning. It was mid-morning when Polly entered with her breakfast. She crossed the room to set the tray on the table, then pushed aside the draperies and let the sunlight pour into the room. The sunlight danced off the articles of clothing which were strewn around the room. Polly cleared the room of clutter and scattered clothing and returned to the bed with a robe as Jessica rolled over, stretched and sat up, yawning, "Morning, Polly." Suddenly Jessica remembered the task she had given Polly this morning and jumped out of bed. She thrust her arms into the sleeves of the robe and said, "Don't forget the doctor. You may go now, and I will make short work of the breakfast."

"Don't rush, miss. You'll faint again. Besides I've already been to talk with Dr. Forsythe. He says if you are to take an ocean voyage, the sooner you leave, the better—though you may get seasick a little more easily than normal for the next month. He said that you would surely have a bad crossing if you sail in the dead of winter."

"Oh. I didn't even think about the weather. Is the Atlantic Ocean worse in the winter?"

"I wouldn't know, ma'am." Polly kept busy making the bed and calling for a bath while Jessica slowly ate her breakfast. While she luxuriated in the bath, Jessica pondered her alternatives one last time. The time for action had come and she must decide what to do.

As she stepped out of the bath, she said, "Polly, will you see that the carriage is brought around? I see no reason why we should not go for our usual drive today."

"Oh, Miss Jessica, do you really think you should? After all. . ."

"After all nothing. We need to talk and I need to see Mrs. Mattingly."

When Jessica descended the stairs prepared for a ride in the park, Edward gaped at her. He quickly recovered himself and hastily grabbed the doorknob. "Good morning, madam," he said as if he were not a bit surprised. Jessica heard Mrs. Winters rushing toward her, but walked on out the open door and straight into the carriage. She did not want to argue with anyone today. There was too much to be done.

Polly told the driver to take the usual drive and climbed into the carriage after her mistress. "Well, now, miss, what do we have to talk about?"

"Polly, I really do not know what I can do, but go to America myself while I can still travel."

"Oh, no, miss," Polly quickly answered. "You can't go by yourself." She frowned at her mistress and rushed on, "You must wait for Mister Jonathan. Ladies can't possibly travel unchaperoned."

"Hush, Polly, and listen to me," Jessica said as if exasperated with her. "What can I do? Jonathan cannot stay here until I am recovered enough to travel. His father said he cannot leave his business that long. If I wait for him, I will be at least halfway through my time. It will be at least two more months. If I allow time to unload and reload the ship twice and time to sell the merchandise here, that will be another month before we can sail from England. I'm sure you have figured out that I am expecting a baby—in March. I will be at the end of my fifth month. We will not arrive in America until the end of my seventh month. That surely cannot be the safest time to be on the high seas. Besides, we would be at sea in December and January—the worst possible times."

"But Miss Jessica, you know how easily you can make me think you are right, but you know you cannot go alone." Polly shook her head and smooth her skirt.

"Polly, couldn't you go with me? I could see that you returned with someone to protect you."

"Me, miss? Oh, I couldn't. Jimmy wouldn't like it."

"Would you ask him at least?"

"I figured you would be difficult this time, so I sent for him yesterday. I told him to tell Mr. Geoffrey you needed him. Let's wait to see whether he comes or not."

"Yes, we'll wait to make definite plans after he arrives. Tell the driver to go to the dress shop now."

Jessica swept into Mrs. Mattingly's shop with all the pride she had ever displayed. The sweet little woman greeted her with her usual gusto, but Jessica headed straight for a fitting room while Mrs. Mattingly trailed behind her. "Do you want to see some fall gowns, Mrs. Selby?" she questioned when Jessica had seated herself in the chair.

"Mrs. Mattingly, I do need some new gowns, but first I want your promise that you will be very discreet and mention them to no one."

The older woman nodded her promise and waited for Jessica to continue. But the girl sat silently with stiff shoulders, trying to maintain her businesslike manner. "I need gowns appropriate for an ocean voyage in the fall. Do you know what I will need? I have no idea what the weather will be like. I would like you to find out and make whatever I will need."

Mrs. Mattingly smiled at the girl and bubbled, "Are you going to join your husband? That will be wonderul!" She smiled and rushed out to return in a moment with drawings. "Do you like any of these?" she said as she spread them out in front of the girl.

Jessica glanced at them briefly, but shook her head. "You decide, Mrs. Mattingly. I trust your judgment completely. You have always done well by me. There is one adjustment you must make though. Can you make them loose below the bosom?" She nodded at the woman's inquiring glance and smile. "Yes, for the usual reason. I would like to hide my condition from those aboard the ship. I may not be able to find passage if anyone knows. Also, I will need some gowns for the end of my term that will do in Louisiana. I believe that is in the south of America."

"How much time do I have, my dear?"

"My arrangements are not yet complete, but I hope to sail within two weeks. Will that be time enough?"

"More would be better, of course, but we will start at once and be finished before you go."

Jessica stood to leave and threw her arms around the little woman. "You have been so good to me. I will miss your kindness when I have gone."

Mrs. Mattingly patted her and said kindly, "It has been a pleasure to dress someone so lovely. You try to appear harsh, but you are really a kitten. Do not try to be too brave, my dear. You need some protecting."

Jessica rode home quietly. Polly looked at her several times as if to decide whether or not anything was wrong. However, Jessica's face revealed nothing. In fact, she was merely tired after an emotional morning and a sleepless night. She closed her eyes and leaned her head back. The next thing she was aware of was Polly shaking her and shouting, "Are you all right, Miss Jessica? Are you all right?"

When her eyes fluttered open, Jessica could not remember where she was. When she started to move out of the carriage, Polly jerked her back. "You're not awake enough, miss. You'll fall."

Jessica sat back down until she awakened completely. Then she announced, "I am awake now, Polly, but I do believe I'll have lunch in my room." She hurried into the house and had started to climb the stairs when Mrs. Winters stopped her.

"The doctor was here and was shocked to find you gone. He will return late this afternoon." She turned to stamp out in anger.

Jessica ran after her, almost tripping on the stairs. "Mrs. Winters, don't be angry. I honestly thought it would be all right for me to resume my daily routine. The doctor told me only to remain in my room lying down yesterday. He said nothing about today, so I assumed I could go out since I felt so well. However, I have already overextended and fell asleep on the way home."

Mrs. Winters softened immediately and became all concern. "Are you sure you feel fine? You almost fell again. You must lie down and have your noon meal in your room. Let me help you upstairs."

"Please do. Polly seems to have disappeared." Mrs. Winters slid her strong arm around the girl and they ascended together. When she had closed the bedroom door, Mrs. Winters unfastened Jessica's gown and helped her into bed. Jessica asked, "Do you think the doctor will forgive me if we ask him to stay for dinner?"

"He just might at that," the older woman smiled. She found it impossible not to forgive the young woman anything and imagined everyone reacted in such a way to her charms.

Two weeks later Jessica lay on the bunk in her cabin. She had lain down after saying goodbye to England through the porthole. Her heart seemed stuck in her throat as she bade her homeland farewell, but she shook herself free of memories and resolved to look only ahead.

Now she lay utterly amazed at what the three of them —she, Polly and Jimmy—had accomplished in so short a time. Jimmy had arrived the day after her trip to town and entered into the deception wholeheartedly. He had found passage for them on a ship bound for New Orleans. He had made all the arrangements, selling Jessica's garnet necklace for ready cash. Everyone in London, except Mrs. Mattingly, thought they had gone to Briarly Hill yesterday. Everyone at Briarly thought the trio in London. With good luck no one would discover their absence for two weeks, the time they were to visit with Geoff. Only Mrs. Mattingly knew of their departure from the country. Jessica could not involve the woman in their schemes, but the gowns had been delivered to the ship so there was no help for it. It would be awhile before anyone would think of the dressmaker, if they ever did.

They had stayed the night at an inn near the ship, and only yesterday had Jessica discovered the reason for Jimmy's quick agreement to her plan. On their way to the inn he had pulled up to a small chapel. Thinking to offer prayers for their safe journey, Jessica rushed inside, only to discover she was to be the witness to their marriage. When she saw the glowing happiness on both their faces, she thought, "This is what a wedding should be like. How fortunate they are to love each other so."

To avoid questions, Jessica was to travel as the recently widowed sister of Jimmy. She and Polly had planned to room together, but Jessica determined the newly weds should have this time to themselves, so the rooms and the cabins had been rearranged at their arrival. Here she was, posing as Jimmy's widowed sister, making her way to a new land and a husband who may have changed his mind once he returned to Carolyn. "How can I make him love me? When I arrive I will have lost my figure. What can I do to attract him when I am so misshapen? What will I do if we pass each other at sea? Maybe that would be better because I could be established in his household by his return. When our baby has arrived, between us we will be a match for Carolyn. We must become important to him." Thinking there was nothing she could do until her figure returned, Jessica determined to wait out the months as calmly as she could.

The crossing was soothing to Jessica's jangled nerves. She relaxed with the conviction that she had chosen the only sensible course of action. Polly and Jimmy still glowed and Jessica was shocked to realize she envied them their happiness. When the ship slid into the dock two months later, she was eager to face the challenge before her. Heavily veiled as the bereaved widow, she walked down the plank and stepped onto American soil for the first time. Jimmy had discovered Jonathan's absence from town, so Jessica now sat in his partner's office.

"Do you know when Mr. Selby will return?" she asked the handsome tall man across from her.

Steve stood with a puzzled frown on his face. Who was this woman just off a ship from England? Suddenly he smiled, walked over to her purposefully, and lifted the veiling and hat from her head. Jessica stared at him, but moved not a hand to stop him. "You are Jonathan's wife, aren't you? You are Jessica?"

Jessica smiled and nodded. At least someone over here knows he is married, she thought, and relaxed in the chair. "I had word from Jonathan that he was coming for me, but I decided not to wait and crossed to him. I am not entirely surprised we passed each other on the Atlantic, but I had hoped we would not."

She watched Steve frown again as he crossed to pour a glass of wine. Handing her the glass of amber liquid, he muttered, "Drink this. You will need it when I have finished." Now Jessica frowned. She waited for Steve to continue, but he paced up and down the room and finally dropped into the chair behind the desk.

He wondered how much he could tell her. Jonathan had left her behind to protect her from Carolyn. Did the girl need that much protection or was she as strong as she was lovely? No wonder Jonathan had married the girl. Leave it to him to come up with the best every single time.

103

Jessica realized immediately that something was wrong. She had not expected enthusiasm, but his smile had been friendly. Why had it vanished? Why did he not say something? Stiffening her body under his close scrutiny, she asked, "Well, what is the problem? Can I not go to Jonathan's home and wait for his return?"

"Yes, you can, but. . .uh. . ." he stammered.

Impatiently Jessica blurted, "Will you get on with it? Are you trying to say I made a serious error coming here and you don't like cleaning up my husband's messes?"

"No, no, that is not the problem." Rushing around the desk, he pulled a chair over beside hers and grabbed her hand. "I'm sorry my hesitation caused you even to think such a thought. Jonathan told me he had every intention of going for you, but he didn't return to England."

Jessica looked at him and said in a very level tone, "Maybe you had better start at the beginning. Did he change his mind?"

He could feel her hand shaking in his and knew she struggled to sound calm. "The day he arrived from England Jonathan told me to unload the ship and load another cargo at once because he wanted to return for you. Did you know he is building a new plantation in the wilderness in the northern part of the territory?"

Jessica shook her head, so he continued. "Well, he is. He has a penchant for starting from the beginning and carving his own way."

"That I did know," she smiled.

"Before he returned, I had reports of trouble up there. Jonathan said he would have to go up there to see about it, but he would leave the day after he returned from the interior. The trouble is, Jessica, he never returned."

"Oh, no!" Jessica slumped against the chair and tears filled her eyes. Blinking them away, she suggested, "Maybe the trouble was more serious than he thought it would be. He will surely return soon."

"Don't you think I thought of that? When he had not returned within two weeks, I sent someone to check on him and find out when he planned to sail. My man returned eventually with the news that Jonathan had left the plantation in time to be back here in New Orleans to sail when he had intended. In short, Jessica, Jonathan has disappeared."

Jessica jumped to her feet. She must think. Activity kept her from fainting. She paced back and forth and finally whirled to face Steve. "Have you done anything else that you have not yet mentioned?"

This is really quite a woman—a real match for Jonathan. Did nothing stop her? "I sent my man back to the interior with the instructions to search under every stick and stone and not to return without him."

"Is he a capable man?"

"The best. Tim can track as well as any Indian. If there is anyone who can find Jon, he will. But there is something else you should know."

"What is that?" But he didn't continue. Instead he looked at the floor. If he could not look in her eyes, Jessica could guess the source of the problem. "Well, tell me. What about Carolyn?" At his shocked look, she continued, "Yes, I know about her. Did Jonathan see her before he left? Do you know?"

Shaking his head in surprise, Steve said, "Yes, at least I think he took care of that—he went to her house from here, but she still acts as if nothing happened between them, though she no longer talks incessantly about marriage. She can be a mean, vindictive creature. I do not think it wise to reveal your identity to her."

"Surely she cannot be so bad as you paint her. Besides, how can we possibly avoid her finding out?"

"Whatever you do, don't trust her. She may be even worse than I say. You seem to like plotting. Shall we continue the masquerade? Jonathan was willing to sell his plantation when he moved north. Why don't you, a grieving widow, buy it? Since Jonathan has not appeared, you can keep the others in line. If you stay close to the plantation, no one will bother you except your closest neighbors. I will pass the word that you are still in mourning, and even they will not intrude on your privacy.''

"You are a plotter too, Steve," Jessica cried with a wide smile on her face. "Let us try to see how well we can keep the secret." Reaching for her hat, Jessica replaced the heavy veil over her face. Striding toward the door, Jessica called behind her, "Let's go see how well we can handle Callie. I'm really anxious to meet her. I wonder what she will think of me," she mused.

"She will think you are lovely and pamper you no end," replied Steve as he followed her out the door. He had noticed her condition when he scrutinized her closely and could easily guess her reasons for crossing the Atlantic as she did.

Jessica, Polly and Jimmy rode quietly, watching the strange countryside. They were amazed by the vastness and the distance between houses. "Jonathan said this country had space. Can you find some for Polly and Jimmy? I would like them to have a place of their own.''

"No, Miss Jessica," Polly put in quickly. "We will not leave until you are with Mister Jonathan." Jimmy nodded his agreement.

Steve interrupted with, "I think they should stay with you until Jonathan is found. Then maybe we can find something for them close to you. How would that be?''

Jessica readjusted her skirts as they turned from the road to a drive. "Is this Jonathan's home?" she asked as she tilted her head forward to look out the window once more.

"It is still quite a way to the house, so don't get nervous yet," said Steve calmly.

"Is all this Jonathan's land?''

"Your land, remember? You just bought it.''

"Yes, I remember." Finally she turned back to face

the strange glances of the pair across from her. "That is how it is to be, Polly. It seems we are never finished with schemes. Jonathan has disappeared and Steve thinks I will be safer if no one knows I am his wife, so as the Widow Germayne I just bought Fairhaven. We will tell Callie, but no one else is to know. When we arrive, Jimmy, give the rest of the jewelry to Steve as payment. You, Steve, can have them appraised and go through all the motions as if I were really buying the farm."

"Oh, my dear, don't let anyone around here ever hear you call it a farm." He laughed while Jessica chuckled a little. "It really makes a difference to these people. Here we are."

The carriage stopped before a huge rambling house. A few children jumped up and down, shouting, "Company's coming. Company's here."

The largest woman Jessica had ever seen rushed outside and down to the carriage. She moved quickly in spite of her size and smiled broadly. "Well, Mister Steve, who do we have here?"

"We have the new owner of Fairhaven, Callie." At her gasp of surprise, he continued. "Could we see you in the study, please?" and strode toward the door without giving her a chance to answer.

"I never heard of such a thing, selling the plantation while Mister Jonathan is missing like he is. How could you do such a thing? I thought you were his friend." She mutrtered the entire way into the study. With the closing of the door, Jessica turned around and hugged the older woman and ripped off her hat. "Oh, Callie, I'm so glad to see you at last. I'm Jessica Selby."

"Mister Jonathan's Jessica?"

Jessica nodded and found herself engulfed in a real bearhug. Callie listened patiently and agreed wholeheartedly with Steve and entered into the plan. "That Miss Carolyn mighty mean, ma'am. Jimmy and Polly can be guests, not servants, and I will take care of Miss Jessica."

"I can see you will be quite well taken care of by Callie. Goodbye Jessica. Let me know if I can do anything else for you," Steve said as she walked with him to the door.

They looked at each other and smiled their approval of Jonathan's choice of the other. Jessica extended her hand to him as she replied, "First of all, don't become a stranger. I may need moral support from time to time. Don't you think you should let Jonathan's father know what has happened? Try to be encouraging though because he worries so."

She waved at Steve in the departing carriage. Then she turned around to take her first long look at her new home before Callie whisked her up the stairs.

Chapter Nine

As Callie opened the door to a huge bedroom, she soothed gently, "You come right in here to Mister Jonathan's room, Miss Jessica. I'm sure Mister Steve has someone coming with your things. Let me help you out of that pretty gown, and you can rest until they come. Then we can unpack and get you a bath, or would you like a bath first?"

"No, Callie, this has been a trying morning. I think I will rest first. I don't think, however, that I should take over Jonathan's room."

"Sure you should, Miss Jessica. This is your house now and this is the master bedroom. Where else would the owner settle herself?"

"Will you see that Polly and Jimmy have. . ."

"Don't you worry yourself about them. Did Jimmy work in the stables before he came here? Maybe I can find something for him to do—men like to keep busy if they are worth anything."

"Thank you, Callie. You seem to know instinctively how to handle everything."

"I've been handlin' everything here since Mister Jonathan came. You just leave everything to me until we find Mister Jonathan for you." With soft blankets she covered Jessica, closed the draperies, and left the room quietly.

Jessica heard noises in the room next to hers and

climbed out of bed to investigate. She noticed a door in the wall and went to open it. Callie stood there, having opened the trunks, holding up each of her gowns. "Miss Jessica, did those clumsy men awaken you? I told them to be quiet."

"It's all right, Callie. I'm surprised I slept so long."

"You just sit down and I will have your bath ready right away."

Jessica walked on into the room as Callie left it. She looked around her thoughtfully, opening drawers and doors to inspect their contents but found everything empty. "Callie," she said as she heard her bath being brought in, "Don't you think I should settle in this room? It looks comfortable enough. Jonathan will want his room when he returns."

"Mister Jonathan will want you in his room when he returns, if I know Mister Jonathan at all."

Jessica blushed brightly, saying, "Would you bring me a clean shift and see that one of my gowns is pressed while I bathe?" Callie knew Jessica was trying to get her out of the room before she undressed. She frowned but walked into the other room. Jessica could see her rummaging through the sea chest and presently she returned with a shift and a robe. Placing them on the arm of the chair beside a towel, she left again. Jessica undressed and slid into the bathtub. She lay back and relaxed against the back of the tub. The warmth of the water almost put her to sleep again. Shaking herself out of her reverie, she picked up the sponge and scrubbed. It was so good to bathe her entire body for the first time in weeks.

Callie whisked through with an armload of dresses, hung them in the wardrobe and slung Jonathan's clothes over her arm to carry out. "Just unpack the chest, Callie. We can work on the trunks later." As Jessica stood to reach for the towel, Callie burst in again. She dropped her load on the bed, but handed Jessica the towel on her way by. "Does Mister Jonathan know?'' she asked.

Shaking her head, Jessica murmured, ''No one knows but Polly and Jimmy and now you. That's the reason I couldn't wait for Jonathan to come for me. I'm so glad I didn't. I would much rather be here to get news of him first-hand than be sitting over there as big as an elephant, thinking he had changed his mind.''

''He won't change his mind, especially with a little one on the way. We've never had a baby here, but Mister Jonathan likes children.''

The girl turned a forlorn face to the big woman. ''Don't you see, Callie, I want him to want me, not only the child I bring him,'' she said with tears in her eyes.

Callie hugged the wet girl to her big bosom and patted her back. ''Don't you worry, Miss Jessica. Mister Jon will be back soon. And you will see that all of these little problems will work out, especially with you in his bed,'' she added with a gleam in her eye. Callie helped the girl into her clothing and then combed her hair. By the time she had finished, Jessica felt ready to cope with her new problems. ''I'll show you where I put your friends and then you can eat in the dining room.''

They went together into the wide hall and Callie pointed to a door across from Jessica's. Polly opened the door at Jessica's knock. ''Have you eaten? Will you come talk to me while I eat?'' Jessica asked after Polly had nodded.

Polly smiled her relief. ''Oh, Miss Jessica, I don't know how to be a lady. What do I do with myself?''

''Please just stay with me and keep me company.'' Jessica slid her arm around the trembling girl's waist. ''I couldn't do this alone.'' Callie beamed and slipped downstairs, knowing Polly would bring the young miss downstairs.

Later Callie insisted on showing Jessica the entire house and introducing the entire staff of house servants. ''I never thought a bachelor's home would be so large,''

111

she exclaimed. "I will never get used to it."

"Mister Jonathan always thought of this place as a temporary home for him. He started building that other place because he knew that no account Carolyn would never move that far from town. If you ask me, she's responsible for the trouble up there. He always says I talk too much, but you have to know what she's like. You're too sweet to deal with the likes of her."

"I probably won't have to deal with her. Jonathan can take care of that when he returns."

"You can be sure she will be out here as soon as she hears you bought the place. She won't be at all happy about Mister Steve's selling the place to anyone."

"We must cross one bridge at a time. I am much more worried about Jonathan now. Do you know the man Steve sent to look for him?"

"Tim O'Leary? He will find the master, just you wait and see." Callie's confidence made Jessica feel better.

"Should I look at the books if I'm to be the new master? I suppose I should at least interview the man in charge." Jessica knew this masquerade could go on indefinitely and was not at all sure she could cope for long, but she must try, for Jonathan's sake—for her own and her baby's too. She must do something about Polly too. The girl would be miserable in no time with nothing to do. Thank heaven Jimmy could occupy himself at the stables without anyone's questioning his status. Gentlemen were at least allowed to interest themselves in the working of an estate—no, a plantation.

"Polly, come upstairs with me. I'm so glad we are about the same size." As they walked into the room containing Jessica's trunk, she could see Callie had started to unpack it. She led the girl inside and said, "I've heard this is the land of opportunity. You can see it would never do for you to be my servant here. Can't we be friends instead?"

The girl muttered through her sniffles, "Oh, miss, it wouldn't be right."

"Of course it would be right. You forget we are to continue as we arrived. If anyone should inquire about the ship's passengers, we must be what we said we were. Besides, it's just a matter of time until you will be what you pretended to be. You don't have nearly enough clothes. Will you take some of mine?"

"I couldn't. I wouldn't feel right."

"Nonsense. Did you see Jimmy's face light up at the idea of a place of his own? Do you really want to be a drudge and hold him to a small cottage because you were afraid?"

"That would make him miserable. He had such grand ideas in his head when he agreed to come to America." Polly was truly uncomfortable, and Jessica pulled more gowns out of the trunk while Polly sobbed behind her. Finally the girl quieted and came over to see what Jessica was doing. "I could do that for you, miss. No one would see with the door closed."

Jessica spun around to face her, anger flashing in her eyes. "You can only do for me what I can do for you. Haven't you been listening? We are sisters! Let me help you out of that dress. Now try this one on!" said Jessica determinedly as she picked up one of her gowns, dropped it over the girl's head and fastened it. They were about the same size so the fit was perfect. Polly was only a little taller. "I could never part with any of the dresses Jonathan bought me, but you are to have all of those I brought from Briarly. Go to the sewing room and get what you will need to lengthen them a little. Shall I got for you?" she asked when the girl did not move.

Polly smiled at her reflection and suddenly fell in with Jessica's plan. "I can go, miss." At Jessica's frown she said, "I mean I can go, Jessica."

"That's better. I will help move these to your room." Grabbing an armful of dresses she stalked from the room as Polly tiptoed down the hall as if afraid of being caught doing something wrong.

Callie said nothing about the missing gowns when she came back to finish the unpacking. "That girl may be able to handle Miss Carolyn after all, but she hasn't seen anything yet." She knocked on the door to Polly's room and charged in. "Mr. Bolton will be here to speak to you soon, ma'am. He's the overseer. When you finish with him, I will help you dress for dinner. I will send someone to help you too, Miss Polly."

Jessica sat at Jonathan's desk when Mr. Bolton entered the study. Standing inside the door, he hesitated to enter further. "Come in, Mr. Bolton. We probably have much to settle," Jessica said matter of factly. "I know nothing about running a place this size, but I learn very quickly. Please tell me, first of all, do you plan to stay on when Mr. Selby moves to his new place or do you plan to go there?"

Surprised by her businesslike manner, the man stammered, "I. . .I really haven't decided, ma'am. I suppose you might say it depends upon how we get along."

"Very well. I will settle for that answer for the time being. Now will you please tell me about the operation of this plantation. May I stop you if I have any questions?" Jessica had Jonathan's ledger in front of her as if she knew how to read it. She hoped she could follow the entries well enough to make sure all the facets of the operation were covered. The man settled into a chair and hesitantly started to discuss the current harvest and plans for the next planting. Jessica nodded in agreement and asked about the horses. By the end of two hours, she had a fair idea what went on. She had interrupted many times to ask questions but saved some for Jimmy. Finally she stood and extended her hand to the man across from her. He jumped to his feet as she said, "Thank you, Mr. Bolton. I think that is as much as I can absorb at one time. You are a careful guardian of Mr. Selby's enterprise. May I request that you continue as usual? If you would normally clear something with Mr. Selby, come see me about it. You may tell me what he would probably do, but I cannot promise to make the same decision. You may be sure, though, one thing I don't like is surprises. If you deal fairly with me, I shall do likewise."

Mr. Bolton crossed the room swiftly, shaking his head. Outside he said, "Boy, Callie, she's quite a woman. I wouldn't be surprised if she can take over this place."

"I've a feeling, Mister Bolton, we ain't seen nothin' yet. This is only her first day," Callie chuckled gleefully.

For the next several days Jessica settled into plantation life. Jimmy took her for a ride in the landau to inspect her holdings. She saw only the fields, the stables and barns, and the lumber mill and quarry. She was determined that each man in charge realize she was not a token mistress here. They must understand she was in charge because she had bought Fairhaven.

One week after she arrived she was resting in her room when Callie came in with the news, "Miss Carolyn's come to call, Miss Jessica. I couldn't get rid of her! Let me help you into that gray dress. It will pass for mourning." She bustled to the closet and held the dress for Jessica to step into. "The nerve of that woman showin' up here." Jessica trembled as she waited for Callie to fasten her. Whatever could she want?

"I may as well meet her and get it over with, though the very idea frightens me." Jessica glided down the stairs as if she were in a trance. Someone had closed the drawing room doors. Thank heaven she will not see me shake. Bolstering her courage by drawing herself taut, she flung open the door. "I understand you wish to see me, Miss Whitaker. What can I do for you?" she challenged.

Carolyn whirled to face her and Jessica felt her overpowering presence at once. The tall woman was generously endowed and exuded strength. "Why have you taken over my Jonathan's home?" she demanded. Jessica knew instinctively she was no match for Carolyn's strength. So she must try charm.

"Won't you sit down? Callie, will you have one of the girls bring tea?" Jessica indicated a chair which Carolyn ignored. "Perhaps you will forgive me if I sit down. I have been so busy getting settled and I was resting. I am not sure I am fully awake."

Carolyn could do nothing but nod. "You have not answered my question," she went on rudely.

"Your question? Oh, you mean about Jonathan's home? I presume by Jonathan you mean Mr. Selby. But, Miss Whitaker, this is my home. I paid a very handsome price for it, I might add," Jessica said, her voice dripping with saccharine. "May I be so rude as to inquire why the purchase is of interest to you?"

Carolyn never took notice of the slur against her manners. "Surely you would not steal his home while a man is missing."

Ignoring the implication of Carolyn's choice of words, Jessica retorted, "Surely you would not expect this house to sit empty. What if he never comes back?"

"Jonathan will be back, and he will want this house," she said venomously.

"His partner—do you know Mr. O'Neill?—told me that Mr. Selby had instructed him to find a buyer as discreetly as possible. He found me. As far as I am concerned, that is the beginning and the end of the matter. You still have not said why it matters to you what happens to Fairhaven."

Polly entered with Callie behind her. "Jessica, Callie said you had company. Am I intruding?" Jessica noticed that she asked but sat down so that Jessica could not send her away.

"Miss Whitaker, may I present my sister-in-law, Polly Jamison? She and my brother are interested in settling here too, though they are staying with me for the present."

Carolyn barely scowled at the girl. She glared at Callie who set the tea tray in front of Jessica and left. "Something funny is going on here. Callie never brings the tea herself," sneered Carolyn.

"You must be mistaken," said Jessica sweetly. "She has been very helpful to me, but quick to inform me she stays only until Mr. Selby is ready to move to his new home upstate." Jessica offered her a cup of tea, but Carolyn ignored her so she handed it to Polly. Jessica gave Polly a warning glance because the girl twitched so in her chair.

"Don't you think, since Jonathan and I were promised to each other, I should have been consulted?" Carolyn had changed her tactics too.

"I am sorry. I did not know. Mr. O'Neill told me he was to act as the agent. Was I incorrect in assuming that this was Mr. Selby's property? I'm afraid all those legal documents I signed looked the same to me. Mr. Powell, at the bank, said all was in order and the property is mine."

"Well, that may be, but I want an inventory of Jonathan's property. I don't want to see him cheated by some conniving little. . .widow."

"Who is conniving, Miss Whitaker?" Jessica jumped to her feet. "Polly, hush!" she shouted at the girl's gasp. "This is my home now. Steve already has an inventory of what was in this house when we arrived. Since I left everything behind in England, I am to use what is here until it can be replaced. Some of the furnishings may be for sale also, but that has not yet been determined. I think you had better leave and not bother to honor me with your presence again!" She strode from the room and forced herself to march up the stairs. She could feel Carolyn watching from below and refused to give her the satisfaction of running away. She hesitated at the top only a second before she turned to walk into Jonathan's room.

"Well! She's even taken over his bedroom," Carolyn said scornfully.

Polly could not help adding, "It's her bedroom, Miss. She's the new owner, you know." Carolyn swung her arm back while Polly squealed with fright, but Callie moved into the doorway and Carolyn spun and stalked through the front door.

"Wow! She sure is somethin'," muttered Polly.

"She sure is," answered Callie as they climbed the stairs together to check on Jessica, who was stamping across her room with fists clenched, shaking with rage.

"Who does she think she is that she can speak to me that way?" Jessica shouted. "The rude people at home don't even know how to begin. I have never known anyone so. . .so brazen."

Callie and Polly watched helplessly until her rage had burned itself out. "Most of the folks around these parts are real nice, Miss Jessica. She shames all of them," said Callie as she fussed around the room, picking up and putting away as usual. "I'll get you both a bath to wash away the stink. Besides you should not be upset in your condition."

Jessica and Polly looked at each other and then threw back their heads and squealed with delight. "Her answer to all the cares of the world is a bath."

They unfastened each other and Polly crossed to her own room just as the servants entered with hot water and filled the tub. Jessica eased herself into the water and sat back.

Suddenly Callie rushed in, "Tim O'Leary's comin' up the drive with someone. You stay right here."

Jessica scrubbed furiously while calling Polly at the top of her voice.

"Whatever's wrong?" Polly screamed as she flew into the room.

"Someone's coming. It may be Jonathan. Help me!"

Polly grabbed the towel and helped Jessica stand up

in the tub. "Be careful, Jess." She dried her one-time mistress and helped her dress. They cleaned up the room as quickly as possible but could hear people on the stairs as they flurried all over the place. Polly stuck her head out the door. "It's him, Miss Jessica, but they're carrying him."

"Turn down the bed," said Callie as she burst into the room. Jessica flew to do as she was told. A stranger, must be Tim she thought, and Callie half carried and half dragged their load to the bed.

"Oh, my God!" screamed Jessica and fainted dead away.

Chapter Ten

Jessica awakened in the room adjoining her husband's. "What am I doing here?" she asked Polly. Suddenly she threw back the covers and climbed out of bed. Polly tired to hold her but couldn't begin to stop her. She threw open the door and saw Jonathan asleep on the bed. Tiptoeing in, she touched his hand but couldn't bear to look at him. "What have they done to you, my dear?" she whispered, but received no response.

Running on her toes, she grabbed a gown and returned to the other room. "Polly, help me. How long have I been here?"

"Just a few minutes, ma'am," she answered as she helped her dress. "The gentleman that brought him is still downstairs."

"I must talk to him," she said as she ran from the room. She practically flew down the steps, calling Callie all the way.

Callie appeared at the study door. "Take it easy, Miss Jessica. We're in here." She waited for the girl in the doorway and they walked into the study together. Jessica walked over to the dirty man and flung her arms around him. She kissed his cheek, murmuring, "Thank you so much for bringing him back to me."

Even beneath the grime the man turned scarlet and dashed for a chair. "And who might you be, ma'am?"

Callied smiled broadly at the pair and interrupted

saying, "Let's all sit down and set things straight. Tim, this is Mrs. Selby, Mister Jonathan's wife." Holding up her hand to silence him, she continued, "It's a secret. There are those who will question you. Just say you took him home and the widow took him in because Fairhaven had been his home and he was in too poor condition to travel further. That all right with you, Miss Jessica?"

Jessica nodded her approval.

"You can stay here and rest up or you can go on and report to Mister Steve. We will take care of the master and get details from Mister Steve later. Can you think of anything else, Miss Jessica?"

"What about Donald?"

"What do you mean?"

"I assumed Donald was with Jonathan. Wasn't he?"

"No, he's with Mister Jonathan's ship. He may be looking for you all over London town. I forgot you would be worryin' about him too."

"Mr. O'Leary, I will forever be grateful to you. I'm sorry I fainted at the sight of him. When you next see my husband, you will be the one shocked at the change in him. Callie, send me warn water, salve, bandages, all the things I will need. I'll go upstairs to him. You take care of Mr. O'Leary and get other details we might need to treat him effectively."

"See," said Callie, "she's pretty tough. Once she is awakened to need, she can do almost anything. Come on to the dining room. You must eat. By the way, try to sneak in to see Mister Steve. That poor little girl already had one row with Miss Carolyn today and she doan' need another soon."

Jessica walked into Jonathan's room and steeled herself inside the door before she advanced to the bed. She touched his forehead and jerked her hand away as if burned. One of the girls came in with warm water. "Put it down here and get me some cold water too. He is burning up." The girl nodded and scurried out.

Not wanting to awaken him, Jessica gently pulled the covers back. But he didn't move. She washed his face and realized he was not sleeping, but was unconscious. Then she proceeded with speed, stripping his clothes from his body. When he was completely exposed to her, she gasped with shock. "What he must have been through!" His body was one gigantic bruise with a few flecks of normal-looking skin. She didn't even think about his being naked. At this point he wasn't really a man anyway, just a beloved body to be restored to health with gentle care. Very tenderly she washed all of his body she could reach but threw a sheet over him as the girl returned with more supplies followed by Callie.

"Help me turn him over, Callie. I need to wash the rest of him."

Callie also gasped as she saw him, "Good Lord, who would do somethin' like this? At least the bullet hole is healin' pretty well. Tim said he was definitely left for dead. He had to tie him to his horse to bring him in. They traveled all night because Tim was afraid he couldn't get him back on the horse if they rested and was afraid he would die if he left him to come for help."

Together the women rolled him onto his stomach. They gasped anew as they saw his back, which was crisscrossed with stripes of raw flesh. Someone had whipped him as if he had been a dangerous slave. Jessica felt sick as she tried to wash the gore from the wounds. Nauseous though she was, she swallowed gallantly when she thought herself about to vomit and finally had his back clean. The stripes had opened again between the ripping off of the shirt and the washing, but it was absolutely necessary anyway. The healing process would have to being all over again. The dirt and poison had to be cleaned out if he were to have a chance at recovery. Callie helped dress his wounds but they both thanked God Jonathan was already unconscious and not able to feel their ministrations, which would have been very

122

painful no matter how well intended. Callie had a salve which would help draw the poison and Jessica took her word for it. Working together over the man they both loved, each in her own way, gave them complete trust and respect for each other.

They changed the bedding and left him naked on his stomach. "If it doan' bother you, Miss Jessica, I think he will be more comfortable undressed under that sheet. Right now he can't tell the difference, but when he comes to, he will toss and turn and be forever twisted in his clothes."

"I can handle it, Callie. All I care about is that he is comfortable. Look at this bump on his head."

Callie leaned over her mistress' shoulder to see better.

"What should we do about it?" asked Jessica.

"We must clean it out. You cut the hair while I find his extra razor. Someone should be shot for this. You can bet Mister Steve will find out who did it."

The women worked together and finally had done all they could. He was clean and reasonably comfortable. Because he was always so immaculate about his personal appearance, Callie shaved and manicured him while Jessica applied cold compresses to his forehead. Jessica wiped his face and neck continually and bathed down his body with the cool water. She must bring him out of the fever.

When Callie returned with broth, she tried to push Jessica to the other room to rest, but the girl refused to budge. "I will feed him. I hate to ask you, but would you please move me to the other room. He needs all the rest he can get, so I will sleep there." She trickled a spoonful of the hot liquid into his mouth. "Jonathan, swallow."

"He must have nourishment, Callie, or he will never get well. We could count his ribs and he had such a magnificent body." She blushed a deep pink when she realized what she had said. "I mean. . .I never. . ."

"That's all right, miss. He suie doan' look like he used to. If any of that broth goes down, it will surely help."

"How long do you think it will be before he wakens?"

"Not until the fever goes. It could be hours or it could be days."

"Well, that's all I can get down him now. We will try again later. Maybe you could tell Polly and Jimmy about what has happened. I want to stay with him."

Jessica sat in the chair and caressed his forehead. She leaned over and whispered into his ear. She held his hand to her heart and prayed. "I must be patient," she thought. "This may be a long process." Aloud she said, "I will not let you die, Jonathan. Don't you dare give up."

She nodded in her chair when Polly came in and lighted the candle. Touching Jessica gently, she whispered, "I will feed him this time, miss. You go lie down for a while."

"No, I'll feed him. You light the other candles." Once more she fed him about four spoonfuls before she could force no more liquid down him. "How can he recover on four spoonfuls at a time? Oh, Polly, what am I going to do?"

"You are going to rest so you don't fall to pieces yourself. All this rolling him over to eat is too heavy for you. I will sit with him and leave the door open so you can hear me if there is any change." She pushed Jessica toward the door. Jessica lay down on the bed and was asleep instantly.

"Jessica, Jessica," she heard as she woke with a start. "I'm going to bed now. There has been no change."

"I'll be right there, Polly."

"There's really no need, miss."

"If I get tired, I'll lie down later." She undressed and washed herself and dressed in nightgown and robe. She sat beside Jonathan, holding his hand, but still he did not move. She moved over the the window and looked out at the clear night for what seemed a long time.

"No! No! You bitch!"

Jessica jumped and ran to Jonathan. Grabbing his hand she said, "What is it? You're safe, Jonathan." She lay on his twisting body to quiet him, but he threw her aside and she fell to the floor. He was still burning up. She dried his body and bathed him in cold water once more.

The remainder of the night passed quietly. In fact, several days passed in much the same manner. Each day she forced a little more nourishment down him. He screamed several times during his nightmares and he opened his glazed eyes briefly. His weakened body recovered even if he was not conscious. The bruises turned yellow and the gunshot wound was almost entirely healed. His head looked better—it did not have to be reopened—they had done a good job. "Maybe," Jessica thought, "his mind needs this rest to recover. What terrible nightmares he must have to make him scream so." When his eyes fluttered open, Jessica tried with all her strength and love to keep them open. She crooned, she pleaded, she swore at him to come back to her. So far she had been unsuccessful. There was still no sign of recognition when he awakened for however brief a time.

Steve appeared one day and stayed long enough to see Jonathan's condition for himself and to tell them he had sent Tim out again, this time to try to track Jonathan's attackers. When Jessica pleaded with him to stay awhile, maybe he could bring Jonathan out of his coma, he insisted on returning to town. "Carolyn is as yet unaware of his return. Surely you don't want to arouse her suspicions."

"No, I don't," Jessica answered quickly. "I am too weakened to go a round with her anytime soon. Should I send you word when he awakens?"

"Nothing will keep me in town then," he promised.

Should I send for him today? she wondered. I can just tell he is going to come out of it. It will be soon. As convinced as she was of this, she would leave his side for nothing. She tidied the room so he should not awaken to a mess. She heard him stir and turned to meet his eyes on her. How long had he been watching her? He started to rise, but she rushed to the bed and pushed him back to the pillows. "Don't move," she whispered.

His eyes were still glazed but his fever had broken. He was completely cool. She answered a knock and took broth from the girl bringing it, saying, "Tell Callie he's awake."

She set the bowl on the table and helped him raise his head a little. Then she fed him every drop of the nourishing broth. He ate complacently with his eyes never leaving her face.

Callie rushed in just as he uttered his first words, "Who are you?"

Both women gasped and stared first at each other, then at him. Before they recovered from their shock, he continued, "Where am I?" Callie grabbed Jessica's arm and led her to a chair.

"Where do you think you are?" she asked.

His brow knitted into a frown as he finally said, "I'm not sure. Why don't you tell me?"

"You must tell him all about it, miss, while I send word to Mister Steve," said Callie as she left the room. "I'll send for the doctor, too," she added.

"Do you remember anything?"

"Not really. I know I awoke in this bed and watched you for awhile, but I couldn't remember who you were. Should I know you?"

"Not necessarily. I have been nursing you for over a week, ever since Tim brought you here. Do you remember Tim?"

"Tim who?"

"Tim O'Leary." Jonathan shook his head.

"He brought you here," Jessica contemplated how

126

much to tell him. Could he take it all? Maybe he had better have the same story as the others, she determined.

"I am Jessica Germayne, widow. You are Jonathan Selby, bachelor. I own this plantation. I bought it from you while you were gone."

"Hold on a minute. You bought it from me while I was gone? How did you manage that?" He smiled encouragingly.

"Let me start over. You are building a new plantation in the interior, so you told your partner, Steve O'Neill," she paused for a sign of recognition, but receiving none continued, "to sell Fairhaven. All the people on this plantation are your people except for me, my brother, and his wife. Tim brought you here because he didn't know about the sale. You went north to your plantation about two months ago and have been missing ever since. You arrived here well over a week ago and finally regained consciousness this morning."

"Well, I can't stay here if it is your house."

"You are certainly not well enough to travel anywhere. Besides, Mr. Selby, if you have really lost your memory, you will probably recover it more quickly in familiar surroundings. At least I think that is what the doctor would say. You must feel free to stay here until you are completely recovered. Callie sent for Steve. He can fill you in on the rest of the details. Now you lie back down and rest until he comes. Let me help you get comfortable." She reached forward to touch him, but he recoiled as if afraid.

"Good heavens, woman, I have nothing on!" he almost shouted. "Besides I'm too heavy for someone in your condition."

"What condition?" she asked as she jerked back.

"I am not blind, madam, but you have disguised your condition rather well. Is it a secret?"

"People on the place know, but no one else, not even Steve. If you noticed so quickly, it won't be a secret long. Look, I've been pushing and shoving you around for over a week now with no help from you at all. You hold the sheet, I'll move the body. My room is next door," she said after she had made him more comfortable. "I am going to take a bath, but will let the door opoen in case you need me." She was certainly glad Callie had moved her the day Jonathan showed up. How was she going to handle this? The doctor had better cooperate or we're in trouble.

Jessica rushed through her bath before Steve came. When he charged into Jonathan's room, Polly was just finishing her hair. "Steve," Jessica called, "you fill in the details he needs. I already told him what the people in town know about me."

She wanted to listen to the conversation, but was too embarrassed to be caught eavesdropping. "If you need anything, I will be downstairs," she said as she passed throught the room. She could hear Callie coming up with the doctor, but she said only, "Could I see you, doctor, before you leave?"

Jessica waited for Callie as she trudged down the stairs. "Oh, Callie, what will I do now? He doesn't even know me." She fell into the woman's comforting arms.

"There, there, Miss Jessica. It will be all right. Did you tell him who you were?"

"I couldn't," she sobbed.

"Why not? It would be all right, now we know he's alive."

"But he's just barely alive. How can I ask a man who doesn't even know me to be my husband?"

"You sure made a mess of this, Miss Jessica. What if he doan' ever remember?"

"Then he will have to decide he loves me all over again," she said defiantly. "Please tell the doctor I will be waiting in the drawing room."

When the doctor appeared, he had little to say. Jonathan would recover physically with rest and cure. His memory? That was something different. Probably he would start remembering soon and gradually fit the pieces together. Yet what happened to him may have been so horrible he wouldn't want to remember. If that were the case, it would take longer. The doctor was sure though that he would eventually remember everything. Jessica felt relieved when the doctor suggested he remain here in familiar surroundings—recovery would be much quicker that way.

When Steve appeared, he was as disturbed with Jessica as Callie had been. "What a damn fool thing to tell him! You'll be sorry if Carolyn finds out he has returned," he warned. Before he left, he went to the stable to talk to Jimmy. Two days later Jimmy and Polly had left. They were to oversee Jonathan's new plantation and start building their own on land Steve had acquired for them.

Jessica and Callie nursed Jonathan, who fumed at the fussing. Too weak to get out of bed himself, he had little choice. He insisted on trying to get up himself and fell flat to the floor. It had taken both women to get him back into bed.

A few days later Jessica announced Jonathan fit to travel as she pulled a chair in front of the fireplace which contained a roaring fire. The effort exhausted both of them, but Jessica insisted on changing the bed linens and cleaning up the room.

Exasperated by her refusal to rest, Jonathan shouted, "Dammit, woman, will you leave that for the servants and sit down a minute!" Callie walked in just then and tears filled Jessica's eyes. "Callie, would you get this girl a chair?" he continued. "She's doing far too much."

"You leave that to me, ma'am," she said as she picked up the sheets. She returned quickly, followed by servants who brought a chair in with them. They set it beside Jonathan's, and Callie brought each of them a stool and insisted they put their feet up. As if to goad him for shouting at the little lady, she then wrapped Jonathan in a blanket, saying, "You doan' want to get chill, do you?"

Conversation between them was severely strained until Jonathan said with pleading eyes, "I'm sorry for shouting at you, Mrs. Germayne. But you are forever fussing about when you should be taking care of yourself. I can't stand this inactivity."

"I know," she murmured. "Patience does not seem to be your strongest virtue. Maybe Mr. O'Neill can find something for you to do." Suddenly her eyes opened wide. "I have an idea. Your overseer has been helpful and I'm sure he must be trustworthy if you chose him. But if I brought the ledgers up here, could you show me what they mean?"

"I don't know, but I could try. Please let someone else carry them upstairs. They are too heavy for you."

Her eyes rounded as she said, "How do you know that?"

"I don't know that either," he said smiling.

"But, Jonathan," she squealed clapping her hands, "don't you see? You are starting to remember."

After lunch Jonathan struggled, this time with Callie, back into bed. Still, from that time on he progressed and was out of bed for a longer period each day. He was able to translate the ledgers for Jessica and they spent many hours working on them together. They ate their meals together in his room and became good friends. Jessica left preparations for Christmas to Callie while she spent her free time making gifts for Callie and Jonathan, but Jonathan's recovery was uppermost in her mind.

After a late breakfast on Christmas morning, Jessica swept into Jonathan's room just as he finished dressing. "Merry Christmas, Jonathan. You certainly look handsome this morning. I have a special gift for you." As Jonathan moved to put his arms around her, she adroitly turned, pulling one of his arms over her shoulder and sliding her arm around his waist. "You will need all your strength," she said slyly. "Callie and I have decided you are to go downstairs today." She led him to the top of the stairs where he insisted he could hold the bannister because he did not want her to fall. Not at all sure his strength was enough, she preceded him and waited at the bottom.

When he reached the bottom, perspiration poured down his face. "You are certainly safe now, madam," he gasped. "Just lead me to a chair."

"Not so spry as you thought, eh Mister Jon," called Callie while winking at Jessica. The big woman helped him but let him lead. She and Jessica grinned as he headed directly for the drawing room. He practically fell onto the settee. "Now you stay there awhile," she ordered.

"Don't fuss so, you two, I couldn't move if I wanted to."

Late in the afternoon Jessica sat in a chair by the fireplace sewing a garment for the baby. He watched her with pleasure. She seemed so delighted about having a child. He wasn't sure why, but felt certain that many women he knew tolerated pregnancy rather than delighted in it as this woman did.

"Well, isn't this a domestic little scene," snarled someone from the doorway. Jessica jumped to her feet at the sound of Carolyn's voice. "I heard you had returned, Jonathan, and couldn't bear to spend Christmas without you. In fact, I've come to take you home with me."

"And who might you be?" Jonathan demanded.

Carolyn gasped but recovered quickly and rushed to his side. "Oh, you poor darling," she crooned as she bent to kiss him, exposing her body to her waist as she did so. "I just couldn't believe you would not remember me after all we have been to each other. We are engaged to be married and will be immediately so I can nurse you back to health," she said in a sugary sweet voice. She sat beside him and blatantly dropped her hand on his thigh.

Jessica stared, mouth wide open. Thank heaven, she sighed as Steve walked into the room followed by Callie carrying refreshments. "Carolyn," cried Steve. "What trouble are you trying to cause now?"

"Trouble? Why would a visit to my fiance's house cause trouble?" she asked innocently.

"Because he isn't your fiance and we both know it even if he doesn't. You are trying another of your famous tricks. If you get out of here right now, I won't tell everyone in town what you have tried today."

"What is he doing here with this slut? You know he was to marry me."

Jessica gasped and the slap on Carolyn's face echoed throughout the room. Carolyn sprang at her, but Steve quickly stepped between them. Grabbing Carolyn's arm, he spun it behind her and pushed her toward the door. "Get out! Jonathan is here because this is the best place for him to regain his memory. I am sure you are no longer welcome in Jessica's house, if you ever were." He closed the door behind her.

Jessica sat back down and struggled to control the tears in her eyes. "Jessica," Jonathan started in a quiet voice, but she ran from the room and up the stairs. Jonathan cursed the weakness that prevented him from following her.

"Steve, you had better fill me in on what has happened here today. Jessica doesn't need another scene like that. Call Callie."

When both of them returned, Jonathan said sternly, "Now between the two of you I want to know everything." They looked at each other apprehensively. "Callie, tell him I am improving. I even knew my way around the downstairs. Can't you see I must know the entire truth?" he demanded.

Jonathan scowled at both of them as they revealed the whole truth to him. There had to be facts known only to Jessica, now that he did not remember. Something had happened in England that caused her to continue all this pretense even with him.

Jessica finally sobbed herself to sleep. She awoke when Callie burst into her room hours later. "Please, Callie, I will have my dinner here. I can't possibly face them after that."

"Mister Steve already left. He didn't think you needed company for dinner." She left quickly, shaking her head but giving no argument. She went straight to the drawing room and announced, "She says she won't come down, Mister Jonathan. She's feeling really bad." Callie looked as miserable as Jessica must have felt.

Struggling to stand, Jonathan said, "Can you help me upstairs? If she wont' come to me, then I must go to her." The need to be with her seemed to give him the strength to climb the long staircase. Turning to Callie, he asked her to return for the gift Steve had brought, which she hastened to do. She found him collapsed on a chair in his room. "We will both have dinner here," he announced. He motioned for quiet and she nodded.

He could hear Jessica pacing in the other room and called, "Jessica, please come here." The pacing stopped, but she did not come to the door. "I'm too tired to come over there," he added. Still he heard no movement, so he struggled to his feet once more. Using the furniture as props, he made it to the doorway, but fell into the room when he opened the door.

"Jonathan!" she screamed and ran to his side.

She could hardly believe her eyes when he raised his head and she saw his trembling was caused by laughter. "How much lower can I go?" he asked. "I really threw myself at your feet, my dear."

Callie, when she arrived with dinner, found them both on the floor laughing. She set the tray on the table and stole from the room.

Chapter Eleven

The relationship between Jessica and Jonathan changed after Christmas day. Now that he knew who she was, he protected her as well as he could. He made all kinds of excuses to keep her at his side. And she seemed willing enough to spend her time with him. She certainly seemed to like him well enough. He frequently wished he knew all the parts of their story because she showed very little interest in their relationship advancing beyond its present boundaries.

Each day Jonathan gained strength, and each day Jessica tired a little more quickly. By the time he no longer required help descending the stairs, he insisted she did. With great tenderness they cared for each other. Jessica did not stop to think that Jonathan was gradually running her plantation as if it were his own. If she had, she might have realized he knew more about their relationship than she had told him. She could no longer tell what he remembered from what he had learned. She did know he refused to remember what had happened to him when he had ridden north. Many nights she spent sitting at the side of his bed trying to calm his thrashing about during his nightmares.

One morning she awakened in his bed. Startled, she almost jumped out but caught herself before she awakened him. When she was fully awake, she remembered she had been able to calm him only to have him shake the bed as chills racked his body. Desperate because extra blankets and a built up fire did not help, she had slid between the covers and held him in her arms. The shaking gradually abated, but he held her so tightly she could not escape without awaking him. Now she slipped from the bed, as agilely as her awkward body would allow, and tiptoed to her room.

Jonathan watched her scurry away from him through narrow slits. It would frighten her more to know he was awake. He knew from the twisted bedclothes in the mornings that his nights were restless. Only now did he understand how much worse they might have been without her silent ministrations. No wonder she tired so easily he thought as he heard her dressing in the other room. When did she sleep? How can a woman give so much of herself and want nothing in return? He determined to rely on her much less from now on.

Jonathan knocked smartly on her door to escort her to breakfast. Threading her arm through his, they descended with her hand on the railing as if she did not fully trust him to keep her safe. Jonathan secreted himself in the study with Callie who could shed little light on the problem. "I don't know, Mister Jon. She says you have terrible nightmares, but she takes care of you herself. I can only tell how bad they are when I make your bed, and almost every morning it's bad. She says you are trying to keep from remembering some awful thing."

Jonathan spent the day outside with Mr. Bolton. He knew the overseer manufactured little chores for him to keep him near the house, but today he would have none of it. This time he finally rode to the lumber mill to find that no one had been hiding trouble from him as he had suspected. However when he returned, he was so tired he realized all over again how much protection and care he had received in these last two months.

Jessica flew to his side when he stumbled up the first step. "You've overdone it today. Let me help you," she said as she reached for his arm.

"Let me alone!" he snarled. "Do you think so little of your husband's memory that you would endanger the life of his child?"

As soon as the words were out and he saw her stricken face, he regretted them. But she had run away again and he was in no condition to follow. Callie charged down on him and practically lifted him to his feet. Without a word she guided him up the stairs. After he had settled into the bathtub and was lying back relaxing, she stormed, "You stay up here and rest until you can treat people decent!" and left the room.

Jonathan came down for dinner very much refreshed. Though he resented being ordered about by Callie, he realized the wisdom of her words. He ate a silent dinner, staring gloomily at Jessica's empty chair. Knowing he must apologize, he mounted the stairs and knocked on her door. When she did not answer, he stalked into his own room and opened to door to hers. "Jessica, I. . ." she slept soundly, but with a troubled frown on her face. Jonathan pulled a chair to her bedside and slumped into it. "Now it's my turn, my darling," he murmured and her eyes flew open. "Go back to sleep, Jessica," he whispered. "I'll watch over *you* tonight." She smiled, closed her eyes, and snuggled into the covers. His heart was heavy at the hurt he had caused her.

Callie opened the door but closed it quietly when she saw him. "The master's sure changed his ways since she came. He couldn't do without her now."

Jonathan guarded her well. He held her hand when she unconsciously thrust it from underneath the covers. When she moaned and rolled away from him, he moved to the bed and gently rubbed her back. When her moans turned to purrs, he slid back to his chair. "Why do we comfort so well when the other is asleep?" he thought.

Jessica awakened to see Jonathan sleeping in the chair beside her. When she moved to crawl out of bed, he stared at her. Smiling, with only gentleness in his eyes, he stammered, "I. . .I came to apologize for my nasty behavior yesterday, but you were asleep. You seemed so uncomfortable and distressed, I stayed." The question disappeared from her face and the smile that replaced it made his spirits soar. "I am truly sorry, Jessica. I spoke without thinking because of my frustration over my lack of energy. Please know I would never hurt you intentionally."

"Jonathan, you need your rest, too. How are you going to get energy by sitting up all night?" she asked quietly.

"I slept in the chair. Don't scold me. I wanted to be near you." Realizing she would not move until he had left the room, he rose saying, "I'll meet you in a few minutes for breakfast."

This day they spent together, each watching over the other. Not even Callie intruded on their quietude. When Jonathan escorted her to her door that evening, Jessica's smile disappeared until he said, "Sit with me by the fire as you did when I was too weak to move farther," he almost pleaded.

Jessica replied solemnly, "I will come through when I have changed. Would you unfasten me?" she said turning her back to him. Surprised by this familiarity, Jonathan fumbled with the buttons, finally unfastened them, and strode into his room to cover his embarrassment. Smiling to herself as she undressed, Jessica considered staying in her own room. How could she let things go farther when he thought her to have been someone else's wife? Would he ever remember her?

As if he knew of her hesitation, Jonathan knocked on the door separating them and opened it without waiting for an invitation, half afraid it may not be forthcoming. He had not waited long enough even to change, but had merely removed his coat. Jessica opened a drawer and removed a package. "Jonathan, I made this for you for Christmas, but the day was such a disaster I didn't have a chance to give it to you. Would you accept it now?" She handed him the box and sat down while he opened it. She watched him remove the green velvet robe from the box and put it on.

"It's beautiful and it fits perfectly. Thank you, my dear. It means so much more to me now than it would have on that horrible day." With his arm around her shoulders he guided her to a chair in the other room. It was a sign of their intimacy that they could sit quietly beside each other. Jonathan remembered well the days when Jessica was so nervous in his company she felt compelled to fill every silence with chatter. Now they were so comfortable in each other's presence that silence did not create a vacuum between them, only a contentment. They simply held hands and watched the fire.

Jonathan knew she was so serene that, if he did not grasp this opportunity to clear the trouble between them, another might not come for weeks. "Jessica," he started gently, "are you ever going to admit you are my wife and the baby you carry is mine?" She started to pull her hand back, but he held it fast.

"You don't remember that," she snapped, not looking at him.

"No, I don't, but I have known for months now that it is true. Don't blame Callie and Steve. I forced the rest of the story from them after Carolyn made that vile accusation against you." He lay his finger under her chin and raised her head until she looked straight into his eyes.

With tears in her eyes, she said, "Don't you see, Jonathan, you recall all of the past now but the last year. The doctor said you continued to reject what was too horrible to remember. If marriage to me was that repugnant to you, I could not possibly tell you the truth."

She looked wretched and he felt the same. He pulled her to her feet then down onto his lap. When she would wriggle out of his grasp, he said sternly, "Sit still."

"Don't you see, Jessica," he began, "I love you now. We need the truth between us. Tell me why you think I was repulsed by our marriage."

Finally she put the last pieces into the puzzle Jonathan had started to fit together. She ended her story with, "I came here under false pretenses. I told everyone you were coming for me and I was believed.

"Did it ever occur to you that they believed you because I had told them the same thing?" he asked. Seeing her agony change to surprise, he continued. "Both Callie and Steve admit I told them that fact."

She relaxed in his arms and snuggled against his body. "Jonathan, are you sure you are just not grateful for my taking care of you? Surely no man could fall in love with a woman shaped like me," she persisted.

He sighed, "The boldness of that cow on Christmas tells me I know much of bodies, but little of love. I am not proud of that fact, my dear. You have given me loving care for three months now, and I *am* grateful for that. But what I feel for you is most assuredly not gratitude. A man does not love a body, he uses it. A man does love a woman, and you are all woman." He let the silence envelop them like a cocoon while she contemplated his words. Should he push her further or be content with this much progress for one night. His lips against her hair, he whispered, "Come to bed with me, Jessica."

Pushing against his chest, she sat up to stare at him. "But. . .surely you. . .I. . ." she could not go on. Surely he would not insist.

"My God, woman!" he exclaimed when he read her thoughts on her face. "I am not a monster. I love you. I want you to lie with me because I sleep easier when you are in my bed. Was it not so two nights ago?" he asked with a sly grin.

"You knew?" she asked quietly. "You had such terrible chills and I could not warm you."

"I know," he said holding her close to him again. "I

will not insist if you are afraid that I will hurt you or the babe with my thrashing about. But I would like to lie with you in my arms and love in my heart and give you whatever comfort I can. Sleeping is difficult for us both. Together we can probably rest better. Besides, you get no rest at all running back and forth," he smirked. He felt the surrender as the tension drained from her body. He took off her robe and stood with her still in his arms and carried her to the bed. He threw his own clothes in the direction of a chair and slipped into bed beside her. He slid his arms around her body. "What's so funny?" he asked as she nearly convulsed with giggles.

"Oh, Jonathan, you say you want to hold me in your arms, but there isn't any place to put them. I am one large lump."

He moved his hands to cover her distended stomach and felt a firm kick from inside. "He certainly is lively, isn't he?"

"Very. He kicks often but not so much as he did. Do you think he approves?"

"Isn't the kicking his approval?" he teased. He squeezed one arm under her and pulled her back against him. His arms barely fitted into the groove between her breasts and belly. "Jess," he whispered in her ear. "Are you afraid?"

"Of what?" she cried and jerked away. "Of having a baby? Not if it's yours," she smiled.

"No, I meant are you afraid of me? What if I have another nightmare?"

"Darling, you are so relaxed you couldn't possibly have another nightmare tonight." And she was right.

In the morning Jessica heard Callie open the door to the other room, close it, and trudge away singing. Jonathan stirred beside her and she turned her head to see him watching her. She smiled and rolled into his arms, though her burden kept them apart. She giggled and held his hand over her tummy. "See. He still approves."

He slid out of bed and held out his hand to her. She crawled out too and went into the other room to dress. "I'll tell Callie to move you back in here. That's too far away." Though she seemed embarrassed for him to see her unclothed, he refused to let her call anyone to help her dress. "Jess, let me do whatever needs doing. I know little of being a lady's maid, but I want to be the one to help you these days. I don't want to be separated from you for even the time it would take to dress. You are beautiful to me. This project is ours, not yours alone. You've been through enough alone." He folded her into his arms.

From that time on Jonathan was at Jessica's side constantly. If Mr. Bolton came to the house for a conference, he included her in the conversation, as if he could not bear even that short a separation. He read to her as she sewed. He took her for short walks. They talked about a myriad of topics. He talked of the coldness of his father's house after his mother's death. She, of the warmth his father had showered on her. And Callie clucked over them both like a mother hen.

One night after they had retired, Jonathan's eyes flew open as he felt her body jerk. "What is it?" he questioned. "Is it the baby?"

Her body convulsed again and he jumped from the bed. He lighted a candle and threw on his clothes. Then he ran for Callie. He met her in the kitchen. She had seen the light, guessed the reason, and had awakened the staff and had them busy. He raced back up the stairs. Callie tried to push him out saying, "Mister Steve is coming. You go down and wait for him."

"Callie, I'm staying," he said determinedly. "How can you think I would leave her after what she's done for me? Just tell me what to do."

Even Callie knew there was no arguing with him them. "Just don't you faint when I have to tend to the missus." She went to talk to Jessica.

"It will be a long time, Miss Jessica. The first one

always comes slow. Save your strength until you need it. Stay as relaxed as you can—don't fight the pain.''

Jessica nodded that she understood. When Jonathan came to her side, she said, "Don't worry, darling, or I will have Callie put you out. You look too gloomy.''

Jonathan smiled weakly but his face drained of color as another pain gripped her. When she breathed easier again, he said, "I will not leave, no matter what Callie says. You don't need to worry about me.''

Through the hours of the long night Jonathan sat by his wife, holding her hand, wiping her brow, trying to make the ordeal as easy for her as he could. "Mister Jon, she's holding up better than you. Why don't you rest for a while?'' Callie tried once more to ease him aside but he was adamant.

Knowing full well if he ever left his wife's side, Callie would keep him from returning, he shook his head. "I will be strong enough. Why don't you rest until there is something you can do?''

Callie was much more practical than he and flopped into one of the chairs by the fireplace. She secretly admired her master more each day. The little miss has sure gripped his heart, she thought. Not many men are strong enough to take childbirth, but I believe he is. He won't let her suffer alone. These two will lead a happy life with each other. They care so much for each other.

Jessica felt enough embarrassment about what she knew was to come to ask Jonathan to leave, but was really pleased at his refusal. Somehow she gained strength from his presence.

"Jess, I know you. Don't be embarrassed. If I can be with you for the beginning of a baby, I want to be with you at the end. You are always beautiful to me—even with a few strands of hair out of place.'' She saw the love in his eyes and smiled weakly.

As another spasm of pain shook her small body, Jonathan almost cried out with pain from her grip which felt as if it would crush his hand. My God, where do these little women get such strength? How much can they take? What a fallacy to call them the weaker sex and protect them so. No man would be willing to go through this, even for a son, and she endures all of it so quietly.

Soon wave after wave of pain convulsed her, one on top of the other, until he could not tell when on pain stopped and another started. Callie bustled about the laboring woman and, seeing the stricken look on Jonathan's face, said quietly, "It's about over now, Mister Jon," and went back to work. With one final push and her only scream of the night piercing the air, Jessica gave birth to their son. Jonathan shook as her body relaxed. He sat as if in a stupor while Callie and her girls bathed mother and baby.

When Callie brought the child to Jessica, murmuring, "We have us a fine boy, Miss Jessica," and put him in his mother's arms, Jessica smiled with great satisfaction.

Still somewhat in a daze, Jonathan gazed at mother and son and vowed, "Never again, my darling, will I put you through an ordeal such as this."

Jessica frowned but was too tired to argue and immediately fell asleep after he kissed her very tenderly.

Callied removed the baby to his cradle and, taking her master's arm, said, "You go get some sleep now, Mister Jon. She will sleep for quite a while. The little missus needs her rest and so do you." Knowing how much love was between them, she shook her head as he walked into the other room. "He'd better forget this night, as she will, or we are in for some rough times in this house," she murmured to herself. "But I think the missus can handle him and never let him know he's being handled. He found himself quite a woman.

Jonathan awoke to bright sunlight and rolled off the bed quickly. Anxious to see his family but not wanting to appear as bedraggled as he felt, he hastily washed in cold water on the stand. The coolness revitalized him somewhat. As he shaved he suddenly realized his clothes were in the other room so he could not dress. Then he spied a clean set of clothes draped over the chair and realized once again that Callie thought of everything. Declaring himself presentable, he opened the door to his wife's room, not knowing what to expect. From the other side of the door he had heard activity in this room and had been worried about what was going on. The room seemed full of women, all going about their business.

"Come on in, Mister Jon," called Callie. "The young master's been fed and we're moving him to the nursery. Daisy's going to be in charge of him because I must look after the missus."

Jessica sat in the middle of the big bed, looking more beautiful than ever. She wore a frilly gown and her hair had been brushed and tied back with a ribbon. She smiled and extended her hand. "Come, see your son, Jonathan," and reached for the baby as Callie and Daisy left to carry the cradle away. They created a picture which he swore to remember always. As he strode to her side, she asked, "Isn't he beautiful?" and patted the space beside her.

Staring at his wife and child, he worked his lips, but was too moved to utter a word. "Do you approve?" she asked, smiling happily.

"I approve most heartily, madam, and yes, he is beautiful," he finally managed.

"What shall we name him?" she asked.

He stared at the depths of her eyes and was relieved to find the ordeal of the previous night had left no traces. Picking up her hand in his, he finally sat beside her where she had indicated. He leaned forward, as if in a trance, and would have kissed her chastely, but Jessica slipped her arm around his neck and held his mouth to hers. Lips seeming to soften and melt apart, their kiss deepened and each could feel the pounding of his heart.

144

He collected himself first and backed away from her, first removing her hand and holding it tightly.

The surge of passion for this beautiful woman coursed through his body, almost frightening him with its intensity. "My God," he thought. "How will I ever live with her platonically?" and finally said with a forced smile on his face, "A name? Shall we keep on with the J's? There's James, or Joshua. Whatever you want."

"Jonathan, if we are not to pander your ego with a junior, could we call him Jeremy for your father? He really brought us together, and I think this is the best way we could thank him."

Jonathan wondered at this woman who could be so forgiving, for hadn't she told him his father had brought them together in a most cruel way? His eyes followed hers to the sleeping babe. Sliding a finger into the tiny fist, he felt a wave of protectiveness as the fingers tightened on his. Nothing must harm these two he told himself. "If that is what you wish, Jeremy it will be," he said with great tenderness.

He walked over to the wardrobe and rooted in the bottom, then returned with a package. "This is nothing compared to the gift you have given me, but I want to thank you for my son." He started to open the package for her, but Jessica's hand on his stopped him.

Thrusting the baby into his arms, she hastily unwrapped it herself. Jonathan, completely taken by surprise, looked from the small bundle back to his wife. Awkwardly he held his son as if he were a basket of eggs. Just then Callie bustled in as Jessica cried, "Callie, look what my husband gave me just for producing a son for him!" Delight ran in her voice as she held up a string of beautifully matched pearls.

Taking the baby from his father, Callie replied, "They're mighty nice, missus."

"If he's going to give me such grand gifts, I must present him with a whole houseful of children," the woman answered soberly, warily watching her husband's face.

Seeing Jonathan scowl, Callie hurried from the room. Jessica saw the scowl too and knew she had heard correctly last night. "Don't scowl so, Jonathan," she teased. "You frighten me almost beyond belief. Be happy, my dear," she pleaded, taking both his hands in hers.

Looking straight into those violet eyes, he smiled briefly. "I am happy beyond my wildest imaginings, but," he continued seriously, "you will not suffer such torture again because of my selfishness."

The smile left her face as she looked at him and realized that witnessing childbirth had frightened him more than any of his own sufferings. "Jonathan," she said, every bit as serious as he, "I did not become pregnant because you were selfish." When he would interrupt her, she rushed on abruptly. "Let me finish. I thought I had made it perfectly clear you were being thoughtful, comforting, and kind. Even last night I didn't think anything else. Never once did it enter my mind to say, 'why did he do this to me?' Why must you blame yourself for something that is the natural way of things? This was certainly not your own little brand of torture."

"It may not have been original, but it surely was torture," he replied scornfully. Knowing he might not be able to resist the pleading in her eyes, he stared at the floor. When he stood up to leave, she held onto his hands so that he could not leave her. "Jessica, if I had had any idea of what a woman goes through to have a baby, I would have not lain with you in the first place."

"But if you hadn't, my dear, I would never have experienced the wonderful sense of fulfillment that I have now," she countered.

Sighing loudly, he sat gently beside her and looked into her eyes. She could not miss the torture written in his. "Darling, we have so much—we have money, a fine home, and a wonderful son. We also have each other and are more fortunate than most people because we are married and find ourselves in love. Can we not be content with what we have?''

"Yes," she replied with love in her eyes. "Let us be content." Seeming to surrender, she fell back on the pillows. He also heard the "for the time being" that she barely whispered and knew the issue was not closed.

Chapter Twelve

Now Jessica really settled into life as the mistress of Fairhaven. All household decisions were clearly deferred to her. Even Callie asked her advice, though Jessica was certain that she needed none. If there was a whisper that someone was not feeling well, Jessica was at his side with comfort and healing broth. She rode over the plantation at Jonathan's side and all who worked here recognized their love and regard for each other. This had always been one of the best plantations to work on, and now the two of them made it even better. Each worker was respected and the love and respect was returned.

Jonathan watched with delight as he saw the growing regard for her, but he worried that she overtaxed her strength. She worked from dawn to dusk at some task or other, never neglecting either him or Jeremy. Their pleasure was increased by the amount of time spent together with their son. One morning before going down for breakfast, Jonathan had walked into the room where Jessica was nursing the baby. Surprised to find them both, he started to retreat but remained when Jessica invited him in. He watched, almost mesmerized, until she was finished, then lingered on while she bathed and dressed Jeremy and returned him to his cradle which Daisy had changed. Somehow he had thought Jessica only fed the baby and Daisy did the rest. Taking care of her son was obviously a delight to Jessica and his heart warmed to her even more. From that time on they met there each day for the morning ritual, and love and contentment surrounded them in that room.

Because she had been working so hard and he thought she needed some enjoyment, Jonathan decided to give a huge ball so she could meet his acquaintances and friends from the area. Jessica had insisted the baby's christening be private, but he was anxious to show off his lovely wife. Feeling perfectly capble of caring for her now, he quickly dispelled his doubts about their safety. The invitations had been sent out and the preparations begun. Now he silently cursed himself and his idea while he watched her work day after day to get ready. She looked even more worn out than before, though she seemed tireless on the surface. Though Callie had helped with the guest list, Jonathan felt he would recognize the people when he saw them.

The day of the ball Jonathan gave strict orders that Jessica was to relax and rode off for town. Jessica did attend to a few last minute details, but mostly she followed the orders and spent the day with Jeremy. At three months he gurgled and cooed and giggled, and Jessica counted each second she was with him very precious. Even though she seemingly did nothing more difficult than change the baby's linen, she indulged in some heavy thinking about enticing her husband back into her bed. She knew his nerves were ragged to the point that he now almost jumped when she touched his hand. There had to be a way to erase his fear because neither of them could continue this way much longer. At first she had refused to move from his big bed, but had finally capitulated when Jonathan had moved next door. After several nights of listening to him bang his head or feet on the headboards, she understood the strength of his determination and took the smaller bed herself. He had insisted she not be embarrassed in front of the staff by moving her clothes from his room, but

Jessica knew they hadn't fooled anyone. She had hoped that there would be so many overnight guests at the party that they would be forced together, but Jonathan had planned too well. There was just enough room for everyone.

She felt today was a poor day to do anything about it, but she could not stem the anger rising within her. With Jeremy sleeping in the middle of her bed, she made trip after trip between the rooms, each time carrying an armload of her belongings to the room where she slept and carefully putting them away. When she finished, she took one last look to make sure no trace of her existence remained behind. Then she called for her bath and smiled pleasantly at the startled faces of those who brought the water when she directed them to the other room.

When she was undressing, she asked as casually as possible, "Callie, do you know where I can find a key to that door?" pointing to the door connecting the rooms.

"Now, Mister Jonathan doan' like locked doors, Miss Jessica. What you want to cause so much trouble for, especially today?"

"I don't want to cause trouble," she answered innocently. "I want my husband back. You heard him the night Jeremy was born, didn't you?"

The large Negress nodded with a worried frown. She did not like the action the mistress was taking, but she also knew someone had to do something or these two might never get together. Mister Jonathan was a stubborn man when he had made up his mind. Callie marched silently from the room and, returning quickly with the key, locked the door. When she would have left, Jessica said softly, "Leave the key, Callie. I may not want it locked long if all goes well."

Jessica was still relaxing in the bath when she heard Jonathan bounding up the stairs. Momentarily she quivered at what she had done, but stiffened her resolve for the battle which she knew would come shortly. She heard him stop as soon as he opened the door to his room then pass hers on his way to the nursery. As she was tying her wrapper around her, he quietly opened the door. Taking in the details with one swift glance, he stepped inside and closed the door. "What the hell have you done?" he exploded.

"Keep your voice down Jonathan," she stated calmly.

"Why should I?" he shouted. "You have told the household more with this move than I could, so I may as well shout to the heavens that my wife has locked me out of her room." He glared at her menacingly, but she stood firmly in her tracks and stared back.

"But I didn't, Jonathan. I only made a reality what you did three months ago—locked me away from you. You are welcome in my quarters anytime you choose to be here."

"I want that door unlocked! And you can carry all those things back immediately."

Suddenly her temper flared as violently as his. With eyes snapping, she straightened her body as tall as possible and said from her lofty perch, "I am not your servant and I will not be ordered about—by you or anyone. You want me separated from you. That is your business, but I will no longer be a party to this farce that we are husband and wife in all ways."

When she saw him clench his fists, she quieted and walked over to him and took his hand. Holding it up for him to see, she said, "Will you feel better if you hit me, Jonathan? Go ahead." She brought the fist even closer to her face. "Go ahead, Jonathan. I will not resist," she goaded. Watching the thunder in his eyes dissipate, she sensed the worst was over and opened the fingers to kiss them, one by one, softly.

With a sudden moan, Jonathan pulled her against him and her soft form melted against his taut body. Jonathan knew he had lost more than this little skirmish which he really did not want to win. As he ran his hands over her soft body, he knew he would never be able to deny her anything. "Jess, Jess," he muttered hoarsely. "Don't you know that I want to possess you in all ways that a man can possess his woman? But I am so afraid for you."

Reveling in the delightful sensations the feel of his hands created in her, Jessica wanted the moment to last forever, but she knew they must dispel this ghost once and for all. Looking deeply into his tormented eyes, she slipped her arm around his neck and forced his mouth to her parted lips. His mouth covered hers hungrily and their kiss deepened until Jessica's head swirled. She could barely remember having felt this way—as if nothing mattered but being with this man—once before. A delicious warmth spread throughout her and she knew only his embrace held her upright. Feeling his reaction against her loins, she pushed gently at his chest and turned her head away. He released her with a questioning gaze and then his eyes clouded over as he said snidely, "Are you playing the tease, madam? If so, you have done it well."

Hurt that he would allow such a thought to cross his mind, let alone utter it aloud, she felt her eyes swell up with tears. Determined that nothing ruin the moment she had waited for so long, she blinked away the tears and led him to the lounge chair and pulled him down beside her as she sat. Hesitantly she began, "Jonathan, I know so little about loving a man. I have been a wife for a year and a mother these few months, yet I have only faint memory of one night of loving you. I am not even sure what 'playing a tease' means, though many whispered conversations of school girls are becoming clearer. I do know, though, that the night at your father's house is my most precious memory and that I would never use my body to force your surrender." Seeing only tenderness on his face, she quickly summoned all her courage and continued. "I want you to understand why I behave as I do. And we certainly could not talk or think clearly as we were," she added with an impish grin and a sparkle in her eye.

Jonathan slid behind her so that he was stretched out on the chair. Leaning back as if completely bored, he rested his head on his entwined fingers. "All right, madam," he said gently this time. "What do you want to talk about?"

"You make me feel so silly," she muttered with embarrassment, staring at the floor. He sat up quickly but allowed her to push him back into the pillows when she said, "I can't think when you touch me and we must have this out."

"We are both young and, I hope, have many long years ahead of us," she started. When he said nothing, she continued, "I may not know much, but I know—and you do too if you will but admit it—that we cannot go on indefinitely as we are." He started to interject but she rushed on, "You are frightened for me, but I am terrified that you will turn to someone else to comfort your needs."

"That will never happen, Jessica," he said, gently pulling her to his chest. "I am not an animal."

"No, but you are a man who needs a woman, not an ivory statue. Is it wrong for me to want to be that woman?" she asked meekly. "Shall I tell you what would have happened if we had continued a few minutes ago? I have it pictured so plainly in my mind so many times. You would have made love to me and tomorrow you would set me away from you again. You would watch warily for a month or so to know whether or not I were carrying another child. I can hear your sigh of relief now if I were not until we lost control once more and you had to go through it again. If by some awful chance I were pregnant again, I would have to watch the agony and self-condemnation in your eyes for months while I wanted to be joyful. How long could we go on that way? You would eventually take your ease with someone whom you wouldn't worry about and I would die." Panic-stricken at the thought, he hugged her to

153

him tightly. "I would, Jonathan. I would know and I would die inside."

Sitting up abruptly, she became very matter of fact and sure of herself. "I am healthy and strong. I certainly recovered from Jeremy's birth quickly. And I will not go on living with you as polite strangers who can look but mustn't touch. If we cannot live as man and wife, then let me go back to England."

His heart jumped into his throat at the thought. Swallowing hard, as if to keep from choking, he pulled her back to him, murmuring, "I could never bear to lose you, Jess."

"Miss Jessica," Callie started as she burst in the door. She stopped momentarily then charged on into the room. "Everything is ready. This is sure going to be a wonderful party. Do you want me to help you dress now?" she said striding to the dresser.

Jonathan felt Jessica tighten and held her so she could not jump away. Scowling, he muttered, "Isn't there such a thing as privacy in this house?"

Not paying a bit of attention to the scowl, she answered, "Didn't have no idea you'd be here, Mister Jonathan. Dinner is almost ready."

Reluctantly he sat up with his wife and stood up. "Dinner can't be ready. I forgot to tell you we are having two guests. My lovely wife made me forget that was what I rushed up here to tell her. You will have to rearrange again because they will be staying to visit. One of them can sleep in this room. Get my bath ready. And one last time, I hope, see that my wife's things are moved again. But let that door locked! It has been too easy for us to escape each other through it."

Chuckling with glee, Callie called as she walked out, "Yes, sir, Mister Jonathan. Leave it to you to make all this extra work at the last minute."

Changing the subject quickly lest Jonathan's mood darken, Jessica asked, "Who is coming, Jonathan?"

"Wait and see," he said, striding to the door and unlocking it.

Jessica followed him into the other room as if it were completely natural. "Tell me," she begged.

"No," he said. "You will have to wait as punishment for today's little episode, though I have to admit I am glad you took matters into your own hands and I am looking forward to the outcome later on." He slipped his arms around her and they stood together as the door from the hall opened and a man came in carrying a huge box.

"Donald!" Jessica cried. "When did you get back?"

"Just today, mum," he answered, turning scarlet as she threw her arms around him and kissed his cheek. He backed out the door as quickly as possible after setting the box down.

Jessica quickly set about taking care of her man and got out clean clothes while he bathed, both of them humming all the while. Suddenly she giggled and cried with delight, "Oh, Jonathan, I'm so happy. Tonight will be a wonderful party." Then she strode to the other room and started carrying her own clothes back into their room while he dressed. "Go see if Jeremy is ready to be fed," she said as he started to embrace her again. "We'll take care of you later," she teased. "I must dress too." She unfastened her robe and Jonathan gasped at the sight of her exquisite body and left the room hastily. When he returned carrying Jeremy, she had donned all of her clothing but her gown.

She sat in one of the chairs by the fireplace to nurse her son while Jonathan sat in the other to watch. Both of them remembered the times they had sat thus while he had recuperated. Their eyes met over their son's head and contentment surrounded them. His eyes wandered back to her breast, and he muttered huskily, "My God, Jess, I'm jealous of my own son."

She smiled and held her hand out to him, indicating she had enough love for both of them. As if hypnotized, he leaned forward and dropped his eyelids as he lowered his lips to hers. Soon both their senses were swimming and only noise in the room next door drew them apart.

155

While she returned the baby to the nursery, he opened the box Donald had brought and was holding its contents in front of him when she walked into the room.

"Oh, Jonathan, it's gorgeous!" she squealed. "It has to be the most beautiful gown I have ever seen. Where did you get it?"

"Donald brought it from London. I ordered it months ago," he said off-handedly as he dropped it over her head and fastened the back. Then he sat to watch while Callie dressed her hair. Suddenly he could not see enough of her and couldn't let her out of his sight for a minute. How could he have remained celibate for so long with her in the house? He had consciously avoided acknowledging, especially to himself, just how truly lovely she was. The gown was all black, but she certainly did not look like a widow in it. The lines were simple but accented her tiny waist. The neckline was so low her bosom threatened to pop out, but Jonathan smiled to himself as he thought of his guests waiting for the threat to become a promise. They can wait all night he told himself. Only I will see the promise come true.

He jumped to his feet as Callie finished his wife's hair and Jessica walked over to him. "Shall we go down, dear, or do we wait and make a grand entrance after the dinner guests have arrived?" she asked impishly.

"We go down," he said, pulling her hand through his arm. It was too much to ask of a man in the bedroom with this vision and not touch it. "Callie. . ."

"It will all be taken care of when they get here. They'll never know from me what a fool you almost were," she called from the other room.

"She's at it again," he barely muttered. "But she's right, as usual, darling."

"She called me a fool too when I asked for the key," Jessica whispered. "Isn't it wonderful that two fools can be so happy?"

Jonathan threw back his head an laughed heartily for the first time in months. Jessica smiled demurely and they descended the stairs together.

Jessica fidgeted in the drawing room while Jonathan smirked. That made her more irritated than his refusal to tell her who was coming. Finally, he handed her a glass of madiera, saying, "Drink this. You will wait easier if you do." Then he added seriously, "Don't spoil my surprise, Jess. I want to see the delight on your face."

"You've sent for Polly and Jimmy," she guessed because she could think of no one else.

"I wish I had thought of it," he answered seriously. "In fact, I did think of it, but decided they might feel too uncomfortable to start meeting society in droves. We will introduce them a few at a time."

Silently Jessica was thankful for this considerate husband of hers. Left to herself, she would have blundered badly and insisted they be here. Actually, she had assumed they would, but she had never seen the guest list because she didn't know anyone on it but Steve.

She jumped to her feet when she heard a carriage roll up the drive. Jonathan roared with laughter as she coyly sat back down and pretended a lack of interest. "Come, dearest, let's answer the door ourselves this time," Jonathan said.

Jonathan yanked her forward gently, saying, "You look perfect. You will dazzle whoever it is."

He swung the door open wide and she squealed, "Geoff! How good to see you!" and ran into his arms. She felt her feet leave the floor as he swung her into the air and kissed her. "Father Selby!" she cried as Geoff set her down and she nearly knocked him over as she threw her arms around the old man. Jonathan caught them both and quietly closed the door. Then everyone was talking at once while Jonathan leaned on the door and beamed. He finally heard Jessica say, "This is going to be a wonderful party," and thought to himself how many times have I heard that today? I hope she never changes her mind.

They had barely entered the parlor when Adam announced dinner so they herded to the dining room. Jessica didn't even remember what was served she had been so busy talking and listening and gazing fondly at her husband. They had eaten early because of the party, and she knew the men should be shown to their rooms to freshen up, but she took her father-in-law's hand as they left the table. "Come with me," she said softly, and he, who wouldn't deny her any whim followed her down the hall, up the stairs, and into the nursery. Picking up her son, she laid him in his surprised grandfather's arms. "Here is the grandson you wanted so badly, you old manipulator." Then lest he think her unhappy with his manipulations, she added, "Father Selby, meet your grandson, Jeremy."

Tears welled up in the old man's eyes and he unashamedly let them course down his wrinkled cheeks as he gazed from mother to child. Geoff and Jonathan, who had followed behind, appeared in the doorway and heard her murmur gently, "Take time to get acquainted. Then Callie will show you to your room. We expect you to attend the party, not spend the evening in the nursery." She walked straight to her husband with her love for him beaming in her eyes. Sliding her arm around him, she walked to their room, knowing Callie and Daisy would see to the others.

Once the door had closed behind them, she burst into tears. "My God, Jessica, what's wrong?" Jonathan queried frantically. Try as he might, he could make no sense of her answer through the sobs that shook her body. She was not even aware of his unbuttoning her gown and slipping it from her body by lifting her from the middle of its folds. Sensing she was near hysteria, he moved to put her on the bed, but she clung to him and would not let go. He held her as a mother with a hurt child and let her cry, rocking her back and forth and crooning tender words in her ears. When she had cried herself out and lay quietly against him, he asked again, less frantically this time, "Jessica, what's wrong?"

"Nothing," she sighed.

"That won't do, Jessica. Tell me."

"Nothing," she insisted. As his expression started to change to one of irritation, she rushed on, "Whatever could be wrong, Jonathan? I'm so happy I'm almost delirious. I'm sorry I frightened you, but I could contain my joy no longer and it simply overflowed."

Realizing that she was telling the truth—that they were tears of joy—he roared as if a joke had been played on both of them. Soon she was laughing too and he sobered immediately before she became hysterical again.

"Was there ever so fortunate a woman as I, Jonathan?" she asked quietly. "I always thought the expression 'kill with kindness' was just an expression, but you may really do it."

Shaking her roughly then enfolding her in his arms as an apology, he whispered sternly, "Don't even joke about it, Jess. We've been so lucky so far I like to think we always will be."

"What an intense day this has been. The excitement of the day was to be the party, and I'm exhausted from excitement before the party even starts. I suppose I have you all wrinkled. What will Callie say when she has to have your trousers pressed?" she teased.

Realizing she would be all right now, Jonathan stood her on her feet in the middle of the dress and helped her pull it up and button it. "One thing for sure," he answered, pretending to be cross. "We are not going to find out. I will change to another outfit, and you can hang this one away, and she can spend the night guessing about what happened. It will serve her right."

They both laughed at the thoughts that might run through Callie's head and prepared to meet their guests.

Chapter Thirteen

Jonathan, Jessica, Geoff, and Mr. Selby stood at the door receiving guests for hours—it seemed to Jessica, anyway, that it was hours. She was so deliriously happy she hardly remembered a single name. Knowing she was on display caused her no alarm whatsoever and Jonathan thoroughly enjoyed the obvious reaction to his beautiful wife. Jessica thought these the friendliest people she had ever met.

Finally Jonathan led her from the door to the dance floor. No one would dance until the host and hostess started the ball. He swept her onto the floor and the ball began. The love between them was apparent to all who watched. "Well, Mr. Selby, do you approve of this wife your son found?" asked Maude Atkins, who lived on the neighboring plantation.

"Approve? I helped him find her," he retorted as he swept the widow onto the floor, much to her surprise.

As the dance floor became more crowded, Jessica and Jonathan left to chat with their guests. The evening swept by as rapidly as the music, and Jessica became more exhilarated with each passing moment. She was laughing gaily when she saw Steve watching from the veranda. With a sly grin she stepped out to talk to him. "Thank you, watchdog."

Shifting his feet, somewhat embarrassed, he asked, "Why, Jessica, what does that mean?"

"Steve, you of all people should know that I can take pretty good care of myself. Go have fun and stop worrying about Carolyn and Jonathan. Let her do her worst. You'll see it won't be enough." As she and Steve danced, Jessica giggled at Jonathan's feeble efforts to extricate himself from Carolyn who brazenly tried to wrap herself around him. He finally led her to the dance floor but had little more success with her there. "Should we both rescue him this time?" she asked, and Steve waltzed her over to the doorway through which the other pair had just disappeared.

"Maybe we shouldn't go out there, Jessica," he said quietly.

"Have you no faith, Steve?" she admonished. "You don't know Jonathan as well as I thought."

They stepped out the doorway and saw Carolyn molded next to Jonathan while he was frantically pulling her arms, not even participating halfheartedly. "Goddammit, Carolyn, you are like an octopus. Will you please let go of me!"

"Come on, Jonathan," she wheeled. "Be fun."

"However hard you may find it to believe, I do not find you fun," he retorted.

"Are you enjoying yourself, Miss Whitaker?" Jessica asked sweetly. "For shame, Jonathan, I should think you could see that she had a better time than this."

With a sigh of relief Jonathan grabbed his wife's arm and whirled her through the door. "You little minx," he grinned. "I love you."

"I know that, Jonathan," she whispered. "How long does this party go on?"

"If you want to go upstairs, I'll make your excuses and say your goodnights."

"I don't want to go upstairs alone."

"You're becoming as brazen as Carolyn, my dear," he said sardonically.

"You're right," she answered. "You're absolutely right."

161

"Go on upstairs. I'll be up shortly," he said as he danced to the door and escorted her to the bottom of the steps.

"Do hurry," she whispered and practically sprinted up the stairs while he watched with a broad smile of anticipation covering his face. He noticed her go directly to the nursery so he realized he would have a little extra time because his son was such a glutton.

Walking up to his father, he said with humor, "Don't believe anything this reprobate tells you, Maude." His father had hardly left the widow's side all evening.

"You Selby men are a bunch of sweet talkers, Jonathan. And your wife is delightful," she added.

"Thank you. I can't agree with you more. Jessica is tired, Father; so I'm putting you and Geoff in charge of my guests. Good night."

As Jonathan spun away, his father gleamed and Maude said, "Someday, Jeremiah, you must tell me the whole story."

"I just might," he said, winking as he replied.

Jonathan meanwhile walked into the nursery but found only his sleeping son and Daisy. The feeling of awe that small child aroused in him still amazed the father. "He will be all right now, Daisy. The party is about over and my wife and I will listen for him." As Daisy quietly left the room, Jonathan looked once more at his son; then he followed her out the door. As he approached the bedroom, he felt himself quiver with anticipation and said to himself, "My God, I feel like a virgin." When he closed the bedroom door behind him, he did not see Jessica and he felt his heart sink into his stomach. But then he spied her on one of the chairs. He walked softly to the wardrobe where he undressed and pulled on his robe. Was she asleep? Had she changed her mind? She couldn't have after this afternoon. Maybe she was just too exhausted to stay awake. Oh, well, I guess I can wait for one more day since I have waited so long. When he walked over to look at her, her eyes were closed too tightly and her shoulders shook slightly. He didn't move but just stood over her; and she waited too. Finally, swooping her up into his arms, he said, "Come on, you little vixen, enough tomfoolery." And she squealed and collapsed against him in a fit of laughter.

Carrying her to the center of the room, he set her on her feet and started to unfasten her dress. But she turned to wrap her arms around him. "I love you," she whispered as she pulled his head to hers. Jonathan kissed her briefly, struggling for control of his body. After all, with only one memory, he must be gentle with her—memories too often prove better than realities and he was determined that this should not happen to her. They had a lifetime of pleasure ahead of them if he could just control himself and not frighten her. He finished the unbuttoning with his arm around her. When she dropped her arms and her dress fell from her shoulders, he started on the shift buttons in the front. Soon she stood like an alabaster goddess before him.

"Oh God, Jess, you are so lovely," he moaned as she untied the sash of his robe. He shook the robe from his shoulders and picked her up behind the knees and carried her to bed. "I have waited so long. I thought we could never be together like this." He fell on the bed beside her and ran his hands over her body. She shivered with delight as his lips dropped gossamer soft kisses where his hands had wandered. She was as hungry as he and let him know in every way she could. Instinctively she ran her hands over his chest and back. She felt dizzy as his tongue toyed with her breast and his hands caressed her thighs, the outside first then moving to the inside. When he rolled her over onto her back, he lifted his body over hers probing gently. But she impatiently spread her thighs and reached to guide him to the haven he sought. She was shocked when he gasped at the intensity of his pleasure when she touched him. Then

163

he moved within her and her ecstasy built until she was mindless of anything but the pleasure that engulfed her. They moved together faster and faster until the bubble of pleasure exploded. Jonathan hastily covered Jessica's cry of pleasure by covering her mouth with his and probing deeply until she thrust her tongue into his mouth and they were entwined another way.

Satiated and fulfilled, they lay in each other's arms. Jessica traced Jonathan's profile and he nibbled at her finger. Leaning on his elbow and looking down on her tenderly, Jonathan smiled as she fell back on the pillows. She clutched his hand which had been tracing designs on her breasts and whispered, "Oh, Jonathan, aren't you glad we took Callie's advice and stopped being fools?" She sighed loudly.

"What was that for?" he asked.

"I'm just sorry for the time we wasted," she replied.

"Jessica, think of it as only a few weeks since you were well enough after Jeremy's birth. Than think of all the years we have to love each other. In comparison what are a few weeks?"

"There is never enough time. Forever is not long enough to love you, so I am sad we wasted even a few weeks."

The intensity of her feelings touched him as much as anything ever had, and his hands started their smooth caresses again. Jessica responded immediately and dawn was sifting in the windows before either of them slept. And their love, which had so carelessly been crushed many months ago and budded anew during Jessica's confinement, blossomed from that night on.

It seemed as if she had just closed her eyes when Jessica felt Callie shake her gently. "Mister Jeremy's demanding his breakfast, Miss Jessica," she whispered. "I'll get a wet nurse for him."

"No, bring him to me," she said sitting up. Realizing she was naked, she tugged the sheet to her chin. Thank heaven Jonathan had pulled the covers up sometime after she had fallen asleep.

Jessica felt embarrassment surge through her when Callie handed her a warm, wet cloth with which to wash before she put her child to her breast. When she felt the first hard tug on her breast by now familiar, she looked at her baby then her husband with glowing warmth. These two were her world, and it was a world filled with contentment.

Callie made no comment but silently picked up her scattered clothes and put them away. By the time Jeremy had finished, the room was quite presentable and Jessica's gown and robe were draped over the foot of the bed. When she carried the baby out, as silently as she had entered, Jessica thought that never before had Callie moved so quietly and said so little. When she scooted back down into the bed, Jonathan's arm snaked around her and pulled her close. She smiled with a delicious happiness pervading her body and was surprised when she turned, to be looking straight into his emerald eyes. "You've been playing possum," she giggled.

"Watching the dreamy happiness you feel when nursing our child is a thrill I want to keep for myself," he said huskily.

"Jonathan, you're afraid of Callie," she murmured.

"No," he retorted. "But that old lady knows too much and sees too much. You turned scarlet when she silently suggested you might be contaminated," he growled.

"She was right, you know," she teased with a gleam in her eye. "Two should never drink from the same cup." Pushing the sheet back, she moved to slide from the bed, but his arm held her still. "I must get up now and bathe Jeremy," she said sternly.

"Our son is well taken care of; he will not miss you this one day," he stated. Then his eyes filled with passion as he murmured, "Stay with me." When his mouth descended on hers, she rolled toward him and

165

their passions ignited again.

Much later when they descended together, their happiness was apparent to all. They saw their guests fed and preparing to leave. Jessica stood with Jeremy in her arms and Jonathan's around her waist.

"You have a most beautiful child, young woman," stated Maude Atkins.

"Thank you, Mrs. Atkins," murmured Jessica with a broad smile.

"Mrs. Atkins! My friends call me Maude. Jonathan's been my friend since he came here so that goes for you too."

"Yes, Maude," Jessica answered hesitantly, for she had never addressed an older woman by her given name.

"Now, Jonathan," she roared. "You bring this little girl around to visit me. Don't keep her hidden away."

"I will, Maude." Squeezing his wife to him, he added, "But you can see why I want to keep her to myself."

By late afternoon everyone had left, except of course Geoff and Mr. Selby, and the household had settled into its quiet routine. After a light dinner the four sat in the drawing room and Jessica was nodding slightly while Jonathan was saying, "Tomorrow we will show you around the place. I think you will like it, but this is very different from anything you have in England." Noticing his wife's sleepy expression, he added, "That's tomorrow. Now I must take my wife to bed before she falls asleep in that chair."

Jumping at the mention of her name, Jessica said, "I'm not tired. I want to hear how you discovered I was gone."

"You really put us through our paces that time, young lady," said her father-in-law. "But that too can wait until tomorrow. Go to bed," he said gently.

The next few days were idyllic for the inhabitants of

Fairhaven. All four of them toured the plantation, and Geoff became excited with what he saw and seemed in no hurry to return to his own estate. When the story of the discovery of her disappearance came out, the men applauded her cleverness but admonished her severely for causing them so much worry.

"Just think, she had been at sea for over two weeks before we even missed her," stated her brother with a scowl.

"It would have been even longer if you hadn't made that trip to town," interjected the old man. "Both of us thought she was with the other—just as she intended."

"And here she was flying, or should I say sailing, to my side," said Jonathan sliding his arm across her shoulder and hugging her to him.

"But what else could I do?" she asked innocently. "Besides, you know you're glad I did," she added softly.

"You have no idea of the stir you caused; and if you ever return to England, beware of Mrs. Winters. She nearly lost her mind with worry." The old man tried to sound angry, but Jessica knew he wasn't at all.

"Why don't you start at the beginning?" asked Jonathan. "I'd like to hear all of it so we can devise a just punishment for this wench."

"Well," started Geoff, "for the first time in months I had to make two trips to town in two weeks."

Mr. Selby took up the tale immediately. "Just as I was about to ask when you were coming back, he shocked me almost to death by asking about you, young lady. Then we put our heads together pretty quickly." Mr. Selby leaned forward as if he had been waiting to tell this juicy tidbit for ages. "Geoff and I thought we were pretty clever when we discovered the three of them—Jessica, Polly, and Jimmy—had disappeared together. That took about five minutes. Then," he stated leaning back in his chair, "we discovered we were not so clever after all, for you three had simply vanished. You, my dear," he stated sternly, "command great loyalty among your friends."

Jessica thought warmly of Mrs. Mattingly and Dr. Forsythe. "You mean they didn't tell you?" asked Jessica, clearly surprised at the revelation. She had expected they would wear down, but too late for her to be stopped.

"Neither that infernal dressmaker nor the good doctor would tell us anything," said Mr. Selby angrily.

Geoff continued. "After questioning everyone we knew you had contact with and putting up with Mrs. Winters' rantings for another two weeks, we admitted defeat and hired someone to find you. When he discovered the dressmaker's delivery boy had delivered gowns to the inn by the wharf, we were on our way again."

"Then that dragon of a housekeeper figured out why and sent for the doctor," interjected Mr. Selby. "Once we proved we knew where you had gone, he became more pliable and told us of your condition, and Polly's trip to him, though he had not realized she was your maid at the time.

"My house never did return to normal until we heard from Steve that you had arrived safely." He added slyly, "Only to enter into more plotting."

Jessica flushed but she teased, "Steve says I have a knack for intrigue."

"You certainly have, dearest," replied Jonathan. "But you are finished with it now."

"Yes, dear," she answered meekly when she saw concern written on his face. Turning to the other men, she moaned with a pained expression, "You have no idea of the condition Jonathan returned to me in. I still don't know how I stood it. It was weeks before we knew he would live; and when he finally regained consciousness, he didn't even know me." Jonathan felt her body tremble and caressed her arm softly. When she was still again, his finger traced her jaw line until she dropped her head on his shoulder. She found it hard to believe she could be so relaxed and thrilled by his touch in the presence of others. Shouldn't she be embarrassed? I don't know and I don't care, she told herself.

Jonathan, wanting the story telling finished, stated simply, "Jessica nursed me back to health. Then I took care of her until Jeremy was born. And we grew to love each other together this time. That's the whole of it."

Much later, lying in each other's arms sated with love, Jessica shuddered as if a chill had coursed through her.

"What's wrong?" Jonathan asked in a worried tone.

"That's not the whole of it and you know it," she replied.

Frowning and cuddling her close, Jonathan, because he had forgotten his earlier words, asked, "What are you talking about?"

"Will we ever know the whole of it, do you suppose?" she asked timorously.

"Of what?" he asked blankly.

"I will never forget how you looked when Tim and Callie dragged you in here. Sometimes I can still hear you screaming in your nightmares."

"It's over, Jess. You cured me, remember?" he teased. "How desperate we both must have been to lie together without knowing each other," he added tenderly. "But then. . ." he sighed.

"But what?" she asked.

"But your big belly would have made any other activity difficult and I was so weak," he added with a gentle pat on her stomach.

She wanted to join in his gentle teasing, but she could never joke about this. It frightened her too much. Realizing her mood immediately, Jonathan said softly, "Jess, we may know the whole of it soon."

"What do you mean?" she asked. Her fear was evident. She propped her head on her elbow and looked down at him, because he didn't answer.

Finally, without looking at her, he muttered, "I'm going back."

She threw her body over his and cried, "You can't! I won't let you!"

"I have to," he said quietly and encircled her with his strong arms. When he felt tears dripping to his chest, he rolled her over on her back and rose above her. "Will you stop crying and listen to me?" he demanded. When she refused even to meet his eyes, he added scornfully, "Where is the strong woman who refused to let me die? Has she disappeared and been replaced by a sniveling weakling?"

She sniffled a few times while he dried her tears with the sheet. "When are you leaving?"

"I should go in the morning." He rushed on before she could contradict him, "I have put off visiting the new place far too long. The ship which brought Geoff and my father also brought many supplies and furniture I had ordered in London." He lay back and sighed, "God, I don't even know what to expect in those crates. I don't remember ordering anything."

"We'll all go," she cried, sitting up and clapping her hands. "It will be such fun to open boxes with no idea what's in them."

"No," he answered stubbornly. She knew that idea had once and for all been rejected. "Tim is back and he and I will transport the crates. You can open them later. I'll save them for you, but you must stay here where I know you're safe."

"But what about me? How do I know you will be safe?" she moaned.

"You will know. You have a sixth sense about these things. Weren't you the only one who refused to believe I was dead the last time?"

Nodding at the truth of the statement, she waited for him to continue. "Do you know," he asked, "that I can't even remember what it's like up there? I can't take you until I find out. Figuring on the amount of time involved, whatever is being done should be finished, but I just don't know.''

"It can't be bad if Polly and Jimmy have been there for six months,'' she argued.

"That's reasonable, but they are used to more hardship than you. I put off going because I didn't want to leave you alone. Your brother's and my father's arrival put an end to the problem.''

"Until right now I was so happy they had come. Now I wish they hadn't.''

"Jess, you don't mean that. Be content that they are the solution to one of my worries. Try to understand I'm not going to find out what happened but to reacquaint myself with our home, the place we will spend the rest of our lives.''

"What is going to happen to Fairhaven?'' she asked.

"I don't know,'' he answered unconcernedly. "Something will turn up.''

"I will miss it because we found each other here,'' she said softly.

"We've also had some very bad time here,'' he reminded her. "I should think you would be glad to see the end of it.''

"I will be content wherever you are. This is only a house. You and Jeremy will make any house my home,'' she answered and only then realized the truth of her statement.

Snuggling next to him, she asked in a small voice, "Jonathan, could I ask one favor of you?'' When he waited for the request instead of promising, she stroked his chest, and looking very much like a little girl asking for sweets said, "Will you put off your departure and give us one more day together?''

His only answer was a broad grin as his hands set her small body afire.

Chapter Fourteen

Two mornings later Jonathan and Tim left. Jessica stepped onto the porch to watch the wagon roll slowly down the drive. Jonathan, having just mounted his stallion, turned for a final look at the house. Surprised to see her because he had just left her in the nursery moments earlier, he jumped down and strode up the steps to hold her in his arms. "Try to come back as soon as you can, darling," she said softly but smiling brightly.

When he kissed her and she felt the familiar excitement surge through her body, she knew that her very existence depended on this one man. Without him life would be nothing. When he set her down, he winked and said with that teasing grin but husky voice, "I most definitely will be back for more, madam." He turned her around and with a pat on her fanny started her for the door before he ran back to his horse and started on his way.

Jessica filled her days with menial tasks about the house, not wanting to think. She was glad both her father-in-law and Geoff had removed themselves from the premises during the daylight hours because she could not have forced herself to be entertaining. By evening, however, she was glad for their company. The nights stretched interminably and she tossed and turned and slept very little. Even though they had spent few nights in the big bed, she constantly reached for Jonathan and finally fell asleep hugging a pillow.

Several days passed in the same way. Jessica was surprised that Geoff seemed to take to life here. He was all over the place from early morning to evening. "I didn't realize Jonathan had asked him to take over," she thoughts. "But I'm glad he fits in so well."

In the drawing room after dinner the men easily observed the agony on her face and tried to keep her entertained with chess or funny stories. Finally, Jeremiah sat beside her one night and patted her hand. "He will be all right, my dear. You cannot fall apart this way every time he is gone overnight. Jonathan can take care of himself. Don't you know yet how strong he is?"

Smiling weakly, Jessica moaned, "But you don't know. . ."

"Don't I?" queried the old man. "Don't you imagine that if I kept track of my son's doings across the Atlantic, I can do it here? He will want to cause you as little worry as possible, so I expect someone will be here any day with the news of their arrival."

When she heard a carriage roll up the drive the next day, Jessica stepped onto the porch to see who was coming. As Polly stepped from the carriage, Jessica flew down the steps and threw her arms around her. The two, so excited to see each other, danced in the drive. When Jessica finally stepped back to look at the girl, she cried, "Oh, you naughty girl! Why didn't you tell me? When will your baby come? Soon by the looks of you."

"Now how was I going to tell you? We don't have mail service, you know," Polly retorted, sounding angry. Anyone seeing the shining faces of these two young women would know immediately neither was angry.

"Come on in. How long can you stay?" Jessica asked, slipping her arm around her former maid's back.

The two young women gossiped and giggled for hours, especially after Polly relayed the all important message that Jonathan had sent with her. Polly was hesitant about sitting to eat with the masters of the two households in which she had formerly worked, but Jessica tossed her fears aside with, "You are my best friend, Polly. No one would dare insult you at my table," though she was relieved when both Geoff and Mr. Selby did indeed treat Polly as if she were a friend.

As she and Polly sewed for the baby, Jessica realized that part of her problem before had been having so little to do to run her household that she had too much time to think. She finally made that visit to Maude Atkins, who guessed immediately what the relationship between the girls had been.

"So what?" she said. "No one will find out from me, and only a snob would care. You and your husband are welcome in my house, Polly, because you are the Selby's friends." Jessica could have hugged her, but knew the older women would be embarrassed by such a gesture.

One evening after both Polly and Mr. Selby had retired early, Jessica and Geoffrey sat playing chess in the parlor. Finally, after looking at the board for some time without being able to decide on a move, Jessica pushed the board from her, moaning, "I just don't seem to be able to concentrate, Geoff."

Following her across the room to the settee, Geoff said, "That's all right, Jess. I'd like to talk anyway."

Jessica looked up at him quickly but he said nothing as he sat beside her. When he still remained silent, she knew he wanted to discuss something important and had been waiting for just such an opportunity as this. Unable to think of anything he might say that would cause this much hesitancy, she almost snapped, "Come on, Geoff—out with it. I didn't think anything would make you afraid," she teased.

Looking levelly into her eyes, he answered, "I'm not afraid, Jess. I just can't decide for sure what I want to do."

"What do you think you want to do?"

174

Almost flinging himself against the back of the sofa, he thrust his feet straight out in front of him, looked at the floor and mumbled like a spoiled child, "I want to stay here in America."

He did not see the delighted grin break out and spread across her face. "Geoff, that's a wonderful idea!" she squealed. She forcibly restrained herself from throwing her arms around him, but she frowned suddenly when she realized he still would not look at her. "Why is it a problem?"

"Briarly."

"What about Briarly?"

Now his eyes faced hers again. "When I practically forced you into this highly questionable marriage, I told you that you could always return to Briarly if it didn't work out. Absentee landlords are no good for long periods of time. Briarly would just go downhill if I stayed here, but I can't break my promise to you. You've done too much for me already."

Now she understood his problem and knew she had been remiss for not telling him of her feelings before this. Looking deeply into his eyes so that he would believe her, she said quietly, "Geoff, the fault is mine. I have neglected to tell you in so many words that I have thanked you and Mr. Selby a thousand times over for forcing—your words, not mine—me into a marriage that has made me one of the happiest women alive. You have not been seeing a great actress these last few weeks, but a truly happy woman. My misery since Jonathan left, which I am sure you have noticed, is not for my plight but for my husband's safety. Do whatever you want with Briarly. I will always remember it fondly as my childhood home, but I have no further need of it."

"I thought maybe when you and Jonathan moved to the interior, I would buy Fairhaven. Do you think my brother-in-law would sell at a reasonable price?" he questioned with a teasing grin.

"I suspect he just might," she smiled. "But are you

sure you want to give up Briarly after all you have been through for it? You have cleared the debts, haven't you?'

"Oh, yes," he interjected quickly. "The debts are paid and the ownership is clear, but I didn't really exact the revenge we once thought so necessary."

"Tell me about it. I've been ever so curious, but half afraid to ask."

"Jessica, I couldn't do it—deliberately ruin a man. When the time came, I simply couldn't do it. Does that make me a coward?" When his sister, who had always been quick to state her opinions, said nothing, he started at the beginning, shuffling uncomfortably. "The day after the wedding Lord Eden paid off all the debts. I'm sure you know that much." She nodded slightly but said nothing. "Then the work of finding the culprit began. Jeremiah discovered enough to convince me that Williams and Courtney had abetted Roger Trevalyn's plans without knowing their full scope. In fact, they had insisted on the extension of time for the debts to be paid. So I set out to ruin Trevalyn. When his son Ross, my former friend, was called home suddenly, rumors were rife that for some reason he could no longer afford the life of debauchery he had been enjoying in London. But I am not the only one of our generation who is made of sterner stuff."

"Would you believe he came to see me? He had found out who was causing his father's problems. I told him why. Of course, he did not believe me. But he demanded the truth from his father and returned to Briarly. It seems he and Father had both courted our mother and he had always resented Father's winning her. Their happiness rankled him until it was an open sore he could not hide. When Lady Trevalyn died, whom everyone knew he had married for her money, he set out to destroy our father for making laughing stock of him."

Jessica, wide-eyed by this time, shook her head, "But

who was laughing? None of us knew about it. Surely we would have heard something if all this were true."

"He was such a consummate actor all these years that everyone had long since forgotten, save his wife. She always knew she was the second choice and never let him forget that he owed everything he had become to her." He sat quietly for some time before ending the tale. "Anyway," he started again, watching her eyes for a reaction, "when Ross told me all this and insisted I had the right to finish them off, so to speak, I couldn't do it. There was no satisfaction at all in making the kill. I knew I would never be able to forgive myself for being so heartless, so I helped Ross make a new start from the shambles his father had created. Was I wrong? and cowardly?"

Jessica beamed with pride in this brother who was too much a man to be mean. "I think you did exactly right, Geoff. And if you think it best to sell Briarly, do so. But please be sure the help will be well taken care of. I couldn't bear for them to be shunted aside when they have served so well."

"On that point we are in complete agreement," he replied.

Jessica was completely delighted with the world. She clucked over Polly as Callie had over her. Yet she was glad as Polly's time drew nearer because Jonathan and Jimmy had promised to be here for the birth and she wanted to be with her husband. Polly had assured her she would be able to move any time and Jonathan had stayed so long only to help Jimmy work on their place. Even though Jessica missed her husband, she was pleased he would do so much for her friends.

Jessica seemed to exist in a bubble of excitement. She glowed with contentment so much that an onlooker would have thought *her* the expectant mother. Her spirits soared when she knew that Polly's baby would come any day now and so would her Jonathan. She sometimes felt guilty that she was so happy for her friend because of her own selfish desires. Little did she know how suddenly that bubble would burst.

On a particularly hot day, about three weeks after Polly's arrival, Jessica sat in the shade of a huge oak tree with her baby sleeping inside her. After lunch Polly had gone to rest and Jessica had had Jeremy brought here. "The gentle breeze is so much nicer than the warm house," she thought. She nodded so much that she put her book aside and lay down beside her son on the blanket where they both slept peacefully.

She stirred when she heard Polly calling her and sat up to chat with her friend. Noticing the baby was gone, she thought only that Daisy had come for Jeremy and not wanted to awaken her. When they finally went into the house, she headed for the nursery.

Daisy looked up when Jessica entered and said, "Where did you leave the baby, ma'am?" The bottom dropped from her stomach and Jessica flew to the stairs screaming, "Callie! Callie! Jeremy's gone!" She missed the top step and grabbed frantically for the railing, but her momentum was too great and she rolled to the bottom.

She knew nothing as the servants carried her upstairs and Callie undressed her after setting in motion the search for the missing baby. When she awakened hours later, she could see Callie's huge form in the shadowy darkness. "Has he been found?" she whispered. At the woman's grim silence, she groaned and rolled away from her, sobbing uncontrollably. Exhaustion finally overcame her and she slept fitfully throughout the night.

With the dawn of a new day she pushed the blankets aside and sat up, swinging her legs stiffly to the floor, but a wave of dizziness overcame her and she flopped back onto the bed with a groan. When Callie peeped in the door some moments later, she muttered weakly, "I'm awake, Callie." When she came on in, Jessica could read on her face that Jeremy was still missing.

"Help me up, Callie," she said.

"No, Miss Jessica," the sober woman answered. "You stay where you are."

"I must look for my son," she insisted.

"Everyone on this plantation is looking for him," she answered quickly. "There's nothing you can do." She gently pushed her struggling mistress back to the pillows. Dizzy once again, Jessica could not argue. She awakened only briefly twice during the long day, long enough to be told her precious son had not been found.

When she was next awakened, it was by her own hysterical screaming, "Jeremy! Jeremy! Someone has stolen Jeremy!" Iron-strong arms pulled her back to the bed. She fought against their constriction with all her strength, never hearing the loving words being murmured to her.

Finally some of the words—or the tone of them—got through and she lay still. "Jonathan?" she queried quietly.

"Yes, darling, your wandering husband has returned," he answered quietly.

"Someone has stolen Jeremy," she moaned desolately.

"I know, dear," he said confidently. "But don't worry. We'll find him." As if confident that he would indeed take care of things, she snuggled against him and fell asleep. Jonathan lay awake for hours wishing he had as much confidence as she did. Thank God it was too dark for her to see me, he thought, for he knew his lack of faith would be discernible to her in a minute.

He had returned admist the hue and cry that afternoon and immediately joined the search himself. How could anyone disappear so completely in twenty-four hours, especially a baby who must be fed at regular intervals? No one had seen him or any other baby. Word had been sent to every plantation within a day's ride in hope that maybe someone would know something. Steve was still having every nook and cranny in

179

the city searched and that would take a while. Only one ship had left the port without being searched, and several men had sworn no baby had gone aboard. That someone had indeed stolen him had been obvious from the first. Several people about the plantation had seen both Jessica and Jeremy sleeping in the shade, but no one had seen a stranger about. Did that mean anything? Had one of his own people committed this despicable act? Why? If someone had wanted money, wouldn't he have heard by this time? Somehow he didn't think a demand for money for the return of his son would be forthcoming.

Jessica felt well enough to attend to her duties the next day; but as each day passed without word of Jeremy, she became more mechanical and withdrawn. She refused to visit Polly who had remained in her room since the time Jessica had burst into tears at the sight of her.

Not even Jonathan could reach her. When they lay together at night, she lay like an iceberg, moaning half the night. He had thought the arrival of Polly's baby would help, but it pushed her farther into her shell. She had paid one courtesy call to the room which housed the pair, but had murmured only, "How cute," and left the room. She convulsed into sobs as soon as she reached the hall. Most of the time she maintained rigid control outside of her room. Her trancelike movements caused the others to let her alone. She knew they were concerned, but could not acknowledge their futile attempts to arouse her interest.

News of failure came from far and wide. As each report arrived, Jonathan felt his heart sink again because he knew her depression deepened. He had accepted the fact that they might never find their son, but she seemed completely incapable of coping with the fact, so he refrained from mentioning it. When she looked at him, he saw her disappointment at his failure to keep the promise he had so easily made the night of his return.

Gradually she ignored even the simplest of her chores, almost completely retiring within the bedroom. All the decisions were left to Callie who had long since given up grumbling to her mistress because it did no good anyway.

At dinner one night Polly finally brought part of the issue into the open. "Jimmy and I are leaving tomorrow, Jonathan."

Not really surprised, he murmured, "But little Jeff is too young to travel."

"Well, he will have to make do," she replied matter of factly. "You know as well as I do Jessica hates having a baby here while hers is gone. The best help we can give her this time is to leave her."

Jonathan admitted she was correct. Even he found it difficult to watch the happy pair and no one would want them to restrain their happiness. Nothing could have subdued either his or Jessica's delight when Jeremy was born. Nodding affirmation, he rose from the table and motioned Jimmy to follow.

Polly ran upstairs and started packing. But after tucking her little one into bed, she walked to Jessica's room. Knocking smartly as she had done in her serving days, she walked in without waiting for an answer. "Jessica, you've got to pull yourself together," she said irritably.

Surprised by the intrusion, Jessica almost flared back, but she dropped her shoulders and turned away. Polly rushed on, "Well, maybe you will do better after we leave tomorrow."

"You can't go yet," she replied scornfully.

"Say you want me to stay and I will," Polly challenged. At the girl's silence, she continued, "See!" You can't even lie to be polite. Surely you can see I can't possibly stay here one more day." Jessica did not even look at her friend, let alone say anything to her. "Some-

181

day soon I hope you can accept what's happened. Probably nothing is going to bring him back. You are acting as if no one but you has troubles." While Jessica stood gasping as if she had been struck, Polly flounced from the room and down the stairs to tell Jonathan what she had done.

"I'm sorry, Jonathan, after you two have done so much for us, but I thought maybe I could shock some sense into her," Polly wailed.

"Don't worry, Polly. At least you tried. Everyone else cuts a wide path around her." When he entered their room a few minutes later, Jessica lay huddled on the edge of the bed. After undressing, he slid in beside her. He could tell by her irregular breathing that she was only pretending to be asleep. When he reached to pull her into his arms, she resisted and held herself stiff.

He lay back, thinking over all that had been between them in the last year, and a loud sigh escaped his lips.

"What was that for?" she asked.

"I'm thinking only that, if I had listened to you and not gone away until you could go with me, none of this would have happened."

"It's not your fault," she said, her eyes widening in surprise. That he would blame himself had never occurred to her. She had thought only that he would blame her for losing the son so precious to them both.

"I should have stayed here to protect you better," he stated flatly.

"You left us with a great deal of protection—Geoff, your father, all the workers." As had happened before suddenly their roles were reversed and she was holding him in her arms. "I can't stand the idea that I failed you and lost your son through my own carelessness. How can you ever forgive me?" she moaned.

Jonathan groaned at her words; and because she couldn't see him, she misinterpreted the sounds completely. When he murmured, "I don't blame you, Jess," she did not believe him, even when he added, "I never have." She was still skeptical because she had blamed herself for so long.

Maybe if he had pursued the issue and forced her to believe him, they could have reached an understanding. But Jessica had been out of touch for so long that Jonathan was grateful for one tiny step of progress. Dealing with a wife was still new to him, and he was well aware that this unusual wife of his would not be pushed too far. She had certainly proved that.

She stood on the porch waving goodbye to Polly's little family in the morning, though she still could not exclaim over the baby. She settled in once more to attending her chores and, on the surface at least, she had put the loss of her son behind her.

Only Jonathan knew how slight had been her progress and how taut she was, as if she were a violin string about to snap from too much tension. They played the loving husband and wife so well that the others suspected nothing of the estrangement between them. Behind the closed door of their room, she had become completely remote. If he reached for her, she skittered away like a shy colt. When his hand touched her body, even accidentally, as they lay in the huge bed, she brushed it aside or moved away, saying "Don't touch me."

Finally Jonathan snapped himself; and after being rebuffed one night, roughly pulled her into his arms, knowing full well she would not protest loudly enough for the rest of the household to hear. He held her tight and his arms felt like iron bands around her. She tried to push him away, mumbling, "I don't want to."

"But I do," he said with determination. Never had he forced himself on a woman. And this was not one he wanted to commit such an act upon, but desperation had led him so far that he felt he must continue or chance being rejected forever.

He smothered further protest in a manner that offered no chance for resistance. She struggled against him, trying to hold him off, but knew she was no match

183

for his strength. Her head swam dizzily from the fervor of his kisses; and a few moments later, when his lips wandered down her throat to her breasts, her resolve deserted her completely and she became possessed by a voracious desire to have him. She moaned with pleasure as his hands caressed her body, and she never realized when he had removed her gown. His deliberate caresses made her forget everything but the two of them until she writhed with so much ecstasy she begged him to take her. When he only laughed and tormented her further by nibbling at her throat and breasts, almost as if punishing her for holding him at bay so long, her caresses became as bold as his. She trembled with passion as she tantalizingly ran her fingers down his chest, then slowly, soft as a gossamer wing, down across his stomach to his groin. He gasped explosively and shuddered when her hand closed over him and he firecely pulled her beneath him. Their passion carried them to dizzying heights until it exploded like a bursting dam and showered them with warmth and peace.

The following morning Jonathan had dressed and left before his wife awakened, confident that they were one once more. Dreamily Jessica stirred with a contentment she had not felt for months. With the memory of her brazenness, a hot flush stained her cheeks. Not a word had been spoken last night about the thoughts troubling her mind. And now she realized how much her body controlled her mind. He would be able to arouse her desire at will and make logical thinking impossible. But the thoughts she had pushed aside last night returned to haunt her in the day.

She slowly crawled out of bed and woodenly donned her clothes, thinking all the while, how could she live with this man whose son she had lost? Maybe things would work out; she would have to wait and see whether he had taken her with love or forced her as punishment.

Meanwhile her husband had awakened earlier, feeling both love and shame at the events of the previous night.

He loved her even more than he had before, but why could he not have waited? He knew she had experienced her womanhood in full measure, but he was not proud of his method. How could he have forced her? He had humiliated her completely by reducing her to jelly and making her beg for him. Even then he had tormented her, arousing her to a pitch of frency which he knew would embarrass her in the cool light of day.

Both of them were busy throughout the day—Jonathan outside, as if he didn't want to see her, and Jessica inside. After dinner Jessica begged for chess lessons from her father-in-law. When they finished their game, Jessica bounced onto the settee and chattered nervously, trying to interest the men in conversation. Jonathan, watching his wife carefully, felt sick in the pit of his stomach because he could see her fear beneath the rambling. Silently he vowed to let her set the pace for their future relationship.

Later they lay in bed, each on his own side—she wishing he would reach for her and he wishing she would turn to him. The wall between them grew higher and higher as each maintained his own counsel and misunderstood the other. Their lives continued in this way, each waiting for the other to make a move, for weeks.

Jessica finally started making trips into the city. Jonathan could only think she hated him seeing that she grasped at the feeblest reasons for leaving Fairhaven. Though he made himself agreeable to her wishes, he asked no questions. She was so delighted with a dressmaker she had discovered, and Jonathan was so happy with her delight that her many trips to town for the fittings bothered him not at all. She bubbled each time she returned with tales of her trip. Once she even brought Steve with her, saying she had met him on the street. Had it been anyone but Steve, Jonathan might have worried. But he also thought he knew his wife well enough to know she was too virginal for an affair. But he was not aware of her acting ability, though he had known of her love for intrigue.

When the day finally came that she did not return as early as usual, he raced into their room, throwing clothes in all directions. He had to see what had happened. He couldn't lose her too. Shoving his shirttail into his trousers, he spied an envelope propped on the table by the bed. When he saw his name on the front, the knot inside him grew and twisted until he thought he could not pick it up. The message she had written brought him only more agony.

Jonathan,

I am leaving you. I cannot go on pretending we care for each other.

I would appreciate your not following me, though I will tell you I am sailing today for London because it is the only place I know.

I imagine you could divorce a wife who ran away from you; and since I will not be returning, I would not object. You will find someone else if only you will look.

Jessica

Jonathan sank into a chair as if hypnotized. He felt Callie shake him out of his stupor, excitedly asking about the missus.

"She's all right, Callie," he said woodenly.

"Then come down to dinner now. What you doin' up here all alone?" she asked on the way out. "You didn't even hear me knock."

When he reached the dining room, he said in a dead voice, "Remove Jessica's setting from the table. It will not be needed again."

As the shock on the other faces registered, he threw her note onto the table and muttered, "It seems she has left us, gentlemen," and sat down as if he were a zombie.

Eyeing him warily, they both reached for the note. When his father had read it, he handed it to Geoff. "Of course, you're going after her," the old man stated. "When can you leave?"

Jonathan looked at him coldly. "Of course I am not going after her. I am leaving for my new home in the morning since there is nothing for me here."

Not wanting to believe him, his father argued, "Surely you don't want to lose her."

"No, I didn't," he said in a frigid voice. "But she has made her decision and I will not beg. If you're so worried, why don't *you* follow her?" The absolute lack of emotion in his voice chilled them both.

"All right, I will!" thundered his father and stomped from the room.

"Geoff," he started in an utterly flat voice. "I will not chase her. I hope you can understand, but there will always be a place for her if wants to return. I am leaving Fairhaven at first light and I never want to see it again. If you still like the place, and want to buy it, take care of the legal details and send the papers to me."

Geoff nodded imperceptibly. He understood but did not know how to help these two people who were more deeply in love than any pair he had ever known.

When Geoff arose in the morning, true to his word, Jonathan had gone.

Chapter Fifteen

The long trip across the Atlantic gave Jessica much time to think about her actions. She knew her decision was irrevocable and she must learn to live with it. Small as it was, the bed in her cabin was lonely. Only now did she understand how much comfort Jonathan's nearness had given her. Even if he had meant the words he muttered that night so many weeks ago, she blamed herself for their loss. She could not find it within her to forgive herself for her carelessness. Every day she was carried farther from the only man she would ever love; and she knew, even if he had forgiven her for the loss of their son, she had hurt him too deeply for him to follow. She must stop this dreaming and fantasizing. He didn't want her anyway or he would have told her so, especially after that night he had driven her mindless with desire. He had quickly made it obvious he had wanted relief, not her. She supposed she should be grateful he had aroused her desire rather than just used her as a receptacle for his passion.

Jessica left America almost exactly one year from the time she touched it and arrived in England two months later. What a year she had spent! Luckily she was able to hire a carriage with little difficulty and went straightaway to her father-in-law's house. She was surprised at its appearance. She had never thought it might be closed and deserted, but that was certainly logical with Mr.

Selby in America. She banged the knocker loudly but heard nothing inside. She knocked again; and just as she had given up and turned away, the door opened.

When she turned back, Mrs. Winters cried, "Why it's Miss Jessica!" Jessica lost the tight control she had held taut for months and fell into the older woman's arms, sobbing hysterically. The housekeeper led her inside and closed the door. She led the girl upstairs and put her to bed. "You must rest now, miss, and I'll be right back." Shaking her head, she left the room so the girl could cry alone. By the time Jessica's crying had reduced to a few hiccoughing sobs, Mrs. Winters returned with tea. "I'm so happy to see you, my dear. I've been here alone since Mr. Selby left and I could do some some lively company."

"I'm so glad you were here. I had no idea where else I could go."

The older woman wisely did not ask any questions, but sat with the young woman until she quieted. The distraught Jessica looked around the room, avoiding Mrs. Winters' eyes. Setting the teacup on the table beside her, Jessica moaned, "Oh, Mrs. Winters, it all went wrong," and convulsed into sobs again.

The woman folded the girl to her ample bosom and patted her on the back until she quieted yet again. "There, there, Miss Jessica, it can't be that bad," she said tenderly.

"But it is," moaned Jessica.

Seeing that crying might overcome the girl again, Mrs. Winters sat away from her and stated very calmly, "You have had so many adventures in the last year, miss. You really had us all worried last year. Tell me all about it," she added even though they had long since pieced the story together.

"You know all about my leaving, don't you?" asked Jessica.

"We finally got that figured out, though it took a

189

while. You were very clever, my dear," the woman soothed.

A little smile crept across Jessica's face, and Mrs. Winters was relieved that a subject change had helped.

"When we arrived in Louisiana, Jonathan was missing," Jessica recounted the events of the past year. Mrs. Winters' face turned horror-stricken when Jessica detailed Jonathan's condition and care.

"And you expecting, too. It's a wonder you didn't lose the babe." She knew she had said something wrong when a horribly agonized epxression crossed Jessica's face. Almost instantaneously the girl shook it away and continued. Just from Jessica's tender expression Mrs. Winters could see the love and happiness this young had once had. "Why don't you rest for a while?" The woman hoped this brave young girl could glow a little longer, and she knew the worst was yet to come.

"No, there is so little left. I ran away again because I did lose the baby." Mrs. Winters was appalled when the girl finished. How could this little mite of a thing take so many hardships! No wonder she sobbed so desolately. "Don't worry, Miss Jessica. We will take good care of you. You stay here with me and we will make you feel better," the woman comforted.

"But there is an added complication," she insisted. "On the ship I discovered I am pregnant again. Jonathan might have forgiven my losing his son if I gave him another, but he will never forgive my running away from him. It's hopeless!" she wailed.

Platitudes are sometimes called for; and when Mrs. Winters retorted, "There is always hope," the beginnings of a tiny smile sneaked on to the girl's face. Mrs. Winters, in a crisp business-like manner, snapped, "We must make plans. First, I will send for Edward and Cook. Then I must interview maids. But we must send for the doctor the very first. You just leave all your problems to me, young lady."

Jessica did just that. She became a pampered little girl

again, though she would not allow Mrs. Winters to send for the doctor. However, a healthy person with Jessica's nature cannot remain idle for long. And the kindly housekeeper judged her mistress's recovery complete when Jessica asked for a carriage.

She headed directly for Mrs. Mattingly's shop. The greeting she received there was enthusiastic and the two women chatted excitedly for several minutes before Jessica told her she would once again need clothing that had room for expansion. The girl looked so much like a wounded doe that Mrs. Mattingly thought, "There's a sad story here. Some time I must hear it, but it's too new now. Her wounds are too raw." With friendliness and just the right touch of dictatorship, she arranged for an entire wardrobe for her favorite customer. Many had dealt with her much longer, but none had touched her heart as this girl. After their first encounter the dressmaker had felt almost as if this wounded chick were her daughter. She was somewhat surprised but said nothing when Jessica informed her she had returned from America with none of her clothing. She saddened when the girl insisted only on daytime gowns. Something was very wrong.

While Jessica was out, Mrs. Winters sneaked out to see Dr. Forsythe. In spite of her mistress's orders, she felt the rapport which existed between Jessica and the doctor earlier called for his help. Jessica badly needed a friend. She recounted most of the girl's story, and they agreed he would call at the house later.

Jessica sat in her room when a smart rap on the door interrupted her. In answer to her summons, Mrs. Winters walked in saying, "You've got company downstairs, ma'am."

Barely looking up from her book, Jessica asked, "Who is it?"

"Dr. Forsythe."

"Tell him I'm resting and can't see him today," said Jessica.

"That won't do, Miss Jessica," said Mrs. Winters, shaking her head.

"Why ever not?"

"You know him, miss. He'll decide you're sick and push his way up here to examine you."

"Oh, very well," sighed Jessica as she put her book aside. "Tell him I will be down in a minute."

In a few minutes when she walked into the drawing room, Dr. Forsythe jumped to his feet, saying, "Jessica, how glad I am to see you! But you look terrible. Aren't you feeling well?"

Jessica tried to sound cheerful as she responded, saying, "Well, doctor, you certainly are not very flattering to a girl. It's good to see you. How did you know I was here?"

"I didn't really," he said quickly. "I noticed signs of life here for the first time in months, so I decided to inquire about you. You can imagine my surprise when Mrs. Winters said you were here."

Jessica looked at him closely, but could detect no hint of falsehood in his demeanor. Mrs. Winters slipped in with tea, and they indulged in several minutes of small talk. Jessica made it obvious that she would offer no information, yet she answered every question he asked about America. She offered no reason for being here without her child. In fact, she did not even mention her child. He wondered whether or not he should ask. He didn't want her to think he was prying, but she might think his not inquiring odd indeed. He dare not let her know Mrs. Winters had come to see him and Jessica was shrewd enough to guess if he slipped even a little.

He breathed a sigh of relief when she switched the conversation to him, except there was nothing to tell. Yes, he was very busy. No, there was no woman in his life. No, he had not taken a vacation lately. Yes, he got tired of the city but was too busy to get away. In the course of the conversation he asked her to call him David. On and on they talked with neither really saying anything. Finally, he saw relief cover her face when he rose to leave. At the door he turned to say, "If I return on a day when you are less tired, may I see your little one?"

Agony replaced the relief instantaneously. She burst into tears and ran for the stairs. Following quickly and catching her at the bottom, he asked, "What's wrong? What have I done?" She turned to face him but collapsed against him and he led her back into the drawing room. When she lay back on the settee, he closed the door as though to protect her privacy. Then he sat across from her and waited until she had quieted.

Finally, she sat up sniffing and he silently handed her his handkerchief. "I'm sorry for putting you in such an embarrassing position," she muttered weakly.

"Good heavens, girl, I hope I can claim the honor of being your friend," he exclaimed. "Why would I be embarrassed when you are so upset? I can only hope you will forgive me for causing you so much distress."

"There is nothing to forgive, David. You had no way of knowing."

"Dare I ask knowing what?" he inquired.

"That my beautiful son was stolen from our home while I was supposed to be watching him. Some mother I am," she added with scorn.

"Jessica, I'm sure you are an excellent mother," he contradicted. "Is it too painful to talk about or could you tell me what happened?"

"It's painful," she admitted, "but I ought to tell you." He listened quietly while she relayed the story of her son's disappearance. When finished, she said with sarcasm, "Now you can see what a good mother I am, David. And now I find myself about to be a mother again and frightened to death of the responsibility. And no wonder."

"Jessica," he said softly as he crossed to sit beside her and held her hands in his. "Jessica, why don't you look upon this turn of events as another chance?"

"I don't deserve another chance," she scoffed.

"Maybe you don't, but through some miracle you've been given one. We don't always have control over these matters."

"David, you're just trying to make me feel better, and I thank you for the effort, but I can't believe God thought I was so wonderful a mother that He is giving me another chance."

He strode across the room then turned and said angrily, "You can't believe it because you don't want to believe it. Sit here in this empty house and wallow in self-pity if it makes you feel better. Let me know when you decide to rejoin the human race. I don't have time for such nonsense."

Jessica jumped as he slammed both doors on his way out. Then she slowly walked upstairs. Who did Dr. David Forsythe think he was anyway? What right had he to talk to her that way? He acted as if she had no problems at all. He just doesn't understand.

But he did understand and was extremely happy to find Jessica in his office a week later. "I decided to rejoin the human race," she said shyly.

With a smile spreading across his face, he walked to her, saying, "I'm so glad." He closed the office and walked her home. During dinner he heard the other parts of the story when he inquired about whether she had sneaked off this time too. That this beautiful young woman was clearly in love with her husband made him sad for both of them. Even though he knew she was not ready to believe it, he knew this Jonathan Selby would never divorce such a wife. When she talked about happier times, she glowed with a radiance he had seldom seen on a woman. He knew these two must be together again because he doubted her husband was any happier than she. Who could be happy after losing a wife like her? He probably was just as stubborn, too.

"What does your Jonathan say about this baby?" asked David. When she sat silently looking at the floor, he added, "You did tell him, didn't you?"

She shook her head and defended her action, saying, "When could I tell him? I didn't find out until I was halfway here."

"Don't you think he has a right to know?" When she didn't answer, he asked, "Did you even let anyone in America know, anyone at all—your brother, your husband, or your father-in-law? Did you let anyone know you had arrived safely?" Again her silence told him the answer. "As you have joined us mortals, don't you think that you should let someone know? If you want to forget the Selbys'," he saw her cringe and continued, "write to your brother."

"All right, David. You are right. I should have written before this," she agreed meekly.

David visited often after that evening. He saw that Jessica maintained contact with the world outside her father-in-law's house. In fact, she became so dependent on him that he worried even more.

Mr. Selby arrived home one week before Christmas and was delighted to find his daughter-in-law, though he admonished, "Why are you always running off, girl?"

"How's Jonathan?" she asked.

"He's as bad as your are. He left the day after you, for the interior. Geoff bought Fairhaven and my son said he never wanted to see it again."

"My goodness! What a lot of changes," she said calmly.

"He is as stubborn as you are, too. He said you had made your decision and, since you wanted to leave him, he would not follow you. You know he won't, Jessica."

The old man looked so tired with all the traveling that Jessica coddled him over the holidays. When David joined them for Christmas dinner, Mr. Selby's suspicions were aroused instantly. Why did she contact a doctor and no one else? He knew how much she loved his son, so romance did not hold these two together. He grinned mischievously and Jessica knew immediately what he thought.

"Stop gloating, Father Selby. David is a good friend," said Jessica with irritation.

"He is also a good doctor," he replied with a twinkle. "Why would you need a doctor? I didn't imagine a slight thickening in the middle, did I?"

"No, you didn't. Now let's not talk about it anymore. When you have finished your cigars, I will challenge you to a game of chess," she said sweeping out of the dining room.

"What is going on?" demanded the old man of the doctor.

"Jessica is afraid of the responsibility of a baby since she already failed as a mother once," the young man answered.

"Does she think that? She was a perfect mother. No woman could have loved a child more."

"But she doesn't see it that way. She cannot forgive herself; therefore she insists Jonathan won't forgive her either."

"Jonathan doesn't blame her at all," Mr. Selby asserted. "He's convinced the theft of their child was a reprisal against him. The only thing that could have hurt him more was losing her. And now he's lost both of them. God only knows what Jonathan is doing now. He left home as soon as she ran away."

"Well, Mr. Selby, what are we going to do about these two? Jessica is damned touchy about anyone interfering in her life."

"How well I know," the old man sighed. "She's caused me so much worry I think I'll just mosey in there and trounce her at chess," he chuckled.

Jessica remained adamant in her decision not to inform her husband of the expectancy of another child. She hoped to control her father-in-law by threatening to run away where he could not find her.

"Mr. Selby, I mean it," she insisted.

"Mr. Selby! What happened to father?" the old man asked.

"You are not acting like a father to me now. You are being a willful old man again. Don't you see no matter how much I love your son, I will not allow this child to be taken to that savage land where helpless babies disappear never to be seen again. I can't go through all that again."

"It would never happen again, Jessica," the old man soothed.

"That is a chance I am not willing to take. If you want to see this child, don't cross me in this matter," she threatened.

"You have become a hard woman, my dear," he stated flatly.

"I learned it from you, sir," she retorted and swept out of the room.

So went every interview between the two in which the matter was mentioned. He soon realized the futility of such conversations and initiated no more for she had clearly demonstrated her determination when she had made up her mind.

Jessica awaited the arrival of her child much more calmly this time. Mrs. Winters fussed over her as much as Callie had, but there was no reason to fuss. As soon as her condition became obvious, she discontinued her few trips outside the house. She had nothing to occupy her time. David Forsythe visited frequently because he insisted on attending her. Though she had no idea whether she could remain friends with someone, even a doctor, who knew her so intimately, she quickly agreed to having a doctor since she couldn't have Callie with her.

On a beautiful sunshiny day in May, Jessica was delivered of her second son. Even though she had not thought it possible, she responded to this child with every maternal instinct she had within her. Though she did not want to add another link to the chain she and Jonathan started, she acquiesced to her father-in-law's wishes and called him Joshua.

To the chagrin of Mrs. Winters, Jessica was up out of bed quickly. The baby was always to be found in her arms if she left the room. Jessica finally relented to her father-in-law's badgering and allowed him to hire a nurse. Jessica and Elsie had little difficulty reaching agreement who would do what because Jessica insisted on doing everything for her child rather than just seeing him occasionally. There would be no wet nurse for her child. She had honestly intended to have this child and turn him over to someone else—carrying none of the responsibility herself. That she couldn't ignore her child came as a gratifying surprise to her. That she had arrived at the other extreme of the spectrum instead and refused to allow the baby out of her sight surprised no one. She refused to allow him to be moved from her room—he didn't need a nursery. To point out that no one else used the room would not move her; if Joshua couldn't be in her room, she would simply leave.

"You really have become a hard woman, Jessica," her father-in-law muttered. "Would you like to have me set you up in your own establishment? I will do it, you know. But I cannot allow you to control whatever life I have left with these constant threats to run away." He looked at her with flinty eyes which challenged hers until she looked away.

This had never occurred to her—that he would send her away. She had not meant to weild her power so cruelly. "But I am so afraid," she moaned.

The eyes softened, and Jessica, feeling him take her hand, looked down at her small hand almost completely hidden in his large veiny hand. "I know," he soothed. "But you can't raise a child alone. It isn't fair to him or to you."

"But he's so little! I won't raise him alone when he gets bigger," she pleaded.

"How big is bigger?" he demanded. "If you start this way, you will become dependent on him and keep him dependent on you until you are both miserable—you if he leaves you and he if he can't. Nothing will happen to him in this house. A stranger could never get past Edward, and Jonathan has no enemies here in London who would kidnap his child."

"Just a little longer, Father," she pleaded again.

"We must start now," he insisted. "But we will take small steps."

"What do you mean?" she asked.

"A three month old baby sleeps through the night, doesn't he?" When she nodded reluctantly, he added, "It's been so long since my son was a baby I had forgotten."

Jessica showed no reaction at all to the mention of his son. He had hoped for something more than nothing. Sighing, silently wondering whether anyone could help these two, he returned to the discussion at hand.

"Move his cradle to the nursery." The old man could see her fear and continued. "No, Jessica, I don't mean to remove him from you completely. Get Mrs. Winters to take you to the attic where all of Jonathan's baby things are stored. My wife kept him at her side in a large basket which could be carried from room to room. See if you can find it. You can't stay cooped up in this room forever. Take him with you during the day and let him sleep in his own room at night.

Acknowledging the truth of his summary of her situation and feeling relief that she would not have to give up more, Jessica and Mrs. Winters rooted through the attic all morning. Even if Mr. Selby had not planned it that way, he had given Jessica a new project that quickly claimed her interest. While they were hunting the basket, Jessica found a rocking horse that had been her husband's. With that discovery she decided to explore through all the nursery items and soon decided the room must be redone.

Her father-in-law agreed to her plans quickly when he discovered a new interest was the reason for not moving the boy. He had kept his house in good condition, but redecorating had never interested him. When Jessica timorously asked to have new wallpaper for the nursery, saying it was much too dull, he readily agreed. The next morning Mrs. Winters came in with the basket scrubbed and newly ruffled and padded with pillows. Jessica lay the baby in it, noticing he would not fit for long.

"Mrs. Winters, you are a miracle worker!" exclaimed Jessica excitedly. "How did you accomplish all this over night?"

"We have a full staff again, miss, which you would know if you ever left this tomb," the woman announced. "Everyone helped. I came to carry the baby downstairs because Mr. Selby sent around painters and wallpaper hangers and all kinds of workmen. They are waiting to talk to you."

Picking up the basket, she left the room. Jessica followed hastily and soon was in deep conference with them. She set the carpenters to work immediately making the few repairs that were necessary. Then she chose paint and wallpaper and allowed that the workmen should start work as soon as they would not fall over one another. When Joshua fussed Elsie appeared quickly and took him away. Jessica retired to her room to feed a freshly-linened baby; and before she had a chance to move, Mrs. Winters appeared with the noonday meal. Noticing the older woman still standing by the door, Jessica asked, "Is there something I could do, Mrs. Winters?"

"I was wondering, Miss Jessica," she began hesitantly. "Shouldn't we do something with Elsie's room too? It's right beside the nursery and wouldn't cause any extra mess."

"Of course, we should! Don't let the carpenters go until I can look at it." Gulping down her lunch, Jessica muttered to herself. "What happened to me? I should have thought of it myself."

Soon she was off on another project with Elsie saying, "It really isn't necessary, miss."

"It most certainly is," said Jessica, overriding her maid's hesitancy. "My son can't have a shiny new room with this dowdy old place for you beside it."

That afternoon Jessica allowed her son to sleep with Elsie beside him rather than her. Thought she would not leave the house, she sent for fabrics from which she could choose new curtains for both rooms. "These won't do," she told the woman in charge. "None of them. I want my son's room to be bright and cheerful, none of this heavy old stuff is right. Do you have any other samples at your shop? I'm trying to create cheerful rooms for a child and a young girl."

The woman ordered her helpers to carry everything away and returned an hour later with all kinds of appropriate fabric and many suggestions beside. "No one uses this for draperies," she said. "But if you make two pairs, plain white under the thin fabric, it won't fade badly and the rooms will be lighter."

"Miss Crocker, you are a genius. this is exactly the kind of thing I had in mind."

That night Jeremiah Selby was surprised, but pleasantly, when his housekeeper informed him he was to dine upstairs with Miss Jessica. He could tell when he entered the room that she wanted something else, but decided to play the role assigned to him and see how she would get to it. He wore an amused grin while she babbled throughout the meal of all that had happened that day. "I hope you don't mind about Elsie's room," she said quietly.

"You may do over the entire house if you want," he answered. "How did my grandson fare during all this activity?"

"Joshua is just fine as you well knew he would be. Elsie was glad to have something to do, though she carried the basket all over the house." She smiled at this man who had become an important part of her life. How much he knew about people! His gentle humoring of her wishes endeared him to her, yet he could be firm so kindly. "Well, if you really don't mind, I may find a few other things to be done around here," she said hesitantly.

"I don't mind at all. I'm just happy to see you so interested in a project outside of this room," he added.

Jessica smiled at this man who knew how to handle her so well. "Thank you, Father Selby, for loving me so much," she said as tears filled and threatened to spill from both their eyes.

Chapter Sixteen

When Jonathan stole from Fairhaven just at dawn, the morning after vowing never to return, he rode like a madman. He thundered down the trail toward his new place at breakneck speed, having no concern whatsoever for himself or his beast. Not even a horse as magnificent as his huge chestnut stallion can take such treatment indefinitely. Snorting his protest, the horse reared and almost threw his violent rider to the ground. Jonathan caught himself and finally regained some sense, at least as far as his horse was concerned. He did not really care whether or not he killed himself, but the stallion had served him too well to be treated so badly.

Pushing forward as sensibly as possible, he arrived at his destination in the middle of the third day. Then he plunged into the work that remained, and there was plenty to keep him busy. His men had been clearing land and Jonathan worked beside them, driving himself much harder than he drove them. He worked far into the night and dropped exhausted onto a cot each night. He ate whatever was put before him, not even noticing what it was. After several weeks he unpacked only a bed from the many crates he had had delivered earlier. He needed no other furniture. He didn't want to be comfortable. He went through the motions of staying alive but thought himself dead inside.

After his arrival he had told Jimmy what had come to

pass at Fairhaven and never mentioned it or Jessica again. Polly had invited him for dinner, but he refused, saying he worked well past the dinner hour. When the first planting had been harvested, he sent Tim to the city with the crop, having no desire to return himself. He ignored messages from Steve, not caring what happened to his other interests as long as he could bury himself here.

And bury himself is exactly what he did, though he spent part of Christmas with Polly and Jimmy. He could not work his men on that day and could find no good reason for refusing their invitation. He was gruffly polite for the few hours he was there, and Polly tried to keep little Jeffrey out of sight. He jumped out of his chair when he heard a small cry and started to leave. As he was thanking Polly for her hospitality and apologizing for his grimness, Jimmy came from the bedroom with the little boy. Jonathan's heart wrenched when he saw the smiling baby, now content in his father's arms and exploring his nose with his little fingers. He cackled delightedly as Jimmy nipped his fingers and sobered when he saw the huge stranger at the door.

Jonathan literally ran from the happy household. As he walked home, he allowed himself to think for the first time in months. Jeremy would be over nine months old now, if he were alive. If he felt so much pain at the thought of his son, how much more must Jessica have felt—she who carried the child within her body and learned to love him months before his birth. How had he let Jessica creep into his thought? He had successfully avoided just that for several months. Even after eating a complete Christmas dinner, he felt empty inside—just remembering her name made him feel so empty. Why had she run away? Obviously she didn't love him enough to stay and face their problems together. All her pretense at closeness after that last night was just that—pretense to lull him into acceptance of her trips to town which were so necessary for her escape.

Did she call it escape? Had she felt so trapped that she escaped rather than ran away? Why did he even think of that word? God, he hadn't meant to trap her.

Why could they not discuss their loss and comfort each other? Always before she had made him listen while he teased her for talking a problem to death. But the problems did die when she insisted they talk them through. This time, when her loss was the greater, he had taken all the action he knew to take but they did not talk as she would have forced him to do.

What did she think? The only clue she had given him was that she blamed herself, and he had told her that he didn't blame her. What else could he have done? He could have made her believe him, he told himself. But would I make love to the woman if I blamed her? Surely she knew I loved our son too.

Maybe she thought I just wanted her. No, he thought, she had to know I needed her as badly as she needed me. But she left me alone with my loss and doubled it—no, even more than that. I could have got along without the child if I had her. Well, that's no matter. Somehow I must muddle along without either of them.

From then on he could not successfully shut her out of his thoughts again. He awoke angry because he'd been dreaming of her. He exhausted himself with work only to imagine her lying in his bed. How did she get such a hold on me? Soon he had to get ready to get away from here too.

Leaving Jimmy to oversee for him again, he left for town in answer to an urgent summons from Steve. "What the hell's going on?" he asked, pushing the door to Steve's office open.

"Jonathan! Thank God!" exclaimed Steve. "I was beginning to think you were dead." He jumped to his feet and pumped Jonathan's hand until Jonathan jerked his hand away. He knew full well how Jonathan had spent the last several months. Even though he had not intruded on his friend's misery, Tim and Jimmy were in constant touch with him.

"In a way I was dead," Jonathan stated flatly. "But I decided to rejoin the living."

He watched Steve observe him carefully. With each passing moment, he felt more and more as if he were on trial or maybe undergoing an examination of some kind. "What is it, Steve?" he asked impatiently. "You said I was to rush and now you just stand there watching while I squirm."

"I've heard some pretty wild tales of your behavior up there,' he said, smiling.

"All I did was work like a demon," he defended. "Why does hard work make a wild tale?"

"Like a demon is right. Some people who came from there thought you *were* a devil or else possessed by one."

"Come on, Steve. You don't believe in that nonsense," he said grimly, shuffling his feet and staring at the floor.

"Do you remember the man you sent here who refused to return? He called your place *Terra Diablo*." Steve was smiling broadly now. And Jonathan could see that the test was over and turned the conversation away from himself. They discussed many details of their business but Jonathan could tell Steve was still holding back the most important detail.

Suddenly there was a commotion outside and Carolyn flung herself through the doorway and into Jonathan's arms. "I am so glad you've returned," she murmured as she kissed him over and over. "I knew you couldn't leave me for long."

Disentangling himself, he stepped back while saying, "But I didn't return to you, Carolyn. I returned to my business."

"Oh, that!" she scoffed as if it were nothing. She plopped into a chair and said, "How about a drink, Steve, to toast Jonathan's return to civilization."

Jonathan looked out the window while Steve poured

a glass of wine which he handed to Carolyn. "Aren't you drinking, Jonathan?" she asked coyly.

When he returned from the window, he was surprised to see Steve had disappeared. Hadn't he caught Jonathan's signal to stay? The last thing he wanted was to be alone with this witch. Then Carolyn drained her glass and, taking his arm, said, "Come on, darling, we can talk better at my house; now that you've got rid of that slut and her son, nothing can prevent our happiness."

She was so wrapped up in her own plans that she did not feel him stiffen. When he stood still, refusing to step forward, she said, "Come with me, Jonathan. You must be starved for a woman, and my house is empty."

Pulling his arm free, he said very quietly as if struggling to control his temper, "I don't know how you got here, practically on my heels, but you have some incorrect information. I did not get rid of my wife—she left me."

Coyness replacing the surprise that had slipped momentarily over her features, she murmured, "That is her loss. I would never leave a man like you, darling."

She moved toward him and reached her hand to his face, but Jonathan grabbed the hand and thrust it away from him. Staring at her with hate blazing in his eyes, he retorted, "No, Carolyn, it is *my* loss. And don't you ever call her a slut again," he threatened menacingly.

"Are you refusing me again?" she roared. "You choose that slut over me?"

Jonathan, for the first time in his life, slapped a woman and the slap resounded in the outer room. Steve bolted through the door as she shouted, "That does it! You'll never see your son again!"

Steve pushed Jonathan back and grabbed both her arms. "What do you mean?" he asked, shaking her like a rag doll.

Carolyn clamped her jaws tightly. Realizing her danger, she gasped, "I don't mean anything." When he loosened his hold, she stuttered, "It's just that. . .that everyone says he has to be dead and Jonathan isn't going to bring back a dead child." She strode from the room as they both stared at her.

Finally someone had said it aloud. At the pained expression on Jonathan's face, Steve said, "She was angry. She didn't know what she was saying."

"There's more to it than that," he said. "She knows something."

"Carolyn? Surely not. What could a woman do?"

"A woman with her money might hire all kinds of people," Jonathan insisted. "Damn! Why didn't we think of her?"

Steve left Jonathan standing by the chair and hastened outside, only to return a few minutes later to find Jonathan slumped in a chair.

"Jonathan, I heard most of what you said. Do you want Jessica back?" he asked solicitously.

"I've always wanted her to come back, but I can't go after her," he moaned. "Why do you ask?"

"Someone from this company has to go to England. I want you to go. Think about it on your way and maybe you can see her while you're there if you want."

"I know I don't want to go to England," he said morosely.

"I can't sail a ship," Steve insisted. "And we've cargo loaded. If you left tomorrow, you could be there by June."

"Tomorrow? I couldn't possibly leave so soon," he said.

"Why not? What is there to keep you here? You have much more waiting for you there."

But did he? She had mentioned divorce. Well, he could, as Steve suggested, think about it on the way. "All right, Steve. I guess I'm off for England," he admitted reluctantly.

"Jonathan, there is much to discuss before you leave. You will have to be there several months, so maybe you should tell me what to do about things here."

When they boarded the ship a few minutes later, Jonathan cried, "My God, Steve, you were certainly sure of yourself. You even have my clothing aboard."

Somewhat embarrassed at being found out this way but happy that Jonathan seemed so light-hearted, Steve said, "I told you all was ready for you to leave tomorrow. Don't you believe what I say?"

Jonathan laughed and looked around the ship—at his cabin, at the cargo, at the rigging—while Steve followed, smiling at the mood of his friend. Finally Jonathan was satisifed and turned, saying, "You're right again, Steve. All that's left for me to do is to find Donald. Let's go."

"We'll go to my house first. Do you want to stay the night with me or aboard the ship?" asked Steve, leading the way this time. "I assume you will not be visiting Carolyn."

"You assume correctly," retorted Jonathan dryly. "And don't be so cute or I may hit *you* next." Slapping Steve on the shoulder, Jonathan walked with him off the ship while they both laughed. Jonathan basked in his good mood so much that he barely noticed the familiar figure outside the office door. "Donald!" he shouted. Turning to Steve, he exclaimed, "Now I'm really ready to sail!" And the friends who were also partners discussed business deals and techniques and strategies far into the night.

Jonathan sailed with the tide the next morning and stood on the bridge trying to decide what to do about his wife. God! Why am I worrying about it now? We aren't even out of sight of land. Nothing can be accomplished for weeks, so I will think of out later.

Later was a long time coming. Everything that could possibly go wrong with a sea voyage did. Two weeks out of port a mysterious fever hit the crew and rampaged through the ship at will. Donald ran all over the ship trying to relieve the suffering of those afflicated while

Jonathan did all sorts of jobs to keep the ship sailing. He worked as he hadn't since his very first trip. He had piloted frequently, for he enjoyed it, but he hadn't climbed the rigging in years. Yet he was so exhilarated, even with the troubles aboard, that he actually thrilled to it. He was so short-handed he had barely any rest for two weeks. Somehow there was hot coffee available at all hours, but he was too tired to inquire how. He rarely even walked into his cabin; and when he did, he flopped into a chair only to tramp back on deck after a half hour's rest sitting up. Finally there had been no new cases for two days and most of the crew were on the mend. Two men had died and were buried at sea, and Jonathan finally stumbled into his bunk to sleep the clock around.

When he awakened, he rolled over to see Donald clearing up the discarded clothing in his cabin. "Good to see you awake, sir," smiled Donald. "That was a terrible two weeks."

"I hope we never have to go through another time like that," he muttered. "Did you get any rest?"

"Yes, sir. I'll bring your food and water to wash soon."

"There's no rush. I want to go on deck and have a look around."

"The men would appreciate it, sir, but most have returned to their jobs so it really isn't necessary."

Nevertheless, Jonathan toured the ship, chatting with his crew and making sure those who were on the job were strong enough to be there. Finally satisfied that the ship had returned to normal, he returned to his cabin to eat and bathe. While leaning back in the tub, he thought for a second about how Jessica loved to luxuriate in a bath. Damn! How does she creep into my thoughts? All my life I could take or leave a woman. Why does this one little girl have such a hold on me? If I can get along without the others, I can manage to get along without her. I will not chase her all the way across an ocean and beg her to come back.

A week later the ship ran into a fierce storm which buffeted them about for days. Once more the crew, including the captain, was passed into extra duty with very little sleep on the rolling ship. Since difficult voyages had to be expected, Jonathan was thankful that the storm had not hit them while the crew had been weakened with the fever. They would never have survived if it had. However, the ship was badly damaged and they sailed for the nearest port for repairs and provisions. All in all by the time they reached their destination, the worse of the summer had disappeared and the warm, not hot, September air greeted them.

Jonathan was very much afraid his business would take too long for them to sail before winter set in. He was not interested in returning during the dead of winter when storms at sea were common. His crew had had a hard enough trip one way without asking for worse on their return. He was determined not to seek out his wife, for he was almost certain she would be with his father. Yet how could he be this close to her for months on end without even seeing her? And what would she think? If she gave any thought to returning to him and discovered he lay in port without seeing her, she was bound to interpret his actions as a complete rejection and never return.

He remained on his ship until the cargo was unloaded. Then he went ashore and started on the business he had crossed the Atlantic to conduct. Steve had thought Jonathan should plan to stay aboard maybe as much as a year, but Jonathan determined to find agents to do the majority of the work after he set the wheels in motion. If they were to have a line of ships, rather than just one, it only made sense to have a full complement of offices at each end of the journey. Steve had been adamant about the other end being England rather than France or Spain, though Jonathan knew he had visions of fur trade from the North and

211

molasses and rum from the West Indies.

Jonathan tired of returning to the ship each night and moved to a nearby inn, which proved even more unsatisfactory. The rooms were too small, the common rooms downstairs too public. Besides, privacy or—better yet—security were unheard of in these parts. He could never leave his room without worrying about it being ransacked during his absence—not that he kept valuables there other than the papers which he did not want to fold away every time he stepped out. If he posted a guard, every thieving cutthroat would soon be convinced he was protecting something valuable.

He sat at the table in his room—that was inconvenient as hell, too—when Donald announced a visitor. Expecting no one, Jonathan frowned questionly.

"It's your father, sir," Donald said quietly in answer to the unspoken question.

Jonathan smiled to himself; he should have known the man would be aware of his arrival. "Well, Father, this is an unexpected surprise," he said walking to the old man. "Do you know you have never come to the dock area to visit me?"

"When I discovered you had been here a week, I was afraid you didn't intend to come to me this time," the old man replied. Both men stood in the middle of the room, their last parting fresh in their memories and neither knowing exactly how to proceed.

Finally Jonathan said sincerely, "I'm glad you came." The old man's reserve broke down and he pumped his son's hand vigorously.

"Why do you stay here in this awful place?" he asked.

The other man shrugged resignedly and realized for the first time just how old his father looked. He's tired or worn out. Surely Jessica isn't giving him such a bad time as she gave me. She always seemed so fond of him. Suddenly Jonathan admitted to himself that he too loved this old man who had tried to many times to rule his life. "I would never let myself believe that he did the things he did because he cared for me. I stubbornly insisted he wanted only to control me. He has been wherever I needed him without saying a word because I had too much pride to ask his aid or acknowledge it when I knew him very well just the name of Selby opened doors for me because of him. Now he has taken the responsibility for another of my problems without a word. And look what it's done to him. It's time I take over my own problems."

Little did Jonathan know that his wife was usually the light of his father's life. The situation between his son and his wife caused the desolation in his father's appearance, not the woman herself. Their happiness, when they found it, had lasted such a short time.

Realizing that someone must break the silence, Jonathan asked softly, "How is she?"

"Her health is excellent," replied his father.

Jonathan frowend at the evasion. Then he knew he must take a step he had not taken for years. "Father, would you do me a favor?"

The light that sprang into the old man's eyes embarrassed his son. How selfish he had been all these years to deny his father this small pleasure. It would have cost him so little to kindle this light. At his father's eager nod, he continued, "I need a place from which to conduct my business. I cannot spread out here and I can trust no one. Can you help?"

"Jonathan, my son, pack up your papers and come with me. I wanted to talk about your wife, but I am not going to take a chance of causing another misunderstanding between us," he added.

Guilt stabbed Jonathan's gut as he packed up all but his clothing and carried them to his father's carriage. As they rode through the city, Jonathan wondered what his father had wanted to say about Jessica, but basked in their new relationship and didn't want to ruin the fragile friendship. When the carriage stopped, Jonathan stepped outside and said with surprise, "But this is your office."

"I know, but there is plenty of room for us both," said the old man. "Come on in." He unlocked the door and led his son to his own large office. "I am almost never here anymore. For all practical purposes I have retired, but I've kept the office so that I could still feel the pulse of the business world if I missed it too much. I would be very pleased if you would use if while you are here—provided, of course, that I can drop in to use the clerk's office for myself now and then."

Jonathan smiled teasingly, "I should have known there was a catch." Seeing the old man freeze, he hastened to add, "You may spend as much time here as you want. How am I to see your otherwise?"

"You know where I live," Jeremiah answered softly. Jonathan shifted his feet and looked away from him. "Son, I will not urge you to do anything against your inclinations. It is a big house and you are welcome. You could probably come and go in such a way that the two of you would never meet, but I can't turn her out to make room for you."

"I wouldn't want you to do that. What did you mean earlier when you said 'her health is excellent'?"

When his father considered before answering, Jonathan said, somewhat impatiently, "Blurt it out, Father. You chose your words very carefully then, too."

"She is in the midst of some redecorating," he replied.

"Redecorating?" Jonathan questioned incredulously. "That is not like you. Why did you let her involve you in that mess?"

"Jonathan, I am so delighted that she is finally interested in something. I have no idea how far it will go or how long her interest will last, but I'm glad for anything that takes her from her prison." He knew prison was a harsh word, but maybe harsh words were called for.

214

Besides, he defended himself, Jonathan had asked.

"I don't understand," said Jonathan, waiting for his father to continue.

"She made herself a virtual prisoner in her room for months. For a while she came downstairs when the doctor visited. No, there is nothing wrong with her. He called as a friend. Remember he was one of her cohorts when she ran off *to* you." When his son's face relaxed again after the worry which had leaped onto it faded, he continued, "For months she did not leave her room for more than five minutes until I finally talked her into a little redecorating of my house. Suddenly she became alive again. But she still doesn't go outdoors. She can do over the whole damn place if it keeps her alive. The zombie who lived in my house broke my heart. I don't want it to return."

Jonathan knew the old man worried about Jessica, but realized he considered it no burden that his son should take from his shoulders. Jessica was his daughter and he loved her as such, not as his son's wife.

"Don't you think, if I moved in, she would retreat to her room again? After all, she ran away from me, you know."

"Yes, I think she would. But I think she would be hurt more if she ever found out you were in town and didn't come to your own home because of her—especially if you stay several months as I understand you will. Do as you think best, my son. She will not find out from me that you are here. Keep in mind I do not want her hurt any more than she has been by us Selby men. I do think her running days are over, so you won't chase her away."

"I will think on these things, but I can promise nothing. I do thank you, though, for the office. I must get to work. Do you want to watch me so soon?" he asked, grinning.

"No, no, I won't bother you. I must go," answered the old man quickly.

"Father, I mean it—you would not bother me and, no matter what I decide about living quarters, I expect you to call here often. Agreed?"

"Agreed," said Jeremiah shaking his son's hand again. When he left his office, Mr. Selby felt more enthusiastic than he had for ages. Why had it taken him so long to discover that people were more interesting than money?

Chapter Seventeen

After his father had left, Jonathan unpacked his papers and settled down to work but soon discovered his mind kept returning to what he'd heard about his wife. Damn! The vixen's ruined my concentration again. Throwing down his pen, he paced the room, trying to decide what to do. Finally, he called a runner and penned a message to his father. "Now mind," he instructed the boy, "give it to no one else; if he is not there, wait for him."

"Yes, sir," bobbed the boy and tore off down the street.

He sat at the desk again and looked up from his work only when it became too dark to see. "It's amazing how much I accomplish when she is off my mind," he thought. He had much to do in the next few days so it was a good thing his concentration had returned. "Everything depends on her now," he said as he left the office and headed back to the inn.

When Jessica appeared for dinner, she asked her father-in-law, "Did that boy find you? He had a message he would entrust to no one but you." She smiled as though everyone knew she was perfectly capable of transmitting messages.

"Those were his instructions," he answered. "Tell me, my dear," he asked, taking a deep breath and obviously changing the subject, "what new plans have you made for our house today?"

She liked the way he said 'our house.' She had long since ceased to think of it as his or Jonathan's. She started—where had that name come from? She had thought she'd pushed him from her thoughts. Why today? Shrugging her shoulders, she turned her attention to her father-in-law to answer him. "I had thought to do one room at a time, but it takes so long that way. Should we do all the downstairs?"

"Anything you want, my dear," he answered.

"No, Father. I know you are trying to keep me busy and I thank you, but *you* must want it too. You're the one who just said 'our house'."

"All right. Let's finish dinner and discuss it in the library. I will forego my cigar to spend the time with you."

"Some sacrifice," she teased. "You know David said you should not smoke them anyway." She suddenly dug into her dinner as if she could hardly wait to being planning again. He hoped she would not change her mind when she heard his news. These two kept him in the confoundest, awkwardest position. Why couldn't he love just one of them? It would be so much easier. But then, the other would have no one. sometimes he wanted to damn them both.

"Come, Father Selby, you're delaying," he heard Jessica say. How long had he been musing? When he stood, she took his arm and led him away, saying, "Do you really want to get involved in a mess down here? I could finish the upstairs first, but we might not finish down here for the holidays. I can't decide."

"I really want you to make the decisions. You know I like my comfort but other than that I don't care. I thoroughly enjoy walking into those rooms you have already done. Never has any room in my house looked so cheerful. You have real talent for this sort of thing and I know any mess will be worth the outcome, so you decide how much you can take on."

He sat her on the settee in the library and crossed the room to close the door. She knew something was wrong even before he returned to sit beside her. If it wasn't the house, what could it be? "The message?" she asked, fear coursing through her body.

Holding her gaze with his eyes, he said, "The message was from Jonathan. Jessica, don't look away. We *must* talk about it," he insisted. "I saw him today. He will be in town for some months and I told him he was welcome here. He is, isn't he?" he asked quietly.

She moaned softly and dropped her head, but he put a finger under her chin and raised it. She had closed her eyes, but he held her head in place with one finger until she looked at him. She gulped, "This is his home," but he saw the misery in her face.

"No," he said, shaking his head. "This is your home as much as it is his." Sitting back so she could look away if she wanted to, he picked up her shaking hand and held it tenderly. "You are the reason the messenger would deliver the letter only to me. He will not come here unless you approve. I told him he could come and go without seeing you if he wanted, but he refused to sneak in and out behind your back. What shall I answer?"

"What have you told him already?" she asked.

"Only that you kept to your room for months and had just recently left it to oversee some redecorating. He is afraid if he appears, you will retreat into your room again. Will you?"

"Probably," she answered honestly. "I don't think I could stand to see him. Can't he stay somewhere else?" she asked wretchedly.

"Of course, he can and he is willing to if you want. You two are at odds most of the time and I promised not to interfere again. But think carefully about sending him away."

"Why should I?" she asked with resentment. "What's he doing here anyway?"

"He will be here at least until spring. He and Steve are opening an office here, for they will have a fleet of ships rather than just his. Jonathan doesn't think so, but it will take that long to find help he can trust and to get things running smoothly. You can avoid much idle gossip if he moves in with his wife."

"What about Joshua?" she asked.

"As far as I know, very few people know about Joshua and his father is not one of them. We cannot control gossip among the servants, so some others may have learned that way, though I doubt it. Jonathan will attend to the loading of his ship for the next few days. In any case he will not come here until the ship leaves port. Leave me or him know your decision. He is using my office."

The old man left the library quietly while she sat too deep in thought to notice. He was well aware of the turmoil caused and wished he had not troubled her when she was finally making progress, but some things must be faced and Jessica could not avoid coming to grips with her feelings for her husband much longer. He was almost sorry he had suggested they meet and marry almost two and a half years ago. During all that time they had been happy less than six months. But then, he reasoned, never had he seen such love and happiness as theirs during that brief time. Maybe it was not too late and they could find it again.

Jessica reluctantly walked up the stairs. She headed directly for the nursery. She had hoped her son would need her even though she had fed him just prior to going down for dinner. He had been sleeping the night through lately, but he might have been awake. Elsie stepped into the doorway between the rooms; but when she saw Jessica, she slipped back to her own room. Jessica gazed at her son with loving eyes. When she thought never to hold a babe again, she was blessed with this dear boy. What would Jonathan say? It would surely be impossible to keep Joshua's existence a secret for months. Dare she even try? If he came here and discovered the boy, he might never forgive her for not telling him. But things between them could hardly get worse, so what did it matter? She could not ask him to forgive her for losing one son by presenting him with a substitute.

Should she prevent his coming here? If both he and Mr. Selby said so, she did believe the choice was truly hers. Could she endure his presence without his love? But even more important could she endure his presence in the city and never see him? She knew that no matter what, she could not harden her heart against her father-in-law. His son must be welcome in the house in which he grew up. She would tell him so at breakfast. That decision made, she finally slept, peaceful at last.

Several mornings later Jessica heard a great commotion in the hall and opened her door without thinking. Hearing Mrs. Winter's constant, "Be careful," she thought the painters must be working in the wrong place and stepped out of her room in time to see a sea chest dropped to the floor. Rooted to the spot, she suddenly recognized the man and cried, "Donald! It's you!"

"It sure is, mum," he said, bowing low. Smiling broadly, he added, "It's good to see you again."

"Oh, it's good to see you, too." Sobering, she asked, "Is your master here, too?"

Sadness swept over his face as he saw the fear on hers. "He won't come until this evening, mum," he said quietly.

"Are you staying here or returning with his ship, Donald?"

"I be staying, mum. Let me know if I can help you," he added. He didn't care if he did sound disloyal to Jonathan. He didn't want anyone to hurt this little lady again.

"Oh, I will, Donald, and thank you. You were always

so good to me. Visit me when you can," she invited.

"Thank you, mum," he replied as he moved on into Jonathan's room with the baggage.

Jessica moved downstairs to confer about wallpaper and fabric for the drawing room. The furniture was well built and comfortable, but the fabric must be replaced. If all the samples were shown together, she could choose so much more easily. She would love to go wild—maybe she would as long as the room appeared restful rather than wild. Suddenly she decided this room would be a secret and even her father-in-law could not peek.

When she finished with her planning, she went to find Mrs. Winters. "I hate to make extra work," she told the housekeeper. "But I think I will have breakfast in my room—starting tomorrow," she added before the woman could protest. Yes, it could be arranged, she could avoid Jonathan. Next, she gathered a wide selection of reading material from the library. Thank heaven her father-in-law still purchased any book he thought might interest her, though she was behind on her reading. Lugging the books upstairs, she thought, no, she would not retreat behind closed doors entirely. This would be entirely different. She could be about the house while Jonathan was at the office. She would stay in her room only when he was home, which really shouldn't be often.

And it worked exactly that way. She heard him come in after she had retired to her room and she remained in her room until she was sure he had left the house. One evening several weeks later she slipped to the nursery to check on Joshua who had been fretful all day. When she saw Elsie rocking him, she smiled and said, "Let me," and reached for her child. Holding him to her bosom, she rocked them both to sleep. When she awakened, he still slept soundly, so with a kiss she lay him in his cradle and tiptoed from the room. As she neared her room, a huge shadow loomed before her. Leaning against the wall, she gasped and covered her mouth with her hand, hoping whoever it was had not heard.

"Who's there?" he asked and she recognized his voice at once.

Trying to make herself invisible, she didn't move a muscle. But he started walking toward her. "Oh, Jonathan, it's you. You frightened me," she said as she left the wall.

"Jessica!" he gasped. "I hadn't thought to see you. You have avoided me so well up to now," he teased. Stiffening her spine, Jessica said as haughtily as she could, "I? Avoiding you? I had rather thought it was the other way around." She started on toward her room.

"Whatever were you doing down there?" he asked.

She stopped short and grasped for an answer. "Down there? I. . .uh, I. . .uh, was taking care of someone who is ill." She walked on into her room and collapsed against the closed door. That was too close. The next morning Jessica awakened later than usual so she went down for breakfast. She spied him as she swept into the dining room. She could hardly turn and run as if she were afraid. Gulping for courage, she walked on toward her chair, aware that both men watched her carefully. "Good morning, Father Selby, Jonathan," she said, nodding her head at each in turn. She sat down as Jonathan rushed over to hold her chair. "Thank you," she said. When he returned to his chair, she looked him in the eye and said demurely, "Jonathan, you really should join us for dinner one of these nights. Your father's household serves marvelous meals. Besides, this may be your last chance. The drawing room will be finished today and the workmen start in here tomorrow."

The gall of the girl, he thought. She's really blaming me for this ridiculous situation. "I would be delighted, madam," he answered in much the same tone as hers. "Besides, I must bear witness to your decorating talents which my father has been raving about. I've seen no

223

evidence of them so far. Just what have you decorated already?''

"Uh, well, I started with my room. If you would care to inspect it," she could not continue, so she shrugged, hoping he thought she didn't care.

"I wouldn't dream of intruding on your privacy," he replied sarcastically.

Mr. Selby watched this exchange anxiously. Pleased that Jessica had fared so well, he was hoping the situation was not so explosive it would burst around them. "Well, that settles it," he said, trying to sound business-like. "We will meet for the unveiling at six thirty and have dinner at seven. Well, I'm off," he said, wiping his mouth and throwing his napkin beside his plate. "Don't overdo today, Jessica," he was saying as he walked into the hallway with her. "We want your charming company tonight. Are you coming, Jonathan?"

"Yes, sir," he said, walking over to them. He turned to watch Jessica run up the stairs and noticed her turn in the direction she had come from last night. "Just who is so sick that she is so concerned?" he asked his father.

"Sick? Is someone sick?"

"She was coming from the back when I saw her last night. She said someone was sick."

"Oh," muttered the old man, "must be one of the maids. You know how Jessica clucks over her little chicks. Come on."

Jessica shivered as she dressed for dinner. She was expected downstairs momentarily but she couldn't face him. Both encounters with her husband had been accidental, but they had left her shaken. She had heard the men return a few moments ago but she had not stirred. She flopped onto the lounge chair with a moan. There was no way she could force herself down those stairs. Why had she ever invited him to dinner? She might have known his father would jump on the suggestion immediately. She would have a tray in her room. She had started to undress when there was a knock on her door.

"Come in," she said, expected it to be Mrs. Winters.

She gasped and pulled her gown to her chin when Jonathan walked into the room.

"I thought maybe you had lost your nerve," he said with a wicked grin. "But I should have known you never would." He walked toward her as she backed away.

He's deliberately being rude, she thought. He knew I wouldn't come down. She glared at him until he walked behind her and started to button her dress. She hastily thrust her arms through the sleeves. When he finished, she strode from the room, furious at the humiliation of being forced to endure his company, more especially his help. She'd show him, she thought as she stamped down the stairs and grabbed her father-in-law's arm.

"You look beautiful, my dear," he said. Then he leaned close and whispered, "Don't let him know you are afraid," and smiled.

When Jonathan opened the doors to the drawing room, he gasped in surprise. The room had changed character completely, and both men saw immediately what was still not obvious to Jessica. Instead of its heavy formality, the room appeared spacious and bright. She had chosen light-weight fabrics of bright colors. No heavy satins and brocades. Even though the woodwork remained dark, the delicate gold design on the wallpaper kept the room from appearing somber.

When Jonathan said drolly, "Well, Father, it appears we have Louisiana in London," Jessica realized what she had done. The room was almost a replica of the parlor at Fairhaven.

"I didn't realize. . .I just thought. . ." Jessica stammered.

"It is charming, Jessica," her father-in-law cut in. "The colonies have something to offer stuffy old London town after all."

"The room was so dark and formal, I thought. . ."

she defended.

"And you thought correctly," he insisted. "I love it." He shot a warning glance to his son as if to say he dare not embarrass her more. Then adroitly he changed the subject until Edward appeared with drinks. Jessica's hand still shook as she reached for her glass, and she hastily brushed from her gown the few drops she spilled.

Jonathan, who had been watching his wife out of the corner of his eye, blinked when his father asked abruptly, "How are you progressing in your search for a manager?" What was the old man doing? He knew very well how he was progressing because he had spent all day at the office.

"About as you predicted, sir," he answered. "My one goal for the future is still to prove you wrong just once."

Jessica sat silent as the men conversed about business and was happy their attention had turned from her. All she had to do was sit unmoving while her rampaging embarrassment quieted. Suddenly she realized the old man was addressing her. "I'm sorry," she stammered. "I. . .I wasn't paying attention. What did you say?"

"I asked whether you would like to go to the continent for the holidays. They are coming soon, you know."

"Oh, I couldn't," she replied hastily. Thinking she may have answered too quickly when she sat Jonathan raise his eyebrow and look at her strangely, she was greatly relieved when Edward appeared in the doorway to announce dinner. Jumping to her feet, she grabbed Mr. Selby's arm, saying, "I don't think I could enjoy Christmas in a strange place with strange customs."

She thought dinner would never end. Why had she ever got involved in such a situation? She pushed the food around her plate, eating very little, until she heard Jonathan say, "You bragged so about my father's meals, Jessica, yet you don't seem to be eating. Aren't you hungry?" he asked sardonically.

"I guess not," she muttered. Why can't he let me alone, she thought? Must he always make fun of me? Jessica finally could endure no more and ran from the room.

"What the hell is going on?" shouted Jonathan.

"You just had to bait her, didn't you?" his father snarled.

"One little time. She used to be able to take much more than that," he retorted.

"I told you she was unsure of herself. You are surely not so insensitive that you could not tell how uncomfortable your remark about the drawing room made her. But you weren't satisfied, were you? You had to pile it on," he scoffed.

When Jonathan saw the old man walk into the hall and turn toward the stairs, he caught him partway up, saying, "Let me. You go back downstairs."

"Jonathan, if you hurt. . ."

"Trust me. Let me go to her," he pleaded. Because he really would rather his son apologize for himself, Mr. Selby left him alone and grumbled his way into the library while Jonathan slowly mounted the stairs. Why did he forever do the wrong thing where she was concerned? Knowing how much seeing her had affected him, he should have known better than to act like a perfect boor. Still, he had expected her to rise angrily to his bait, not to dissolve into tears.

He walked to her door and knocked. When she did not answer, he called softly, "Jessica? Jessica, please let me talk to you." He opened the door and looked into the empty room. Where was she?

As he was closing the door, he heard her behind him, "Jonathan, what do you want?"

Spinning around, he said, "Where have you been?"

Straightening, she asked stiffly, "What concern is it of yours?" and spun past him into her room. When the door would have slammed in his face, he caught it and followed her in. "Please leave. I want to dress for bed."

"Go ahead," he drawled and sat on the lounge.

"Jonathan," she said, walking back to face him. "Does it make you feel better to humiliate me? Go ahead. Be your nastiest. I will not grovel as you seem to want me to, but I can lock you out of my room. Now will you go or do I have to change rooms?"

"Jessica," he said, reaching for her hand. When she pulled away, he stood quickly and apologized, "Jessica, I'm sorry. I came here to apologize, not to make matters worse. I'll do the groveling if you want me to but, please believe me, I am sorry."

"All right, Jonathan, I'll believe you. Now will you go?" She turned her back to him and waited.

Clenching his fists at his side, he tried once more, "Jess, please, can't we talk?"

"I don't think we have anything to say to each other, Jonathan," she said stubbornly.

"I'll stay out of your path. Just don't lock yourself away. Maybe you can even take Jeremiah up on his offer to go to the continent," he added.

"I can't," she said quietly.

"Why not?"

"Besides," she continued, ignoring his interruption. "I'm done with running away and that is really what I would be doing."

"I'm glad to hear that," he said as he walked to the door.

"Jonathan," she called before he opened it. "You can come and go as you want. Don't stay out till all hours just to avoid me. If we are both to be part of this household, you should be here more often. All I ask is that you not taunt me in front of your father and the staff."

"Agreed. And I thank you," he said quietly and left the room without turning around.

The following Sunday Jonathan dallied at the breakfast table as long as possible, but Jessica did not come down. When he rapped on her door, she did not answer so he sought out Mrs. Winters. "Do you know where my wife is, Mrs. Winters?"

"She's probably in her room, sir."

"No, she isn't. I've already checked."

"Then I wouldn't know, sir," replied the woman as she walked off, not giving him a chance to ask more questions.

There's something going on, he thought. That woman always knows where Jessica is. He walked back up the stairs, deep in thought, and met Jessica in the hall. "Where have you been?" he demanded. He saw her bristle and hastened to explain, "I have been looking for you. I wanted to invite you for an outing today."

"Oh, I couldn't," she replied hastily.

"Jessica, you can't stay cooped up in this house forever."

"I know that, but I can't go out today," she returned.

"Why ever not? What can you possibly have to do today, Sunday?" he asked.

"Jonathan, please don't insist," she said, staring at the floor.

"I have no right to insist, Jessica, but I do wish you would change your mind," he requested.

"When would you want to leave?" she relented.

"Whenever you say, Jessica," he answered.

"Let me talk to Mrs. Winters. Maybe I can make arrangements."

Grateful for this concession, Jonathan said nothing but did wonder what arrangements had to be made. What did he want from her? She had once said she could not live with him as polite strangers. Could they ever be more? Well, if he could take the frightened, stricken look from her eyes, he would feel less guilty. Would he be satisfied then? He honestly didn't know. He knew they had to take one step at a time. To see her smile easily would make him feel better. God! Was he interested only in his own feelings? If so, she was really better off left alone, but he really didn't think so.

Jessica had sent word that she would be ready at two, and he awaited her at the door. When she came down, he thought her as beautiful as he had ever seen her, but hesitated to mention anything so personal. He hoped they could survive an afternoon together without battling. "I hope you have no plans for the rest of the day," he said as they went outside.

Stopping quickly, Jessica murmured, "I have to be back early, five o'clock at the very latest. What did you have in mind?"

"I thought we would take a drive, even if it is cold, and then have dinner later."

"No, I must be back before dinner," she said quickly. Seeing his disappointment, she added, "Could we enjoy the time we have rather than argue about it?"

"You're right. Let's enjoy the time we have." But he had every intention of keeping her to himself as long as he possibly could. He helped her into the carriage, saying, "I thought we would see some of the sights in London that we did not have time to see the last time." She looked out the window and ignored the remark.

Both of them remained on edge throughout the drive, but neither snapped at the other. Jessica smiled wearily a couple times, and Jonathan congratulated himself on his self-control. Both of them were happy they had survived the afternoon without a major clash. The weather was not conducive to outside driving and especially the walking from place to place that Jessica seemed to prefer. He knew very well she did not have to talk to or look at him outside the carriage and she preferred these conditions. Jonathan finally insisted on stopping for tea so they could warm themselves. When they left the teashop, Jessica asked the time and fussed all the way home learning it was shortly after five: they were over half an hour away from home.

Stepping out of the carriage when it had stopped

before the house, she murmured, "Thank you Jonathan," and ran inside.

When he followed her inside, she was running up the stairs and a maid he had never seen was saying frantically, "You're so late, ma'am. I didn't know what to do."

Jonathan looked at his father who stood in a doorway. "What is it?" he asked.

"Follow her, son; it's time you know," he said gently.

Jonathan bounded up the stairs, but Jessica had disappeared. Receiving no answer when he knocked on her door, he sat on the top step to wait for her. She always seemed to be disappearing up there. He could open every door on the floor. He looked into her room, his, his father's, and one more in the front of the house. She must be at the back. Surely that maid wasn't still sick. Jessica would have had a doctor before she let anyone lie in bed sick for almost a week. Not wanting to walk into some stranger's room, he sat again on the top step to reason through this situation. Soon, however, his mind wandered to the afternoon. If possible, Jessica was more beautiful than ever. She was no longer a girl, but an exciting woman and he loved her still. He smiled wryly thinking of the prim gown she had worn, as if trying to disguise her loveliness. Modesty had been the order of the day—high collar and long sleeves. But when she had removed her wrap in the teashop, nothing could disguise her full breasts pushing at the buttons. Full breasts? No! It wasn't possible! He jumped to his feet and strode down the hall.

Silently pushing open the nursery door, he gasped audibly at the sight of his wife rocking in the chair, crooning softly to the baby sucking contentedly at her breast. At the sound she looked from the child into his eyes. Fear sprang into her eyes as if she thought he might hit her.

"Why?" he asked as he walked into the room.

"Can we discuss it later? I don't want him upset any more than he is by my lateness," she said quietly.

Nodding his assent to her wishes, he sat in the straight chair which he assumed was often occupied by the child's nurse. Looking around him, he observed dryly, "So this is what started the redecorating. You did well in here too, my dear."

Flinching at the familiarity, Jessica murmured only, "Thank you," and looked again at their son. She could not meet her husband's eyes. Panic and fear surged through her. What is he going to do? Thank heaven whatever it was would not occur here. Joshua was upset enough without having a raging battle in the room. Jonathan would not have caught her had she not taken the time to quiet her son before feeding him. But she had never left him for hours before today, and both he and Elsie had been almost hysterical when she had run into the nursery. She must not take a chance of repeating the performance.

She felt Jonathan standing behind her, but kept her eyes riveted on the baby. He had fallen asleep but she made no move to return him to his cradle. Finally Jonathan reached for him, saying, "May I?"

Not wanting to give up her son, Jessica looked at her husband. She started to shake her head, but could not deny the pleading in Jonathan's eyes, so she tenderly laid her son in his father's arms. Overcome with emotion, Jonathan cuddled the little boy, for he was over six months old, close to him. Jessica rearranged her shift and dress while Jonathan lay his son in the cradle.

Jessica stood at the door watching them; but when her husband came toward her, she started down the hall. "Wait," he said softly but sternly. She stiffened, almost afraid to move, while he closed the nursery door then dropped his arm around her shoulder as they moved down the hall.

Chapter Eighteen

Jessica trembled at his touch but dared not move his arm. Had she wanted this to happen all along? Was that the reason for inviting Jonathan to come here? She would do anything to avoid the anger that was about to explode, but she had to admit this interview was months overdue. She tried not to cringe—she must not let him know how frightened she was.

Jonathan, resorting to his sly grin to mask his feelings, said calmly, "Your room or mine? Or should we choose neutral territory?" he hastened to add.

"I don't care," she answered hopelessly.

He winced at her tone. Was he that monstrous to her? She sounded as if her world had collapsed. "Jessica, take heart. We have talked things through before, with excellent results; can't we try it again? If you had talked to me instead of running away, we might never have come to this."

Hearing the sincerity in his voice, Jessica led him to her room, the place where she would feel the most comfortable.

"Why?" he repeated behind the closed door.

"Why what?" she asked. Jonathan gasped at her effrontery. Were they at impasse already? "Jonathan, I'm not being difficult. I guess I don't know where to start." She glanced around the room as if seeking a place to hide. Finally she sat on the stool before her dressing table as her legs refused to hold her any longer. "Do you mean why did I leave or why did I keep Joshua's birth a secret?"

"Joshua? You kept the J's. I'm surprised," he added. What a stupid thing to say. But he had to say something and he was afraid he might push her into a corner.

"Why should you be surprised? I thought we had agreed on J names for our children."

"Jessica, I thought you hated me so much you wouldn't feel obligated to continue our agreement," he said sadly.

"I never hated you, Jonathan," she said, keeping her voice level.

"Then, why? Why did you leave me?" he asked incredulously.

"I. . .I thought you hated me for losing our son."

"Jessica, I never, ever blamed you. I told you that," he insisted.

"I guess you weren't very convincing," she murmured. She looked away from him but felt him kneel beside her and slip one arm around her waist as he covered her hands with his.

"Jess, how could I have convinced you?" he asked. "You wouldn't talk to me. You shut me out."

"I couldn't help it."

"I suppose not, but you acted as if only you suffered. Jeremy was my son, too. We needed each other, but you wouldn't even let me comfort you."

"You did once," she whispered.

"God, Jessica, I was hoping you'd forgotten that." Leaving her side, he murmured, "I've never been so ashamed of my actions as I was that night." He walked over to stare out the window.

Jessica truly did not understand. "Forget? How could I ever forget? She heard him moan and walked over to stare out the window with him. Why did he want her to forget one of her loveliest memories? In truth she

234

had long ago forgotten the short tussle with which the night started. Groping for understanding, she lay her hand on his arm. Not realizing instinct is often better than understanding, she murmured, "I will never forget that night, Jonathan," and felt his arm stiffen. "You gave me Joshua that night," she added with tenderness.

He started to pull her into his arms until she cast her eyes about the room, saying, "And he's all I've got." It was as if she had dashed cold water over him and he dropped his arms to his side.

Summoning up more courage than she'd known she possessed, she walked back to her chair, saying stiffly, "I waited two days after that before it became obvious that you were interested only in my body. Then I made plans to escape. When I discovered I was to bear another child, I was almost here. When your father arrived, he wanted me to let you know, but I couldn't. I knew you would want your son with you, and I might have let you have him. But after his birth I knew I couldn't bear to give him up. Now you've found out anyway, but I'm begging you not to take him away from me. I can't lose a second son," she wailed and burst into tears. Great sobs shook her entire body and he hurried to reassure her.

"I won't take him from you, Jessica. But I can't live in this house and never see him. Do you want me to move out?" He prayed silently that she would concede this point because he needed to be here to convince her to return home with him. God, we were stupid—each hugging his own side of the bed and waiting for the other to make the first move.

Jessica shook her head and his spirits soared even if she did look miserable. "No, Jonathan, you need not move."

"And may I see Joshua?"

"Yes. A father should not have to ask to see his own son, and I am sorry for putting you in such a position. You may visit the nursery whenever you wish, but please check with me before you ever take him out of that room," she begged.

"Jessica, I would not hurt you more. You have my word on it." Then with a hearty laugh he added, "There is more we need to clear up between us, but this has been an extremely emotional afternoon. I'll come back in a few minutes to take you down to dinner."

"No, I think I will have a tray here."

"Jess. . ." he started to object.

"I'm not hiding, Jonathan, really I'm not. But this *has* been an emotional afternoon and I'm tired. Please make my excuses to your father." She walked over to the wardrobe, unbuttoning her dress on the way, and he exited hastily as a desire started to rise in him.

While Jessica undressed for the day, Jonathan passed along her message to Mrs. Winters and his father.

"I heard no fireworks," commented his father dryly.

"When she saw I had discovered her secret, she looked like a whipped dog. I couldn't hurt her more. But I could kill you for not letting me know," he snarled.

His father continued eating as if nothing had been said. Jonathan waited angrily for a response. Finally he snarled again, "Have you nothing to say in your own defense?"

Setting his fork on his plate with all the patience he could muster, he looked his son in the eye and said, "Jessica needed a friend she could trust much more than you. Would you have me betray her?"

Shuffling uncomfortably Jonathan muttered, "I suppose not. But I should have known."

"Would you have rushed over here to be at her side? You who refused to follow her?" he inquired sarcastically.

"Of course."

"Not of course, Jonathan. You were angry and she was afraid. You can see how changed she is, how easily defeated. I could not take that chance that you would

236

explode in here and crush her completely."

Jonathan thought over his father's words carefully. Christ! What a mess! Was it too late to restore order from this chaos? If this were any other woman, he would know what to do; but Jessica had confounded him from the beginning. Even if he tried to tell her he loved her, she had a bee in her bonnet that wouldn't let her believe him.

Jonathan bided his time, waiting for an opportunity to reach his wife to present itself. They met often in the nursery, though he stayed away at his son's mealtime because she seemed uncomfortable. When Mrs. Winters mentioned Christmas preparations to Jessica, Jonathan offered to go to the attic to see whether there were any decorations for the season. They climbed to the top floor together and finally found some boxes that had not been unpacked since Jonathan had lived at home. He dragged them down for her and they unpacked the remaining pieces of a childhood nativity scene. "There's no stable," she cried.

"I'll make one," he answered unhesitatingly.

The whole family spent a day in the country gathering greenery and vines to be woven into wreaths and to decorate the mantles. Jessica wouldn't go without Joshua, so they packed him up too. Jonathan rented a room in a nearby inn where they could have a hot lunch. Jessica needed privacy to nurse their child. He would never ask her to endure the stares of those in the common rooms. After many reassurances she was finally persuaded to allow Elsie and Josh to stay behind while he napped. Jonathan had never seen so many greens, but Jessica kept thinking of new uses for them until he was afraid they would not be able to get the load home. They picked up Elsie and Joshua at the inn and arrived home just before dinner. All in all, the day was perfect except for Jessica's reticence to nurse her fussy son on the way home.

When bouncing him on her knee didn't quiet him,

237

Jonathan finally muttered, "You know what he wants."

"He will have to wait until we get home," she retorted.

Jonathan grinned ironically, saying, "Go ahead and feed the little glutton, madam. I won't attack you with Elsie here."

Jessica turned scarlet but unbuttoned her dress and suckled the child, turning her back to his father.

When the carriage stopped in front of the house, Jonathan handed the boy to his waiting nurse before he turned to Jessica. He lifted her from the carriage and slowly lowred her to the ground. When her body brushed his, even with all their heavy clothing, they were both surprised at the intensity of their reactions. Struggling for control, he murmured huskily, "This has been a most enjoyable day, my dear," and hugged her to him before releasing her.

Jessica ran into the house without a word. When he entered, after giving the driver instructions about the greenery, she had disappeared. When she pleaded tiredness and did not appear for dinner, Jonathan arranged for a tray for two and carried it to her room himself. Jessica gasped as he walked in and attended to the business of setting a table, saying, "I didn't think you would want to dine alone, madam." Both of them knew she had wanted to avoid him, and both knew that the other knew, so the first few minutes were tense. But Jonathan pretended nothing was wrong and soon Jessica assumed the same attitude.

Jessica hoped he would leave as soon as they finished dinner, but he rang for a maid to take away the tray and sat by the fire. "Jonathan, what is this about?" she asked angrily. "I wish you would leave."

"I want to talk," he asked calmly.

"What could we possibly have to talk about this time? Please don't ruin a nice day." When he still made not move to leave, she flounced into a chair across the

238

room. "All right, talk, she said, her exasperation obvious.

"I love you," he said quietly.

This simple flat statement knocked the wind from her. What could she say to that? She certainly didn't believe him. "You want me, Jonathan. That is not the same thing."

"Do you think I don't know that?" he retorted angrily.

"I don't really know. The last time you made love to me, you turned away from me afterwards. As far as I am concerned, that makes it lust, not love."

"Jesus Christ, woman! How can you sit there and babble such nonsense? He strode to her side and dropped to his knees. When he reached for her, she jumped to her feet and skittered away from him.

"Don't touch me," she gasped.

"Oh, hell! I've certainly heard that often enough. If you recall, those were the only words you knew after we lost Jeremy. Why do you think I feel so damned guilty about that last time Jessica?" He started in a softer tone, "You say you remember because Joshua was the result. Have you forgotten how that night started? With your usual, 'don't touch me.' Never before had I ever forced myself on a woman. But that night I insisted and you fought me with all your strength, which surely doesn't match mine, so the outcome was inevitable."

"See! You've as much as admitted it was lust," she answered.

"No, I deliberately drove you nearly wild with passion to make you think of me. You had shut me out of your life and I wanted to come back in. I still do."

"That doesn't mean you love me."

"Dammit! What must I do to convince you? If I only lusted for you, I would have broken this door down weeks ago!"

"You wouldn't dare!"

"But I would if I didn't want something lasting

between us. My father would be furious if he ever found out, but he *wouldn't* find out. I know you well, little one. You'd be too embarrassed to tell him. Besides, I could make you enjoy it."

His sly grin infuriated her. Yes, he could make her enjoy it. He could even make her beg. Was that what he wanted? Well, he would wait forever! Striding to the door, she said, "Yes, Jonathan, you can reduce me to shivers and make me want you. I cannot control my body that well, but I will never again come to you willingly. If you insist, you will have a fight on your hands every time to try to take me. I am going to check the baby, and I expect you to be gone when I return."

She slammed the door behind her. Who the hell did he think he was? Her husband, that's who said a small voice inside her. Good heavens, he had her cursing—she'd soon be as bad as he was. There was no way she wanted to start up with him again. She couldn't take all the disappointments and hurts that came from loving him. She needed serentiy, not the chaos he attracted.

Jonathan had never struck out so completely. And the days that followed made him aware of feelings he had not known he possessed. He had liked David Forsythe from the instant they were introduced, for he knew the doctor had Jessica's welfare at heart. However, as he took to coming home earlier in hopes of reaching understanding more to his liking with his wife, he also became aware of how much time the doctor spent with her. If he arrived for tea, David was there. If he arrived after tea, David had been there. If he arrivd just in time for dinner, David was staying. David, David, David! He was sick of David. He knew they saw each other only in open view of the staff, but Jessica so obviously enjoyed his company. Sometimes when he opened the door, he could hear peals of laughter coming form the drawing room; yet when he stepped into the room, the laughter died.

Usually Jessica and David sat in chairs facing each other, but one day she had carelessly flooped onto a settee. When Jonathan entered, he quickly sat beside her and slid his arm across her shoulder. Jessica froze. She was trapped.

"You're home early, Jonathan. Let me pour you some tea," she said too gaily.

"Don't bother," he said, holding her still with pressure from his finger, just over her shoulder when she started to move forward. He knew David had observed the exchange but he did not care. Jessica was his and he would not give her up to this doctor who also loved her. Thank God Jessica, in her innocence, was not yet aware of his feelings, for it would not occur to her that a man would fall in love with a married woman, especially one had had had two children. He nuzzled her neck instinctively with a bent finger and felt a tiny quiver course through her. He was glad David had not been able to see that—was his touch that repugnant to her?

"You must help me, Jonathan," she said quickly. "I have been trying to persuade David to have Christmas dinner with us, but he insists on leaving town."

"I'm sure Doctor Forsythe knows he would be welcome with us, my dear, but you cannot expect him to desert his family during the holiday season."

Jessica started when he dropped his hand over hers in her lap. What is he doing, she wondered. He's practically wrapped around me here in the drawing room. She flushed bright pink and turned to appeal to him silently with her eyes. But he shocked her even more by whispering, "You are lovely today, darling," and kissed her lightly on the cheek.

"Thank you," she answered with as toss of her head. "I must feed the baby," she practically shouted and jumped to her feet. She sprinted for the hall and disappeared.

Jonathan sighed and leaned back to pull off his

boots, one foot tugging on the other. "She is still running from me," he mumbled.

"Do you blame her? You deliberately humiliated her," snapped David.

"I know," he muttered wretchedly. "But I wanted you to. . ."

"I got the message, Jonathan, but it was not necessary. If you weren't so damned jealous, you would see I never had a chance. It's you she loves and always has."

"Loves!" he scorned. "She managed to hide it well."

"Be patient," David said quietly.

"Patient! What the hell do you think I have been? I'm married to the most beautiful girl in the world—beautiful in more ways than appearance too, I know her worth—yet I haven't touched her or any woman for a year and a half. How much patience must I have?"

"I'm sorry. I doubt I could have had the willpower you have had."

"You were right, David. I am jealous—jealous because you can make her laugh. God, it just about kills me admit it. When I walk into a room, she turns into a piece of wood. I want her to come with me when I leave; instead she can hardly wait to be ride of me."

"Would it help, do you think, if I didn't come here anymore?"

"No, David, I don't think that would help at all. She needs every friend she can get. In fact, you know you really are welcome for Christmas. I know you were here last year." The two walked into the hall together, shook hands, and separated—David to go home and Jonathan to find Mrs. Winters.

When he found her in the kitchen fixing a tray, he asked, "Is that for my wife?"

"Yes, sir," she answered.

"Better make it for two again, Mrs. Winters. Call me when it's ready." She moved to get another tray, shaking her head. These two, she muttered. Well, at least he will carry the trays for me.

"Come in," Jessica said to the knock on her door.

"Your servant, madam," said Jonathan when he entered, trays in hand.

Jessica closed her book and asked, "What are you doing now?"

"I'm bringing dinner again. Would you please clear the table?"

"No, I won't. I don't like this game you are playing." She angrily threw her book on the bed and, arms akimbo, paced across the room and back. "Get out, Jonathan," she said determinedly.

"Jessica, I have tried to refuse you nothing, but this request I am refusing."

"If you will notice, it was not a request."

"I asked David to reconsider about Christmas," he said, taking her offguard.

"Why did you have to fondle me in front of him? You are constantly humiliating me."

"I am constantly trying to tell you I love you. If *you* didn't get the message, it seems David did."

Elsie interrupted with Joshua. Jonathan took the fussing child from his nurse and swung him high into the air. Joshua squealed with glee while Jessica gasped with fear. He pulled the baby back into the shelter of his arms and slipped his other arm around his wife, who immediately escaped to arrange the table. When she had finished, he set his son on the floor, letting him scamper away on all fours.

"Jessica," he said while they were eating, "are we to continue this way the rest of our lives? You once said you could not stand for us to be polite strangers. Must I be exiled in my own home—allowed to look but never to touch my beautiful wife?"

"I don't want to discuss it." When he said nothing else, she finally raised her eyes to see a broad smile covering his face. Her anger flared until she realized he was looking past her. Spinning in her chair, she giggled at her son who was sitting by the wardrobe trying to flail his way from under several gowns he had pulled down on himself. Jonathan sensed the boy's frustration and plucked him out of the material before he cried. Jessica felt a pang in her heart when the boy put his arms around his rescuer's neck.

Christmas came and went. Jessica was touched when her husband presented her with a gift of the jewelry Jimmy had pawned to gain passage for them so long ago. With a leering gleam in his eye, Jonathan said, "I expect you to hold on to it this time. It has taken me a long time to accumulate your family jewels you disposed of so carelessly."

"Thank you, Jonathan," she said fondly. "Nothing could mean more to me, and I thought they were gone forever."

Jonathan's spirits soared but briefly. She was grateful to him but not enough to give in. Still, he reasoned, she's not angry today.

January and February flew by with matters between them pretty much at a standstill. If Mr. Selby was not home, they often dined together in her room. His ship returned and he kept putting off his departure; he had found a completely reliable man and could have left weeks ago. He was determined that she would come with him, but she had never even given him a chance to voice the idea. Jessica looked relieved when he announced at the dinner table he was sailing for America March fifteenth, one week away. he was sick at what he was going to do, but he could think of no less cruel way to handle his wife—he had to take her with him. She was so relieved he was leaving that she had gone over all his clothes, mending and seeing to their laundering, cleaning, pressing. It seemed she intended him to be a neat bachelor.

"Jonathan!" she shouted as she charged into his room the night before he was to leave. "What is this about taking Joshua with you? You can't! I won't let you!"

"What do you propose to do about it?" he asked coldly.

"Well," she said, casting her eyes about her frantically. "I'll do something."

"Madam, there is nothing you can do. He is my son and I am taking him with me to my home when I leave tomorrow. You didn't really think, did you, that I would let you keep him here?"

"But you promised!"

"Promised what? I never promised to sail off and leave him behind."

Jessica was frantic. She could not lose another son. She would have nothing. Her life would be over if she lost Joshua. "Your father won't let you. I'll speak to him," she flung over her shoulder as she turned to go.

"You should know he will be able to do nothing but call me names. The law is on my side. A man is in control of his family and I say the boy comes with me." Jonathan did not feel so cold as he sounded. She may never trust him again, but he was as desperate as she. God, her agony nearly crushed his resolve—he wanted to wrap her in his arms, not crush her like some defenseless fragile moth. No! He had played the waiting game long enough. Even if she hated him, he could not let her win this time.

She was unaware that her eyes betrayed her resolve—she grasped at a plan—and he knew she planned to run away with Joshua during the night.

He moved slightly to the side and swept his arms to reveal the cradle behind him. "As you can see, my dear," he said, "Joshua will sleep here tonight. There will be no running away this time."

She collapsed on the bed in tears, and he almost relented. But he must remain hardened to her sobbing to save them both. Finally he said, cruelly, "Crying will win you no concessions. You've worked that magic on me for the last time, so you can stop that little act right now."

"Act?" she raged, her tears suddenly gone. "You tear my son from my arms and say I am acting? I never thought you so callous, you cold unfeeling brute. I hate you!" she spat.

"Why should you be surprised? You have always known I value my family above everything else."

"But you promised!" she wailed. "I trusted your word as a gentlemen."

"I'm sick of being a gentleman. If I were less a gentleman, you would have been in this bed with me long ago."

Realization dawning on her finally, she asked incredulously, "Are you saying you are open to bribery? You will leave my son behind if I share your bed?"

"And will you resort to bribery, madam?" his voice taunted her wickedly. "Will you exchange your body for your son?" Sensing her surrender as she thought one night wouldn't be too bad, he added nastily, "I'm sorry to disillusion you. There will be no such bargain. I am not interested in such a noble sacrifice."

Humiliated that she had even thought to use her body as an instrument and then to be so completely rejected, she rose to pound him with her fists. He knew how despicable he was or he would not stand here and let her beat on him. "Your word is worth nothing!" she raged.

Grabbing her wrists to stop her ineffectual pummeling, he said slyly, "My word? Exactly what did I promise you?"

"You promised not to take my son away from me," she wailed.

"But I'm not. Only your stubbornness is separating you from your son." Questioning eyes gazed at him. She clearly did not yet understand his plan. "You can come with him," he added softly.

"You can't mean that!" she exploded as the full

meaning of his words reached her. "You wouldn't want a wife who will hate you for this!"

"You're right, but I do want a wife, the wife who is already mine. Make no mistake, Jessica. I do want you but whether or not you come is your choice. Our son is coming with me and you are welcome to accompany him if you want. But there will never again to running away to escape your hateful husband. If you decide to join us, you will stay and be my wife."

There was only firmness in his voice and Jessica knew he had truly outwitted her. She could give in to his demands or she could lose her son forever. The choice was hers. Woodenly she walked from his room, utterly defeated at last.

Later Jonathan said to his father, "What do you think she will do?"

"I don't know," the old man answered in a subdued voice. "Couldn't you have found a kinder way?"

"Father, do you honestly think I wanted to be so cruel? I hope she believed me because I don't think I could, in the end, take our son from her. But I must go and I can't leave her behind either."

The old man nodded his understanding. He didn't want to lose her either. When Jonathan invited him to come along, it took all his resolve to say, "No, son, if I come, she will turn to me. You need time alone to smooth out the difficulties between you. I just hope it's not too late."

Chapter Nineteen

The next morning Jonathan paced at the bottom of the stairs, waiting to see who came down prepared to leave with him. Would she give in? If she didn't, could he take Joshua? He loved this son every bit as much as he had loved his first, but he also loved his wife. What might she do if he left her with no child? He was spared contemplating those possibilities when she swept down the stairs, eyes averted from him. "We are here as you commanded, master."

He was so relieved to see her he didn't care how haughty she acted. Elsie followed with Joshua, who squealed with extended arms when he saw his father. Smiling at his son, he said quickly, "I'm so glad you decided to be reasonable, madam."

Jessica moved toward the door, saying, "I had little choice, my lord. See to my baggage, will you? I understand Joshua's is already gone."

Holding his son, Jonathan helped his wife and then Elsie into the waiting carriage before climbing in himself. She stared out the window, saying nothing, all the way to the waterfront.

"Wait here," said Jonathan. "I will have to signal a boat to come for us."

In a few minutes he returned to lead them to the waiting boat. Elsie was clearly frightened so he handed her down to Donald first. After handing the boy to

Donald, he stepped into the boat and turned to lift down his wife. She stiffened but allowed him to help her.

During the short ride to the ship, the boat tossed on the high waves, and Jessica could feel her breakfast rolling in her stomach. She would not be sick, she vowed. This would be the crowning blow to her ego. Swallowing hard, she felt a little better and smiled wanly at her success. Jonathan heard a moan escape her and turned to watch her struggle. Yes, she had as much fight as ever, he thought.

Finally the boat bumped against the ship and the sailors quickly grabbed the rope ladder on the side. Donald scampered aboard, still holding the boy, who gazed in wonder at the strange sights around him. Elsie climbed up awkwardly, and Jessica was about to follow suit when Jonathan picked her up in one arm and carried her up the ladder as if she were weightless. Elsie and Joshua had already disappeared when he set her on the deck.

"Where is my son?" But he had turned to speak to a sailor at his side. When he had given the orders for the sailing, he led Jessica below deck to his cabin. "This will be your home until we reach New Orleans," he said, opening the door. "You will please remain inside except for a turn on the deck on a nice afternoon or evening."

"This is not my first sailing, sir. I know the deck belongs to the men in the mornings. Where is my son?" she asked angrily. "I shall want him with me."

"He is already in the cabin he is to occupy with his nurse," he answered. As she moved toward the door, he added, "It is much too small for another. You will stay here. When he is awake during the day, he will be brought here to you."

"Where are you staying?" she asked coyly.

"Right here with you, my dear," he answered with a leer.

Shrugging her shoulders, Jessica turned and began to

unpack the sea chests Donald had tugged through the door. After one hasty glance, she avoided looking at the narrow bunk against the wall. She supposed it was big enough for two, but what did it matter if she must be submissive? She blushed at the thought and turned to find her husband watching her. Angry that he might have read her thoughts, she slammed the lid on the chest, knowing full well there was little room to unpack anything and she must, one more time, accustom herself to living from a chest.

The tension between them was relieved when Donald banged in again, this time carrying two cups of strong coffee. "Thought you might want to warm up after that ride in the wind, mum." Setting the cups on the table, together with a plate of biscuits, he backed from the room.

"Come, Jessica," said Jonathan pulling out a chair for her, "we are going to be in very close quarters for some time. Let us strive to make the hours we will be together as pleasant as possible." She sat down without a murmur. When she noticed him smiling at her, she tilted her chin and looked down her nose.

"I will leave you now," he said, rising. "Try not to miss me too much, darling." He ducked just in time to evade the cup flying toward him. Throwing back his head, he laughed heartily. She fumed behind the closed door. She would never be able to take this humiliation. She had been a fool to think she could. What else was she to do? She threw herself on the bunk as if to cry over her plight, but the tears refused to come.

After tossing the turning, she arose to loosen her garments, but decided instead to seek her son. When she stepped out of the door, she faced Donald who clearly was guarding her. Bowing low, he opened the door across from hers. Her son slept soundly in his cradle carefully watched by Elsie. So Jonathan was not so cruel as he would have her believe.

When he returned in a thoughtful mood, she had

bathed and changed. He noticed she had unpacked and rearranged until the cabin looked roomier and even homey. There was a cloth on the table and the bed was turned back for the heat from the stove to warm the sheets. Very little was said while they ate. When Donald came for the dishes, the air was heavy with silence. He blushed as Jessica thanked him profusely and left quickly. She glanced about the room nervously and bounced into a chair by the stove. She quickly picked up some handwork and began punching her needle through the material until she had a complete mess. Pulling the needle from the thread, she started pulling out the threads she had just sewed. She felt rather than saw Jonathan's grin as he watched from the corner of his eyes.

"Damn!" she said, throwing the sampler across the small room. Walking over to pick it up, he put it on the table. Then he lifted her from her chair and stood her on the floor. "Jessica, my love, is sleeping with me so terrible that you will ruin perfectly good work and stay up all night to avoid it?"

"Jonathan, please don't make fun of me," she asked.

"I am sorry, my pet, but you seem to ask many things of me without giving anything in return."

"You know I want no part of this. Why do you insist?"

Spinning her around and unbuttoning the back of her dress he said softly, "I keep hoping you will change your mind, love." She was surprised when he stalked to the door—even more so when he added, "I will leave you now and give you the privacy you so obviously desire. It is not my intention to embarrass you, though why you always want to hide that beautiful body is beyond me. When I return, I expect to find you in bed, not nodding in some chair."

Grateful for the time he had given her, she scurried to undress, don a nightgown, and fold her clothes. She hung up the coat he had thrown over the desk chair and straightened up the cabin. When he returned, she was indeed in the bunk with her back to the room. He put out the candles before undressing and slid under the quilts beside her. He knew she was only pretending to be asleep because her body was stiff and her breathing uneven. Sighing heavily, he lay down and turned so his back touched hers. He felt her relax gradually and knew when she did really sleep.

When he awakened near dawn, the room was cold and she had fitted her body into the contours of his for warmth. She had flung her arm around him and her breasts teased his back as she breathed. He could feel his manhood rising and barely controlled himself from rolling over and taking her right then. She would be furious if he took such advantage of her, but she had better give in soon or he might lose his willpower. He rolled on to his back and she caressed his chest in her sleep.

Her hand became still and he looked down into her eyes. "My dear," he said lightly, trying to keep his voice even. "I'm going to think you are not so reluctant as you say if you keep doing that." She flung her body away as if struck, and he slid out of the narrow bunk before she could see how she had aroused him. Pulling on his breeches and jacket, he rushed from the room. When he returned, she wore a robe but she had heard him talking in the companionway. "I told George we would be four for breakfast, so you had better dress quickly."

She practically flew across the room, throwing her robe aside as she went. He watched her back as she stood at the chest with her gown half off, trying to find a shift. When she reached up to put her arms through, she let the gown fall and wriggled her enticing body into her underwear but not before he glimpsed the length of her. Did she know what she was doing, he wondered, or was she so unaware of the effect she had on a man? She started to brush her hair, dressed in the shirt, until he muttered hoarsely, "God, Jessica, cover up!"

"Well, you don't have to look," she retorted. But she reached for a gown at the same time—one that opened in the front, thank heaven. He could not have buttoned her dress without grabbing at her. Elsie carried Joshua into the cabin, and Jessica was playing with him— bouncing him on her lap—when George came in with breakfast. Jonathan tied the happy boy onto a chair and Elsie fed him porridege from one of the bowls. "I can see you are trying to make me an unnecesary part of my son's life," said Jessica quietly.

"You will never be unnecessary to him, Jess. But it's time he was weaned. When we get home, he will be over a year old." Elsie hesitated, not knowing what to do. But Jonathan nodded at her to continue and dropped his hand over his wife's. Holding her firmly when she tried to pull away, he said with emotion, "We both need you, darling. He will be every bit as lovable as a boy as he was as a baby. Let him grow."

"I couldn't stop him if I wanted to," she said quickly.

"But you do want to, don't you?"

She knew he was right, but that didn't stop the hurt of knowing her son could get along without her. She had thought her position so safe only to realize she couldn't get along without him instead. She ate mutely and left the table to make up the bunk as soon as she was finished. Elsie left to clean up Joshua, for he had slobbered all over himself and his clothing. Jessica could feel Jonathan's eyes on her back but she couldn't turn around.

Suddenly his arms snaked around her waist and he pulled her back to lean on him, "Jess, don't hurt so. Don't withdraw and shut me out again."

Turning to cry onto his shirt, she whispered, "I can't help it. It does hurt to know I am no longer necessary to anyone."

Anger and exasperation replaced the tenderness with

which he held her. Gripping here elbows, he held her away from him and a frown creased his brow as his voice rose. "Stop this! Since when has a mother's only duty been to suckle her child?" He shook her roughly until she looked at him, half afraid. "Dammit, grow up! Where will he learn love and gentleness if not from you. I wish I'd had my mother's gentle hand past the age of six. I might not be so mean as you seem to think I am if I had."

"You're not mean, Jonathan," she said and meant it.

"That's not what you said our last night in London."

"I was angry and just as hateful as you were."

"You bring a great deal of pleasure into both our lives, Jessica." Pulling her gently against him he added, "Both of us need you and will for a long time." Then he stalked from the cabin and did not return until well past the time for lunch. He met her coming out the cabin door. "I'll be right back. Did you eat?" He nodded and she carried Joshua into the other cabin and put him in the cradle. When she came back, he was working at the desk and did not look up. She picked up the few things scattered around, saying only, "Little boys can wreck a room in no time. I kept him from the desk. Is there anything else he should not touch?"

Looking askance at her and the cabin, he murmured, "No, he can explore all he wants." No mention was made of what had occurred earlier. Jonathan dreaded dinner but aboard ship dinner is early. He was relieved, when Elsie carried Joshua in, to see Jessica tie Joshua into the chair and feed him from the table herself. She made quite a game of it and all of them enjoyed it, especially Joshua. Before turning to her own now-cold dinner, she handed her son a bread crust, saying, "If only your father had some nice fat book, you'd be able to reach the table and feed yourself in a week."

God, this woman amazed him. When George cleared away the remains from the dinner and Elsie and Joshua retired to their cabin, Jonathan returned to work at his desk. He watched through lowered eyelids as Jessica strolled to the chest, picking out a nightgown and robe. She stepped out of her dress and bathed as well as one can from a basin and slipped the gown over her glistening body. The little tease knows I am watching, he thought. As her arm brushed her very full breast, she winced and Jonathan knew the complete and sudden weaning of their son was more painful for her physically then she would admit. Nonchalantly she picked up her sampler and this night she calmly repaired the disaster of last night.

After the first day Jonathan always appeared just before dinner to escort his family topside. Elsie thought she should stay below, but Jessica quickly insisted she needed air and exercise even if they did not need her services, so the four of them, Jonathan holding his son, made a pleasant group; and the crew, especially Donald, enjoyed seeing their captain so content. Joshua excitedly pointed at clouds, men, whatever captured his interest, while his father pronounced the names for him—rope, Donald, wheel, sail, on and on went the list.

Meals were sometimes a little messy since a few days out to sea Donald had come into the cabin with a box, saying, "For the little one's chair, mum, since the captain don't have any thick books." Jessica soon gave up on table linens but was secretly pleased that Jonathan was so patient and did not seem to mind the boy's fumbling efforts to feed himself. At least her child would never be banished to the nursery.

Jonathan knew Jessica was hiding something from him and worried about it momentarily a few times. A smile covered his face the day he opened the cabin door and Joshua walked halfway across the cabin door, screaming, "Pa! Pa!" Jonathan swooped him into the air just as he lost his balance while the child squealed in delight. "So this is your secret," he said.

"You guessed!" she cried disappointedly.

"Only that you were keeping something from me, my

dear," he hastened to explain, not wanting to spoil her surprise.

With the passing of time, the weather became milder and soon, because they sailed south, the cabin seemed hot. Jonathan awakened one morning barely seconds before he would have taken his wife. She was wearing a gown that barely covered the top half of her body. During the night the skirt had twisted about her waist and she pressed her body to his with her breasts spilling from her gown and tickling his chest. Her hand roamed over his back and buttocks and he was fully aroused. Jumping from the bunk as if he had been shot, he gripped the back of the chair, fighting for control of his body. Gasping from the effort, he threw on his clothing and stormed from the cabin.

He avoided his wife that day except for the stroll on deck. He made up tasks to keep him away from her until she had retired. When he lifted the blankets to slip in beside her, there was only a sheet, the quilts having been packed away. It's not that hot at night, he thought. When she rolled and touched his body with hers, he moaned until he heard her giggle. As realization of her intent swept over him, he lost the control he had struggled for so long. His hands flew over her body as he moaned, "Jess, Jess, I've waited so long." The first time was disappointing, for he had indeed waited so long, but the others following exceeded all her expectations. Over and over his hands aroused her desire to near madness, and each time she felt the pleasure of fulfillment. Her aggressiveness startled them both as she reached for him. They dozed only lightly before their need drove them to possess each other once more. Dawn spilled through the porthole as he moaned, "I wish I could keep you here all day, too. If I don't let you alone, you'll never be able to chase our son all day."

He started to turn from her, but she reached for him again, whispering, "Elsie can chase him." Groaning with renewed hunger, he rolled toward her, and once more the mindless ecstasy enveloped them.

Donald peeped in with breakfast but withdrew quickly with a pleased grin. He and Elsie watched Joshua in her small cabin and allowed Jessica and Jonathan the day together. They did not spend the entire day in the narrow bunk, but neither left the cabin, not wanting to be away from the other's presence. However, the next morning they were ready to face the others and Jonathan opened the door to demand breakfast for four.

The remainder of the journey sped by too quickly for Jessica while their love blossomed anew. She had never been so happy. When she asked where they would go, Jonathan told her about *Terra Diablo* and jokingly said he expected her to choose a more appropriate name. Gradually she became aware of his suffering when she left. Was he the devil? He must have been terrible. Finally the morning came when Jonathan bound his books into a large box and led his family ashore.

Steve smiled when he saw Jessica, but frowned in puzzlement at the boy in Jonathan's arms.

"I'm glad you're back," he said tenderly, hugging Jessica. "But who is this?"

"It seems my wife takes to the sea when she is expecting a child," Jonathan teased.

"You don't really look very happy to see me," Jessica said quickly. "Why are you frowning?"

"I was hoping to send your husband on another trip, but I can see that's out now," he answered.

"Maybe we can all go," Jessica said laughing. "Don't take me seriously," she hastened to add at his new frown. "I hope I never set foot on a ship again, though this trip was very pleasant, especially the last half."

"What is it?" asked Jonathan quietly.

"Come inside," said Steve as he led the way. Once inside, they could see he was having trouble getting to the point as he brought chairs forward, then poured and served him and Jonathan drinks.

"Jessica, would you like to go out to Fairhaven? Callie will be so excited and Geoff is expecting you for at least a quick visit."

"How can he be expecting me?"

"Let's say we hoped you would be coming."

"If you want me off again, Jessica can know about it, too. What is this all about?" demanded Jonathan. He held his wife's hand when she murmured, "Oh, no!" and smiled reassuringly.

"We've been watching for you for a week. The men on the *Golden Hawk* said you were about ready to sail when they left."

"There was no hurry that I knew of, so we took our time," said Jonathan. "Now get to it!"

"There may be word of Jeremy," he said softly.

Jessica gasped her pleasure and leaped to her feet. "Tell me! Tell me where! Has he been found?"

"Calm down, Jessica. I don't know."

Jonathan held her in his arms as Steve told them what he knew. A child, two years old, had been located in Mexico and there was a possibility he was Jeremy. He needed to be identified.

"Jonathan, you must go," cried Jessica.

"You truly are the most changeable woman I know. A few minutes ago you were saying, 'oh, no,' at the thought of my leaving," he teased.

"But this is different!"

"You've had this news a week?" he asked Steve, who nodded calmly.

"Can't we both go?" asked Jessica, turning to her husband.

"No, we can't," he answered sternly as he noticed Steve leading Elsie and Joshua outside. He sat down in a nearby chair and pulled her down on top of him. "Jess," he said sternly, "I know waiting is one of the things you do worst, but this time you must wait for news."

258

"Jonathan, why?"

"If I am to go, I can go faster alone—twice as fast. Do you want me to send someone else and wait with you? I will, you know."

"No, you go, Jonathan."

"Will you be here when I get back? I couldn't stand it if you take off again."

"Jonathan, you told me to 'grow up.' I thought I'd been doing rather well."

"Darling, you have. But I will not go unless I have your assurance that you will not run off from me again."

"I will be waiting for you when you bring Jeremy home." He winced at her statement. This would not do. "Let's go to Fairhaven," he said, standing her on her feet.

"No, Jonathan, you will end up losing a whole day. You can leave from here. Let me have my way in this, please," she wheedled. "If I know Steve, he has everything ready for you. Just promise to hurry back."

She has grown up, he thought as he held her so tightly she could hardly breathe. "Jess," he groaned. "Don't get your hopes up too high. Steve said it may be Jeremy—not that it *is*."

"I can't help hoping."

"I know, but don't depend on it too much. I don't want you to be disappointed again." She clung to him as if she could not let go, but soon stepped back and smiled bravely. "Take care, darling. Callie will guard us."

She walked out of the room stiffly and he knew her bravery was only a pretense, but he was proud of her determination. She would be all right with Geoff, and Callie would help her to keep her perspective. Besides, this time she had Joshua to need her.

Jonathan did not go out to see his son, feeling that he could not go through another farewell to his wife. He watched her climb into Steve's carriage and give Steve

259

instructions of some kind.

I haven't prayed for years, he thought, but I do pray I can bring her good news this time. An hour later he was riding his chestnut stallion through the back streets, trying to leave town unseen. My God! Could it really be true? No wonder Steve didn't want to talk in front of Jessica! Thank God he instinctively omitted some details.

Chapter Twenty

"Don't try to stop me, Geoff. I am going."

"Jonathan said you were to wait here."

"I can't help what he said. I'm going."

"Jessica, can't you ever do what you're told?"

"Geoff," she said with lowered voice, "try to understand. This is something I can do for Jonathan. Besides, my memories of Fairhaven are not so fond, you know. I lost Jeremy here."

"But to go off in the wilderness by yourself—it's out of the question."

"I won't be alone. There will be Joshua and Elsie and Callie, if you will give her up this quickly."

The argument had raged since Jessica had come down to breakfast and announced her intentions. When the wagons stopped at Fairhaven on their way to the new plantations, Jessica intended to accompany them to the home she had never seen. "Geoff, there is every reason I should go. Now, may I take a carriage or would it be more sensible to take a wagon?"

"A wagon," muttered Geoff, knowing she would defeat him again so he may as well give in. There was no telling when the men would get here—probably a day or two to unload the ship—so he may as well make preparations. "Did it ever occur to you that those men may not want to be bothered with three more woman and a baby? Do you want me to come with you?"

"You said earlier that you are too busy, so I will go alone. What I really want from you is the equipment I will need for several days on the trail and, of course, your blessing."

Geoff stared at her and wondered about this sister of his. Was she just being willful, as usual? or did she truly need something to do?

When Jessica had arrived the day before with Joshua and Elsie, Geoff and Callie had both been delighted. She hastily explained that she had been sent until Jonathan's return. Callie had taken charge immediately and installed her former mistress as if she were still the lady of the manor. Indeed Geoff was more than happy that she assume such a position.

Callie was thrilled with Joshua but more delighted that her master and mistress had found each other again. She was alarmed when Jessica told them where Jonathan had gone because she did not really believe in the success of his mission, but she could see that Jessica had changed and would be able to deal with failure if she needed to do so.

Listening to the argument between Geoff and his sister, Callie recognized Jessica's determination. "Let her go, Mister Geoff," she said after the girl walked from the room. "You should know she's not the type to wait with nothing else to do."

"But Callie, she doesn't know what she's getting into. That is a dangerous trip," he argued.

"Can't you see how she's changed? She wants to go home and have it ready for her man when he come to her—with or without their first son."

"Do you really believe that, Callie? Are you sure she's not running away again because Jonathan left her behind?"

"Look where she is running," the woman answered quietly.

Geoff's brow furrowed with deep thought. "But God only knows what she will find there from the stories we've heard about Jonathan."

"All the more reason why she should go. If Master Jon's news is disappointing, she should not have to face that hardship yet—the trip and the house. They will be behind her and she can concentrate on what family she has left"

"All right, Callie, you've convinced me," said Geoff with a smile. "Do you agree to go?"

"I think everything and everyone that belongs here should go this time. That way you can start to set your life in order too."

Geoff nodded agreement and sent Callie to attend to the matter, but he would certainly miss her—she knew more about Fairhaven than he did, even though he had owned it for almost two years.

"What are you going to wear?" Callie asked Jessica a little later.

Eying the large woman warily, Jessica asked, "Why should I change?"

"Miss Jessica, we will probably leave tomororw. Who knows when we will return? Surely you won't leave without visiting Missus Atkins."

"Oh, Callile, you make me so ashamed," cried Jessica. "Of course, I must see her. Should I take Joshua, do you think?"

"That would be real nice, but why don't you ride over? You may want the exercise before we start our trek tomorrow. If I know you, you'll want to ride on the way 'cause you'll get tired bouncing in a wagon."

Jessica changed into a riding outfit and soon cantered across fields and through trees to arrive at Maude Atkins house a short time later. As she stepped on the porch, the door opened and she found herself engulfed in a great bear hug. "Lordy, girl, how good to see you," boomed the older woman. "How's that husband of yours? A lot better since you're back, I'm sure."

Jessica and Maude, arms around each other's waist,

moved inside where they promptly fell into a conversation that brought them up-to-date on the details of each other's lives. Maude was apprehensive about Jessica's departure but could see her reasoning and reluctantly agreed she should go. "If you're to leave so soon, I'm riding back to see that boy of yours, if that's all right with you," she hastened to add.

"Oh, please do," cried Jessica. "I almost brought him along, but Callie thought I needed to work into riding before we started."

On their way to the stable, Maude asked, "How's Jeremiah?"

"He's fine," Jessica replied. But after thinking about it for a moment, she mused, "I'm sure he must be lonely with us gone. I must write to tell him of the latest developments before we leave."

Maude ended up staying all day and helping Callie and Jessica get ready, though Jessica insisted she had little to do because she hadn't unpacked. How could she ever have forgotten all she had left behind her so long ago? All Jonathan's personal belongings had to be packed as well. Leaving the clothes to Callie, she and Maude tackled the library.

"Geoff says we should take everything from his house that is to go. I have no idea what books Jonathan wants." Jessica looked about her helplessly. "I've hardly even been in here."

"If Jonathan is like most men, his study is sacrosanct. I'd pack everything. Notice that those books have been read. They are not window dressing as they are in so many houses," said Maude.

Jessica nodded her agreement, but was amazed at the enormity of the task confronting her. "I'll have a couple of the boys pack the books, and I'll do the desk myself." Callie sent in some boys who dragged in several wooden boxes with them. They left almost immediately for more boxes when Jessica said all the books were to go. She filled two boxes with Jonathan's papers from the desk, labeling each pile according to the drawer from which it had been taken. The work was tedious and dull, but she finished soon, thinking she had no right to read personal papers—even her husband's.

By the time everything was ready to be loaded onto wagons, it became obvious Geoff's two wagons would never be enough. Maude offered two more, but suggested they tour the house, including the attic, to make sure her wagon would be enough. Jessica, Callie, and Maude climbed the stairs to the storage room at the top of the house, but found very little to add to the growing pile. "Thank heaven my husband is not a saver," said Jessica.

Before leaving, Maude asked kindly, "Do you want me to come with you?"

"Maude, I don't know what to say," said Jessica frowning. "I'd love to have your company, but this is a terrible time to leave your own place. I have no doubt Jeremiah will be here by fall, especially when I tell him about Jeremy. What don't you come with him? Could he stay with you until someone will bring him?"

"I'd love to have him," said Maude. "But don't be surprised if I keep him."

"You're a sly, wily woman, Maude Atkins, and nothing could please me more than for you two to get together. I'll write him tonight, but remember he's wily too and has avoided women for years."

After Maude rode off, the hard work of fitting the accumulated stack of goods on the wagons began. It seemed they had barely started when Maude's wagons rumbled up the drive. One wagon had to be saved for the women's and baby's quarters, and the other three were filled quickly. Jessica was amazed at the amount one amassed, especially as she and Jonathan were seldom here. Of course, the nursery furniture had to go—Geoff certainly had no use for it, at least not yet. Callie insisted on packing a few dishes, cooking utensils, and bed linens; no one knew what Jonathan had purchased for the new home.

Geoff finally called a halt to the proceedings. "You will be too tired to travel if you keep this up," he said, drawing Jessica away from all the activity.

"I must write to Father Selby tonight yet. You will see that the letter gets off, won't you?"

"Jessica, you *have* changed. You would have told me to do it before," said her brother.

"Geoff, I am doing the right thing, am I not?" she asked timidly.

He embraced his sister briefly before saying, "You have convinced me. You haven't spent this day pining for your husband and building up false hope. If you want to do this for him, I'm proud of you."

"I keep thinking he may be angry and not like whatever I do there."

"Jess, you know you could do anything to the house you want and Jonathan wouldn't care—not if you really liked it rather than acted in a fit of temper. You have found a unique man, my dear sister. I would never put up with what he has, let alone bring you back for more."

"I wasn't that bad, Geoff. After all, he owes me his life," she replied, tossing her head in the air.

"Callie would have brought him through. You're lucky she allowed you to tend him."

Jessica had not stopped to think about that. She had always thought they were about equal in their obligations to each other. She knew the good times were good for both of them. Jonathan had guarded her carefully and stayed with her when Jeremy was born. He had suffered alone because she left him even before she sailed away. She had never realized how selfish she had been during that time of their lives. In truth he had made all the concessions. How much he must love her to put up with her silliness and, as Geoff had said, to ask for more! Only now did it strike her how cruel she had been to keep Joshua's birth from him. Always she had considered only herself. Thank God he had forced her to come with him.

Geoff watched his sister from his chair across the room thinking that, yes, she had changed. What was it now?

Dismay appeared on her face at the pain she had so carelessly and selfishly caused both of them. Suddenly smiling in that special way that would win anyone to her, she confessed, "Do you know, Geoff, when I was acting like a spoiled brat because Jonathan wanted me to let Joshua feed himself, he told me to 'grow up.' I think I have. What do you think?" she asked brightly.

He smiled his answer. Yes, she had finally grown up. His sister had become a wife and mother who would put her family first. She was no longer a little girl who ran away from problems. From the first Jonathan had seen the woman she could be rather than the child she was. He should have known that was the reason Jonathan agreed to the unlikely marriage in the beginning. Geoff only hoped he would be so wise when the time came that he considered marrying.

Shortly after a cold supper Geoff went to give the orders for a relaxing bath for his sister. "Come, Jess. You won't have a bath for days. You luxuriate and pamper hourself one last time and write your letter. When Jeremiah comes, as we both know he will, I'll bring him to *Terra Diablo*."

"Oh, Geoff, you don't have to wait so long, do you? Can't you get away before that? Besides," she added with a shy grin, "he's to stay with Maude and bring her to visit."

"You are a schemer, young lady," he teased.

"Yes, I am," she admitted before going into her room, leaving her brother gaping in the hall alone.

Donald frowned then smiled his approval when he learned how large a caravan he would be leading. "Does the missus know what the trip will be like?" he asked Geoff.

"You will take care of her, won't you?" Geoff asked quietly, though he knew the question was unnecessary.

"I've taken care of Jonathan for years, and I will do the same for his family."

Geoff watched the wagons pull out with mixed feelings, but Jessica seemed so happy to be off he could only wish her well. Callie had been right and after the midday meal Jessica moved from the wagon to her horse and rode beside the wagon most of the afternoon with a few excursions ahead to give her mount some exercise.

The first night out would tell whether or not the women could endure this trip, but Jessica found it rather exciting. Geoff had insisted they bring their own food and equipment and Callie made biscuits and a delicious stew. It seemed she was not completely homebound after all. She may have run the house a long time, but she still knew how to cook over an open fire. The women stayed to themselves with the exception of a short visit from Donald.

Jessica even decided to sleep under the wagon as the men did, leaving the cots for Callie and Elsie. Both of them objected, but Jessica cast their objections aside with, "Nonsense. Elsie is too afraid and, Callie, you get the best bed so you will not be too stiff to cook breakfast."

As she crawled under the wagon, keeping low to avoid hitting her head, she realized there would be no snuggling into the hard ground as there was in a bed. She flopped several times with little relief, so with a sight she finally lay still thinking, if the men could sleep, so could she. Her senses were next aroused by the aroma of strong coffee. Surprised she had slept so soundly, she scrambled to her feet and banged her head on the wagon above her. Ducking down, she crawled out, rubbing her head. Joshua spied her and ran toward her, tripping over a root sticking up from the ground. She grabbed him before he had a chance to cry. The boy, after screwing his face into a frown, opened his eyes to see his mother and crackled with merriment and pushed against her chest, squiggling to be free of restraint. Lowering him to the ground, she said, "Now you be careful, Josh." But he ignored her and tottered off in the opposite direction. She had been worried about how the trip would affect him, but he seemed to be holding up better than anyone.

When the wagons pulled out, she set him on the seat between her and the driver. His curiosity was limitless but his little body bounced so much that she pulled him up to her lap. He squirmed to crawl down until she turned him to face forward and straddle her own legs. Since he could see much better that way than he could cuddled against her, he was content and both of them were cooler.

Jessica had thought being among the heavy trees would be cool, but the oppressive heat filtered through the treetops. She uttered her thankfulness at least for the shade. She was surprised that so few people had come with them. She had thought their loyalty to Jonathan was stronger. However, she was secretly pleased that Geoff was able to command their loyalty so completely so quickly. Her brother continued to surprise her. It was too bad their father had suppressed Geoff's natural inclination to work hard because he would have been terribly proud of Geoff now. Of course, Geoff had only himself to blame. Not wanting to argue with his father, he had accepted the man's instructions to enjoy himself a little longer, though he had never thought his situation through deeply enough to realize he did not enjoy the life he was living. Oh well, there was no use mourning the waste now, and he had certainly proved himself. In less than four years he had saved Briarly Hill, paid off a mountain of his father's debts, migrated to America and accumulated a lovely plantation here. Yes, Geoff had done well. I may have begun much more slowly than he, but I'm on the right track now and will do just as well myself, she vowed.

One day on the trail seemed much like another until, five days after leaving Fairhaven, the little caravan moved from under the trees into a cleared area and Jessica knew that they would arrive at their destination soon. The tall grass waving in the gentle breeze was a welcome sight after the dense forest. The sun shone brightly here and a boy chased chased a butterfly through a field. The little blond lad gave up the chase when he heard the creaking wagons and raced back in the direction he had come. Who was this fair child? She knew that the men with them worked for Jonathan, but they were mostly Spanish. They lived here with their families, but she had no idea where. She had thought theirs to be the only house here. Then she saw a large house sitting in a grove of trees and thought that to be her home until the child crawled onto the porch, crying, "Mama! Mama!"

A blond woman rushed out the door to scoop up the boy and turned to look in the direction he was pointing. As she came down the steps, Jessica recognized her and standing in the wagon to wave, yelled, "Polly! Polly, it's me!" Without even waiting for the wagon to stop, Jessica scrambled down and ran across the tall grass. She had completely forgotten the strain between them when they had parted company the last time. She vaguely heard a child's squealing in the background but ran on to her friend who set her child on the ground and ran toward her. They ran into each other's arms and danced in the waving grass like young girls playing for an afternoon. Both laughed and cried and Jessica, with tears streaming down her face, cried, "Polly, I'm so happy to see you. We'll have such good times together."

"Is this Jeffrey?" asked Jessica finally remembering and muttering, "Polly, I'm so sorry."

"Forget it. It's over and I'm just glad to see you here," answered Polly quickly.

Jessica frowned slightly and looked at her friend. Polly beamed with such happiness that Jessica believed her and their last encounter was behind them forever. Questions bubbled from both of them so fast neither has time for an answer. Suddenly they laughed and hugged each other again. The childish squeals finally pierced Jessica's happiness and she said quickly, "I must go. Will you come over? Is it much farther?"

"We can walk from here—your house is just past those trees. Stay with me awhile and I'll take you over."

Nodding to her friend, Jessica ran back to the wagon for her son. "Callie, I'll be there soon. Do you mind going on without me?"

Callie, delighted at her young mistress's happiness, took over immediately. "We can unload and clean. You come when we're ready, Miss Jessica."

"There is no rush. Let the men see their families before you set them to work," said Jessica, and Callie knew her sensitive mistress really had returned. Jessica watched the wagons roll away then turned again to her friend. "Polly, Jeffrey, this is Joshua." The women, each with an arm about the other's waist and holding the hand of her child, walked slowly back to Polly's house.

When they reached the house, Polly rushed to prepare tea and remove a pot from the stove so she could take Jessica home when they finished. Jessica hastened to say, "Polly, finish what you were doing. I waited two years to come to this home Jonathan made for me. One hour more or less won't make any difference."

Polly looked at her friend quickly. Was Jessica now becoming a martyr and punishing herself? But she put the pot back on the stove. As she poured the tea and sat down across from her friend, she asked quietly, "Is it all right now, Jessica? Is the hurt gone?"

Jessica sighed as she looked at her friend's worried expression. All of these people had suffered with her, but she had been too blind to see it. "The hurt will never be gone, Polly." Then she added quickly, "But I can live with it. What I cannot live with is the agony I caused Jonathan."

Polly nodded but said nothing and waited for Jessica to go on. "Do you know, Polly, I was so embittered I didn't even tell him about Joshua. In fact, even after he moved into his father's house, I carefully avoided him—well, we avoided each other. Finally we met in the upstairs hall one night, quite by accident, and I thought I would die for loving him but I was too stubborn even to be civil. We saw each other occasionally after that, but I still kept Joshua hidden from him. How could I have done that, Polly?"

Polly watched while Jessica collapsed in tears. She wanted to embrace her friend, but knew instinctively that Jessica had passed the stage of requiring comfort. Besides, she was somewhat horrified by Jessica's behavior because she could never do such a thing to Jimmy. In a low voice she said, as Jessica wiped her tears and straightened to look her friend in the eye again, "I see Jonathan isn't with you." She wanted to ask why but couldn't bring herself to pry into her friend's affairs. If Jessica wanted her to know, she would explain.

"He thinks I am safe at Geoff's," she said levelly. At the questioning look on Polly's face, Jessica explained, "I must do, or at least try to do, something constructive to make up for the suffering I so selfishly caused him. We had planned to come directly here when we arrived in Louisiana, but he had to go away again. Polly, I have hurt him so many times he was half afraid I'd run off again if he left me—even to investigate a rumor about Jeremy. I think I convicned him I would be here when he returned. But I never had any intention of staying with Geoff as he suggested. After two years Jonathan deserves a home, so I came on ahead, determined it would be not only livable but comfortable when he returned—no matter what news he brings."

Now Polly walked around the table to embrace her friend. As they clung to each other, Polly said, "You're right, dear. He deserves so much from both of us. You stay for lunch and we'll both go over and get started. Between us we will set things aright for him."

When Jimmy came in for the noon meal, he found them happily working in the kitchen together with the boys playing at their feet. When he started with, "Miss Jessica," as he always had, he was soon corrected.

"I understand you are Jonathan's friend and partner in this horse business, so there will be no Miss Jessica." Taking the man's huge hands in her little ones, she said with seriousness to the embarrassed young man, "Jimmy, I owe you and Polly too much for you to treat me like the mistress of the estate. Please, can't we be friends?"

His hesitant smile was enough for now. It had taken awhile with Polly, but she was getting better at waiting.

Chapter Twenty-One

If Jessica lived forever, she would never forget her first vision of the house that was to be her home for the rest of her life. She felt Polly's excitement as they wended their way across the fields and through the trees. She gasped as they stepped from beneath the sheltering branches into another clearing. "It's beautiful!" Perched on a knoll directly in front of her stood a huge brick and wood house of Spanish design. This she had never expected. It nestled like a jewel in its own grove of trees which surrounded it on three sides. The sun shone brightly on the front as if to shower it with approval. The ocher brick had already faded to a tawny gold from the burning rays of the sun. Jessica could easily picture azaleas and honeysuckle vines climbing the rails of the veranda.

As they walked inside, she was surprised at the coolness that greeted her. She and Polly wandered randomly through the downstairs. Finally she realized the house was almost circular with a patio in the center and entrances to it from almost every room. What might have been a fountain had been started in the center and huge flat stones were stacked by the open end. The second floor rooms opened onto a balcony with a sweeping staircase at one end. In effect, the patio was the hub of this wheel-shaped house and could be reached from every room. Jessica wanted to start here and finish the outside room which could be more beautiful than any room inside.

However, she followed Polly up the staircase and they entered all of the rooms, Jessica mentally deciding who should have each room—even Mr. Selby, for she had no doubt he would soon be here. When she opened the door to the only room which had any furniture, she realized all over again that Jonathan had not cared whether he lived or died when he had been here. There was nothing to suggest comfort—a small bed, which he could never fit his large frame onto comfortably, and some unopened packing crates piled with a few tattered items of clothing. Her heart twisted when she saw how Spartanly he had existed during her absence.

"Polly, there is so much to do I don't know where to begin," she almost wailed.

Polly, always practical, said, "First, we must make sure all of you have a place to sleep—you can stay with me if you want."

Jessica immediately straightened her back, saying, "If I get too comfortable, I may take my time and not finish before Jonathan arrives. Let's find Callie."

They found Callie in the kitchen. There at least she could begin and she had not waited for her mistress to tell her what to do. She was elbow deep in soap suds, scrubbing cupboards and everything in sight. Jessica slumped onto a bench by the long table in the middle of the room and pulled Polly down beside her. A worried frown crossed Callie's brow; but when Jessica straightened, she smiled because she knew Jessica already had a plan for attacking the enormous job confronting her.

"First," said Jessica, "is Elsie with the children?" When the woman nodded solemnly, Jessica turned to Polly. "They will need to nap soon. Where can that be done?"

"Why not let them play outside? Your girl can take a blanket out, and they can sleep on the ground if they are really tired.'' When the look of pure pain flashed on Jessica's features, Polly gasped at what she had done. A hand flew to her mouth as if she thought she could call the words back and hold them in.

But Jessica shook the pained expression away and said determinedly, ''That's what we will do, but Callie, she must be careful not to fall asleep herself.''

Callie nodded silently and said, ''Then what?''

''Then, as Polly pointed out, we need places to sleep tonight. You get first choice. What room do you want?''

Callie's face softened at the kindness Jessica had shown her, but she said, ''I'll take one of the rooms behind the kitchen.''

Jessica jumped to her feet, saying, ''Let me see what's there.'' She strode off in a direction she had not bothered with before. Past the pantry there were two rooms with a connecting door. Neither would have much privacy, she mused. A knowing smile crossed her face and she turned to the woman behind her. ''Callie, these are your quarters. I just know that's what Jonathan intended—a bedroom and a sitting room with as much seclusion as you want.''

''But, Miss Jessica,'' the old woman started.

Jessica interrupted with, ''But nothing, Callie. My husband would never want you to be in a room with a connecting door for a stranger. No others live in, do they, Polly?'' When Polly shook her head, she continued, ''These are both for you. Choose where the bed will go and we'll see to it.'' She was back in the kitchen, the matter settled as far as she was concerned, while the other two stood shaking their heads at each other. She could be a whirlwind when she got started and they knew this was just the beginning.

''Callie, I need someone to help open those crates, at least enough to find the beds and bed furnishings. Jonathan and I will take the rooms at the front of the house; but if he thinks they will be two bedrooms, he doesn't know me very well. He did say once separate rooms lead to easy misunderstandings and we will have no more of those. See if some of the men's wives will help with the cleaning—today just the top layer so we won't be having to wash all the bed linens again when we really clean. Elsie can sleep, at least tonight, in the bed Jonathan used, but I want it moved to the end of the hall. Joshua will go next to her. The wing to the right will be for the children, however many that may be.''

She swept out of the kitchen, leaving Polly and Callie gasping after her. "Polly," she said when the girl scrambled after her. "Do you think we should open those crates upstairs first?'' Without waiting for an answer, almost as if she were thinking aloud, she continued, "No, we won't. They are obviously not beds, and that horrible room will be the last I will tackle. Just being able to see it occasionally will keep me at work. Let's look for Jonathan's study. This is obviously the dining room; that, the parlor. Now what about the rest? This has to be the library.'' She was off again opening doors, but not shutting them this time.

Polly followed helplessly, barely able to keep up with Jessica, whose mind had leaped far ahead of her friends. When they returned to the front of the house, where crate after crate filled the hall and parlor, Jessica sat down only to rise quickly when Donald appeared with several men following him, carrying hammers and claw hooks and other tools for opening boxes.

"Donald, I forgot about a room for you. How could I have been so thoughtless?'' she moaned.

"I have a place to sleep, mum. Don't worry about me.''

"Well, I will worry about it, but later if you are all right for now. I need these crates opened, especially those that might be beds.'' He nodded silently and pointed out those the men should unpack.

When the men had set to work, Polly said, "Jessica, I

came to help. What can I do?"

"Do? Why, you are going to sit here and help me decide. We are going to have a grand time—an early Christmas—opening packages." Hesitantly Polly sat on the crate beside her former mistress. She had come to work but this could be fun. She had been dying to see the contents of all those crates. The front of the house looked like a warehouse, there were so many.

Finally the banging stopped and Jessica looked at Polly. There were seven headboards standing against the crates. "Callie!" Jessica called. When the heavy Negress rushed in, thinking something had gone wrong, Jessica said, "These are the beds. Which do you want?"

Hands on her wide hips, Callie stared. Even she had never unpacked new furniture for an entire house at one time. She had also never had a choice before, always taking what she was given. Even though she knew her mistress meant every word she said, Callie chose the plainest of all the headboards. At Jessica's frown she said, "I wouldn't be able to sleep in them fancy beds," and went back to her work.

"That one is certainly for Jonathan," whispered Polly, pointing to the largest bed. It was heavy and too masculine for Jessica's taste, but she knew Polly was correct—Jonathan had chosen this for himself. So she directed the men to carry Jonathan's bed and Callie's to their rooms, put them together, including mattresses, then to move Elsie's. Then they were to open all the other crates so that she could inspect the contents, but they were not to unpack them. "Polly, do you know anything about the patio? We must get someone busy on that. I want it to be magnificent when my husband gets here."

"I do, ma'am," said a quiet voice behind her. When she turned, one of the men stepped forward. "I'm Reynaldo, ma'am. When I was looking for work, I told your husband I knew nothing about horses, but he said to come on up here and he would find something for me to do. I helped build most of the men's houses and this one, too. I worked on the patio until Mr. Selby told me he didn't care about it any more."

Once more the now-familiar pain gripped Jessica's insides. Would she never be able to put this feeling behind her? Laying a hand on the shy man's arm, she said quietly, "I'm sure he cares now. I know I do. Let's go see what's to be done." As they walked through the kitchen and onto the patio, she asked, "How long will it take to finish the fountain?"

"Only a couple of days."

"And to lay the stone?"

"Probably a week if I have help with moving the stones. Rosa, my wife, has some plants we thought would do well here, too."

This was more than Jessica had hoped for. She spent about an hour with Reynaldo listening to his plans, interjecting with an idea of her own now and then, and setting him to work. "When you are finished and we have our first of many meals out here, you and Rosa must bring your family to eat with us."

"That isn't necessary, ma'am. Besides, there are too many of us. We have five little ones. Your husband is to be thanked. We were near starving when he rescued us. Now, because of him, we have more than we ever dreamed of." The man drew on the dried earth with his toe, seemingly concentrating on some important task.

Jessica smiled warmly. "That's the reason this must be done for him." That she loved Jonathan she had no doubt, but here from these people who worked for him, she was learning about facets of his character she had not known existed. The more she learned, the more she loved him. He was not a simple man bent on getting what he wanted as she had once believed. She knew he had really rescued her, too, even though she had been too bull-headed to admit it. That he could want her and love her after her childish behavior was a constant wonder to her. Was he a hero to everyone here or only

279

to her and Reynaldo? She supposed she would find out eventually.

Jessica strolled inside to look for Polly, finally finding her making up the beds upstairs. "Polly, you were to have fun today," admonished Jessica.

"Help me," said Polly. "You grab that end." She continued whipping the sheet through the air to unfold and spread it at the same time. They made up all the beds, one on either side, quickly.

"Polly, do you think we should set up one of the smaller beds for Joshua? Does Jeremy still sleep in a cradle?"

"Heavens, no! He outgrew his cradle ages ago. But maybe his first night here is not the time for Joshua to change," she added hesitantly.

"Let's set up one of the beds and let him choose at bedtime. Can we carry it up ourselves?"

"Of course we can," she answered. But when they started up the stairs with the headboard, Donald would have none of it and motioned to the men to help.

"In the second room from the end," called Jessica after them. "Where did you find those bed linens?" Polly rushed to the appropriate crate and rooted around until she came up with something the right size.

"I never did find pillows." So they rooted through more crates and finally found what they were looking for. "How many do we need?"

"Well, let's see—two for me, one for Josh, one for Elsie, and two for Callie. You did make up her bed, didn't you?"

"Yes, Jess. I knew you'd want hers done first." After they had encased the pillows and deposited them on the beds, Polly said, "Let's find the boys. Then I must go, but Jeff and I will be back first thing tomorrow."

"Polly, don't rush. I love having you here, but don't neglect your own family."

"Jess, you know Jimmy and I could never repay Jonathan for all he's done for us."

"Don't talk that way, Polly. Jonathan doesn't want to be repaid." Jessica squeezed the other girl's hand and they went outside to find their sons.

When Jessica awakened in the morning, she practically leaped from her bed she was so anxious to start a new day. How much could she do today? The kitchen could keep Callie occupied for days she supposed. Well, there was much she could do. By the time she had skipped down the stairs and eaten breakfast, she had practically an army of women with buckets in hand at her command. Every woman on the place was at her disposal. "But what about your children?" she exclaimed.

"The older ones watch the younger ones," said Rosa who had introduced herself earlier.

"Callie, do we have enough cleaning supplies to keep everyone busy?"

"Sure, Miss Jessica. We got supplies to last a year or more. I finally found them this morning."

"Then, let's shine the second story today so we can uncrate the furniture and move it upstairs before we start down here." When the women moved off to start their work, Jessica said to Callie with surprise, "Why are they doing this?"

"Rosa explained Mr. Jonathan's arrangements to me. Almost every family here was down and out when Mister Jonathan hired them. Knowing you don't approve of slavery any more than he, he hired the men on the condition that their wives would help in the big house as needed. It seems one is to to cook—under my direction of course, or should I say ours?—some are to clean and others are to do whatever we say. Some men work the horses, others clear land, and still others build and repair as needed."

"My God, Callie, we have an entire community here with everything but a store." Jessica's laughter rang throughout the house. "What is left for me to do?"

"All you have to do is please the master, ma'am."

"Well, I certainly plan to do that, Callie. Do you think I've made a good start?"

"He would probably not be pleased to see you working so hard, young lady."

"Callie, I must. Let me talk to this new cook we have."

"Conchita, this is the mistress, Mrs. Selby," said Callie to the woman kneading bread dough on the table.

"Conchita, you can't possibly do all there is to do in my kitchen yourself. How many children have you?"

"Three, ma'am," answered the young woman with questioning eyes.

"And what is your husband's name?"

"Paco, ma'am."

"In this house we are at least six, plus Donald and maybe out first son. If you are to cook for us, when will you cook for your family?"

"Before I come, ma'am, and after I go home," answered the woman quietly. Strange, thought Jessica, I should think of her as a woman. I don't think she is as old as I am.

"Conchita, that will not do," Jessica stated matter of factly. "This is what I have decided we shall do, starting today." Jessica ignored the shock that registered on the girl's face. "You will, first of all, find one of the other women to help you. Can you do that?"

At the woman's slight nod, Jessica continued. "Try to find someone whose family likes food cooked as we do. I assume my husband chose you to cook because he thought you had the best food. Then at every meal time you will cook enough for all three households. Your helper can deliver to her and your houses. Your families will eat what we eat. Do not cook special for anyone. It seems to me that, when you finish here, you should not have to go home and start all over there. If you have free time during the day, you may go home to attend to chores there. I certainly do not expect you to cook from sunrise to sunset. Is that satisfactory?''

The gaping woman still stared at Jessica's back when Callie said, "Our Miss Jessica is sure something, isn't she?" She cackled and followed her mistress, hoping to keep up with her.

"Callie," called Jessica when he heard her approach. "Do you think the women will have scrubbed out the cupboard for the linen and blankets yet?"

"Probably, Miss Jessica."

"Then I shall carry them upstairs, an armload at a time, and you will put them away."

"Why don't I have the men take the boxes upstairs? There's no need for you to make all those trips."

"I thought I would keep the crates down here," she said, filling her arms with pillows. "Come, Callie, we don't want to make a mess upstairs while the women are cleaning it. When we're finished, we'll open the carpets and choose which go to the second floor—no sense putting furniture down then lifting it to put the carpet underneath. We must also put some of the women to sewing tomorrow."

Callie could do little but pick up more pillows and follow. When Jessica returned, Polly walked in, asking for something to do. "Tell Conchita, in the kitchen, how many extra for lunch and grab an armful." Many trips up and down the stairs later, both young women sat again on the same packing case as they had the day before and watched the men unroll the many carpets, eyes opening wider and wider as each was opened before them.

"This is no good," said Jessica. "Let's see the fabrics and see what we can match."

Then they unwrapped bolt after bolt of fabric, each seeming more beautiful than the last. "Polly, I simply cannot make up my mind. Let us try to choose for my son's room and see if we can get that in order. Maybe if we do one room at a time, I will be able to make up my mind."

"You always did try to do everything at once, Miss Jessica," said the young woman, slipping back into a habit of years gone by. "How about this?" she said, picking up the end of a bolt of fabric with small yellow and white flowers on a light blue background.

"It's lovely, if I had a daughter," said Jessica with a wry smile. "Still I don't want velvet or brocade in a child's room. We must have missed a crate."

"What about those upstairs?"

"We should have opened them. Instead, I forgot. But those have been there since before Jonathan knew of the existence of either of his sons." Finally in the far corner of the parlor, they found another crate of fabrics. Pulling out a bright, multi-colored stripe, Jessica cried, "Here it is! Now what carpet can we put with it?"

Almost every other bolt in the crate was unbleached muslin and Jessica smiled as she savored Jonathan's thoughtfulness. "Callie! Callie, where are you?"

"Right here, Miss Jessica," panted the older woman for she had run to answer her mistress's call again.

"Find out which women sew best and start them on draperies tomorrow. I want muslin for this room, the little room at the back right wind, and my son's room. The draperies in my son's room will be double. The other set will be these."

"Two sets, ma'am?" questioned Callie.

"Yes, one set of white and one of the stripes. The blue with the flowers will go in the back downstairs room. Polly and I are going to take the boys for a walk. Have Conchita pack a lunch."

Lugging the heavy bolt of fabric, Jessica carried it to the dining room where the men had arranged the various carpets. With the bolt in hand, she quickly selected the best carpet to accompany it and called Donald. She instructed him about the carpet and the furniture. "Wait here a minute," she said and ran from the room. When she had put Joshua to bed the night before, he had crawled into the bed to sleep rather than

284

into the cradle. She needed to know whether or not he had changed his mind during the night. Upon her return, she said, "Donald, it seems as if our baby is growing up. Move the cradle out of the room and set up both beds."

"Both in the same room, mum?"

"Yes, Donald. If Jeremy returns, our sons will need to be together, at least for a while. If not, Josh may have friends overnight—yes, both beds. In fact, by the time we return, Polly and I will have two very tired young men with us."

"Then what, mum?"

"Then have Callie chose the furniture for both her rooms. Make sure she does. And can you get rid of the extra crates?"

Noticing her friend's stare, Jessica asked, "Am I being a tempest in a storm again, Polly?"

"No, Jess, I think you'll last to see this through now that you've become sensible again."

"Good. I want to talk to Reynaldo a minute. You get the lunch, the boys, and the nursemaid and meet me by the kitchen door, all right?"

Again she was gone without waiting for an answer, but Polly merely shrugged and did as she had been bidden.

Chapter Twenty-Two

Jessica and Polly sat in the kitchen telling Callie about their walk and picnic. Elsie had taken the boys upstairs to nap. "Jonathan is a wonder, Callie. Behind that stand of trees is a house for each family. Every home owner has his own garden, though one of the men said they planned to have one large garden next year with everyone working it. Do you know all these people were impoverished when he found them?"

"Mister Jonathan always said all people needed was a decent chance," she responded.

"Well, he has proved that theory here. None of the families knew any of the others before they came together here. Yet everyone gets along so well."

"Miss Jessica, could we talk about my room?" began Callie.

"Sure. What's wrong, Callie?"

"I can't pick any of that furniture, ma'am. It's not for servants' quarters."

Realizing Callie's embarrassment, Jessica waved her hand, saying, "All right, Callie, we'll find something for you—something suitable."

Downing the last of her lemonade, Polly pushed herself to her feet, saying, "We'd better start before the boys awaken, or we won't get anything else done today."

"Come, Polly, help me choose carpets and draperies

for Jonathan's and my rooms. If we get them done, at least we will have a comfortable place to relax."

"Miss Jessica, the rug that goes with the flowered material is too big for the back room. Mister Jonathan must have meant it for your bedroom."

"Oh, he did, did he? Well, we'll see about that," she said with a sly wink. Taking Polly by the hand, she led her back to the hallway. "What do you see as right for Jonathan's room?"

"Does he favor red or green?" she asked.

"His room at home is dark—red, I think."

"We could do one room in each," Polly said thoughtfully. Suddenly she whirled, "Jess, does everything have to match?"

"I don't know. Why? What are you thinking?"

"Well, he likes heavy Spanish—look at the furniture. You like light and airy. Can you mix them? Put one on the bed and hang the other?"

"We'll do this much," she said, tagging two rugs, one red and one deep green, for the two rooms.

Gradually the house took shape. She had been so foolish to rush at it headlong. She soon found that Reynaldo was not the only non-horseman among the men. One had been a farmer. He was responsible for raising food for both animals and people and came to her to say that Jonathan had wanted a garden for the family when they arrived. Knowing the season was late to start a garden, she told him to do what he thought best. Two days later her indifference disappeared and she hunted Jed Brady to ask a myriad of questions— did he have help? what could be planted? was the land cleared? Finally, she got to the most important: if the men were combining their gardens the next time, could they combine the Selbys' too and have just one very large garden for everyone? Could they have a grove of fruit trees? what would grow here? what about nuts? Actually they planned an entire farm with Jed in charge but, of course, all subject to Jonathan's approval when he arrived.

When she tramped into the house, she attacked Conchita. "If we have no garden for this house, where are you getting the food you cook?"

"From the others," she answered calmly, as if it were unimportant.

"But it's not right!" Jessica exclaimed.

"It's right that you should starve?" After a long pause during which Jessica paced the kitchen and said nothing, Conchita continued, "Look, Mrs. Selby, your husband said we are in this together. I haven't asked for a single thing, just taken what's offered. No one will go hungry."

Subdued, Jessica turned to Callie, "What can we contribute? This can't go on."

"Leave it to me, missus. You know Mister Jonathan's fair. I'll find out what we are to do."

Jessica set two more men—Pablo and Juan—to work on the lawn. She even foraged in the woods one day for bushes and flowers they could move to the house. By the time Geoff arrived, three weeks later, the house had taken on some semblance of order. The second floor was finished except for some of the sewing of draperies and bed hangings and coverings. The library, with Jonathan's study just off it, had been easy to furnish; so had the dining room, though she had avoided finishing it because she so enjoyed the pleasantness of meals in the kitchen.

She ran to the porch when she heard a rider, and Geoff saw the disappointment that flashed across her face for only an instant before she smiled a welcome. Knowing she had hoped he was Jonathan, he said softly, "No word yet," and squeezed her hands.

Jessica appreciated the 'yet.' Then pulling him inside, she said, "Come see what I've done. There's hardly any place to sit down yet, but I'm glad you've come." She showed him to his room, apologizing for the lack of furnishings, then through the entire house. She asked, "Do you think Jonathan will like it?" so many times he finally laughed aloud.

"Jess, you know he will."

"I know he would let me do as I want, but what I want is to make him happy, not me," she retorted somewhat angrily.

Geoff was just beginning to realize what kind of woman his sister was. And she was a woman now. Her behavior at Fairhaven had left him not quite convinced, but he was sure now that her husband came first. Not many women would forsake the pleasures of town for such a life in the wilderness. It was true she would have every comfort, but what did she do for entertainment?

True to her word to Reynaldo, they had their first dinner on the patio that night, with his and Polly's families present. Geoff hoped he wasn't rude, but he spent much of the evening watching her in amazement. She wasn't the gracious hostess at the foot of the table. She helped carry food from the kitchen, she piled books on the benches for the children who were too small to reach, she talked to these people as friends just as Polly and Jimmy were. The Mexican couple were ill at ease at first, but Jessica's ravings about the glory of the patio made them glow with pride—in short, she made clear they had done her a favor she could never repay. "Christ, she really means it, too," thought Geoff.

He stayed two full days and invited her to come back with him. Shaking her head, she said, "Maybe someday soon. Right now there is still too much to do before Jonathan gets here."

Hugging his sister whom he had always loved but now respected as well, he said huskily, "Jess, Jonathan will be as proud of you as I am."

"I hope so," she murmured.

He gripped her arms and held her away from him to look in her eyes. "Don't worry. He will be here and soon."

"I know he's safe, Geoff. Somehow I can tell. But I wish I knew how much time I had before he comes—there is so much to do."

Releasing her, he stepped off the porch to his waiting horse, calling over his shoulder, "Just make sure you are well when he returns. Working yourself sick will be no welcome to him."

She nodded as he turned toward her again. Astride his stallion he patted his shirt pocket. "I have the list and will see that you get all that's on it." With one final wave he was off, and Jessica turned to contemplate what was in store for her in the weeks ahead. Silently she allowed herself two more weeks to finish the house. Two weeks! She scrambled inside to her tasks.

During the two weeks Jessica had allowed herself, she worked harder than ever. But the house was respectable, at least the last of the crates had been emptied. When the supplies—mostly outdoor furniture—from Geoff arrived, she concentrated on the veranda and patio. Joshua played there most days, often with a bevy of children, almost always with Conchita's, who also stayed for lunch.

Geoff had sent trees and they had been set out. She hated to go much farther without Jonathan. "Well, Callie," she said walking into the kitchen. "Have we done well enough? Do you think Jonathan will like his home?"

"He'll be right pleased, Miss Jessica," the older woman answered sympathetically. "Now we've got to get you ready."

"Me? What's wrong with me?"

"Nothing that a couple of days of rest and relaxation won't cure. Look at those hands from all the hard work you been doing. You almost look like a wild woman. Mister Jonathan won't like that. He'll be made at me for not taking better care of you."

"All right, Callie," she smiled. "I put myself in your

hands. Do what you will.''

As usual Callie called with a bath. From heaven only knew where she produced scented soaps and oils which she poured lavishly into the warm water after Jessica had chosen the fragrance. After the leisurely bath Callie insisted upon, Jessica, let her wash and brush her hair and settled into the huge bed for a nap.

Only drowsily awake, Jessica stirred at the memory of her dream that Jonathan was on his way to her. It had been so vivid she knew it to be true, but had he been alone? She thought so. Now fully awake, she pushed the thought from her mind as she crawled from the bed. As if by magic, Callie bustled in practically before she set her feet on the floor.

"He's coming, Callie."

"Today?" was her only response as she pulled a gown and shoes from the wardrobe and stockings from a drawer.

"No, tomorrow, I think," Jessica replied. "Will I be ready by then?"

"We'll just have to make sure you are. Good Lord, Miss Jessica, just look how loose this gown is! You always was a mite of a thing, but now. . ." The gloomy frown on her face told Jessica she should not go to the mirror.

"Can it be taken in? I don't want him to know I've lost weight."

"One squeeze and he'll know. You can't fool him." But she took the gown and brought Jessica a peasant blouse and skirt she had been wearing around the house recently. "I'll just alter a few of these because we'll have to fatten you up. I'm not taking in all of them."

Jessica tied her hair up with a ribbon and went to find her son who had just awakened. Edging Elsie away, for she needed Joshua to herself for a while, she dressed him and promised him a walk. She tried to carry him through the high grass, but he squirmed to be down and promptly ran off, chasing a butterfly. Consequently, it seemed to take forever to reach Polly's. She marveled at his cheerful nature, giggling and squealing with glee when the grass tickled his short stubby legs and pushing himself up from all fours to his feet when he tumbled. Finally he took her hand and let her help him up the two steps to the porch.

"Polly, Jonathan's coming!" she said, accepting a cool glass of refreshing lemonade.

"Good. How do you know? He wouldn't send someone else on with word."

"I dreamed it. Oh, Polly, don't look at me that way. The dream was so vivid I just know he'll be here tomorrow."

Suddenly Jessica was filled with self doubt. These six weeks of relying on herself, making major decisions on her own, faded as if they had never been. Before Polly could even leave her chair, Jessica sobbed uncontrollably across the room. Polly, clearly frightened at her friend's collapse, wrung her hands with indecision. What should she do? Was Jessica going mad? Dreams, sobs, what did it mean? Feeling completely helpless as well as afraid, she sent for her husband. After a whispered conversation in the doorway, she went to watch the children while Jimmy handled her hysterical friend.

What the hell do I do, he thought as he crossed the room to her. I've never seen a woman out of control like this. Thank God for sensible, lovable Polly. Then, as if it were his beloved Polly, he lifted her from her chair and, cradling her small body in his arms, sat down with her in his lap. "Come now, Miss Jessica," the man spoke softly, all the time patting her on the back and holding her head to his shoulder. "You've been very brave, Miss Jessica. He'll be here soon, Miss Jessica."

Finally the soft voice punctured the sobs and pacified her mind and body. Embarrassed at the scene she had caused, Jessica jumped to her feet. Drying her eyes, she growled, "If you call me 'Miss Jessica' one more time,

292

I'll. . .I'll. . .I don't know what I will do," she laughed. The release of the tension left her relaxed and exhausted.

"Polly says you had a dream. Do you want to tell us about it?" He was ignoring the whole episode.

"No, that's not what is bothering me."

"You've been working like a demon to be ready for Jonathan's return and you're ready. What could possibly be wrong now if he's so close to home?"

"What will I do if he's angry with me for coming to *Terra Diablo*? What if he doesn't like the house?" she almost wailed to him.

"If I know Jonathan, after six weeks of traveling, he'll be so damned glad to see you and Joshua, he won't even notice the house," he said, holding his breath and releasing it at her smile. Polly had slipped in to stand behind his chair and he reached up and clasped her hand, tenderly rubbing it on the side of his face. "Besides, he can afford to redo it himself if your work doesn't suit," he added with a shy grin.

That did it. "And he will just have to do it himself," she said with spirit. "Will you three come to dinner tomorrow?"

"No, Miss. . .no, Jessica," he corrected himself at her scowl. "You need to fight that yourselves. You come see us when the battle is over," he teased.

Jessica knew what he meant, even though it was far from what he said. She and Jonathan did need time together. They had been married over three years but had been together as husband and wife such a short time. Maybe this time, she sighed, maybe this time they would have all the time they needed. No, there would never be enough time, but she intended to grab and to hold on to all they had.

When Jessica awakened in the morning, she had no idea what time it was. The peculiar construction of the house did not really allow sunlight to spill into the room at any hour. She knew that the foot-thick walls and the lack of direct sunlight combined to make the house cool and comfortable. She dressed and went to breakfast, surprised to see her place set on the dining room table. Marching into the kitchen, she sat on the bench as she had every other morning. "I'll have breakfast here, Conchita."

She wanted to sew the draperies, but Callie said her hands were too much of a mess and she wasn't pricking them more.

She sneaked into the library and rearranged the books on the shelves, having pulled them out of the boxes in any order when she unpacked. She had always intended to do this, but it hadn't seemed important. She separated types and alphabetized and found several she wanted to investigate later. Resisting the inclination to open them, she finally turned from the shelves when she heard Joshua on the patio. Wondering vaguely where the other children were, she stepped out into the bright sunlight and stepped over to the little fountain where her son happily splashed water, most of which spilled onto his feet. She sat in a chair close to him. He tottered over to her chair to watch her. She ruffled his hair and sat up quickly. "Papa's coming today," she said.

He immediately set up the cry, "Pa! Pa! Pa!"

"Later," she said, "after your nap," while his cries of "Pa!" still pierced the air.

Thank heavens I held my tongue yesterday, she thought. She rose to answer a question about the draperies and the chair she vacated toppled over, knocking the boy down. "You needn't be so vigorous, young man," she said as she extricated the crying child. But after a reassuring squeeze from his mother, he squirmed to be down again. "You're as independent as your father," she said with good humor and set him on his feet and watched him toddle off.

The morning dragged on interminably. But when Josh disappeared for his nap after lunch, Callie rushed her up the stairs. "You can't greet Mister Jon like that," she said sternly. When Jessica stepped out of the tub and Callie toweled her dry, she absolutely refused to siesta, but she did walk into their sitting room and pick up a book. She could not concentrate, however, and jumped to her feet when she heard a rider in the distance. Callie ran in at the same time.

"Help me, Callie, I can't meet him in my shift," she cried frantically.

"He might like that best," she answered with a wicked grin, but from somewhere she produced an exquisite gown Jessica had never seen. In answer to her mistress's questioning eyes, she said, "It's a surprise from the women for this occasion."

"I'll thank them later. Hurry!" She wriggled so impatiently Callie couldn't get it fastened.

"Stand still or it will take longer." Nothing must take longer, but at the woman's soft, "There," Jessica flew out the door and down the stairs in time to step demurely onto the porch as the rider came into view. He was alone. But she had known that from his speed. She just hadn't allowed herself to think about it. Suddenly she was nervous.

Jonathan, after riding as if a devil were chasing him, was nervous too. How much could he tell her? How would she take the news, he thought as he climbed from the sweaty horse and gave orders for its care to the boy who had appeared as if from nowhere. He walked slowly to the porch, watching her face for tears, but she smiled radiantly. Not being able to stand his slowness, she flew down the steps and flung herself in his arms, crying, "You're back! Jonathan, you're finally here!"

Feeling the tension drain from his body, he gloried in the feel of her soft body crushed against his hard, lean body. Then his hungry lips covered hers and their kiss deepened until both of them were shaken with emotion. Jonathan broke away first and looked into her shining eyes.

"What are you doing here?" he asked.

"Where else would I wait for my husband but in our own home?" she questioned, still looking at him levelly. He pulled her to his chest again. Then, keeping an arm around her waist, he turned her toward the house. He glanced only casually at the inside as they walked through the hall and up the sweeping staircase. Jessica didn't care because he was looking at her as if he would never see enough of her.

"Oh, Jess, I was so afraid you had run off again," he said, his voice shaking with emotion. "Steve told me you were here, but I had to get here to see for myself."

"Never again, my darling," she murmured.

Jonathan stiffened slightly when she opened the door and led him into a decidedly masculine bedroom. Jessica felt the movement and smiled to herself. "These were to be our rooms, weren't they?" she asked innocently. At his slight nod she pulled him to the doorway between the rooms.

At least the door is open, he thought to himself, but relaxed visibly when he saw the door was gone. Then she led him into a rather feminine sitting room, a very restful room with no bed. His breath exploded as he crushed her to him. After a kiss of some length, she asked shyly, "Do you approve?"

A wide grin broke over her face as he said, "My dear, you are forever the tease." His laughter mixed with her giggles and echoed through both rooms.

Suddenly she jerked away, "Oh, Jonathan, here I am being such a fool. I forgot your bath and you haven't eaten, have you?" She raced to the door calling for Callie to give orders for both.

"Jessica," she spun to face him with fear in her eyes at his stern tone. "I must tell you about my trip," he said in a softer tone.

"Later," was all she said. "Let me be happy you are here first. Bad news can always wait."

"It's not all bad."

"Later. . .please," she pleaded. And he had no

choice but to wait as Callie burst in with a tray.

"'Bout time you got here, Mister Jonathan," she said. "The mistress sure could use some help around here." She arranged the tray on the small table by the window and bustled into the next room to oversee the bath.

Jessica gasped at her frankness, but Jonathan smiled and said, "She's right. I know. But I am here to stay now."

Jessica sat with him as he ate and moved into the bedroom, gathering a clean outfit while he stripped and picking up the sweat-stained clothes, caked with dirt, while he bathed. On one of her trips past the tub, she reached down and flicked some water into his face, but she could not back away before he snatched her arm. Tugging her forward, he said playfully, "So you like the water, do you?"

Trying to pull away, she squealed, "What are you doing? Jonathan, don't. I'm sorry."

He released her arm and she flew back, but he rose and stepped out of the tub to close in on her. "Jonathan, what are you doing?"

"Well, I thought since you wanted to play in the water," he said hugging her off her feet.

"Jonathan, put me down." She beat his chest with her fists when she felt him lower her over the tub. "You will ruin my new dress!"

He swung her over the side and down to the floor. "New dress, eh?"

"O look what you have done! It's soaking wet. Now I'll have to change."

"I'll help," he said turning her around and unhooking the gown from behind. "I'm honored you wore a new gown to greet me," he said sardonically while bowing.

"The women here gave it to me just this morning," she said stepping out of it with a little pout.

"We'll let it dry here and you can put it back on

297

later." He lay it carefully on the chest at the end of the bed.

"And in the meantime?" she questioned.

"In the meantime we will have a siesta like everyone else around here. It is siesta time, isn't it?" he asked with his sly grin.

She smiled broadly as she walked into his arms. He pressed his lips against her white throat and Jessica tingled with delight at his touch. She felt his hand at the buttons on her shift and could barely refrain from helping as his hand slid from the first to the second and finally to the last. Was she shameless for wanting her husband so badly—in daylight? She didn't care. When he raised his hands to part the shift and bare her breasts, she dropped her arms and let the garment fall to the floor. She trembled under the fiery heat of his kisses on her soft flesh. She lost her hands in his thick hair when he stooped to strip her of her stockings and caressed her thighs softly. When she thought she might fall from the intensity of her passion, he lifted her in his arms and carried her to the huge bed. There with roving hands and mouths they brought each other to new heights of ecstasy until that final joining when wave after wave of pleasure washed over them. He brought her to the peak of frenzy, moaning her desire until a dam within her burst and she cried out his name as a soaring bliss neither of them had experienced before swept over them and left them spent and shaken.

They lay in each other's arms, saying nothing, until breathing evenly once more, they slept.

Chapter Twenty-Three

Jessica stirred then jumped when she recognized Joshua's squeal in the hall. Feeling weight beside her, she started to lie back, remembering what had taken place moments before. When she lay down, she found herself looking into Jonathan's eyes as he propped his head with his elbow. "Stay," he murmured, gently caressing her body.

Smiling at the warmth of his tender touch, she whispered, "Tell me now, darling." Lying back on the pillow, he leaned on the headboard, because he could not talk if he looked at her body, he pulled her up beside him and recounted his story of the past six weeks—how he had ridden two weeks to a small Mexican village, arriving only to find the woman and child gone, how he had waited another week hoping for word and receiving none, and how had had ridden back to tell her and found her gone again. "And you really thought I had run off again?" she asked quietly.

"Darling, I didn't know what to think. I believed you when you said you would be waiting. Steve insisted he had sent supplies only two weeks earlier, but I could not wait for the wagons he was sending now. I just knew I had to be with you as quickly as possible. The whole way here I didn't know whether to kiss you for coming or spank you for not waiting."

Rolling her body onto his so she could see his eyes,

she grinned slyly, saying, "I'm so glad you didn't spank me." Raising to her knees, she said, "Let's find Josh and then I want to show you what I've done while you were gallivanting over two countries."

"Gallivanting! I may spank you for that." He grabbed for her arm but she bounded from the bed with a delighted squeal, much like her son's.

"Jonathan, do you think they heard us?" she asked, flushing with embarrassment.

"Allay your fears, my dear," he said as he finished hooking her dress. "Thick walls serve many purposes. Which way?" he said looking from the hall door to the balcony and back to her.

"You decide," she said seriously. "I know where Josh is, but it's the best room to see. Do you want to see the best first or last?"

"Last, if it means I can have you to myself longer."

"There's no satisfying you, is there?" she teased.

"I will never get enough of you, Jess," he said huskily and pulled her back against him after encircling her waist from behind.

Turning to slip one arm around him, she said with mock severity, "Will I have to fight you off in every bedroom? If so, we will omit the second story."

Releasing her with a pat on her behind, he followed her from room to room. He approved her division of wings and raised his eyebrow at the two beds in Joshua's room. "It's all right, Jonathan. If Jeremy returns, I want them together while they are so young. If not, Joshua will need company occasionally. Jeffrey and he often nap together when Polly is here."

With a sigh of relief, Jonathan admitted to himself that Jessica really would be all right. She was now strong enough to survive her loss, if need be. She had borne this disappointment much better than he had dared to hope. She remained hopeful but was not consumed by hope. He could not resist encouraging her, "He will be here, my dear. We will find him."

She smiled her thanks and led him downstairs. Starting with the small room she had chosen for herself at the back, she said as they entered, "You will tell me if you don't approve or if you had different plans for a room, won't you? Here, especially, I didn't know what you had in mind."

But he smiled as he looked around him. He had known there had to be a bright cheerful room like this since he had seen his father's house. And he approved even more when his study was next door. She would be close. She took him to every little nook, even into Callie's rooms, and finally she led him to the patio where sunlight poured through the trees onto the evenly laid stones. Vines and bright flowers climbed the walls and dazzled the eye. While his eyes swept over the spectacle, drinking in the impact, he saw his son leave off his play and run on tottery legs toward his mother. Suddenly he veered slightly and reaching for his father's hand, said almost with a question in his voice, "Papa?"

Jonathan swooped the boy high into the air while his delighted shrieks pierced the air. "Yes, Joshua. I am your wandering Papa who is home to stay." Elsie, knowing she was no longer needed, slipped away while the little family, Jonathan with his son in one arm and Jessica embraced with the other, basked in the sunlight showering them with happiness.

The next week flew by as both Jessica and Jonathan gradually settled into what would be their routines. The first few days they were almost never separated. They rode together over the little settlement with Jonathan inspecting what had been done during his absence. The only decision Jessica had made that he did not agree with concerned the gardens.

"But it was their idea to combine them," defended Jessica. "I agreed only that, if the others were to have one together, ours should be with theirs—not the only private farm."

"I still think each family should be responsible for its own. It is natural for a person to work harder for himself or his family than for the good of all."

"But the sugar is for everyone."

"We use here very little of what we harvest. Sugar cane is our only money crop on this plantation—that and the horses. The men work the sugar because that is what they are hired to do. Don't fuss about it. I'll talk to each of the men and maybe we can work out something."

Even when Jonathan left the house early to work with Jimmy, they breakfasted together and set about their duties quickly. He and Jessica often rode in the early afternoon when others rested, even though it was the hottest part of the day. Since almost everyone followed the Spanish custom, their rides were very private. Jonathan particularly enjoyed remembering the afternoon he had persuaded her to swim with him in the creek. Once he had overcome her natural tendency toward modesty and convinced her to shed her clothes outdoors, it had been a most pleasurable afternoon. And Jessica, seeing how aroused he became while watching her undress, had known exactly how the swim would end but had enjoyed it every bit as much as he.

The idyllic atmosphere was first broken by the arrival of Tim O'Leary. The moment Jessica saw him, she knew the sheer peacefulness they had enjoyed was at an end. Nevertheless, she sent Pablo, Conchita's oldest, scurrying to find Jonathan. When he burst into the study where Jessica and Tim were waiting with, "What is it, Tim?" Jessica knew her hopes that this was merely a visit were futile.

"Jonathan, can't you at least welcome him to our home?" she admonished. Both of them were startled because she had never corrected him before and certainly not in front of anyone else.

However, Jonathan grinned sheepishly and did so, but Tim was even more direct. "You know I ain't one

302

for niceties, Jonathan. Sorry I've been away so long, but Steve said I should see you. About a year ago I ran onto the place where you were held. Do you want to see it? Or do you just want me to tell you about it to see whether you think it is familiar?''

"I want to go there."

"No, Jonathan!" Jessica exploded without thinking.

"Jess, I want to clear all this up once and for all. I don't like having blank spots in my life. If I go, I may remember all of it." He slid his arm around her, trying to allay the fear he had seen spring into her eyes.

She knew he would have his way in this, but she felt absolutely empty inside. Stiffening within his arms, she asked, "When do we leave?"

"Jess," he started instinctively to protest. "I don't have time to argue with you."

"Then don't." She pushed away from him far enough to look straight into his eyes. "Don't you see, Jonathan, I'm tired of being left behind to wait. I can be ready quickly and promise I won't delay your start." Scurrying out of the room, she spoke to Callie and ran up the stairs.

Within a half hour the three rode away, Jessica wearing old pants of Jonathan's she had cut down and riding astride. She giggled as she remembered Callie's expression of horror as she stood on the porch. Jonathan had done the packing so she had no idea what lay before her except that she was with him. She *was* tired of being left behind but that was not the only reason she wanted to come. She remembered far too well what he had been like when Tim had returned him from here the first time. Just the thought of those nightmares, which had lasted for months, sent chills down her spine. If they were to return, he might well need her again. She certainly did not want him to be alone should such an eventuality come to pass.

When they finally stopped for the night, Jessica was so stiff she almost fell off her horse. Jonathan was at her side immediately to lift her to the ground. He walked with his arm around her until she was limber enough to manage on her own. Meanwhile Tim built a fire. The men, being much more accustomed to traveling on the trail, did all the work—preparing supper and bedding the horses for the night—though Jessica observed carefully so she could pull her own weight in the future. After eating, they sat around the campfire, the quiet night sounds adding to their relaxation.

"What do you expect to find?" asked Jessica quietly.

The look that passed between the men told her only that the matter was serious. Tim, who rarely had much to say, was not about to be loquacious for the first time now. Finally Jonathan said, "We really don't know. Maybe nothing. Maybe everything. Tim found the place deserted a long time ago; either one or both of us have been away since. He's followed a lead, but there's no sense continuing if it's not the right place. I may recognize it. I may not. We just don't know anything for sure," he shrugged.

"I know you must want to remember once and for all, but I can't help wishing you wouldn't. After all, we've been happy without your remembering meeting me." She looked into the fire pensively, remembering the awkwardness of that first interview between them and secretly happy he did not remember.

"Who said I don't remember?"

Turning to look at him, she said, "Jonathan, you remember only what I told you."

"You forgot to tell me how nasty I was," he said. With eyes widened in surprise, she stared at him as he grinned and said teasingly, "How could I ever have forgotten that day? You were absolutely livid when I arrived two hours early. No woman has ever slapped me so hard as you did when I called you a pathetic creature. You did gloss over the details in retelling, my dear."

"Jonathan, when. . .?"

"Ages ago—so that's one ghost you can lay to rest. It

wasn't too horrible to remember after all; only my treatment of you was horrible. Let's get some sleep because tomorrow we cross the river and after that the trip is more difficult.''

Jonathan gathered and spread a thick layer of pine needles for a mattress of sorts. At least it was softer than the hard ground on which Jessica had lain on her first trip through this territory. She smiled to herself as she thought about how carefully she had cleared the needles from her resting place that time. How stupid she was about so many things. She lay awake thinking long after she sensed Jonathan sleeping beside her. Though she resented his leaving her, she realized that two years ago she might not have survived a night in the woods. Certainly she could not have calmly lain awake, as she was now, and thought things out while the others slept. What would this trip bring? She was certain their love was strong enough to withstand whatever happened. But Jonathan—could he go through it again? Smiling because she was sure she had been correct in coming with him, she snuggled into her blanket with a sigh and slept. It seemed as if she had just closed her eyes when Jonathan shook her awake.

''Come on, sleepy head. We must get moving.'' After a quick breakfast they were on their way again with Tim leading, followed by Jessica and Jonathan in the rear. Jessica knew that being in the middle was for her protection and wished they didn't consider it necessary, but Jonathan had never really felt safe on this trail since he had been kidnapped from here. In fact, so anxious was he to be done with this trail they ate dried meat in the saddle for their midday meal and stopped only when they reached the spot at which they would cross the Mississippi. Jessica had not idea how they convinced the man at the landing to take them across, but Jonathan managed somehow and Jessica found herself on a raft being poled across the river practically in the dark.

The terrain and vegetation were different from that

they had ridden through on the eastern side of the river. The land was flatter and very few trees shaded them so that Jessica, by the end of the third day, felt perspiration dripping down her back and was sticky. From somewhere Jonathan had produced a wide-brimmed hat that shaded her face from the sun's rays. And she was thankful that he had insisted on her wearing one of his old shirts to cover her arms and shoulders rather than the blouse she had in mind.

"How much farther?" she heard Jonathan ask as they slid from their mounts in a grove of trees near a stream.

"About two hours more ride," Tim answered.

"Why don't we push on tonight?"

"You probably wouldn't recognize it in the dark."

Jonathan and she bathed upstream a little where they found a fairly deep pool. Jessica even washed their shirts and spread them on the bushes and grass to dry. Both of them seemed to sense that the other felt nervous about what they might find tomorrow and said very little, preferring instead to enjoy today to its fullest. Tim disappeared shortly after they stopped, leaving them to set up camp and build the fire. He appeared shortly after they had heard two shots—with fresh meat for their dinner. In the morning while they had slept later than usual, he was off early and cooking fish for their breakfast which he had just caught. Jessica had never realized life on the trail could be so ideal and peaceful. Now for the first time she could understand why Tim preferred the wilderness to people. He was in his element out here.

Jonathan remembered nothing on the trail. He had been fairly sure that he would not. When they reached the cabin where Tim thought he had been held prisoner, an eerie feeling came over him. He didn't remember but he did feel as if might have been here.

It was obvious from the fresh, though not warm, coals in the fireplace and food supplies on the shelves that someone had been living here as recently as yesterday. If they pushed on, they might have caught someone here. Whoever had been here left in a hurry.

"I'm going to follow. You and the missus wait for me until tomorrow. If I'm not here, start back without me."

"No!" Jessica automatically protested, but Jonathan nodded and watched Tim ride out of sight down the trail.

"But Jonathan. . ."

"Do not interfere, especially with Tim. Out here, my dear, you must do as you are told." Not wanting the full weight of Jonathan's wrath to fall upon her, Jessica clamped her jaw shut and turned back into the cabin and furiously swept with a worn broom she had found standing behind the door. If she was staying here for twenty-four hours, it would not be in such filth. Once Jonathan barely made it through the door before she threw some garbage at the spot where he had stood a scant second earlier. He did build her a fire and, grabbing an empty bucket, scooted out before a flying object caught him on the head. Several minutes later he returned with water which he put over the fire to heat and again escaped quickly.

After sweeping, Jessica scrubbed the table in the middle of the room and the dry sink in the corner. She washed the dishes and silverware that she could find. In a chest she found some linens—evidently a woman had lived here at one time—and stripped the bed, putting those linens to soak. They looked as if they hadn't been changed for at least a month.

Jonathan had disappeared; but when Jessica stepped outside, she saw a fire with a huge tub of water over it and more water on the porch. Moving the bedclothes to the cooking water, she hoped he returned soon, though she could keep busy for quite a while. While she had moved from the cabin to the small porch, he rounded the corner carrying his rifle and a couple rabbits. Oh God, she thought, what am I going to do with those? But he set to work and soon had another pot on the fire

307

bubbling gently. After he had helped her pull the bed-clothes from the cauldron and spread them to dry, they sat companionably on the porch.

"Is any of this familiar?" she asked quietly.

"I just don't know." Standing and reaching out a hand to pull her beside him, he said, "Let's go for a walk." Arm in arm they strolled toward the path, but Jonathan stopped short and, looking around him, finally started to the left. As they came into a small clearing, he recoiled so violently Jessica almost fell. She thought he would catch her, but his complete attention was focused on two trees in front of them between which a stretched hide had been tied. He stepped forward as if hypnotized and walked around the trees staring up and down the trunks and reaching out to touch them. When he stretched himself between them, Jessica shook, suddenly afraid. He could almost reach from tree to tree. What did that mean? "It's coming back," was all he said as he strode back toward the cabin with Jessica scrambling after him.

Jonathan stalked into the cabin and sat in a rocking chair in front of the fireplace. Jessica pulled the other chair over and sat beside him. They rocked silently for quite a while before she reached over to take his hand. He flinched at her touch then turned to look at her. Smiling at his wife's puzzled frown, he pulled her over to his lap. "God, Jessica, it was horrible."

"I know," she almost whispered. "I just wanted you to know I'm here."

"You will never know how glad I am that you are," he murmured.

"Do you want to tell me about it?"

She could feel him stiffen and knew he would refuse even before he said quietly, "Not yet. I am reacting so strangely that I am half afraid I will hurt you."

She pushed her way to her feet, saying, "Let's eat and that will be out of the way. Do you know how to make biscuits from corn meal? Jonathan, I'm really a miserable cook."

308

He smiled and said, "I never expected you to have to cook. I can help." He showed her how to mix and bake, though she had a fairly decent idea from watching Callie. The stew he had started earlier was tasty and between them they almost finished everything.

"Should we save some for tomorrow?" she asked.

"We will be fine tomorrow. I'll bring in the supplies we carried with us. You were cleaning so furiously earlier I was afraid to cross your path," he teased with a broad grin.

She pushed him gently toward the door and turned to clean up the dishes. After he had stowed their gear away, he sat again in front of the fire, but she brought in the linens, folded them and put them into the chest. Turning to her husband, she said, "Go to bed, Jonathan, so that you will be there if you get violent."

"Jess, don't be silly."

"I'm not being silly, darling," she said stamping her feet. "I can understand if you don't want to talk about it until you have it all worked out in your mind, but you're going to have one of those nightmares you had when you first came home. I can barely hold you if you are flat on your back. I know I can't if you are walking around."

"Are you coming with me, or have I frightened you too much?" he asked seriously.

"Now *you* are being silly. I know you would never hurt me, even if you don't know who I am at the time. You never did the first time and you didn't even know me. I must finish cleaning up the dishes first, but I'll be with you shortly." She turned her back to him, but softened her actions by saying, "I will be there soon. Wait for me."

However, when she turned around, he was in bed as she had requested. She knew he watched her through almost closed eyelids and determined not to fail whatever test he had in store for her. She walked straight to the bed and sat down. Leaning over, she kissed him softly then moved to bank the fire. Slipping out of her clothes, shift included, she slid between the covers beside him. "You know, Jonathan, the nightmares stopped when we lay in each other's arms. Maybe you won't have one tonight after all."

"Wishful thinking, Jess? It's not like you these days."

Finally when he lay still without touching her, she rolled next to him and threw her body over his. "Jonathan, you are tight as a drum. You must relax. How much do you remember now?"

"I remember being tied to those trees just as that hide is. I think I remember being beaten there. I can almost picture faces."

"Jonathan, you are struggling much too hard." She slid up his body until her lips closed over his, forcing them apart. As her kiss deepened, he finally relented and cooperated. Soon he lay back but kept her within his arms as they talked about inconsequential matters. "When we get back home, may we have a party? Not a grand ball as we had at Fairhaven, but something for everyone in the settlement?"

"Considering all the Spanish speakers we have, maybe it should be a real fiesta," he murmured as he dropped kisses onto her hair.

"Could we? Could we really? Everyone has been working so hard we must do something."

"Jess, how on earth was I lucky enough to find you? Remind me to thank my father. Do you realize how few women would even consent to such a party, let alone plan for it?"

Plunged into the middle of plans for Jessica's fiesta, Jonathan seemed to have completely forgotten his previous experience. Soon both of them slept, though Jessica awakened when Jonathan kicked restlessly and threshed his arms and legs under the covers. She quickly slid out to build up the fire. This was going to be a long night. She sat on the bed, trying to decide what to do. Her body had lulled him to sleep, could it quiet him? Slipping her arms into his shirt, she lay beside him. But he only threshed harder at the restriction. When she slid under the covers and lay over his body, he became calmer, jerking occasionally and yelling, "You bitch!" with each jerk. Sweat poured off him, but not from a fever—it was a cold sweat, as if from fear.

When Jonathan had been trying to take Jessica out of herself, he had made love to her to force her to think of him. Was that the solution here? Could she do it? She had never taken the initiative. Unbuttoning the shirt, she lay with her arms around his shoulders with his head cradled against her breast, murmuring love words and phrases all the while. Finally when he shifted slightly so that a nipple slid into his mouth, she held his head tightly so he had either to respond or to suffocate. The survival insticnt in Jonathan, together with a subconscious knowledge of his wife's love, led him to the natural course and he suckled at her breast, driving her almost wild with desire. The agonized groans soon became moans of pleasure as his mouth moved to the other breast and his hand took over where his mouth had been. Still murmuring, but passionately now, Jessica felt his body stiffen then yield as if he were completely aware of the events taking place on this bed. He was aware of "what" and "who" and "why" and took over, though she had prepared him so well, he could hardly wait. Even though he took her roughly, they once more reached the peak of fulfillment as each gave wholly to the other.

In the hushed quiet afterward he murmured, "I cannot remember ever being so pleasantly awakened," and held her tightly to ward off the embarrassment he knew she would be feeling. "Was I bad?" he questioned.

"I. . .I didn't know what to do," she answered meekly.

"It seemed a perfect solution to me, but I was rough on you."

"Jonathan, my dearest, as long as it is you, I don't care. I'm not a piece of porcelain, you know."

Having dried the sweat, now turned warm, from his body, he climbed over her to sit naked in front of the fire. Sliding onto the chair beside his, she asked, "Jonathan, when you have these nightmares, why do you call me a bitch? What did I do?"

He looked at her questioning eyes and knew he must tell her all of it. She had gone on for too long thinking he called her a bitch because of the circumstances of their marriage. "Jess, you are not the bitch. Don't ever think that," and he slowly and deliberately told her what he had been able to remember and what he and Steve and Tim had pieced together. He told her how Carolyn had vowed he would not get away with marrying someone other than her. How she had hired men to capture him and bring him here. How she had shown up and tried to beat him into submission when he had refused her. How she had left orders for them to kill him. "That's the reason she charged into Fairhaven that Christmas day, so long ago. She had heard I'd lost my memory and wanted to be sure. Steve thinks she's responsible for Jeremy's disappearance too."

"It must be terrible to want someone so much," murmured Jessica, more horrified than ever before.

"Don't feel sorry for her. She's a monster who must have her own way. It's all my fault for underestimating the lengths to which she would go to get what she wants."

"I've caused you so much pain," said Jessica, almost to herself.

Leading her back to the bed, he muttered very seriously, "You caused none of this. I can blame no one but myself. I am truly sorry you had to reap the disasters that have fallen on us because I let her think I would marry her. You have brought me the only real happiness I've ever known. Let's get some sleep so we can go home tomorrow."

But they didn't sleep for a long while after they lay on the bed.

Chapter Twenty-Four

Several days later when Jonathan and Jessica arrived home together, it was with the feeling that this was home and nothing could mar their happiness now. They had survived all the horrors they had been through and found their love equal to any test. The last morning they had waited briefly for Tim; but when he hadn't arrived by midmorning, they were too anxious to be on their way to wait any longer. Jessica wondered what Jonathan would do about Carolyn but didn't dwell on it because she knew he would keep all of them safe, whatever he decided about her. Knowing how dangerous she was comprised half the battle, and Jessica did not make the mistake of calling the contention between them anything less.

Jonathan was sending a message to Steve to ask about supplies for her fiesta. She immediately plunged into plans for the party and left Carolyn to him.

"Callie, I want everyone to enjoy himself. I don't want half the women serving and cooking. What can we do?"

Callie nodded and strode off to consult with Conchita while Jessica and Polly visited each home to issue verbal invitations. Most of the women were overcome with pleasure at her calling and insisted on showing Jessica their homes. This was exactly what she had been hoping for. When she had visited to get acquainted, she had seen only the main room; and she had a feeling most of the houses were too small for as many children as there were. That would be her next project, starting with Reynaldo's and Rosa's house. Five children in one bedroom was ridiculous. She had no doubt that, if they had more bedrooms, the others would want them too.

Everyone ran to her drive or to some vantage point when Paco was due back and they heard a carriage as well as a wagon. Who could it be she wondered. No one comes here. Maybe Jonathan sent word to Geoff, but it wasn't like Geoff to arrive two whole days early or to bring a carriage rather than ride.

As the carriage rolled to a stop in front of the house, Jeremiah Selby thrust his head out the door, saying, "I couldn't wait any longer to see my grandchild again."

Jessica squealed with delight and hugged him so hard he could hardly breathe. Then she heard a booming voice say, "Don't I even get a hello for bringing him to you?"

"Maude!" She hugged her just as hard. "What have you been up to?" she asked with a sly grin.

"Not a thing but coming to visit you," the old man replied smartly. But she did not miss the gleam in his eye.

"You're just in time," beamed Callie. "We're havin' us a party." And she immediately took charge of seeing their baggage moved to their rooms while Jessica led them through the house to the patio.

"You can go to your rooms later. Come, rest out here a minute." They had barely sat down with cool drinks when Jonathan entered and all the greetings were repeated. Jessica caught the unspoken question in her father-in-law's eyes when he shook hands with his son.

"Father Selby," she said, "everything is out in the open here. Jonathan and I made up on the ship, as he knew we would. We have only one son, now asleep in the nursery at the present, but there will be more—even if Jeremy is never one of them."

She took Maude to her room from the patio. "We have three guest rooms—one for you, one for Jonathan's father, and one for Geoff—though I had hoped we might combine you two and have a spare," she added teasingly.

"Jeremiah is a good friend. I would never want to lose his friendship by pushing for a marriage I'm not sure I want," Maude replied. "At my age friends are more important than husbands."

"Regardless, you are still family to us. May our children consider you their grandmother? They will never have another."

The older woman smiled and Jessica knew she was pleased. Dinner was a treat for everyone. Joshua entertained spectacularly after the adults got used to his being at the table with them. Both Maude and Jeremiah doted on him and gave in to his every whim. For the first time he screamed when Elsie took him off to bed until his grandfather went with him. Though she knew Mr. Selby was delighted, Jessica was not and said as much to Jonathan later when they were undressing for bed.

"My love, if we're not careful, they will spoil him until he is completely out of hand." "We will not allow that to happen," he promised. "But you are too enticing for me to consider Joshua's problem tonight."

As he put out the light and took her in his arms, she murmured, "We'll save that problem for tomorrow. We must take care of his father tonight."

The two days until the fiesta, as Jonathan insisted on calling the party, sped by. Jessica was almost delirious with happiness as the preparations continued. Both Geoff and Steve would be here so that last room in the children's wing had to be prepared—the one Jonathan had used and she had avoided. Finally, though, it was as homey as the rest, and she and Jonathan lay on their bed talking during siesta time when they heard another carriage. "I thought Geoff and Steve would ride in," she said. "I wonder who that can be?"

Having thrown on their clothes, they raced down the stairs and out to wait for the approaching carriage. Steve jumped out, calling, "Look what I brought you," and reached inside. Then he turned, holding a small boy, the very image of Jonathan, in his arms.

"Jeremy!" screamed Jessica and grabbed him, hugging him to her so hard he cried. She whirled with him in her arms, but he cried more.

"Darling, you frighten him with so much love." When she finally stood still, Jonathan asked quietly, "Is your name Jeremy?"

The boy nodded and his cries quieted to sniffs. Good God, thought Jonathan, what does one do with a three-year-old stranger who is frightened, especially when it is your son? "Maybe Josh would help him feel more comfortable, Jess." Extending his arms, Jonathan waited to see whether or not his son would come to him. When Jeremy came willingly, Jonathan said softly, "I'm your papa."

Jessica ran as quickly as she could into the house, and Jonathan and Steve walked around in the yard with Jeremy holding onto a hand of each. They casually strolled into the house, motioning to Callie not to make any noise. They reached the patio as Jessica descended with Joshua.

"Josh, this is Jeremy, your brother," she said as she set him on his feet. She thought he knew vaguely what a brother was because of all the brothers and sisters he had for playmates. He toddled to his brother and stood looking him up and down. Then he flashed a wide smile every bit as captivating as his mother's, and pulled Jeremy over to the spot where he usually played. The adults watched warily, but the boys were oblivious to them and soon settled themselves on the ground, busy with the toys.

"Jonathan, do you think. . .?" Jessica started to ask.

But he interrupted before she could express her doubts. "Jessica, don't worry," he reassured her. "There are too many new people. He will be at home here in no time. Look how much fun he's having with another child." Just as Jonathan said that, Joshua pushed Jeremy and their parents stood, their nerves on the very edge, waiting to see what would happen next. Jeremy simply gave Joshua what he wanted while they sighed with relief.

Shepherding the others into chairs, Jonathan said, "It's obvious Joshua has been king around here too long and will have to mend his ways. But I don't think this is the time. Let them alone and see whether or not they can work it out themselves." The last statement was directed toward his wife who would have gone between them to correct her younger son. But she realized the wisdom of Jonathan's words. Parents could not fight a child's battles for him, especially not the older, larger child's.

"Steve?" He turned to look at Jessica whose large, soft eyes were filled to the brim with tears. "Dare we ask where you found him or should we just say thank you?" she asked in a quiet voice.

"Thank you will do nicely." But he did turn to see Jonathan's raised eyebrow. "I'm just glad he looked so much like his father there could be no mistake about his identity," he laughed.

"Me, too," murmured Jessica, returning her attention to the children. "Steve," she gasped suddenly, "I never even offered you a chance to clean up—not that you really need to. What a hostess I am. Did you eat? I'll bet not, since you got here so soon after the noon meal." She flew into the kitchen while the men chuckled softly, knowing she was embarrassed at her forgetfulness, but aware it was unimportant compared to what had taken place today.

She was back almost immediately, because Callie was Callie and never forgot. When Callie carried a tray to the table, Joshua scrambled to his feet and ran over to climb onto the bench, and Jeremy followed. Jessica's heart seemed to melt as she observed both her sons eating the goodies Callie had brought. Soon the patio was filled with people—Maude and Mr. Selby came down, Geoff arrived, Elsie came to watch her charges—and Jessica was too busy to hover any longer. She bustled through the house with Callie, seeing that rooms were ready, baggage unpacked, and baths prepared. The newcomers took Jeremy's arrival on the scene in stride, almost as if he had always been there.

When Jessica and Jonathan were in their room after a cold dinner, dressing for the party, he slid his arms around her and murmured, "Darling, we could not want for nothing more, now that Jeremy is here. Are you as happy as I?"

"I'm so happy I could burst," she answered. "I don't think I even care any more where he was, though I'm grateful whoever cared for him did so well."

"That was Maria," he said, walking away from her to fumble with his necktie.

Slipping her arms into her dress, she walked up to him and brushed his hands away and retied his tie herself. Patting it flat, she asked, "Maria? Maria who?"

Taking her hands in his he lowered his head and kissed them both, then looked at her with agony. "Jonathan, what is it?"

Sighing loudly, he laid his hands on her shoulders and held her away from him. "Once again I have been the cause of all your troubles, my dear. Maria was Carolyn's maid. Carolyn blackmailed Maria's brothers into kidnapping me. When she could not change my mind about you, she ordered them to kill me. Thank heaven they were so afraid they rowed me to this side of the river and left me."

He felt Jessica waver and saw her eyes close. Afraid she might faint, he led her to a chair and sat on the floor at her feet to finish the story that had started so long ago—well over three years now. When she looked at him again, he continued, "Carolyn really is the bitch I called her in my nightmares. When she found I was still alive, she thought she was safe because I did not remember. She didn't want me that Christmas day. She knew we were through but was afraid my memory would return and I would accuse her. When I wouldn't leave, she bided her time. Then she heard you were really my wife instead of just some widow who had bought Fairhaven and was being kind to me.

"She thought the ultimate agony she could cause both of us would be to destroy my son and she forced Maria's brothers to kidnap him. Somehow in her twisted mind she thought that I would get rid of you and I would return to her. She sent Maria and Jeremy to Maria's old village in Mexico—probably planning some miraculous discovery so she could produce him later."

"If she only knew how close to success she came," said Jessica. "I was such a fool to run away."

"Jess," he said shaking her hand. "She was never close to success. Even with you in England, I never gave her a moment's thought. And now she's gone. You have nothing to fear from her ever again. Steve and I gave her a choice—go to Europe forever or face arrest. Even if we couldn't prove all of this in court, she would be disgraced by the accusation."

"It must be terrible to love someone so much. I would want to die if you didn't love me, so I can almost sympathize with her."

"No, Jess, I told you before. She doesn't deserve any sympathy—not even understanding. She doesn't love me as you do—she didn't want my children or want to make a home for me here as you have. She just couldn't stand not to own something she wanted. I was more like a prize to her. I should have made it clear to her before I ever met you that she would never be my wife."

Jessica stood and pulled him to his feet. Crushing her soft body against his full lean length, she kissed him with all the love she had. "It wasn't your fault, Jonathan. She would never have believed you."

Footsteps in the hall reminded them of the party, and she stepped away from him to button her dress. He turned her around and did up the buttons as he had so many times before. Moving to the door, she reached her hand back to him saying, "Let us say goodnight to our sons before we go downstairs."

When they entered the boys' room, Elsie was just finishing dressing them for bed. Jessica nodded and Elsie slipped into her room as the boys' parents took over her chores; after all, she was to go to the party too. Jessica and Jonathan each tucked in a child and traded beds to kiss the other good night.

Standing in the doorway to the balcony, they turned for one last look at their beloved children who were almost asleep after their full day. Strolling arm in arm toward the stairs, they paused in the middle to survey the hub of activity in their home. The rest of the family were below and Rosa and Reynaldo came into the light of the patio hesitantly. Soon the other workers would follow.

"Jonathan, you have truly carved a land of happiness for us all out of your wilderness," she said. "There is no other possible name but *Tierra Felicidad*."

They gazed deeply into each other's eyes and hearts and pledged their love to each other with that long wordless look. Then they strolled down to welcome their guests. And the flower of their love, now in full bloom, enveloped and warmed them all.